# Quarry

## The Ancient Trackways, Part I

# Quarry

## The Ancient Trackways, Part I

## Richard Abbott

© Copyright 2025 Richard Abbott

All rights reserved

No part of this publication may be reproduced, stored in a retrieval system, or transmitted, in any form or by any means, electronic, mechanical, photocopying, recording, or otherwise, without the written prior permission of the author.

ISBN: 978-1838-0120-3-8 (soft cover)
ISBN: 978-1838-0120-4-5 (ebook)

**Matteh Publications**

Contact:
Web: http://mattehpublications.datascenesdev.com/
Email: matteh@datascenesdev.com
Cover design by: Richard Abbott
Original Matteh Publications logo drawn by Jackie Morgan

Maps generated using Open Source Maps and OpenLayers Mapping software
© MapTiler © OpenStreetMap contributors

*For Roselyn, for family*

# Contents

| | |
|---|---:|
| Prologue – Travelling | 1 |
| Part 1 – Melen | 21 |
| Part 2 – Brannen | 121 |
| Part 3 – Lindirgel | 185 |
| Epilogue – Travelling | 299 |
| Author's Note | 319 |

**Also by the Author**

**Science Fiction**
*Novels:*
- Far from the Spaceports
- Timing, Far from the Spaceports book 2
- The Liminal Zone, A Far from the Spaceports novel

**Historical Fantasy**
*Novels:*
- Half Sick of Shadows

**Historical Fiction**
*Novels:*
- In a Milk and Honeyed Land
- Scenes from a Life
- The Flame Before Us

*Short stories:*
- The Lady of the Lions
- The Man in the Cistern

# Prologue – Travelling

*Richard Abbott*

Bran watched as the men sculled the little boat back away from the beach. The curved wooden hull pieces flexed in the waves, as the withies that held them together stretched and shrank again. The crew turned from him then, and settled into their long-distance rowing pattern as they started to pull back out to sea. Their paddles, broad like a duck's foot, caught the low sun. He admired the working together of the strokes, like the steady beat of a cormorant's wings. It was a very different skill to his own, but talent was talent, however it was expressed.

There had been five in the crew: four working the oars and, on occasion, the little sail, overseen by an older man who had considerably more tattoos than Bran. The youngest was clearly only just starting his apprenticeship, and the solitary oar trademark on his lower right arm still looked new, almost glistening in the spray. Bran grinned to himself; it was evidently the boatmen's equivalent of his own first mark, the hammerstone-and-antler tattoo just above his right wrist, made all those years ago by Morvin map-Deru at the very start of his apprenticeship.

Bran had no idea how secretive the boatmen were about their skills, so carefully avoided asking about them. He suspected, though, that the oldest man was skilled in navigation and the art of travelling well beyond sight of home, while the others, if he was not with them, would stay close to their own port. To avoid seeming too curious, he had looked forward as the mainland shore turned from a faint distant line into a coastline, alive with bays and promontories.

They had landed at the full of the tide, and the water would be falling now, taking the vessel with it. The rowers would be away from the shoreline soon, avoiding the broadening shoals, and from then on, their journey across the great sweep of the bay would be easy. Seals had already started to haul up onto an emerging sandbar in the rivermouth. Their haunting call, the Song of the Falling Sea, drifted over the bay. It was the song of settling, the song of being in one place for a time.

The sea-passage from Innis Mon had taken the better part of the autumn day, and now they had left him here, just inside the

## Prologue – Travelling

broad mouth of a river. As he turned away from the open sea, his shadow stretched ahead of him up the dunes. Night would come before long, and he needed the light of day to navigate the next stages of his journey. So he toiled up the soft slope and cast about here and there, until he found a grassy knoll for his camp. Further inland, away from the sand and the salty marshes, the short trees were coming into greenleaf. It would be more comfortable there, but he was not sure of his way in the gathering gloom. There would be time tomorrow to look for the signs he had been taught.

He lay back against the slope, watching the dayglow fade. Somewhere out to sea in that direction – somewhere out of sight from this low elevation – lay Innis Mon. He turned away from it, changed sides, faced inland to watch the eastern stars appear, little by little filling the bowl of the sky. The moon was on the wane, and she would not rise for him this evening. The sky was darkening rapidly. In the distance he could hear blackbirds calling their evening alarms, one to the other.

He ate a little of the smoked fish bartered from the boatmen, seasoning it with fragments of gutweed from his own supply. All around him, the night-noises carried on the quiet air. For a while, the air sounded with the cries of the wading birds in the estuary – the same cries as had floated around his island home – but little by little they fell silent, leaving only owl-calls to break the quiet of the night.

It was a half-month since he had left the quarries on Innis Mon, since he had packed up there and bid farewell to his workmates and his family. And it was only three months since Morvin had taken him aside and told him, in his careful indirect way, that it was time to leave the place of his apprenticeship behind, and find a place for himself on the mainland. They had climbed together to the top of the nearby crags on a clear early summer's day, well above the top of the workings, and looked east at the crinkled range of hills on the mainland. Two or three high peaks stood a little proud of the rest. Some days the hills were obscured by layers of cloud and mist, but today they were sharp against the skyline. Bran had never been over there, never before left the island of his birth, though he had wandered up and down its length several times.

"You've given me seven years as an apprentice, Bran, and three as a true worker. I made the marks of the stone trade in your body myself. But look now, I'm thinking that you don't need any more time here. Maybe it's a good time to move on, before you grow roots into the rock here, and become like the barn-and-byre folk down there at the little port. You're a traveller; you'll not want to be ending up like them."

"You've been here longer than that."

Morvin laughed.

"So I have. But I'm not recommending that for you. You could maybe go to The Quarry in The Valley over there, work with the gang there for a spell. Ty Caroc is where they all live."

Bran considered the dark ridge along the skyline beyond the wide stretch of water.

"Why not go west, over to where Conegall comes from? I hear they're making all kinds of great monuments over there."

He had half-turned to look that way, even though the bulk of the island stood between him and the western aspect, but Morvin was still facing east.

"Better over that way, I reckon. You're real skill is in smaller work, not these great circles and all. You'll meet Conegall's kindred in the hills over there, for sure, but my feeling is that you'd do better to go east. You'll find stone monuments there too, if that's where your work takes you, but I don't believe that it will."

Bran had drawn a deep breath.

"But will they take me in, do you think?"

"No reason why not. You've learned well. Go to the foreman there – last I knew it was a man called Avank, but that was a few years back. Chances are he's passed it on to someone else by now. But find them, and show them the proof of your work with me."

Bran had taken a little more convincing than that first conversation – the stonework done in The Valley was renowned, and

## Prologue – Travelling

he questioned his ability to match it. And he was settled here on the island, and it was all the home he had ever known. His parents lived here, his friends, his workmates who he had grown up with and learned his trade beside. Even his first lover was here on the island, though she had moved to the south end, and he had not seen her for several years. But he had been persuaded, and now, finally, the better part of a season later in the year, here he was. He settled down to the first sleep of his life away from Innis Mon, and let the same darkness, the same stars, the same night-breezes, the same occasional calls of the wading birds out in the tidal waters watch over him.

The next morning he woke with the sun, and set off around the curve of the bay. He kept to the firmer sand between the waves and the dunes until he had passed a series of reedy brackish ponds, then branched inland to follow the crest of a low ridge. He looked back and left, across the estuary. Thin curls of household smoke rose in the still air from a few places on the other side, but they were of no interest to him. Nor, to the mild surprise of the boatmen, had he journeyed straight to the little port that lay to the east, his right, even though reputation said that they handled some of the trade for The Quarry.

Instead, he was following the directions passed on to him by the elderwoman at his homestead on Innis Mon, who had stored up all kinds of practical wisdom for them all. *Do not go to the port and the traders. Not yet. You must go first to The Quarry. So turn north along the estuary. But do not follow the river for long, for it will take you too far to the west.* So here he was, on the ridge with its low, scrubby bushes. *Continue along the crest until you reach two standing stones; turn half right and follow the line they show you. Keep along that line until you reach a ring of stones.* And so, he was leaving the sea behind.

By late morning he had reached the place. It was a small ring, no more than a dozen or so stones, fringed by an earth bank topped with smaller pebbles. Too small to be a real gathering place, then, and he supposed it was just a waypoint, guiding travellers like himself. The elder woman had not known its original purpose, only that it was there. *Turn north and look at the line of hills. Mynyth Mam will stand out, but you must not visit her yet, not until you are accepted. A day will come when you will ascend her slopes to do her honour, but not on this day of your arrival. Indeed, you must ascend her one day, not just for your own benefit but to stand there for all of us among whom you have lived, but who will never go here ourselves. So be patient, and wait for that day, the auspicious day of your ascent. Climb on a clear day, and you can look back across the sea to this, the place of your birth and your apprenticeship. But for that first day, look again. Pen-y-hal will be to her right, watching over her northern flank. And look a little right again; look for a notch in the hills. Head towards that notch, and well before you reach it you will come to the barn-and-byre village of Dolgolvan.*

It was still a little early in the year for berries and nuts, but he foraged for some leaves to eke out the fish. At least there was no shortage of water. For the rest of that day he persevered generally north, following along a flat stretch of land above the western shore of a long lake fringed with oak trees. The notch in the hills was sometimes in sight, and sometimes obscured by some nearer ridge, but each time he saw it he marked some closer landmark to aim for. It caught his eye, called out to him, and he spun fancies to himself that it had been cut into the long ridge in a past age by some giant, wielding a giant tool. One day, he decided, he would pass through that notch and see what lay beyond. And one day, rather sooner, when the time was right, he would scale Mynyth Mam and do reverence at her summit.

*Keep Lugh Deri on your right, and Mynyth Mam on your left.* Near the top end of the lake he netted and cooked a duck, then carried on a little way into the jaws of the valley before stopping for the night to eat and then sleep. The hills on either side were sheer and craggy from about half-way along the lake. They rose steeply above him, as though warding him away from the ascent and ushering him on northwards.

Mist and low cloud filled the sky when he woke the next morning. Little droplets of water clung to his hair, his beard, and the wool and leather garments he had around him. He glanced

## Prologue – Travelling

up and shook his head. If he was any judge of the weather here, there would be little change until the afternoon, and he might as well set off sooner rather than later. *Do not take any way that opens on your left, even though it would shorten your journey. It must be done properly; your first sight of The Valley must be from its open end, from the east, and you must not intrude half-way. You must learn the life of The Valley as it is offered to you, and not try to seize it for yourself.* So he kept right, ignoring the few places where narrow valley routes opened gaps in the ridge walls to his left.

He crossed finally into a broad valley, keeping part-way up the ridge that edged it, well away from the marshes that bordered a series of small lakes. When the ridge started to dwindle he found a place where he could wade the stream that flowed eastward, and turned along it for the last approach to Dolgolvan. *Follow the stream until it turns south into Lugh Crum, go to the travellers' place, and ask directions there.* And at that point the woman's remembered voice fell silent. Her job was complete.

As he had approached the first houses, he passed through open land where the trees had been cut back. A ragged patchwork of little fields pushed against the edge of the forest. Animals grazed here and there, some scrawny, some thriving. They were mostly goats, with the occasional sheep, and a solitary cow in the distance, guarded by a languid boy who ignored Bran's presence. The crops were equally varied in condition; Bran was no farmer, but he could tell good growth from weeds, and both could be seen here. After a while the houses displaced the fields, and as he approached, a haze of woodsmoke hung in the air.

And so, just before midday, he stood in the travellers' place at Dolgolvan. Here, and to the north, the cloud had started to lift, but the south was still shrouded. The village stood at the head of a long lake – Lugh Crum – and both east and west shores soon faded to shapeless bands of darker grey. The townspeople, seeing the pack, the set of tools at his belt, and the tattoos of the stoneworkers on his arms, directed him up a gentle track west again, due west this time, not the south-west from which he had arrived. For all that, he was not very far from the track he had been using. The people there had helped him, but they had not liked him very much, and showed it. They were glad to see him go, for he was too far removed from them and their way of life.

For his own part, he had also been glad to leave Dolgolvan behind again. There were too many people for his taste: too many people busy in the narrow streets, in the little houses, too many people arguing in the marketplace. Too many cats and goats, too much muck being trodden underfoot. Too much rubbish and filth from the many fires. Too many children running around. Too many faces that looked worn out and haggard, ill-fed and worn-out. Too much sickness lurking in the mucky streets.

They were all barn-and-byre people, fixed in the one place, not travellers through the land like himself. He was out of place in the town, and he felt acutely the focus of their suspicion of him, and all that he stood for. They probably perceived his own distaste for them.

That said, they would need each other again, when it came to trading. They had food and clothing, household goods and women, and the stoneworkers had tools and trinkets to barter, and stoneworking skills that might be needed. So for all the dislike he had felt today, he knew for sure that he would visit Dolgolvan again often enough, always presupposing that the gang at Ty Caroc accepted him.

To either side of his new path lay the little scrappy fields, with their scratched earth and scattered crops struggling to grow. Like the streets of Dolgolvan itself, they were untidy, with broken pieces of pottery and splinters of wood left to lie where they fell around heaps of burned twigs and leaf litter. Just like the cultivated area he had walked through when arriving at the settlement, however, they stretched for a surprisingly long distance along the track, and he supposed that in total they could grow a considerable amount of food. The sight reinforced his ambivalent feelings about the place.

He set out along the track, then all at once he was away from the sight of houses and fields, working an easy way around the side of a crumpled hill. Trees grew all the way up to the summit,

## Prologue – Travelling

well above him, with little crags pushing through here and there. He could no longer see the track he had followed that morning, but it must be somewhere in the valley bottom below, to his left. All of a sudden he came out of a stand of trees, and a broad swathe of grass ran down ahead of him to a rounded tarn.

The afternoon sun was out now, and the air was still, leaving no ripples on the circle of water in front of him. The trees opposite - oak and birch, hazel and holly - stood upright on the heels of their own reflections. He looked down at their length stretched out in the water, and saw below all of them an arc of grey rock, speckled with other colours.

He looked up again, eyes tracing the trunks and the leaves, until he was looking at the real spur instead of the reflected one. It was his first sight of the place where he would be working. From here, it was a two-headed beast. A long curved ridgeback ended in those proud upraised horns. Perhaps it had once settled from the skies onto the valley wall, its fiery ardour slowly solidifying into crag and rock. Or perhaps it had welled up from the world below, forming these shapes as it contended with the outward air. He remembered hearing storytellers speaking of such at the seasonal meetings at the stone circle at the northern end of the island. Whatever its origins, now it was cold and hard, and traces of vegetation and veins of rock streaked its spine and flanks.

He leaned back against the rowan tree which sheltered him just now, and gazed, filling himself with that first sight. A two-horned beast it might be, but the horns were not alike. The nearer one was flattened across the top, but the further one rose into a peak. In time he would come to know them as the Ban and the Brig, but for now they had no names. Parts of the slopes were steep, but as well as those crags there were gentler ridges that looked accessible.

Somewhere between this little lake and those outcrops, he supposed, Ty Caroc was waiting, hidden from him by all the forest between. But once he lived there – if they let him live there – his task, day after day, would be to clamber up between the beast's paws, to find and follow its hardened veins as they wound back into the body of stone. There he would tease out the best of the unformed teardrops of rock, and shape each of them into gifts. Gifts between enemies, gifts between lovers, gifts to celebrate marriage, gifts to end war: each one would be a thing of beauty drawn out from the mountain.

A squirrel chattered nearby, and a family of wagtails began to dabble along the water's edge. It was time to go; it was time to finish his journey into The Valley. He rounded the tarn and carried on westward. The path clung to the side of the ridge where it joined the crumpled hill to the higher ground beyond. Below him, and ahead, The Valley was full of trees – hazel for the most part, it seemed, but with a mix of others. Some were in full leaf already, while others still had bare branches. And before long – a shorter distance than the one from Dolgolvan to the tarn – he had reached his destination.

He had been told what to expect, and so the abrupt appearance of a little cluster of circular houses did not surprise him. He had arrived at Ty Caroc, the House of Rock. This was where the stoneworkers made their home. So far as he could judge, it would still be a fair walk to the peaks at early light, and a fair walk home again as the sun dipped behind the ridge at the far end of the long valley. But this was where they chose to live.

The settlement was well away from the centre of the valley, with its flowing beck, damp rushes, and patches of asphodel. Instead, it was tucked under the northern valley wall, in a little clearing that was much smaller and vastly tidier than the sprawling area around Dolgolvan. Most of the nearby woodland consisted of hazels, and there was a wide band which had been coppiced close by. That would, he reckoned, have been the work of some travelling woodsmen, as none of the stoneworkers he

## Prologue – Travelling

knew would have the talent for it.

There was no real pattern to Ty Caroc, except that the centre was left empty. The houses – round, and stone-built – found themselves, as if by accident, at varying distances from that centre. A decent number were in good condition, and everyday items nearby suggested that they were lived in. But the obvious houses were only a small part of the whole. At least twice as many regular heaps of stone lay further away, fading at a distance into the valley walls. They were in various stages of disrepair; here, the works of man, of nature, and of time all blended into one.

In that very fact of stone lay the village's oddness. Everywhere he had heard tell of, houses were made of wood. Even on Innis Mon Allan, where stone was every bit as plentiful as here, and every bit as sound for building, the little circular homes had wooden walls. He knew that everyday houses could be made of stone – he had learned the skills of building them during his training – but never before had he seen them in real use. Ty Caroc was set apart from other places, and knew it, and cared nothing for the building habits of the world around. The wooden roofs, coming up in a shallow cone to a central point, were the same as anywhere, but the walls were unique.

The village felt old, heavy with the weight of generations, holding a vitality of its own separate from the transient lives of the workers who occupied it. He had heard, back on his island home, that it was indeed old. This valley – called simply The Valley to all who knew it, and Nant-y-Laesach to those who did not – was still older. The towering peaks above it had been the source of both axes and other polished items of beauty for more generations than anybody could tell. Stone had been worked here, and stoneworkers had lived here, long before his grandfather's grandfather had been born.

Several tracks led away from the houses. Bran was arriving from the east, and almost opposite him a well-worn path led further along The Valley. It was easy to imagine himself striding that way every morning to get to his new place of work. But before that, he had to find acceptance here. Other ways led down towards the beck on his left, or wound steadily up the valley wall to his right.

He walked into the hollow centre and halted, looking around. Most of the houses seemed empty just now; with the sun leaning well past midday, he supposed that the men would be away at work in the crags. He called out, turning this way and that, hoping that at least somebody would be nearby.

After a short pause, a woman came out to him. She was noticeably older than him. She carried herself just like the women who lived in the traveller villages of Innis Mon, and was not at all like the women he had seen around the edges of town life at Dolgolvan. She was confident, self-assured, and although her face was deeply lined, she looked lean and well-fed, and well in body. She had tattoos along her arms, showing that she had learned some sort of skill. He thought he recognised some of them from the healer-woman of the community on Innis Mon. Quite apart from all that, she seemed entirely unimpressed by him.

He had not known who would greet him at the traveller settlement, but was not surprised to meet a woman. Just then, arriving new at the site, he assumed that many other women lived there, as that had been the rule at the training quarries on Innis Mon. In time he would learn otherwise. She studied him up and down, seeing his kit, his body-marks, his bearing.

"Who're y'here for?"

Her accent was like what he knew from Innis Mon, and was broadly comprehensible to him. But he soon found that she used odd words, or spoke them in an unfamiliar way, and he stumbled over her meaning.

"Whoever is the foreman here. I don't know his name. I was told it used to be Avank map-Luk, but maybe that's all changed. I've come here to join..." he saw her sceptical expression. "I'm asking to join the crew here, and I need his say on that. Call me Bran. Bran map-Broch."

She nodded approvingly at him.

## Prologue – Travelling

"That's fair. Avank, y'say. Well now, but Avank's not foreman now. It's another man now – Finn, they call him. Finn map-Gwath. Big man, no hair worth speaking of, lives in that there larl hut. Back by sunset. Y'll wait here."

She turned to go, then glanced back at him, over her shoulder. "Got bait with'y? Had some?"

He shook his head, blankly, not knowing what she meant. She frowned.

"I'll fetch some. Y'can owe it me."

With that she left again, ducking under the low door at a nearby hut. The village was silent again, although he had the clear sense that others were watching him. He looked around, saw a convenient boulder pushing out from an earth bank nearby and went to sit on it.

A cascade of bright yellow-green leaves spilled out where the soil spilled over the top of the rock, and he traced it delicately with his hand, enjoying the familiar feel of woundwort. Other patches of it grew near most of the stone huts. He picked a sprig and tucked it behind his ear, a half-conscious appeal for good fortune. It had grown extensively around his old settlement on Innis Mon, and many times before he had wrapped the leaves around the little cuts and scrapes that attended his work.

Then he searched his pack for the sliver of antler he was carving and got back to work on its shape. When he was done, it would become a swan. He was expecting a long wait through the afternoon.

But actually, it was not all that long before she came out again, bringing a large oat bannock and some sort of fish in a wooden bowl, poached with some herbs.

"Bait for'y."

He suddenly understood what she had been saying. He took the bowl from her, then rummaged in his pack and gave her a small pouch of the gutweed in return. She opened the drawstring, sniffed at the kelpy ocean scent, and nodded her thanks. She glanced at the spray of leaves he had plucked.

"Y're familiar with that?"

"Woundwort? I'd never be without it, and supposing I stay here, I reckon that I'll be using it most days."

She nodded.

"All the lads do. Creeping Jenny, they call it here. But the virtue's as y'say. If y'stay, then take a piece from the clump there, and plant it beside where y'll live. This one..." and she held up the gutweed, "this one we call baitweed."

She turned to go again.

"Wait a moment, please. It's kind of you to bring me this. What kind of fish is it? Surely not seafish, not here? And do you know Avank? I was told to ask for him by Morvin map-Deru when I arrived. Morvin trained me on Innis Mon, and cut the trademarks in my body."

She glanced at him, a trace of a smile across her face.

"I know Avank, for sure. But I don't know this Morvin. The fish?" She gestured at the bowl. "Gwinnad, they call it. Lives in lakes and tarns hereabouts. Freshwater, not salt."

"And what should I call you?"

"Lewenith."

She moved off again. He grinned to himself. Just then he could think of no less suitable name than Lewenith, since she seemed distant, wary, guarded: far away from the happy state she was named for. The fish was good, if more bony than the sea-fish he was used to, and he began to feel warmer towards her as he ate. Perhaps if she didn't have to look after a stranger who had arrived unannounced, she might be more pleasant. He finished the bowl, rinsed it in the nearby beck, and settled back again to whittling the antler.

Much later that afternoon, the men of Ty Caroc started to come back. They arrived in ones and twos, carrying tools and fragments of stone in their bags. For the most part, Bran couldn't tell if it had been a good day or a frustrating one for them. Perhaps it was just another day at work amongst the stone pinnacles. A few were younger than Bran: most were older. They wore beards of all shapes and sizes, with hair longer or shorter as each chose. Some outran him by a good many years.

## Prologue – Travelling

Their voices showed a whole mixture of original homes, with accents and turns of phrase from all over the land. But there was a commonality in how they dressed that matched his own garb; all wore leather or suede garments to cover and to protect. Occasional pieces of other fabrics showed as trim, for vanity or reminiscence. One had a red neckpiece of twined wool from some animal or other. Another had a patch of green woven stuff as a pocket. The little personal adornments transformed what might otherwise have been drab uniformity. His own shoulder-patches of black and white embroidery fitted in well.

They glanced at him, curious, as they arrived, but let him be, dispersing to the several huts. They had spent the day up in the high places, and an odd feeling nagged at him as he watched them arrive. Perhaps it was envy.

Most of them had some sort of minor cut or bruise. Bran grinned at that. It had been the same at the quarries back on Innis Mon. Work was hard, and rough on the body, and it was rare to have a spell of time without finding yourself with some kind of scrape. His own most recent marks had healed and faded during the journey days on the boat and on foot, but he had no doubt that they would reappear once he started to work here.

One or two, though, had more serious injuries; a leg that had broken and been poorly set, leaving a limp, or a long scar over the forehead that had come within a finger-width of taking the eye with it. Morvin used to say that the worker who had no wounds on his body had done no work.

Last of all came the man – surely – that Lewenith had described. He was indeed big, with only a thin fringe of hair circling his bald head. Lewenith came out from her home to speak with him, gesturing to Bran. He nodded, set a dusty bag of tools and stone off to one side, and came over.

"Call me Finn. And you are Bran map-Broch, I hear. You're wanting to join us."

Bran stood to greet him properly, aware that most of the other workers were gathering around again.

"I am. I trained with Morvin map-Deru, foreman of the quarries on Innis Mon. He set the marks in my body with his own hands to show I'd learned the skill."

He paused, stripped off his tunic so that the tattoos were clear to them all. Finn considered them all carefully – up and down his arms, legs and torso – and then nodded.

"I never yet met Morvin, but I've heard of him, and I know his work. What I see here is good enough for me." He turned to the rest of the group. "Does any of you object?"

There was a pause. Nobody said anything, until another man spoke up. He had a sharp face, and stood a little apart from the others. Bran had not noticed when he had arrived.

"Well, I for one have not heard of this Morvin. How do we know what training this here man has had, and whether it's to our own liking? Did any of us make those marks on him with our own hands?"

"Drus, just hold your peace. These on him are the right signs of our work, and well you know it. Where's the harm? This lad trained somewhere else, is all. No shame in that. And I know Morvin to speak to, even if Finn here doesn't. I met him at a midsummer festival when he came over once from Innis Mon. He was good for a crack, and good at his work too."

It was an older man who had spoken, perhaps the oldest in the group. He had joined the circle last, shuffling slowly from Lewenith's hut. He must have been there, staying inside under the roof through the day, but Bran had had no idea. His hands trembled slightly as he leaned against one of the adjacent rocks, and his eyes looked filmy in the evening sun, but his voice was still clear. Drus was unconvinced.

"If he comes in, and what he does is no good, it counts against all of us. I don't want to be having to explain it all to some trader in a year's time. Worse yet, that lot at Dolgolvan. I say we should see first what he can do by way of fine work."

Bran put his tunic down on the rock beside him, and bent to pick up his bag. He was intending to pull out the little antler swan he had been working on, but Finn forestalled him.

## Prologue – Travelling

"Well, until I know differently, I'm trusting the marks that Morvin map-Deru made. I'll see what Bran here does best over the next season, and I'll see if there's anything amiss. But I'm not expecting to find that. And nobody here needs to work alongside Bran if they don't want to. That's my call. Does anyone object still?"

He looked slowly around the group, starting with the old man and finishing with Drus, who scowled and wandered away without saying anything else. There was a murmur of assent from the rest.

"That's settled, then. Bran: you're welcome to join us all here at Ty Caroc."

Bran wondered if there would be more ceremony surrounding the event, and this concern nagged at him for some time afterwards. It seemed all very easy. Apparently, though, Finn had nothing more to say about it.

"Pick a home for yourself that's not being used then, settle yourself there. I'll take you up to the workings first thing tomorrow. For this evening, there's food to share with you, as I can well see you've none of your own yet. You can make it up to us another day."

Bran grinned ruefully, thanked him. Finn waved the gratitude away.

"Say nothing of it. And think nothing of what Drus said back there. He'll have his say, that's for sure. He does like his words. But he's a good stonecrafter. It is what it is. If you can win him over, he'll have a lot he can show you. It'll not be easy though, so just don't expect it to happen tomorrow. He'll not even live here at Ty Caroc with the rest of us, has his own hut up on the ridge there."

He gestured up above them. Drus was already some way up the slope, on a little winding track that followed the contours of the land between outcrops and steeper slopes.

"How is that?"

Finn frowned.

"You'll hear soon enough. There was a dispute. Several years back now. A man died: Piat, they called him. His body was at the bottom of an overhang, head quite stove in. Nobody quite knows how it came about, and Drus thought some of the others were accusing him of something foul. Well, he swore he'd never live with us again, he'd only ever see us at the workings, and for when we gathered for a meeting. And so it has been since. He comes and goes as he pleases, and takes his own counsel. As you've found out. One other fellow joined him up there, as an apprentice like, and Drus has taken it upon himself to do the trade marks on this lad as he learns things little by little."

One of the younger lads, hearing this, joined them.

"Spink, he's called, that one. He's soft in his head. Better that he lives up there. But Finn, I reckon that Drus shouldn't be doing the marks without you beside him."

Finn glanced over at him and shrugged.

"Spink is slow, no doubt about it. But he's got a rare talent with stones, to bring the shape and the shine out of them. If he wanted ever to move down here, I'd not stop him. And for now, I'm not minded to take up the other with Drus. And if I'm not, why, neither should you."

The lad subsided, but Bran was more interested in Drus.

"But he's got skill? Drus, I mean."

"Oh, no doubt about it. He knows his stone. Just if you want his advice on something, don't try to hurry him along, and don't let him feel you're looking to getting something for nothing from him. Go easy with him, and make sure he knows what he'll get for it from you."

Bran nodded, and looked back around at the houses.

"And who was that other man, the older one?"

"That was Avank. Used to be foreman here back in the day. A fair few years back now, that would be." He laughed, and glanced across to where one of the younger men was helping Avank back to his hut. But despite looking away, he had not missed Bran's sudden start of recognition. "You've heard the name before, then?"

## Prologue – Travelling

"Morvin knew him, said to ask to see him when I got here. Told me he'd met him once, when he was still foreman. Avank, I mean. I had no idea Lewenith shared that house with him; she said nothing about it."

Finn laughed.

"She's uncommonly protective of him."

"But he's not working any more?"

"Well, he cannot get out to the workings now, that's for sure. A bit far along the track for him to go every day, and too high up. His balance is gone, and his eyes are not so good as they used to be. But see, it upsets him not to be able to get out on the crags anymore. So he'll help you if you've got a piece you can take right in to him, show it to him so he can feel the grain in the stone for himself. We look after our own here, y'know. I dare say it would be the same when you was back on Innis Mon?"

He waited for Bran to nod, and then went on after a slight pause.

"I don't exactly know how it was out there, but here, if one of us cannot work for a time, whether it be injury or just decline, we look after them. Food, goods, whatever. But dignity most of all: I'll not have anyone feeling the less because they need a hand up again."

Again he waited for Bran to acknowledge him and then pointed out some of the other crewmembers. Bran listened to a rattle of names. Prental was the one who had joined their conversation first. Brogat was the youngest, a year younger than Prental. Nant seemed to be more or less his own age, possibly a little older. Don was a big man with a big black beard. Roudhok kept in the background, a nervous man with jerky speech and mannerisms. Cowann was older still, not far off Avank's age. Gan-Mor was someone at a distance that he didn't properly meet, clearly a little shorter than most of the rest. The other names settled into a blur that he would have to hear again, several times, over the next few days.

Prental showed him a vacant hut not far from his own home, and bustled him around all of the other places he would need to know. He stayed close to Bran, carrying things for him, moving them from place to place in the hut, leaning in as he explained the ways in which the community of workers functioned. After a long quiet day it was all too much to take in, and he found himself just nodding incessantly at the explanations. Eventually Finn noticed his quandary, called Prental away, and let Bran settle into his new home in peace.

# Part 1 – Melen

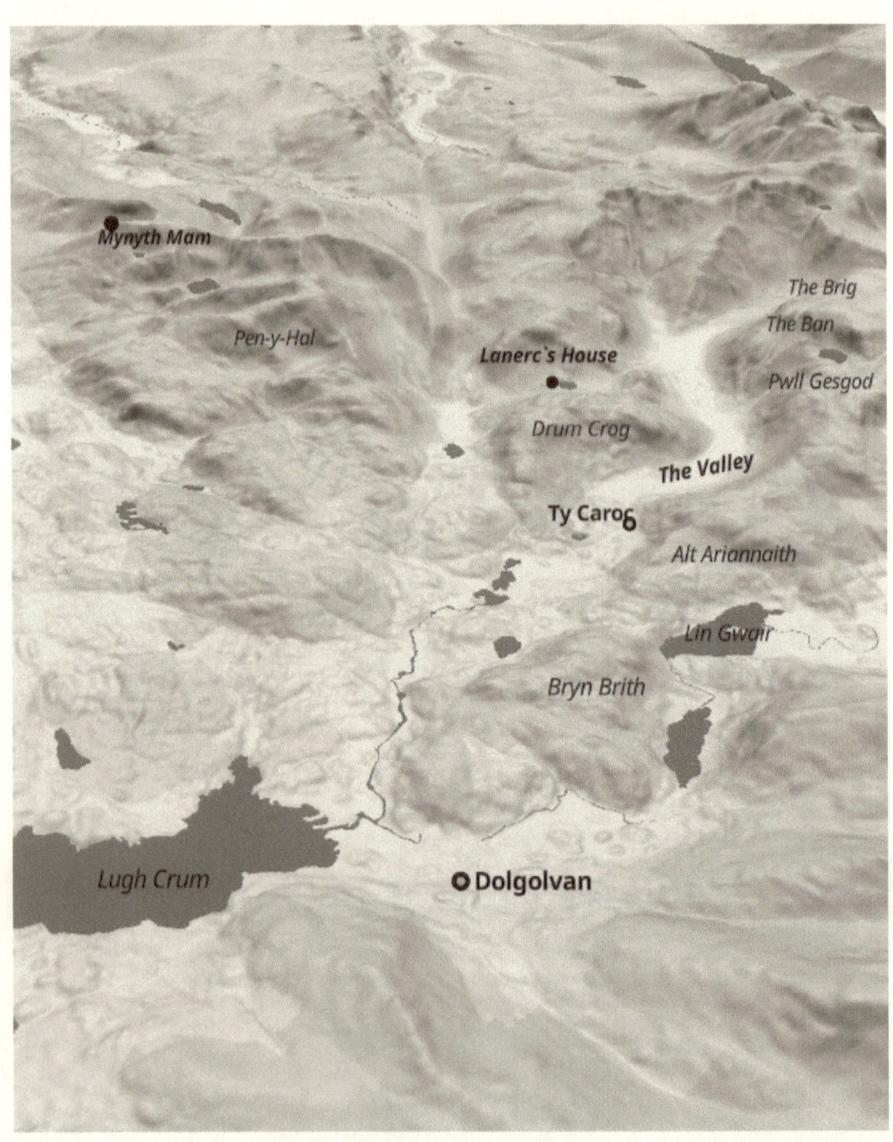

*Part 1 – Melen*

THE NEXT MORNING, Finn came to Bran's new home as the sun came over the hill towards Dolgolvan, lighting up the crest of the long ridge to the south of Ty Caroc: Drum Crog, one of the men had called it. Bran had been awake for some time, making the hut into a new home. His first act, as soon as Prental had gone, had been to set up in a convenient alcove in the wall the small collection of special personal things he had brought with him from Innis Mon for his individual devotions: stone, wood, a squirrel tail, and some bird feathers. He wasn't entirely happy with the arrangement yet, and he would change it again tonight after the day's work.

He had also, with some anxiety, checked his tools several times over. He wanted no foolish omission or forgetfulness to interfere with Finn's first impression of his working abilities. He emerged at Finn's first call, and the older man grinned.

"All ready, are y'now?" He gestured to the interior of the hut. "That was Cavran's lodging, back in the day. He left to go back west over the sea couple of years ago now. To the great island beyond your Innis Mon. Good to see you's filling it now. First the jackdaw living there, now the raven, hey? Well, be that as it may, let's get along to the workings now."

They set off west along the length of The Valley. Some way ahead of them, Drum Crog came to a sudden end, with one last rounded spire standing as sentinel, watching the several finger valleys where they wound up into the crags. The ground rose steeply to their right, but ahead, a well-trodden path meandered through the stands of hazel.

After a while, a broad glade opened up. The sound of the beck was louder here, and the ground fell away to their left down to its banks. A cluster of large boulders bunched around an especially huge rock, with alternate holly and oak trees ringing them all. A small opening in the ring let anyone standing here see up The Valley ahead, to where the twinned mountains stood proud. The main part of the Quarry would be between the two peaks, the flat one and the pointed, the Ban and the Brig. Finn stopped them at the edge of the glade.

"We all come here for sunrise a few days before the midsummer, to see the sun climb right over that nearer peak there. I'll tell you what day it'll be, when I know myself. To pay our own respects as we see fit, as stoneworkers together. Y'll join us for that. But on midsummer day itself we'll go up to one or other of the great circles."

They went over to the boulders then, and Finn pointed to the flat sides facing them. Bran saw at a glance that the rock was a kind of tuff, but not the true tuff. A close relative, perhaps, which had been tumbled down from higher up the slope in a former age. Looking closer, he saw how loops, spirals, cups, and curls had been pecked into the surface. They were the marks of each of the foremen, going back into antiquity. Finn reached up to shoulder height to trace one set with his finger.

"I made this one here, you know. Ten turns of the year now, it must be, since Avank stepped down." He smiled at the memory, then looked sharply up at Bran. "Maybe y'll make your own here, one day, providing y'stay here with us. What do you think?"

Bran stayed silent, stepped slowly around the boulder, looking at all the marks there, seeing how the oldest were now almost invisible, worn away by time, with moss and lichen growing in from the rough rock. Finn let him look for a while, then led him on.

"Now, today, I'm going to take you all the way along the valley and climb up just below the workings. But there's other ways to get there, and y'll find the one you like best. Brogat, now, he likes going up onto the ridge just as soon as he's left Ty Caroc, before he even gets to them rocks with all the marks. Nant, he comes along most of the way before going up. Learned that from Cowann, he did. But he chops and changes about as well. He likes the path going by them dead men's stones."

Bran frowned at him, unsure whether to take the words seriously. The older man nodded to him.

"Oh yes. Stone rings and cairns up there. Ask Nant sometime and maybe you'll get a longer answer than you wanted. He's a

*Part 1 – Melen*

right one for names and places."

They carried on for a while. The track threaded a little way above the valley floor, meandering through the groves of coppiced hazel and avoiding the wetter ground either side of the beck. The towers of rock that Bran had seen from that first tarn, soon after leaving Dolgolvan, were close now, reaching high above them on the right.

Then, on their right, on an outcrop that bulged out from the valley wall, Bran thought he saw a man sitting. As they drew closer he saw that it was in fact a bundle of old workers' clothing, torn and ragged, roughly arranged in a body shape. Some old branches gave shape and height to the cloth, and a heap of stone chippings lay below the cast-off leggings. The two split halves of a broken hammerstone, and a small pile of worn-out hand-tools sat on the rock shelf beside the figure, within reach of the tatty sleeves. From somewhere above, they began to hear the tap-tap, pok-pok noise of hammer on rock.

"That'll be Roudhok and Prental; they're always here earlier than the rest. And say hello to Crug here. Whosoever's arrived first of a morning makes sure he's all right for the day. In case, you know, the wind's knocked him over, or the badgers have messed with him. Now that you're in the group of us, you can add whatever you see fit to kit him out."

Bran stopped and laughed.

"My father was named for the badger: Broch, they called him. So I'm partial to the beasts, like. But they can certainly be a right nuisance when they put their mind to it, and they don't usually leave things tidy like they find them."

He nodded solemnly to the figure.

"Y'alright, Crug?"

Then he leaned back and tried to look for the two men, hoping to see them perched up in crevices or crags. But Finn took his arm and led him on.

"We don't spy out where others are working, Bran. Leave them to find their own pieces and don't give them the idea you're looking to poach on them. I know where every man of them looks for the tuff, but that's where it stops."

"You do?"

His quick scan of the rock had shown him nothing that gave away where the two men were working.

"A right fine foreman I'd be if I didn't know, isn't it? But as for you now, you leave them to their own devices. They'll do the same for you. And like I say, Roudhok and Prental are here early. Sometimes Gan-Mor as well, but not so regular like. Y'll find everyone in the gang leaves their own working marks a stretch or two below where they're working, so y'll know even if they're not there to tell you."

Bran nodded. This was all familiar, and he had chosen the shapes of his own working marks the day after his apprenticeship was over.

They moved on again, to where a shoulder of land ran up between the two great buttresses, Ban and Brig. Lofty crags rose between them, and curved in a great arc to the north and east of Ban. The crags matched the summits they stood beside – the one curving away from Ban was flatter and rounded, whereas the stretch closer to the Brig was pinnacled.

Finn gestured to a rough track, and they started to climb. Beyond them, further west, the great arm of The Valley split into three. In a straight line at the western end, the land rose up to a line of crags like the knuckles on a hand, which crinkled the morning sky. A noisy stream tumbled between boulders to their right, and a slightly quieter one to their left.

It was demanding effort after their casual stroll along the valley floor. In steepness, it was no worse than Bran had known at the workings at the north end of Innis Mon, but the climb continued longer than he had anticipated, or was used to. They climbed steadily, without talking, until the slope eased off a little into a small upland meadow.

"Here, let me show you this first."

He branched right, towards the louder stream. As Bran crested a low ridge, a small tarn came into view, spreading still waters across to an imposing rock wall which rose up to the summits,

*Part 1 – Melen*

still considerably above them. The tarn reflected those heights, and the blue sky wheeling higher still. The sounds of falcons, higher and shorter than the buzzards' calls, sounded from the upper reaches of that wall. Streaks of colour interrupted both the grain of the rock and the watery reflection in places, but Bran was not close enough to see if the colours came from intruding veins of stone, or vegetation. There was a broad stretch of rock and grass between the lip of the tarn, and the outflow where the stream tumbled out, cascading down in a long series of steps to The Valley below.

"On the spring and autumn still days we all come up here together, up to this here Pwil Gesgod, to give the gifts and all that. Your choice: nobody will tell you what's what, least of all me, when it comes to your devotions. Some of the lads come here more often, if they've a mind to, or their families are in the habit of it. Summer we all break for a time and celebrate however we please. Then at midwinter we all go together to one of the gatherings. The chief one is north of here, at the great circle of Dronow Moar. But the main thing you'll need to know about this pool here is that we all gather beside it in the middle of the day, eat up our bait together."

He glanced at Bran, appraising his mood.

"You'll have done the like back on Innis Mon, I've no doubt. We make a habit of being all together to eat, every day. But for the rest, it's entirely your own shout how often you come up here for your devotions. Nobody's counting, nobody's watching you, so do as you see fit."

They turned away again, headed back towards Brig, the western of the two peaks. Finn paused at a high meadow where junipers sprawled over the ground, and blaeberry sprigs clustered between them, dark fruit showing amongst the leaves. Bran looked back south. They had now climbed enough that they could see over the ridge of Drum Crog.

"Come on up this way, now."

They scrambled away from the tarn, back towards the quieter beck, across ground made scrabbled and tricky by loose shale. Bran wondered how much further they would climb before reaching the true tuff. He turned towards the south, scanning around the several crests of hills in that direction.

"Is Mynyth Mam one of those there?"

Finn shook his head.

"I have no idea, lad, I'm not one for names and places. But tell you what: ask Nant sometime, he's got a real talent for all that. But what I can show you is this..."

He pointed down, closer than the peaks Bran had been looking at, to where the valley forked. A tarn, considerably larger than Pwil Gesgod, and almost square in shape, showed there amongst trees. A building stood in a clearing on the far side of the tarn, backing up against an outcrop which stood there.

"That's Lanerc's place, down there, t'other side of Pwil Glas. Y'll want to get to know him soon like. He'll swap you food, or tools, or such like, for well-finished pieces. He's sound. But not everyone around here will honour a debt they've built up. There's some will quietly forget what they owe if you're not sharp about it. I'll tell you who's who."

He turned back again and pointed up towards the summit of the Ban, below the crags which ringed it They climbed a little higher, and under Bran's feet he heard the sound of the rocks change. When the shards came together, they rang clean and clear, with a sharp clack quite unlike the dull clunk of lower down. He bent to pick up a sharp-edged shard which, long ago, some former worker had slivered away from the main mass of a roughout.

Finn nodded, his sudden smile lighting up his face.

"Aye, that's what we listen for. Best sound in all the land, that noise, isn't it though? I'm right glad you know to listen out for it."

He stopped again, and Bran tossed the fragment away to see where he was pointing.

"I reckon you could start up that slope there. Not the first part over to the left, it's been worked pretty clean by now. But further up, from where that spur leans out, I've often thought

## Part 1 – Melen

that there's good material that could be found there. True tuff."

The Ban loomed craggily above the spur. Bran looked across the tumbling stream to the ridge where it peaked to his left.

"So is that the Brig?"

"No, not that. There's a line of crags between us and the peak. Y'll see the Brig better from down below, or from where the valley turns to its close. Or right up the top. But y'll find out soon enough. For now, don't worry about names. Start work there, below that spur, the first few days, maybe the first month, and see what you find."

Bran glanced a question at the older man, not sure if he needed more permission than that to make a start. Finn laughed.

"Look, Bran, you're your own man. If there's sharp words spoken among the crew, as happens every now and again, why then I'll step between them. But we all work when and where we want. If you don't like this slope here, then move across somewhere else. Just don't set your feet in another man's diggings, for they won't put up with that, and nor will I. And put your own working mark below wherever you get to, so's we all know it's your patch. As for me, I'll be across a little that way, and a step or two further down."

He set off, then turned again to call back.

"And don't fret yourself if you don't find anything of any proper size at first. Or if a piece splits unkindly for you. There's plenty of little bits which make fine trinkets to trade for odds and ends. And then there's always the girls at Dolgolvan; y'll need bits and pieces for them. So don't discard a bit of good stone, just because there's not an axe in it. Use the little pieces. Use it all."

Bran looked up and around at the higher crags above him.

"And the true tuff's all here? Nowhere else?"

Finn laughed and pointed further west, towards the end of The Valley.

"Well now, that's not strictly true. They say there's some of the peaks over that way where you can find it as well. You cannot see those peaks from here, you have to go a ways over in that direction. A while back, long before Avank's time it was, a group broke away from the main gang here and reckoned they were going to set up their own crew. And they found pieces there, no doubt about it. The vein runs through the rock in other high places if you know what to look for. Closer by, just above the waterfall you see there." He pointed. "One of the first things Avank told me was how a group of lads had dug an actual tunnel, right into the rubbishy rock over there, to work down to where the true tuff lay. Deeper than a man's height it was, so they say. Took'm an age, it did."

"They do that down south to get at the flint."

He grimaced.

"Aye, so I've heard. It's clay down there, mind, not our proper rock. But it's not for me, rummaging away like a mole." He laughed, suddenly. "Saying that, my father was named for the mole. But that's not for me. If I'm going to die out here it'll be because of a fall or something, through the air, not with a massy piece of rock crushing the life out of me when it comes loose above me. A horrible way to meet your end. But back to your main point. Flint's alright, I've no quarrel with that. But there's folk who'll just fashion an axe out of whatever rock they find to hand, even down in the lowlands, not any kind of tuff nor flint. But what we make comes from this one place. Shaped by the sky and the steepness just as much as the rock below your feet. Y'll find axes made from all kinds of stone, but none of them are ours."

He waved and scrambled away again. Bran worked his way up the slope, past the jutting spur of rock that Finn had indicated, and looked around. He was used to spotting intruding veins of rock from his time on Innis Mon. Some of the tuff was similar here; in any case, he had studied one of the Ty Caroc axes which Morvin had traded for, and he knew what he was seeking. Here, it would be nestling in the rock like an unborn child inside its mother, not trimmed and polished in its final form. But he would, he was sure, know the vein as soon as he saw it.

The first half of the morning passed slowly, as the brightness of the sun moved up the sky behind the sheet of thin clouds,

## Part 1 – Melen

until he found his awareness becoming bound into the rockface. The outer wrinkles and crevices took on deeper meaning to him, opening up their knowledge of the substance within. He forgot the passing of time, stopped hearing the high calls of the buzzards, and let himself sink into the ancientness of the mountain, the past that was sealed up below the surface.

Until, finally, Finn's voice from below called him back into the world of men. He blinked, looked up in disbelief at how high the hazy sun had risen.

The group, he discovered, had gathered all together beside the tarn. He settled himself on the edge of the group, nearest to Don. It was, he decided after a few minutes, a poor choice: the older man had little to say to anyone, and least of all to a newcomer. A few of the others nodded to him, but for the most part they simply continued their own conversations, each pulling out their own bags of food. It was, he decided, going to take time for them to feel him as one of their own.

Nant had arrived late, and sat beside him. Judging by the way the others teased him, it was clear that he normally missed most of the midday time together, being caught up in his own pursuits. But he felt more alive than Don, so Bran turned to talk with him, feeling a wash of relief. He quickly realised that Finn had been right; Nant knew The Valley in a different way than any of the others. He was diligent, almost obsessive in giving things their names, and had a way of making connections between places that seemed obscure.

Bran swept an arm around the peaks to the south.

"Is any of them Mynyth Mam?"

"For sure, yes." Nant pointed. "That one there, in the distance between Pen-y-hal on the left and Drum Mail to the right. A fair bit further away than either of them, of course, but that's her alright. But if you go across towards the Brig you won't see her. The swell of the land will block her from you."

Bran gazed at the distant crest, fascinated by the thought that the peak that the elderwoman had said that he should, one day, ascend, was so clearly visible from here. Nant carried on, pointing out this and that landmark, showing Bran where exactly in the valley he should look for the great rock with the foremen's names.

"Finn told me that you often get to the quarry by a different route."

Nant nodded.

"Come up the regular way, did you now?"

Bran nodded and gestured across to the ridge they had ascended earlier.

"Well, that's alright for your first morning. And some of us always do the same thing every day. Gan-Mor's one of them, day in day out the same path. Reckon it gets them in the right frame of mind for the day, and maybe it does. But that's not what I do. Mostly I come up an earlier path, but I chop and change around. Suits me to do that, it does. Helps me get to know every trackway hereabouts. If you like, I'll show you tomorrow morning. Then you can decide for yourself."

"Finn said something about dead men?"

Nant nodded, his face serious, intent.

"Oh yes. The track goes up right beside the dead men's markers. The men are long gone now, of course; I couldn't tell you exactly how many generations ago it was. I like to think they're just like us, but from an age ago. Stoneworkers, I mean. But nobody knows. I mean, how would we ever know for sure? But I'll show you. The rings are small, mind; you find a lot that are larger than these."

That midday break ended, suddenly, with a collective decision which he missed. No doubt he would become used to the clues, the unseen signals that they were familiar with. Each of them packed away their bait bags, stood, and drifted away towards their own workings, like sprinkles of dust shaken off from a fleece in the spring.

It was late afternoon when he found his first piece of any real size. He had started by clearing away some of the loose shale and flaky stone which had trickled down the hillside over the years of sun, rain, and ice. He wanted to get a sense of the grain

*Part 1 – Melen*

of the rock, how and where it would split apart for him, and just what strength he would need to persuade it to reveal what lay below the veil of the surface.

That first piece could never be an axe. It was far too small, for one thing, and the grain sat wrongly in it. But it would polish up nicely, and in its final form would be a practice piece, and one useful for trading. He turned it over, considered it from all sides. A fish head, perhaps, or a squatting mouse. Maybe a duck. He would uncover its true form as he worked away at it back at his stone hut. But whatever the finished shape would be, it was the true tuff, and it was his first piece.

After a month he felt that he was getting to know not only the quarry and the two peaks either side of it, but the wider area around them as well. From his perch up in the gully, he could look down The Valley. The beck that ran along its length fed no tarn until well past Ty Caroc, and even then, the water there was a half-hearted affair, reedy and shallow with marshy borders. He thought he must have walked close to its southern fringes on that first day, in the last stages of his journey from where the boatmen had left him on the coast. Even further away he could see a great swathe of Lugh Crum, though the little town of Dolgolvan was hidden by the swell of the land.

Closer at hand, the valley bottom below where he worked, stretching east and west, was full of trees that tossed in the breeze like waves on a green thread of lake. From Ty Caroc, the long ridge of Drum Crog sprawled like a tadpole, hiding the taller hills behind it. But by the time he had walked along to his workplace, he was past even the spiked end of its tail, almost level with where a more rugged spur came out from the high land which walled off the far end of The Valley. Over the low end of that, the little tarn that Finn had showed him shone in its cleared circle of land. Lanerc's farm straddled the bridge of land that joined the main branch of The Valley to its smaller sister to the south. He had been to see Lanerc several times now, and had come to appreciate the quiet competence of his ways.

Lanerc was half-traveller himself, and had two children by Gwennol, the traveller woman he lived with. The manner of his household was far more familiar to Bran than anything that he had seen in his brief visit to Dolgolvan. He had been in no rush to retrace his steps back to the town, as the dirt and squalor of the houses stood out clear in his mind. It was only a matter of time until he would need to go again, but for the time being his footsteps turned west, not east, if he needed food or other exchanged goods.

In this first month he had experienced almost every kind of weather that The Valley could supply – though not yet any snow, not so soon after the summer pole of the year. He had been burned and parched by occasional days of continuous sunshine, but more often wettened by drizzle and rain, that some days drifted past in brief showers, and other days was unremitting from daybreak to dusk. But it was the wind that bothered him most, the sudden and unpredictable wind. Twice already, the gusts had been fierce enough that he had stayed at home and worked on pieces he had already recovered; the thought of perching on a pinnacle of rock in those squalls did not appeal.

Most of all, he was learning how the land breathed, how the life within it was fashioned and shaped. The stone he sought, the true tuff, was only one facet of that life. It was the most enduring facet, to be sure, but the life of The Valley also oozed as water from the steep sides, ran with the squirrels among the trees, and soared as flocks of birds above. He breathed in that life as he strode along the wooded paths, and as he perched up in the heights through the working day.

What he liked best were the mornings of low cloud. Some days he climbed up through the layers, to work then in sunshine looking down on a long ribbon of mist filling The Valley like a woman's shawl draped along the ground. Other days, wisps and

## Part 1 – Melen

drapes of cloud hung festooned around the outcrops above him. The peaks were veiled then, appearing briefly and then hiding again from him, and the nearby crags loomed, mysterious and forbidding. If light rain or drizzle misted the rocks into a blur of darker shapes, so much the better.

That aside, he had still not found a roughout of rock of a size that could transmute into a decent axe. There were little pieces aplenty, and as Finn had suggested on that first morning, he kept them to work with. But he really wanted to unearth something of proper dimensions, and so far it had eluded him. The life hidden within The Valley was shy, secretive.

On particularly fruitless days he had explored further afield. This habit was partly fuelled by his own traveller ancestry, to wander the land, to learn its shape and adapt himself to its temperament. But he had also been spurred on by Nant's familiarity with The Valley and all the little trackways that spanned it. A few times each month he had joined Nant on their morning walk to the quarry, sometimes along the same paths but more commonly picking a different trail to follow.

Nant, it turned out, knew not only the names of nearby places, but something of the long history of The Valley. Left to his own devices he would talk without ceasing, pointing out this or that feature of their surroundings, telling tales of days and working habits gone by. Bran had no idea how he had come by his knowledge, but it didn't seem to matter, and he just let the stream of chatter wash over him. In amidst the babble of noise there were nuggets of genuine interest. A little bit, he thought, like the process of extracting the true tuff from the ordinary rock that surrounded it.

On their first journey together, Nant had, as promised, led him up through a series of small rings of stone, each with a raised mound. The oldest of them had already collapsed on itself, the stones which had once stood firm now toppled across each other. But the outside ring was clear to see, with its dusting of finer pebbles. The others were all still intact.

Bran looked at them silently for a while, wondering about the names and skills of those left here. All of the rings faced roughly south, so that the long-dead occupants could still look out from their entrances to the distant sea, and to Mynyth Mam.

Another time Nant led them further on, onto the ridge that led up towards the Brig.

"See this one?"

He pointed out a rough pile of rocks, worn and weathered now, and starting to lose whatever cohesion the structure had once had.

"What is it?"

"I think it's a house. Long since fallen down. I reckon our long-distant predecessors lived right up here, close by the quarry places."

Bran looked around. The site was sheltered in one direction by the swell of the ridge, but was otherwise very exposed.

"Bit of a miserable place."

Nant nodded.

"Fair enough. But maybe whoever it was wanted to live close to the true tuff."

"But there's only one house. And it's not big enough. You couldn't get more than three of us in there. Maybe four at the outside. Not enough for a real lot of workers."

"Again, fair. But maybe this was the foreman. Like Finn's or Avank's long-past forerunner. Maybe he lived up here, and the rest of the gang were down in the valley."

Bran looked at the stones again, then up at the quarry, and along the valley to where their own homes were still covered in mist.

"Finn wouldn't do that. He likes being close to the rest of us. I can't see him perched up here on his own while his gang all leave at day's end." He paused, and turned back again to the hillside. "I don't think I'd like it here either – it's too near the workings. Too near the mystery at the heart of what we do. It's not a place we should live."

Nant nodded soberly.

"Can't disagree with you there."

## Part 1 – Melen

They walked a few paces up the hill, then Bran stopped again. The pressure of past ages was heavy on him.

"Just how long do you think we've been digging here? People like us, I mean. How long have we been digging out the tuff?"

"I have absolutely no notion at all. But there's so much that's really old here. I think we've been doing this forever."

That was the end of their talk for the day, for Nant branched off at an angle and let Bran walk, on his own, to his working place.

Nant's ideas were fascinating, but also wearying, and Bran made sure he only walked with the man every so often. Most days he went alone from Ty Caroc to the quarry. When left to his own devices, he liked to begin and end the day by passing by the great rock that marked the division between the living space of Ty Caroc and the sacred space of the peaks. It seemed fitting to him to honour the memory of the stoneworkers who had gone before, by pausing a moment at the rock to glance at the little clusters of marks they had made.

Once in a while he left the Ban and the Brig to themselves and explored. One day he walked back to the eastern end of Drum Crog and ambled along the length of it, enjoying the sight across towards his usual site, looking from this angle like a sheer stone ring. It was easy to imagine it as the crown of the whole land. Not, to be sure, the tallest place, but the heart of the land's mystery.

Sometimes he climbed up onto the long arm of the plateau that came away from the high peaks. There were a few tracks from the valley floor up the steep side to the north, and he systematically tried them all. The ridge extended eastward towards Dolgolvan but fell short of it, forking southwards into the crumpled hill he had skirted on that first day – Bryn Brith, they called it – and northwards to a final rounded summit, before descending steeply down to two smallish lakes, separated by a marshy area between. He learned, eventually, that the rounded summit that overlooked the pair of lakes was named Alt Ariannaith.

The plateau itself was pleasant enough to wander around,

and granted fine views north and south, but to his experienced eyes it held no places where the true tuff might surface. Once he found some beautifully marbled outcrops of white rock. The vein ran in a perfect line for a few hundred paces along the surface of the ground towards the Ban, the nearer of the two peaks that towered above his workplace. It was quite different from the nearby outcrops of shale and granite, and he chipped off some convenient-sized pieces that he could fashion into pretty things. On some such trips he spotted, from a distance, the two little stone shacks where Drus and Spink lived, but he kept well away from them.

On a day where the high clouds scudded past, high in the bright blue air, he had wandered all the way along the level floor of The Valley, right up to where it ended in steep walls. He turned left to clamber up out of the hazel and birch woods, through the juniper and hawthorn, up to where he could look back at the steep pointed slopes of the Brig. He hardly ever saw it from this angle, neither from Ty Caroc nor his place of work.

Caught by a sudden idea, he climbed higher, until he was on a level with the crags adjacent to the Brig. He frowned at it, trying to imagine how the vein of the true tuff might extend out towards him, if the great hollow of The Valley did not interrupt it. Perhaps – if he drew out in his mind's eye the line of rock he worked at every day, out through the gulf of empty space – perhaps it was still higher than his current altitude. He turned and looked in the opposite direction, to where the land rose higher again. He had asked Cowann to tell him more about Finn's tale of the men who had left The Valley and found another place, another peak where the true tuff pushed out of the ground. The way Cowann told it, he could half-believe that the tale was true. But standing here, it was too hard to work out how the grain of the land might join up one peak with another.

He climbed a little further on, threading his way between sheer crags on his left and a softer ridge on his right, and discovered a little tarn, nestling under steep cliffs that glistened with wet. Ahead of him the land rose up again. He shook his

*Part 1 – Melen*

head, looked at the height of the sun ahead of him, and turned back. He had gone far enough for today, and before his next foray would ask Nant if he knew what lay beyond the next crest.

He chose a different route home, circling around north around the ridge, across a tract of land which seemed more remote, more wild even than the places he knew. To the north another long valley curved away, and he did not recognise the shapes of the hills there. In all that walk he found plenty of stone, but no true tuff.

In the evenings, when he wasn't shaping and polishing the little pieces he had found, he often found himself in Avank's house. The old man bitterly regretted his own inability to climb up to the quarry as he had used to, and made up for that by dispensing advice and skill with open hands. Bran would pass over a piece of rock, and delight in the way Avank's hands fondled it, feeling it on every side for the grain, the bumps and the crevices, before suggesting in a few quiet words how it might be worked. Lewenith had watched him closely, with wary eyes as she mended baskets and nets, squatting near the door to catch the best of the light. But after the first few occasions, she became easier about his presence there.

Prental was another matter. He would turn up outside Bran's door unexpectedly and settle himself to talk. He took no notice of whatever Bran was doing at the time, and sat himself down uncomfortably close, prattling away and offering advice and suggestions that Bran did not want. He had no idea how to change this without causing offence.

One night he arrived, beside himself with emotion. He was clutching something in his hand, and it was a long time, full of incoherent words, before he was willing to show Bran what he held. It was a piece of the true tuff, partly worked but with a ragged split across one end, as though the rock had been torn apart. Finally he pushed it into Bran's hands. He turned it over, seeing the shaping marks that had already been made, and the slightly careless stab that had split the whole thing apart. He nodded.

"You found there was a deep flaw in it."

Prental's face worked, as though he was trying to hold back tears.

"Bran, look, I thought this was a good piece. See here..." He took the piece back again, turned it so that the jagged edge was facing away, pointed at some of the delicate work he had begun there. "It was going so well, then all at once... Well, see for yourself. Just here. What did I do wrong, Bran?"

He looked away. Bran took the rock from his limp hands and studied it.

"This was alright, what you were doing here. Bit previous, maybe: you didn't need to do such fine work until the whole thing was roughed out. And this, just here, this was a clue that maybe you might have noticed." He tapped an indentation on one side, with a discolouration in the deepest part. "See, the flaw inside comes out to the skin just here. It was trying to tell you that it wasn't sound all through. Then this strike here..." He turned it again, bringing the final blow up to the top. "Well, you caught it right at its weakest point, and that put an end to the whole thing."

Prental rubbed his face, frowned at the rock.

"Then I should have seen it. It's all my fault. A perfectly good piece of tuff ruined."

Bran leaned back and studied him.

"Well, no, it was never that good. That flaw was inside there all the time. Even supposing you hadn't split it how you did, it wouldn't have held up in use."

"Is it always like that? I mean, can you always tell from the skin of the rock what the inside is going to be like?"

He laughed.

"No, not at all. Look at this." He turned to one side, rummaged through a little pile of part-worked stone before picking up two particular pieces. He turned the first to show a ragged split not unlike the one on Prental's stone. "This one here – look. Nothing visible on the surface at all, but it came apart when I worked it. I was cross about that one, since I had it in my mind

## Part 1 – Melen

it was going to be a proper axe. A bit on the small side, but neat and handy – but it wasn't to be, as you can see."

He waited until Prental had studied the fragment, then held up the second one.

"But this one now, just look at that stain on the underside. That was the last bit I eased away from the vein, and when I saw it, I was convinced it was flawed. Well, I decided right then to divide it up into several bits for trading. And would you know, the more I worked with it, the more I realised that it was sound right through. That seeming flaw was just on the surface and nothing deep. Too late by then, of course – I'd already divided it up. But if I'd known from the start, I could have made a proper axe out of it, and made what looked like a flaw into a truly attractive feature."

He shook his head, ruefully, and let Prental look over the second piece.

"You see, you don't always know when you start out. Something that's a flaw might show on the surface, or it might not. Or something might look good but be broken inside. You just have to work with it and find out."

Prental let out a long breath and pursed his lips.

"So how do I know? What should I have done?" He paused, and then rushed on. "What would you have done?"

Bran picked up the original piece and turned it over again in his hands.

"Well, there's plenty of good stuff here still. You won't get an axe from it now, but then you were never going to, not with that flaw. But you'll get two, maybe three little pieces for your own trading at Dolgolvan. Or you could save this part here to add to your working set of tools. Look, it would make a nice little shaper if you take off that angle there."

Prental took it back again, starting to study the stone properly again. Eventually he nodded with relief.

"Yes, I do see what you mean. I don't know how to thank you."

Bran waved the comment aside and turned back to his own

work. Prental almost reached the door, and then turned round.

"All this is new to me, you know. I grew up down south, where we use flint. Dig it up from down under the soil: it hardly ever comes to the surface in big enough pieces to use."

Bran leaned back.

"I've heard of flint, of course, and Morvin who trained me had some pieces that he showed me how to work with. Altogether different from tuff."

Prental nodded eagerly.

"It is. You have to learn the grain, else it splits the wrong way on you. Like you say, it has a different habit from the true tuff." His voice dropped, and he leaned closer in a conspiratorial manner. "Finn has a piece of flint, you know, that he showed me once. I didn't tell him, but it's only second-rate. He's so proud to have it, but I know it's not the best stuff at all."

Bran nodded cautiously, not wanting to encourage a line of words that could easily turn into unpleasantness. Prental waited a few moments before continuing.

"Bran, can I come and work alongside you of an evening? Learn more of this."

"Isn't Gwovan the one who's finishing your apprenticing?"

Prental nodded and shrugged.

"But he wouldn't have sat and explained all that like you did. He gets impatient with me, you know. I'd learn more from you, I'm sure of it."

"I couldn't do that. Not with Gwovan being in the same gang. Wouldn't be right. You have to stay with him. I mean, it's fair that I work alongside you, and maybe we'll share some problem or other between each of us as mates, but I won't come between you and him. He's the one that'll put the next few marks in you."

He turned back to his workbench, wanting Prental simply to walk away. There was a long pause, and then he heard his door open and close again. He closed his eyes briefly, breathed a sigh of relief, and got on with his own stonework.

## Part 1 – Melen

The days slipped by, becoming shorter all the while. He was content, except for the lack of proper stone roughouts to begin what he considered to be his real vocation. Little bits to fashion into tradegoods, or pretty trinkets shaped from the true tuff or the white outcrop he had found, were all very well. But to prove himself to the rest of them, he wanted to find a piece that could be transformed into an axe. It had to be large enough to trim down to the right size, properly sound all the way through, and unblemished in appearance. Later, perhaps, when he was truly a part of the group, he would relax a little, but he wanted the first one to be as near perfect as he could make it. Nothing had, so far, met all of his exacting standards.

His life at Ty Caroc had settled into something like a routine. Once each moonphase he went out with one or other of the gang to hunt game or gather food from the wild. He preferred nets and snares to longer-range weapons, so mostly he brought rabbits and hares back to the stone houses, along with a few pigeons. Roudhok was excellent with the bow, and Cegit sometimes teamed up with him to bring back the occasional deer, hanging heavily from the pole slung between them. Don and Prental were not far behind in skill. Several of them fished the becks and tarns. Most of the group worked in pairs or threes, but Gan-Mor always went out to the hunt alone, and brought back considerably more than an equal share. But once they discovered, early on, where Bran's own skills lay, they urged him to team up more often with Lewenith.

Lewenith was much more patient with the snare than he was, though not so adept with the net. But she excelled in the gathering of plants, saying that those pursuits better suited the life left in her limbs. She knew in detail what grew where in The Valley, and Bran rapidly came to enjoy the times they went as foraging partners. She never spoke of her training, but he was convinced now that she had once been apprenticed to a healer, and had perhaps taken that training for a considerable distance. Certainly she took on that role in the village, and was often busy binding sprains or choosing herbs to heal a work injury.

During these autumn days there was no shortage of things to forage. Day after day they brought back roots, leaves, nuts, flowers, and berries of various kinds, most of which could be dried down for use in the winter months. The baskets that she and Cornigil made, and which hung in every house out of reach of the mice, were steadily being filled.

They spent over half a month finding and gathering mushrooms of different shapes and colours, and gradually he got to know the rosegills and the elfcups, the waxcaps and the bonnets. Lewenith would take some and reject others with only scant words to highlight the differences, Indeed, she said little on any particular day, but she showed him a great deal, and they returned after each foray with their reed baskets full of good things. He began to feel that even without her help he would be able to manage to gather enough, in these plentiful autumn months at least.

The food they collected was, he reflected, not very different from how it had been on Innis Mon. In some parts of the year, the land supplied most of their wants, and there was little need to hunt. But as winter closed in, and before the spring would awaken the world of plants again, animals and the occasional game bird would become their chief source of food. But on balance, over the span of a year, the gather brought in considerably more than the hunt, and Bran took great pride in his work with Lewenith.

As the autumn approached, and the sun's track through the sky dipped lower each day, he grew to love the days when the valleys and their western ridges were in shadow. But on the east, the declining sun lit up the ridges as it set, illuminating the yellowing leaves and browning bracken as it did so.

These days away from the peaks, finding the animal trods

## Part 1 – Melen

in the hazel woods, or stalking the larger prey on the slopes of Drum Crog, or patiently seeking out the edible plants and mushrooms, soon taught him which of the gang could be relied on to join in, and which shirked away.

Nant, to his surprise, hardly ever participated, though he did join in the shared meals readily enough afterwards. Brogat reckoned he had no skills in either hunting or foraging, and kept away. Both men rather ostentatiously worked on repairs around the village houses, or helped Cornigil bank up the great fire to cook whatever the others had caught. It would be extremely easy, Bran thought, to get a reputation for laziness at Ty Caroc, and quite hard to lose it once gained. He sometimes heard the other men speak of Cegit thus, despite his occasional forays with Roudhok.

On fine evenings after these foraging days the whole community would gather in the open space between the houses. Cegit, it seemed, had the best voice of them all, and could easily be urged to lead them in song. Salis always brought Cowann out for these times – they were almost the only occasions that Bran saw him outside his own house. Bran would watch him tapping the pulse of the music with his shaky hand, and mouthing silently along with the words, and wondered what it would be like not to be able even to walk along the valley floor to the great rock.

Brogat was the nimblest of them all. Quite apart from his poise high up on the quarry face in places that nobody else would tackle, he would impress them all with handsprings and somersaults between the buildings and over the central fire. All of them took turns at entertaining the others on these nights, and although Bran had not been expected to join in for his first few times, he knew that before long he would be taking his place among the entertainments. He would have to think of something.

But before that could happen, Don died. Bran knew nothing of it, until he heard shouting in the early afternoon from the crags above Pwil Gesgod, a wordless noise that nevertheless told him that some calamity had happened. He thought at first that someone was simply lamenting the loss of a dropped stone tool, falling all the way down the slope into the tarn. But when the clamour continued he frowned, shook his head, and worked a careful way down and across towards the source.

Don's body lay twisted well below the bottom of the crag he had been working, a pool of blood around his broken head where a rock spur had caught him. A little heap of shale was under him, with a scatter of stones leading back towards the high crag. His left hand still clutched a sprig of heather, uprooted from its insecure grasp. Nobody had been close to him, but Roudhok had been nearest, and the first to reach him. He was on his knees beside the body, babbling to Finn, who was standing over him, rubbing his shoulders. The rest of the gang were already in a loose circle around them, or hurrying across from whichever more distant parts of the vein of rock they had been working.

"But I didn't see a thing, not anything at all. I knew he was off to my left, not exactly where, I never looked you know, none of us do, but I used to hear him whistling and talking to the rock like we all do, it can't have been far, not far at all, but I never watched to see exactly where, I wouldn't have done that to any of us. I wouldn't. You know that. But that all means I can't tell you what happened."

Finn nodded, squeezed his shoulder one last time, and looked very sombre. His voice was very quiet, and Bran had to strain to hear it.

"I know, lad. I know. Nothing you could have done. Nor none of us. He must have missed his footing. Could have been any one of us lying there."

He sighed, shook his head, turned, and sat on a nearby stone.

"We'll get the body prepared properly now. Then we'll expose him on the rock at the west end of the valley at sunset tonight. There'll be no more work for the rest of today, not for none of us. Not tomorrow neither. And we'll not be going to Dolgolvan the night after. I'm thinking that it wouldn't be right. I'll get word to Bechan."

*Part 1 – Melen*

"He's been with Braith a few times lately. Might be good to pass word on to her."

"That's fair. And while we're speaking of such, does anyone know whereabouts he came from? If he had kinfolk or anyone that should hear about this?"

They all looked at each other around the group in silence. After a while Nant spoke.

"He came here from up north, across the big arm of the sea up there beyond Dronow Moar and the great hills above it. Where they keep them little black cows with the white band round them. And their tradition is that us travellers first made landfall there, long ago I mean, from over the water."

Gan-Mor sounded doubtful.

"Is that true? We tell a different story back home."

Nant shrugged.

"I have no idea. We tell it another way where I come from, too. But that's what he said to me once." He noticed Finn's expression and hurried on. "But as for kindred? That I don't know. He never talked about such."

Finn nodded, slowly.

"It'll have to do. All he had is us, then, and it'll be on us to send him off proper-like." He stood up again. "Go get your tools from wherever you've been working, if they're not with you already. We're all done for today, so just tidy up your kit and leave the work. Then we'll get him all the way down the fellside. And Roudhok, you gather up his stones and carry them down for him. If you can find them without coming to grief yourself, that is. I'll sort out whatever's half-worked in his house and share the pieces out among us all. Maybe a piece for Braith next month for his memory."

Roudhok nodded, and as most of the others started to scatter back to their different sites, Brogat spoke up.

"I'll go back to Ty Caroc and tell the others. Avank'll want to be there: he put the last marks into Don's body just before you became foreman. If he can do the walk, I mean: I'll see what he says."

He started off down the fell, running where he could and slowing down where he must, and before long he had disappeared from their sight.

Bran stayed near to Don's body; he had brought his kit with him down from his former perch, and knew that the piece he had started to chip at would be safe until he got back. It was still attached to the main vein of rock on two sides, and wasn't going anywhere just yet. Finn came up to him.

"Bran, I'm wondering if you've heard anything about that white crystal stuff they sprinkle over bodies some places down south. Maybe if y'd brought some over from Innis Mon we could put it with him."

Bran shook his head.

"Morvin talked about it, and he showed me some that he'd been given years before. But we never used it out on Innis Mon, and I've not seen it since then. They have it in plenty on the great island out west. Is there some to be found around here?"

"Not as I know. I just wondered. No matter though: we'll make do with some flakes of the true tuff instead. And his own tools if Roudhok can find them."

The afternoon was half gone before they were all down at the flat land below their usual working place. They placed the body on top of the rock that Finn had mentioned, a great slab about as high as a man's waist. At some previous time, signs had been cut into the rock, but nobody knew any longer what they signified. Perhaps, Bran thought, they were just the working marks of some ancient foreman. Or maybe they hinted at a vision some passing seer had had, squatting beside the rock, gazing out from the grove of trees towards the end of The Valley, where the land rose up into crags into its row of giant knuckles.

Whatever the original intent, it was now the place where bodies were laid out and exposed for the wild things to take as they saw fit. From what he had heard, Piat was the last person to have been laid out here, but none of the men wanted to talk about him. Today was Don's story alone. Brogat had run back to Ty Caroc, told the others, and collected Don's few belongings from

## Part 1 – Melen

his hut. Lewenith and Cornigil had walked back with him along the winding trail between the hazel thickets, and Avank was following along slowly. The others could not come; they were too old or too infirm to make the journey, and would remember Don from their homes in Ty Caroc, each in their own way.

When Avank arrived, they stripped the body and laid it out on the rock. Someone had split his hammerstone so it could never be used again, and Finn had set it to rest on his bare chest, with his antler beside it. They shared out such of his other things which had some use or value left in them, and left the scraps to one side. Each in turn stepped forward to recount some story about Don; Bran thought hard about this, having known the man for such a short time, and ended by saying as how Don had once given him a spare antler tine, when his had sheared away in mid-session.

Finally, Finn scattered some flakes of the true tuff over him, and set a partly-worked roughout beside the hammerstone, and then they all turned and went away. The wild things of The Valley would take him, as and when they saw fit, and he was no longer the responsibility of either Finn or Ty Caroc.

The mood was subdued that evening. Nobody sang, or recounted stories, or gathered much in each other's houses. The regular tap-tap, pok-pok sound that echoed around the huts every evening was absent. Finally, his own feelings heavy, Bran wandered out of his house and wandered down to the beck. That was also quiet tonight, quiet in the cooling air of autumn, and the distant call of owls sounded louder than the water's murmur.

He stood there for a while, then, feeling the chill and realising he had come out without an extra wrap, he shivered and went back to the circle of houses. A light spilled out from Nant's hut, and he went towards it. Nant was sitting a little way inside his hut, working away with antler and rag, polishing a piece of stone. His door was wide open, and he seemed unbothered by the colder air. He looked up as Bran loomed at his door.

"Ah, it's you. I reckoned polishing was acceptable, even if proper working wasn't."

Bran shrugged.

"I'm too new to know, but I won't argue with you."

Nant leaned back, stretched, and set the partly-worked stone down.

"I met Don when he arrived here, knew him from that very first day, so I reckon I've an idea what he'd like and what he wouldn't."

Bran squatted down near the door, leaning against the stone of the house wall. Nant passed him a clay mug of water and continued.

"I knew something would happen today; when I got up there were great trails of geese, high up, heading northward. It struck me as a significant day, though I had no idea why." He shrugged. "Perhaps they were here to carry Don back north again."

Bran shivered a little, wanting to change the subject.

"What was it like here, back when you first came?"

"Well, Avank was foreman then; he was still getting up on the crags, no bother at all. He finished Don's training, set the last couple of marks in his skin himself. He'll have been glad to get there today. I thought it'd be too far for him, but he was quite set on being there. I thought he'd only have got himself along to the great rock of names while we were up at the other end laying Don out, so he could join in in spirit at least." He shook his head. "But he was quite determined. Look now, come in properly, don't stand out there like that."

Bran settled himself on one of the wooden stumps inside.

"What was Avank like? As foreman, I mean."

"Oh, he was good. Different from Finn, easier about some things but much much stricter on others. Give him his due, though, he's never once tried to interfere with how Finn does things now." He paused, thinking about it. "I liked the way he did things. I mean, he comes from the same part of the land that I did, so I know the way he thinks. But he always had reasons behind the things he said, so you felt there was, like, a complete plan there, even if you couldn't see it yourself. Finn knows it too, and you'll see soon enough that if there's a hard choice to be

## Part 1 – Melen

made, he'll sound Avank out about it. They're careful with each other – Finn doesn't quite ask and Avank doesn't quite tell him, but they understand each other."

"And Lewenith? Did she just come along to help him now like, when he can't do so much for himself?"

Nant laughed.

"Not at all. She's been with him forever, long before my time here. The story goes that he met her one spring festival at the great circle at the top end of Lugh Laesach. Coupled that night, pretty much as soon as they looked at each other, and they've been living together ever since. All the time while he was foreman and all. He got her with child soon as anything, and in the end they had two children. Neither of them stayed round here, though. Maybe you'll meet one or other some time. Neither took up the stone trade, but they sometimes come travelling this way."

Bran blinked.

"I thought Finn didn't really like anyone in the gang being partnered, and he only tolerated it with the older men out of respect."

Nant laughed again, shortly.

"Well, that's true, he doesn't, not really. Always says that that's what Dolgolvan is for. But he's practical, and he knows the older men can't get along there any more, not easily. It's not as if the women there will trail out here to see us in our own homes. And anyway, from what I heard Avank told him straight up that Lewenith was staying." He paused, thought about it. "I mostly reckon Finn's in the right about it, but then I don't mind me being on my own. Getting on with things. I don't generally go with the other guys on the half waning moon days, you see, not if I'm in the middle of something. It's simply not important enough to me to interrupt what I'm doing. Most of the time I just can't be bothered with it. Sometimes if the other lads nag me too much I go along, to keep them quiet-like, you know, but when I do, it doesn't do much for me. I'm not exactly one for doing anything at all with anyone else, even at the hunting and foraging. As I'm sure you'll have noticed by now. Not for me to say, though, is it?"

"But all the rest go to Dolgolvan? Except Avank and Gowann, I mean? Tomorrow was supposed to be my first time, but I'll be waiting another month now."

Nant nodded.

"They pretty much all go. Gan-Mor misses more than most, though probably not as much as I do. But you'll have plenty of company along the way."

"You with us tonight, bud?"

Bran finished rubbing up more shine onto the little piece he was working on, before looking up and nodding from where he sat, just outside his house. He had decided, just as soon as the piece had come out of the rock to him, that it was a deer head, and he had done just enough flaking and polishing to bring the creature to full view. Brogat had come over to him, was peering over his shoulder. The rest of the gang were already walking across to the start of the track to Dolgolvan.

"That's nice work. You done with it now? Bringing it with you? They'll like it at Bechan's house."

Bran stood up, and put the piece back inside the doorway.

"Not this one: I'm not happy with it yet. I've others with me."

He followed the older man across to join the rest of the group, trying to remember just when he had graduated from "Bran", to "mate", and thence to "bud". It hadn't taken all that long, and he was pleased with how quickly he had been accepted by the team as a whole, once Finn had taken him in.

The afternoon sun was low over the rough crinkled line of crags at the western end of The Valley, and a late chill was in the air. A half waning moon had leaned over the crags for part of the morning, never rising much above the horizon. The crew set off

*Part 1 – Melen*

in a loose gaggle along the track towards Dolgolvan, little knots of men chatting, laughing, jostling. He looked around, assessing who was there. Nant was missing, as was Gan-Mor: a pity, he thought, as he had imagined he would get a chance to talk with them all away from the rocky heights they worked at every day. Brogat was still beside him. He had bent a finger backwards in a rock crevice a few days ago, and the splint that Lewenith had bound it together with the one beside it was ungainly on his left hand.

"This'll be your first time at Dolgolvan, isn't it?"

Brogat knew perfectly well that his first trip should have been last month, but for the death of Don. He shrugged; he had a pretty good idea what to expect, from disjointed comments from the other men, and similar encounters on Innis Mon.

"It is, to be sure."

Prental had heard, and called over from nearby.

"But not your first time ever, I'm hoping. Otherwise whatever girl you get is going to be mightily disappointed."

They all laughed, Bran as well. Better, he thought, to give the men their fun with him now, to let himself be the target of humour. Prental came over to walk beside him now, a little closer than Bran was used to. Of all those who were in the group that night, Prental seemed the least enthusiastic about the night ahead, and Bran felt that he kept trying to cover it over with loud words. In the pause that followed the laughter, Roudhok took up the conversation, his anxious voice rattling the hasty words.

"So listen, Bran. Remember they're not travellers like us. They only know the midden and the byre, not the open land. They're tricksters, so have a care there. They can't be trusted. Don't let them take too much from you, and don't just take their word as truth like you would one of us. And for sure, don't give any of the girls anything before you reckon you've had the value of it out of her."

Bran nodded. He had brought in his bag a little collection of animal shapes, mostly cut from antlers or soft stone - a mouse, a sitting bear, a fish - together with some fragments of the true tuff, not of any particular shape but brought up to a good shine. Spurred by a sudden impulse, he had picked up at the last minute a small duck he had fashioned from a piece of the white marbled outcrop he had found on the upper ridge.

"And you're coming back home to Ty Caroc tonight, isn't it?"

"No: I reckoned to stay over and go back in the morning."

"They'll want more from you for that. Why bother? Just have what you need there and leave again before the night is too far gone."

"Look, Roudhok, it's been a long time since I was with a woman. An exceedingly long time. I'm not going to just rush away after some quick fun. I'll leave when I'm ready, and more than likely I'll see you back in The Valley tomorrow."

"All right, all right, it's your game. If you change your mind, I'll be going back with Prental and some of the others tonight. Just meet up with us if you want. There's a man makes drink out of apples, just a few doors down from Bechan's. Good stuff it is, too, for all he's barn-and-byre. Meet us there if you want. He hangs a wooden sign that looks like an apple outside of an evening. I'm just saying that while you're in Bechan's house, watch what you're giving away, that's all. And most important, make sure you don't upset her. Bechan, I mean. She can make your time here mighty difficult. Turn you away altogether if she takes a dislike to you. Don't get her riled with you, else it might go badly with us all."

Bran had been to Dolgolvan just once since the day of his arrival, and then only to the market area. He remembered little of the town itself. Only the untidiness of the fringing fields, with their background haze of woodsmoke, had stayed in his mind, and also the open space near the centre, where he had been given directions to Ty Caroc. Today, Finn led them through a little network of winding streets that he did not recognise.

They went between the leaning wooden houses, all with doors closed as though in rejection of the men from outside. A few times a dog barked, but they met nobody as they made their winding way along the lanes. Sparrows flitted around the streets,

## Part 1 – Melen

and every so often a mob of jackdaws swirled overhead, but otherwise there was no bird life, and Bran missed it more acutely than he had expected.

Where the houses were more widely scattered and the track opened up more, he could still see the surrounding hills. He had no anxiety about getting back to The Valley, and was confident that he would be able to find his way back to Ty Caroc, but he doubted his ability to retrace the exact same route they had taken. Like the rest of Dolgolvan, the paths between these houses were confusing, untidy. But the other men ignored the houses around, and the occasional half-glimpse of a person who was watching their passage from a window.

The whole town was small, and before too long they arrived at a larger building. Rush tapers flickered their waxy lights and shades into odd corners. A group of young women gaggled at one end. They were not dressed like the travellers Bran knew, either in The Valley or from before: hoods and plain dresses tied with tight sashes, plain coloured, with no personal adornments. It was hard telling one from another, at least at first glance. They stood, all of them stocky in build, so that Bran would never have confused them with traveller women he had known. They were watching the men of Ty Caroc, tucked together safely behind an older woman. Finn strode up to her, towering over her short frame, but she did not look in the least unnerved. Bechan, he presumed.

After a moment, Brogat joined him and the three talked, with Brogat gesturing particularly to Bran where he stood. Finn laughed; Bechan shrugged. Then she nodded, and called a younger woman forward from the rear of the room, behind the gaggle of others. She stepped out, slowly but without real hesitation, her dress tight around her. The scarf over her hair shadowed her face. She stopped when she had come up beside Bechan, and remained silent while the older woman spoke.

"You're the one they call Bran?"

Roudhok gave him a little push. The older woman looked him up and down. The stoneworkers of Ty Caroc were quiet, grinning behind him. He nodded.

"I would like to stay the whole night."

"Very well. This is Melen. She'll be yours for tonight. And, for tonight only, you settle your payment directly with her. I'm sure the rest have told you; behave yourself here, or I'll bar you from ever coming here again."

One of the men chuckled, but Bran couldn't tell which. Melen held out a hand, neither eager nor reluctant, but simply purposeful. She took him through the wide door at the back of the room. As she went, she untied the threads on her hood and let her hair fall down. She led him out into a courtyard and into one of a dozen or so little sheds. Nobody had made any attempt to beautify the place; it was stark, functional, drab.

"What do you have for me?"

Her voice was quiet, disinterested. She scarcely looked at him. He pulled out his pieces of antler-work and stone, along with the marbled duck. She picked at them, turned them around and over, weighed them on her open palm. She completely ignored the odd shapes of tuff, however polished, and focused on the shapes of creatures. Her fingers hovered, lingered longingly over the duck, and then chose the mouse.

"This."

He nodded, surprised at both the smallness and restraint of her choice – she had clearly seen which was the most enticing item – and put the other two items back in his pouch.

She turned away from him, got down on hands and knees, and pulled her dress up around her waist, exposing her woman's parts to him.

He stared at her, baffled. This was not what he had imagined during the long days up among the crags and the scree. His fantasy while teasing the tuff from its hollow, while pondering the rough stone forms he had kept, while smoothing and shaping them back at his home, had been much warmer, much more personal.

She looked back at him, over her shoulder.

"Is something wrong? I thought you'd want to be done with

## Part 1 – Melen

me, to get away from here again with the others. Or am I not to your taste? There are other girls."

She sounded bitter, but unsurprised.

"No, no. It's just... it's only that I don't want something that's quickly over and done. I want..." He stopped. He couldn't say to her that he wanted her to fall asleep in his arms once they had coupled, to make believe that he meant something long-lasting to her, to pretend that she was more to him than just a thing to trade. He ended, lamely, by saying. "I want the whole night. That's what I said to Bechan."

She stood again, rearranging her clothes. She held up the mouse.

"I didn't think you meant it. Well then, you'll have to give me more than just the mouse, if that's truly your wish. I want the duck." She paused, a calculating look briefly crossing her features. "Maybe more even than that. I have to have enough to show Bechan it was a night's work."

He fumbled in his pack again, pushing away the sudden memory of Roudhok's words. He had ceased caring about price. He could always make more trinkets from the rocks where he spent his days.

"Have the duck. And the deer-head." He glanced back at her, reached out and cupped her cheek with his hand, stroked her hair where it curved over her ear. "And look, have this polished piece too. It's a good shape. Worth something."

She still did not pick up any of the pieces, though her hand wavered over them.

"You're the new one out there, aren't you? Bechan told us that somebody different had started out there in the wild fells. It must be you. But none of you came here last month, and I'd forgotten what she said about all that." She stared up at him, puzzled. "Why weren't you here last time?"

"One of the men fell from where he was working, died of it straight away. Bashed his head in and all, so there was nothing to be done. Finn led the death rites and said we weren't to come here. For respect, you know. Don, they called him – did you know him? An older man, shaggy black hair."

She nodded.

"I remember him. He often went with Braith. And Gwinn before her, until her family found her a new home to go into up at Butaintal somewhere. But as for me, well, he never looked at me, not properly. Like I wasn't even there. He never once chose me."

There was a harsh edge to her voice. She took a deep breath, then considered again the shapes he was holding. She took from him each of the pieces he had named, then tied them in a fold of her headscarf. He was distantly aware of noises from the nearby rooms, laughter and the sound of pleasure. But they held no interest for him just then.

"You can't take them back, not now you've given them me. Even if it turns out you don't like what you get."

"I don't want anything back."

She nodded, slowly, and put her headscarf on the floor to one side of the rush matting bedroll. As she straightened again. she turned a little to one side so as to stand at an angle, hiding something of herself from him. Abruptly she pulled her dress over her head, and settled it beside the scarf. Her naked skin had a strong yellow tinge to it, up and down across her whole body. She crossed her arms over her breasts and stared at him, waiting to see his reaction. The abrupt realisation of her name came to him.

"Melen."

The name meant 'yellow' in their shared tongue. She nodded, still watching him, as though challenging him for a reaction. He stripped off his tunic, tossed it to the other side of the room.

"Is that your true name, or just what they call you?"

"It's all the name I've ever had since I was a girl. Is it not good enough for you?"

He pulled off the rest of his clothes, stepped closer to her, held out his arms.

"Then Melen it shall be, and it shan't change what passes between you and me. Tonight nor any other night."

*Part 1 – Melen*

When she finally, reluctantly, faced him and opened her arms to him, he realised that she was weak and wasted all down her left side. Her left arm and leg were thinner, lacking muscle and tone, her left breast was smaller, her left hip did not move so easily, and the skin all down her left side was rough and mottled.

Seeing this, he turned over in his mind the cruelty of his own workmates, quite apart from that of her townsfolk. How, he wondered, had Roudhok, Brogat, and the others expected him to react once he was alone in the room with her? Had they expected her to feel shame when he first saw her? Was he the intended target of their amusement, or was she?

It suddenly made sense of all the joking and teasing the men had put him through along the way. What had life in Dolgolvan been like for her? Had she expected him to look at her with disappointment or repulsion? He felt a sudden surge of anger towards his workmates, and a matching wave of compassion towards Melen. He remembered, all of a sudden, a woman he had seen in the village where he grew up. She had also had one side of her body blighted since birth, but she had learned a trade, had the marks put on her skin, and none of the travellers treated her with anything other than respect. Why should it be different here?

So he said nothing to her, except for little words of encouragement and appreciation, as she let him lead her onto the bedroll. They lay together to couple. And he was patient with the coupling, waiting until she was ready before pressing in, making sure that she had her own pleasure alongside his. He had no idea how the other men of Ty Caroc might favour the women they were lying with, but he had decided that for his own part, he would treat her no differently from a traveller woman.

She lay silently beside him for a long time afterwards, looking into his face as though uncertain what she would find. He could not read her expression, and still had no idea if she considered his tenderness with her normal or strange. Eventually he wearied of the silence between them.

"You said before as how that girl, Gwinn, went away to the

top end of Lin Tios."

She sighed.

"Her family talked with people they knew up there, found another house that would take her under their roof. She's one of them now, and I haven't seen her since." She paused, frowned. "I liked her. She didn't get chosen much either, just like me. Except for that man Don, of course, he kept picking her, said he liked the thought of her pale hair against his dark." She laughed, shortly. "Don't know if I believe that. But anyway, we were a bit like each other, and we used to talk whenever we could. I suppose I won't ever see her again. But the change was good for her family, and most likely good for her. I'm happy for her. Really, I am."

She fell silent again, but he was enjoying the sound of her voice.

"How did she find out about this man at Butaintal? Did she travel there often?"

She propped herself up on one arm and stared at him. Then she shook her head.

"Of course not. I can't believe you don't know. What strange lives you all must lead out there in the wilderness. No, of course she'd never left Dolgolvan before. Her father and eldest uncle went there and arranged it all. Took her brother along so he'd learn the way of it. And it was a good match, you see, because she was paired off into a different settlement. Not just here with somebody she'd known all her life."

"And she's happy there?"

She shrugged.

"Who knows? She's not with her own kinfolk any more, and that will be terrible hard for her. I couldn't bear that. But maybe the family that took her in are good to her. However it is, that's her life now. She'll not be back here, and whatever little ones that come out of her will know nothing about Dolgolvan. She's Butaintal now, not Dolgolvan."

She fell silent again and tucked herself in closer to him. After a little while they coupled a second time, before pulling the rough woollen blanket over them both.

*Part 1 – Melen*

She turned away from the arm he wanted to circle around her, preferring to lie with her wasted side against the ground. She did let him rest his hand on her flank, and fell asleep quickly after that. He lay awake at her side after that, listening to her breathing.

The sounds from the rooms nearby dwindled and, eventually, stopped. Then he heard the other men from the gang leave, one by one. Some would be heading straight back to Ty Caroc, sated for another month, but Roudhok and Prental, and maybe some of the others as well, would be wandering down the lane to find drink.

Bechan's house fell silent, and he kept his hand on Melen as he felt sleep approaching. Even with just one hand against her, he could feel that his fantasy of close intimacy was being fulfilled. He would couple with her again in the morning, he decided, so that she would have no doubt that he was glad to have stayed for the whole night.

He could easily persuade himself that she had wanted this as much as he had needed it, and that he had done nothing to make her more ashamed of her body. He had tried his best to be no different with her than he would with a traveller woman. He was still turning over in his mind what, if anything, to say to the gang from Ty Caroc. Most likely nothing, he decided in the end; he'd play out their game with him, and would simply baffle their expectation by going with Melen again next time. Then he gave himself up to sleep.

A few days later, Bran met Nant again to learn another new route up onto the crags where they both worked. This late in the year, the sky was only just starting to brighten as they set off along the track. Ahead of them, great billows of cloud lifted high above the peaks at the western end of The Valley, their tops rose-pink where they were already catching the first light of the dawn.

Nant had a great bruise on his left wrist, and he was favouring that arm as they walked along. He shrugged as Bran asked about it.

"Just a work-a-day accident. Put out this hand when I slipped a couple of days ago, and jammed it badly in a crevice. Lucky it wasn't worse for me, I reckon. Maybe I'd have been like Don if I'd not stopped myself like that. Lewenith gave me a cloth wrap for it in the night, some sort of herbs in it. It's better today than last night."

Behind them, the morning star was only just visible above the swell of Bryn Brith, almost lost in the sky-glow of the rising sun. Nant gestured to the bright star, quite obviously changing the subject sharply away from his injury.

"Not all that long, and then we won't see her until well into next year. I shall miss her all that time; she's a rare beauty."

Bran nodded, accepting the other man's reticence about the injury.

"Almost a year from disappearance until reappearance, someone told me back on Innis Mon." He frowned, thinking. "It wasn't the elderwoman. Someone else – a man, I think. Yes, a man travelling from the mainland here, he was going off out west to the great island beyond us. He was saying as how some of the bigger stone circles tell you when."

"Not the one up at Dronow Moar. At least, I've never heard tell of it. But oftentimes the builders long ago knew more what they were doing than the stories we're left with. Or maybe it's a secret that the songmakers keep to themselves, and don't share with the rest of us. We all have knowledge that we keep within our own trades."

Bran was still looking back at the morning star.

"Well, at any rate, it's right what you say. And look now, at least we'll get the evening star in a couple of moons' time, to make up for the lack, so to speak."

Nant laughed. They had met at the track that led through Ty

*Part 1 – Melen*

Caroc. It ran along the northern side of the valley, a little way up the slope so as to avoid the wet ground and rushes where the beck wound to and fro. Bran had expected they would go west, but instead they set off away from the peaks at first, towards Dolgolvan.

But then, soon after leaving the group of houses, they turned to branch up the steep valley wall on their left. Bran followed without comment; he was used to Nant's unexpected changes of route by now. They stayed quiet while toiling up the hillside, winding along a smoother way between sheer outcrops. A noisy stream cascaded through a ravine on their right, and at one point they threaded a careful way across it, with the water splashing across their feet.

They had left the oaks and beeches, the hazels and the blackthorn of the valley far below, ascended through belts of birch and juniper on the way up, and were now on open ground with only scattered bushes in more sheltered crannies.

When they reached the top, they paused to look around. The summit of Alt Ariannaith was almost ahead of them, screened by the crest of a ridge. The quarry, and the higher peaks of the Bran and the Brig above, were well to their left. Behind them the head of Drum Crog rose sharply. The morning star was quite lost in the light of day by now.

"It's quite a bit longer this way, but I reckoned you wouldn't mind."

Bran did not answer at first, as he took his time to survey the land around. Ty Caroc was hidden behind a swell of the hillside, but he knew where it was.

"No: this is good." He frowned and pointed into the valley, where the myriads of hazel trees tossed in the gentle breeze, like the waves he remembered from his life on Innis Mon. "I think the foremen's rock is down there."

"That's right."

Bran paused, thinking. The summit of Alt Ariannaith was above and ahead of them, though if they continued on that way the slopes would be much gentler than those they had already climbed. He had come somewhere near here once before, when making his way east from Pwil Gesgod, but had not previously been this close to the sheer northern slope of The Valley, nor discovered the ravine they had climbed. There were, he thought, always new pathways to find in the hills here.

"Don't we pass where Drus lives by coming this way?"

"Not far off." Nant glanced at him. "Not anxious to see him today? No need to worry, he and Spink get up on the tops right early. They've been working the long hump that runs east of the Ban for months now, hoping to pick up where the vein of tuff crosses it."

Bran thought briefly that Drus wouldn't like the idea that somebody knew where he was working, but discarded the notion. Instead, he tried to consider how the seam of the true tuff might bridge the empty space eastwards to the great arc of rockface.

"I can't see that working. The lines don't feel right. The height, the angle and all. I mean, I'm sure Drus knows what he's doing, but I can't make it add up in my mind."

"I agree. Seems a foolish waste of time to me, and I'm right glad to hear that you think the same. But Drus'll not be taking advice from anyone. The two of them have been up there for a long time, and I don't know they've much to show for it. I reckon he'd have been crowing to the rest of us about success if he'd had it."

After a handful of paces Nant continued.

"But I reckon someone could find the true tuff if they went looking on the big fells west of us. They go higher than the Ban or the Brig, and the vein of rock might easily clip through them somewhere."

Bran thought back to earlier conversations.

"Finn talked once as how some men had tried it on the Brig, by digging down to where they thought the lines would cross. And Cowann said something about some diggings over that way as well. Leastwise, I think that's where they meant; I was new here at the time, and wasn't used to the hills yet."

*Part 1 – Melen*

"That's so. I was meaning further away, though. Where Cowann meant, not Finn. There's some truly big peaks across that way. There's nowhere to settle, though. And it's, well, it's not welcoming like The Valley is. I walked over there and stayed a couple of nights a few summers back, just camping out under an overhanging rock. Gave it up again, though, soon enough. It didn't feel like a place where people could live comfortably. Too much strangeness up there, and the rocks are all slabby underfoot, so you don't feel safe. Nasty scree, too. Like you could turn your foot quick as anything. Then where would you be? And the valley beyond, going out west, well, it looks forbidding. Steep crags either side and hardly a strip of land between the valley walls and the lake."

He shook his head at the memory. They continued along the broad ridge, following the thin traces of track as it scrambled up over craggy sections and skirted great wet swathes of peat hags and dripping moss. Every now and again Nant would gesture at a tarn, talking of where the frogs would spawn in the spring, or the dragonflies flit in the summer. This late in the year, however, there was little to see. Once he pointed off to their right, to where another track branched away to the two stone huts where Drus and Spink lived.

Whenever they crested a higher piece of the land, the Ban stood up proud before them, with the curving spine of crags to the right, and the solitary pinnacle that obscured the Brig to the left. The sun was well up by now, and although The Valley itself was still shadowed, the crests all around it were lit up in their autumn shades.

They had stayed silent for a while, enjoying the morning as they walked, watching the tips along the top of Drum Crog catching the morning light in turn. They reached the last rise where the ground sloped down towards Pwil Gesgod. To their right, the ridge continued in a long curve round, eventually running up to the northern side of the Ban. Bran had expected that they would go down the long slope, but Nant gestured towards the ridge.

"Shall we go all the way round? Pop out between the Ban and the Brig? That way we'll be near where you work."

Bran was mildly surprised, as most of the crew maintained the same studied ignorance of where they each worked that Finn had mentioned on his first day.

"That would be fine." He considered briefly whether to be tactful in his words, then abandoned the idea. "Is that near where you're working at the moment as well?"

"Well, that's hard to say. I've been across working at a vein on the far side of the Brig for about a month. Thought it might be promising. But I'm going to leave that now, today even, and find somewhere a bit further over. I reckon that same vein should surface again a little bit north of where I've been working."

Bran stopped and stared at him.

"Only a month or so? That's hardly time to even scratch the surface. Don't you want to stay longer than that? You know, give it a fair chance."

Nant glanced back, then walked on again, but slowly, so Bran could easily catch up with him again.

"Well, that's not my way. If something doesn't come up quick-like, I'll move on. I dare say you're a man who'll stay in one place a while and work it dry. Get every last bit out of that spot." Bran nodded. "Most of the lads are the same. But not me. Quick work, in and out of a place and onto the next. Even if I'm finding things, even good things, I mean, not just bits. You know why? It's because the longer you stay somewhere, the harder it is to move along. You keep thinking to yourself, well, another few days and I'll run this seam out, and then I'll make sure I don't miss even the tiniest little bit that's worth having. Not me. It's not worth the effort, Bran. Just move on to the next place."

He gestured across the wide sweep of land, over Pwil Gesgod to the crags behind.

"I mean, look at it, it's not like we're going to run out of rock. We talked before as how travellers like us have been pulling the true tuff out of these hillsides for ever. And when we're gone, there'll be others behind us. Now, there's a skill to finding the

## Part 1 – Melen

really good stuff, that I won't deny. But there's that much rock here that you don't need to claw and crack away at the same little piece and tunnel after it as though there was no other. Give it a short time, then drop it and move on, that's what I say."

Bran frowned, thinking about it, then waited while they tackled a steeper section, rounding the top of the ridge to an isolated hillock that overlooked the great bowl.

"I guess that's not the way I was taught. And see, I took from the rock just the other day a piece that I'm sure will be an axe. Not just little trinkets. That was after a longish wait."

Nant shrugged.

"I'm very pleased for you. That'll be your first, won't it? But don't you mind what I say about that. You work whatever way suits you best. And most of the lads work just the same as you. I'm just saying that I do it different like. It suits me."

They finished the circuit around the rim, stepped carefully across some rougher ground, and both sat on a great rock at the summit of the Ban, legs dangling over the edge. From several places around them, near and far, they could hear the tap-tap, pok-pok of the crew at work, each in their own places. It was a homely, comfortable sound, and Bran felt his spirits lift at the knowing that his workmates were within earshot.

"You trained on Innis Mon, yes?"

"I did. Grew up there, too. My kin still move around the southern half of the island, though the quarries there are up in the north. The rock's similar enough to here that I had no trouble making the change. And the man I was apprenticed to, Morvin they called him, he was right keen I should come over here."

Nant was nodding.

"It's good here. Better than where I learned." Bran looked quizzically at him, and he shrugged before continuing. "Over on the east coast, and a fair bit north from here too. Oh, the rock's fine if you want pretty things, or just walling, but you only get anything like tuff in a few places here and there. There's a long ridgy outcrop runs east a bit then turns north out to the sea, across to a little group of islands. Very dark: almost black in places. That's decent stuff, for sure. I used to go there and pick some bits and pieces, then go back to the great river bend where our winter camp was and spend time working on them. Not the true tuff, though. It's a good place to live back east, but the rock's better here."

"Would you go back?"

"Never. Why would I? My life's here. I like the rhythm of it here more than there."

"Why so?"

He shrugged.

"The barn-and-byre lot are worse back there. More pushy, less inclined to mix with us lot. Though I reckon it's getting more like that here too, year by year. But even the traveller life isn't the same. You'd not think it'd make a difference, but it does. Don used to say much the same about where he come from. And besides, it gets fearfully cold sometimes over on that coast, but it keeps milder here. The winters are better. What about you?"

Bran glanced westward, though the bulk of the land was between the sea and where they were sitting.

"I might go back there. One day, I mean." He paused, and thought about it. "But not yet a while. I used to day-dream about going back in the early days, especially if I wasn't finding anything worthwhile. But not recently. And now, to be honest, I can't actually imagine myself getting on a boat on the sands here, getting off at the beach on the island, going to talk to Morvin and the rest." He considered some more, then shook his head. "Indeed, I truly don't know if I could go back at all now, not since I've started to settle properly here." He paused for a little while before carrying on. "Well then, now I know where you come from. But I've no idea about all the others. Seems to me they come from all over."

"Indeed they do. Brogat and Roudhok are from the mountain country south of here, across the great bay. Inland, though, not along the coast. Cegit further south, not far from that great river mouth with the great wave that brings the tide. Finn's from the same side of the land as me but further south. Gan-Mor much

*Part 1 – Melen*

the same. Cavran, him who lived in your house before you, he came from the great island west over the water. Further out than your island: the one you talked about earlier. They say he was going back there, and that he became homesick for his own way of life. Prental, well, he's come the furthest to be here, he hails from right down south. Started his learning in the chalk ridges they have that way."

Bran thought back to the time Prental had come to his door, distraught about a perfectly ordinary flaw in a piece of tuff. It all made sense, now that he knew where he had started, and how different the rocks of his native land had been.

"That's a big change for him. In fact, he's done well to change himself to working with tuff instead of flint."

"Yes, he has."

They stayed silent together for a while, until Bran spoke again.

"You know, it's different here in The Valley than other traveller places I've known."

Nant laughed, a sudden amused bark.

"I'd say so. But what exactly are you meaning?"

"Well. There's no elderwoman. So there's nobody holding the memory of us all here, and being able to recite the routes and all. I mean, Lewenith does something of that, but I don't believe it's what she learned properly. And you know more than anyone about the tracks all around here, but it's not your training either."

"Well, a real elderwoman – which of course I'm not – would know all the routes around, and how they join up to others close to. How to connect with other folk and other encampments in the area." He shook his head, decisively. "That's not me. I only learn what's useful for the work, going to and fro. I don't know beyond that, and I don't care to. I'm a practical man, you see, and I don't see that learning all that would have any value for me. But to your main point, not every traveller camp has an elderwoman. There's never enough of them who's ready to take it on, and by and large they're self-willed by nature, and won't go where they don't feel it's right for them."

Bran nodded.

"That's true enough. But that's only part of it. We're not a proper encampment in other ways too; there's too few women, and no children at all. And too many of us are stoneworkers and too few anything else. And we're kind of isolated, except for the festivals at one or other of the great circles. It wasn't like that on Innis Mon."

"Can't say you're wrong. I suppose the answer is that Finn likes it this way. Reckons that it keeps us attending to the stonework and not getting distracted into other things. Once a month to Dolgolvan keeps the gang happy enough, and the lads aren't really asking difficult questions about how we live and work. But that said, from what I hear we've been isolated, as you put it, for a lot longer than Finn's been in charge. I couldn't say why that should be. And talking of work, perhaps we'd better begin our own day soon."

It was true: with their longer approach route, they were starting their own work considerably later than usual. Nant, however, still seemed in no particular hurry to begin.

"I've decided for sure. No more time spent on the far side of the Brig. I'll work my way back towards the Ban. Not too near where Cegit is, nor you, for that matter. But a fresh start somewhere. I just have to get my hammerstone from where I left it last night. With this arm still flimsy I'll be better off just scouting around today."

He stood up and wandered off, rounding a protruding crag and disappearing from view without a backward glance. It was, Bran mused to himself, quite typical of the man. He would talk for long spells of time, and then be suddenly gone. In any case, the day's light would not wait for him, and it was overdue time that he began work.

He realised, as he picked up his hammerstone from the crevice where he had left it, that he had been more strongly affected by Nant's words than he had expected to be. Since the early days of his instruction from Morvin, he had had instilled into him that you persevered with a seam until you were sure that it was worked out. You didn't just leave it half-done.

*Part 1 – Melen*

But he had to admit that this resolve had been swayed. Nant was right; there was ample rock here for many more stoneworkers, and many more years to come. The veins of the true tuff were not going to run out. So – if one seam that he was working started to get difficult, or unyielding – why not just move across to another patch?

He sat back on his heels and thought about it. Being honest with himself, he knew he could not easily set aside all those years of training and habit. But perhaps he could work a little towards that end, by not persevering so very long if a seam was unfruitful.

He frowned at the rock face in front of him. This one now: it had started well, and given up to him a number of decent pieces. Melen would be receiving another one of them next time he went to Dolgolvan: a small chunk which he had tried to turn into a deer head. But lately it had dried up, and perhaps it was time to try out his new resolve. And in all this time, it had only given him this one big piece good enough for an axe. He would, he decided, give it a short time longer, perhaps only a few days. If nothing more of real substance came to him by that next trip to Melen, he would move on.

The moon was at the half waning, and the men of Ty Caroc were once again heading towards Dolgolvan. Unlike last time, the stars were veiled, and a fine mist hung in the air, cold against the skin in the late autumn air, and the men were hurrying along the rough track east out of The Valley.

"But it'll fair up before it gets light."

Bran nodded at Cegit's comment. He had an uncanny ability to see the weather's moods well before their time came, and Bran was quite sure that Cegit would be proved right.

"Alright for me then, seeing as how I'll not be back home before the morning."

Cegit shook his head.

"Look, Bran, change that now, before it turns to habit. Just in and out's enough. Why stay longer? It's not natural, not when it's dealing with the barn-and-byre folk. They're alright for this and that, but you can't rely on them like you do travellers. Their word's like this drizzle we've got just now, all promise and no substance. You shouldn't treat them like you would one of us. You just can't."

Bran walked on in silence for a while, until Cegit tried again.

"Have you thought who you'll go with tonight?"

"Oh well, I'm thinking to choose Melen again."

Cegit glanced across at him with surprise.

"You don't have to, you know. She's an odd one, that girl. That last time, last month, that was just like the lads having a bit of fun with you. Seeing as it was your first go here with us and all. Bechan was in on it too. But you don't have to stay with her, not now that first time joke is over and done with, you can move on and pick anyone you like."

"I know that."

They walked on for a while, until Cegit spoke once more.

"Most of us swap around every time, you know. Don't make them – any of them – think that they've got something on you. Don't get stuck with one of them. Why not try Colomenn this time? Or Braith now? They're both alright. Nice to look at and all. It was just some fun, for that first night. I thought you knew that. Didn't you?"

"Look now, I like Melen. She's alright."

Cegit shook his head.

"I can't tell if you're serious."

Bran laughed, and said nothing, and after a while Cegit turned to Roudhok instead. Bran found himself beside Gan-Mor. They talked for a while along the way, though Gan-Mor was taciturn by nature, never using four words when two would do, and always preferring just a single one. The wind turned against them

## Part 1 – Melen

as they passed the tarn, and both were walking with set faces turned down, and hoods turned up to keep warmer.

They passed the tarn that Bran had seen on his first arrival – Pwil Brith, the men called it, named in keeping with the speckled hill that leaned above it. Then they worked their way along a good path that fringed Bryn Brith, and ended by coming down the steep track, passing through a newly burned area of woodland which had not yet been properly cleared. There was a shallow crossing-place across the beck there, into the fields that surrounded Dolgolvan. The town was at the meeting-point of three streams, on the eastern side of the valley. Most of the houses were there in the low ground, but some had been put up on the lower slopes of the ridge beyond. Finn led them along the winding tracks within the village. Bran thought they went by a different route this time, but he couldn't be sure.

And then they all gathered in the big room, and while Bechan was organising them all, he repeated what he'd said to Cegit, asking for Melen again. Melen herself gave a start of surprise when he said what he wanted, but Bechan stayed expressionless. There was a brief murmur from the rest of the gang, but nobody spoke out.

He went with her out of the main room and into one of the sheds outside, where she picked out several of the pieces he had brought with him. Then they coupled, warm together in the drafty space.

She was still guarded with him, cautious in her words, holding herself so that the weaker side of her body was less obvious. But he could persuade himself that she was becoming more comfortable with him, and more eager to involve herself in the coupling.

She had placed the pieces he had given her to one side before they had started. Turning half away from him she picked one of them up. He glanced at it and chuckled.

"You know, I originally planned for that to be a deer's head."

She pulled a face and turned it this way and that.

"It looks more like a goat."

He nodded, ruefully.

"It's not my best piece."

"I like the shine on it, though. It catches the candlelight well enough."

"That's a kind of tuff, but not the true tuff."

She looked at him warily, trying to decide if he was serious.

"No, really. I mean it. You get veins of that close by the true tuff, so they fool you if you're not careful like."

"So what, you mean it's not proper rock? Looks it to me."

"Oh, it's proper rock alright. Good for pieces like that, and a heap of other things. But if I'd tried to make an axe from it, it wouldn't last properly, not like the real thing."

He warmed to his subject.

"Every kind of rock is good for something. Even rubbishy bits that you chip away can be used somehow, as shapers or sharps. Or soft stuff that you'd think at first sight was just a waste will come in handy somehow. It's knowing what you want to use it for that matters."

She shrugged.

"You've talked about this tuff, and flint. Sandstone. Clay. And..." She paused and frowned, then shook her head. "I'm sure there's other names you used last time."

She put the animal head back on the floor with the other pieces, and he settled her more comfortably against him.

"There's all kinds of rock. Those you've named is all true, but they's like a peck of grain beside a sack-full. Chalk and flint you don't get round here, but they're mighty handy in their own way. You get them down south, a long way from here, Where Prental comes from. Not much sandstone nearby either, except down by the coast near where I first landed, Limestone here and there. But I talked about marble, and onyx, and jet. Maybe basalt and granite. Slate, of course, any amount of that all round us. That's the one that slides into flat pieces if you tap it gently at just the right angle. You've got to be right careful with it, though, or it just goes into flakes. There's a different rock we use for a hammerstone, for heavy work. Every rock has its purpose, and I learned

## Part 1 – Melen

all about them when I trained. Then there's a special kind of crystal stuff, bright white, and it glistens in the light when you turn it into a shingle. You don't find it here, but I've heard that people sprinkle it on the mounds of the dead as a special gift. Finn asked me about it when Don died."

"But you lot mostly just dig up that one type, this true tuff."

"Well, that's how we make a living. It's the only place I know of where it comes to the surface so readily. And there's no better stone in all the land if an axe is what you want. It's strong and it picks up a wonderful shine if you treat it right. I found a real good bit a month or so ago, and I'm still working it. It takes time. But the bits I bring here, they're all from different sorts of stone. Different colours, different hardness, different grain inside of them. That duck you picked out last time, on our first night together here. That was a kind of marble."

She nodded, without any real interest.

"Well, it's all just rock to me. All pretty much the same, except for the colour maybe. You can't eat it like you can plants or animals. Yet you talk about these rocks as if they all had their own nature. So far as I can see, they're all just as hard under your feet when you're walking about. But you say they all have their uses?"

"Oh yes. All of them do. Like I say, you just have to know what each one's good for. Morvin – the man who trained me, that was his name – he showed me a flake of obsidian once. I don't know who'd dug up the original core and chipped away this little piece, but it can't be found anywhere near here. A long way south, he told me, across another stretch of water that divides land from land." He laughed. "I sometimes wonder how many pairs of hands had touched that flake before I did."

"What was special about it?"

"Oh well. Obsidian is fearfully sharp, and it holds its point, or its edge for that matter, better even than our true tuff from around here. You could be using that sliver as an awl, or maybe a needle, and it'd keep sharp for ages, so long as you took care of it."

She nodded and sat up straight, apparently with more enthusiasm than she had shown about the other kinds of rock.

"Well, that's good then. Would you bring me some one day? I could use a needle that never gets blunt, or a knife edge that isn't worn away so quick-like. That would be better for me than a deer head, or a goat, or whatever it is." A calculating expression crossed her face, and she frowned. "But you have to bring me some of these animal shapes and whatever as well, so I can give all them to Bechan and hide the needle from her. She'll have to never know that you've given such a thing to me."

"Melen, I don't know that I can find a piece like that. Not around here. If I find one, or that trader-man who comes around from time to time has one with him, then for sure I'll get it for you and bring it secret like. But I don't know when that might be."

She turned sharply to him.

"That trader, you don't mean Gavur?"

"That's him. Do you know him?"

She shuddered.

"I've never talked to him, nor never would. My family would never allow it. But I've seen him from our window when he comes to the village centre. He's a nasty little man, and I wouldn't want to talk with him even if it was allowed. I wouldn't trust him with anything. And you deal with him, like man to man?"

"I've only met him once. Can't say that I liked him, not like one of the lads I work with every day, but if he's the only one who's got something I want, why then of course I'll deal with him. Be stupid not to, wouldn't it? I'll ask him if he might fetch me an obsidian flake next time I see him."

"You mustn't say it's for me, or any of us girls. He'd take pleasure in making all kinds of trouble for us."

"I swear I won't say what it's for. He'll just think it's for me. And in any case, I don't believe he'll have it with him. Nor yet that he could get it. You'd need to know stone proper like to get the right thing."

She stared at him and then nodded.

## Part 1 – Melen

"Alright then. But I'd rather he never knew anything about it. But then, didn't you just say that there's none of that obsidian anywhere near here?"

"None that I know of, nor any of the lads out there with me. Indeed, I couldn't tell you exactly where it comes to the surface; I've only ever seen that one piece after all its travels to get here."

"Then I suppose you're not able to find me some up there in your mountains, that I might use when I'm stitching?"

"Well. I wouldn't say I couldn't, just that I don't yet know how nor where. There's none near the true tuff, the two rocks don't have an affinity for each other. But maybe somewhere else nearby. Something like it that's not from too far away is jet; they find that over on the east coast of the land, over the backbone hills. That's another one holds an edge really well. More chance of getting some of that for you, even if there's none close by here."

"Ah well. No matter. I'll just have to make do with what I've already got. You see? I thought that all those rock names wouldn't help me much in the end." She shrugged with finality and settled back again. "I suppose you're here the whole night again? I guessed that when I picked out those pieces."

He nodded.

"Yes, I'll leave again at first light. Climb back up to where I can find the true tuff, and just maybe some obsidian. But I won't leave before we've gone together again."

She settled against him and sighed.

"You ought to swap and change around when you come here. Not just pick me. None of the other men keep with the same girl. If you stay with me too often, they'll start to wonder why, and maybe Bechan won't like it neither and it'll get me into trouble. I'm not supposed to be someone that's anyone's regular. 'Cos of how I look."

She gestured vaguely down the length of her body. She had not spoken with rancour or disappointment, but as though simply making a statement of fact. He shook his head.

"I'm happy with you."

She sighed again, and pursed her lips, but said nothing for a while. Then she sat up again and nudged him. He looked sideways at her, wondering what had caught her attention.

"I saw that Gan-Mor was with you all tonight. She's not often here, so I was wondering what had happened to bring her out from your place."

He blinked.

"What do you mean, 'she'? Gan-Mor is one of us."

Melen laughed at his expression.

"I'm sure she is one of you. But she picked me one month to be with her, and I can assure you that she is definitely a she. She's only gone with me the once, she swaps around every time she's here. Which is not often. She's not one to stay the same every time. Not like you, but then none of the others have ever done what you did by picking me out twice in a row. I still don't know why you did that." She paused, and then stared at him in sudden surprise. "Why, didn't you know about Gan-Mor? Aren't there other women living out there with you all? But I suppose then that's why you all come here."

"No, for sure there's women out there. Lewenith, for one. Salis. Cornigil."

"I've never heard those names before. But I have seen Gan-Mor."

He felt compelled to honesty.

"Well, those three don't exactly work with us up in the fells. They're older. They're important, mind, and nobody would ever say they shouldn't be there. Lewenith teaches me a lot about where to forage food and all. And she's good if any of us is sick, or hurt. But Gan-Mor is up on the tops with us, cutting out the true tuff and working it just the same as me, or Roudhok, or Cegit, or any of us even."

"And you didn't ever think that she might not be like the rest of you?"

He frowned and looked away, remembering how he had walked beside Gan-Mor most of the way from Ty Caroc, had talked with her after Cegit had given up on him. He couldn't think of

## Part 1 – Melen

anything that had made her look different; her clothing was the same mix of rough-spun wool and leather, the functional and protective gear that they all wore.

"I suppose I never thought about it." He shook his head, trying to puzzle out her questions and his ignorance. "Look now, I mean it doesn't matter. If someone's got the native skills and the training, why should it matter? Gan-Mor never said much about where he – I mean she – came from, but lots of the men are the same. They're shy about where they've come from, where they've trained. They keep it hidden. Out of sight like. I'm not, but that makes me the odd one out, not Gan-Mor. If any of the gang don't want to say, why would I ask? And she's good with rock, you know. Her work's not like mine, but that's alright. We're not all alike. Finn must have checked the marks of her previous training when she first arrived, so I suppose he must know. Anyway, if her work's good enough for him, then it's good enough for me."

She shrugged.

"Yes, she had those nasty marks all over her." She leaned back and pointed. "She had this one, and that. Not those two. That one again, though I don't think it was quite the same."

He shook his head.

"It might not be; it all depends on exactly what type of stone they were using."

She looked blank, then nodded.

"You mean like your tuff or flint or marble or jet?"

"That's right."

"Why'd she come here tonight?"

Bran shook his head.

"I couldn't say. There's another man doesn't come here much, Nant, they call him. He once told me that he's just not that bothered about it all. He's happier staying away. I suppose Gan-Mor is the same."

"But you don't know? You didn't make sure that he's well and safe, and not sick or something out in whatever houses you live in? You lot really don't know much about each other, do you?"

He felt a surge of annoyance.

"We know what matters. We know what each other's work is like. And what other skills besides stonework that each has got, hunting or trapping or whatever. I suppose you know everything about everyone in Dolgolvan?"

She nodded, not with pride but as if what he said was quite obvious.

"Of course. I've grown up with them. I know them, they know me. My own near family best of all, and then further-away kin, and then other folk who live here. Except for those women who've married in to families here, we've all known each other for always. And women who move in to be here make sure they find out quick. They'll need to know who's who as soon as they're with child, and who to call on when their time's due." She laughed, obviously very amused. "I'd certainly know who's a man and who's a woman. And we wouldn't let someone dress up as the opposite. I can't believe that you lot don't know each other that closely."

He shook his head.

"We've all come from outside, from our own kinfolk. Mine are out on Innis Mon, and I'm not expecting to see them any time soon. Maybe I'll go back there, maybe not. There's nobody living out in Ty Caroc who was born there."

She closed her eyes, and settled herself, as before, so that the wasted side of her body was away from him.

"Ah well. What a strange life you live."

He lay on his back, staring up at the rushes and twigs that formed the hut's roof, as she quickly fell asleep beside him. He would say nothing to Gan-Mor about his new knowledge, he decided. If she wanted not to say anything about herself, he would respect that. But perhaps he would talk with Finn, to try to find out more in an oblique manner.

*Part 1 – Melen*

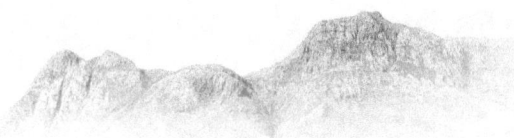

The early winter day was bright, and the blue sky vivid behind the long back of Drum Crog. This late in the year, the ling had all dropped, but it seemed that only scant days had passed since it had been vivid with different shades of purple.

Bran strode, excited, across his valley beneath the leafless hazel trees. Their branches were stark, black against the sky. Up there, wheeling above the crags, a family of buzzards called to each other, but none of his own feathered namesakes were on the wing just now. It was late morning, later than he had hoped to be away from Ty Caroc, but he was sure he had sufficient time.

Low cloud and rain had been incessant for days, and he had grown profoundly weary of the dripping cranny he had been working in, teasing out the tuff where the vein broke the surface. It was a good seam, but open to the sky above, and so open to the dreary weather. At the end of each short afternoon he had returned to his hut as the light faded, wet through and dripping, and each night he had tried, unsuccessfully, to dry his clothes before the fire's embers, to be ready for the next day. Two days ago, the unrelenting drizzle had finally ended, replaced all through yesterday with a thick, dispiriting fog, cold and clammy, seeping through his clothing. But that had finally broken into fierce cold, and wide open skies: a delight to his heart. So now that this utter brightness had dawned, exploration into the high places had called him away from work.

Most of the men were keen to get back to working the crags, finding trinkets to take to Dolgolvan in a few days' time. But not Bran. He already had enough raw material and half-shaped pieces to trade for Melen's company, and plenty of time to finish whatever needed doing. Instead, he was going to climb Mynyth Mam. He was eager – almost desperate – to do something different, something away from the clefts and the pinnacles where he spent most of his days.

He mused, as he walked on, about a conversation he had had with Finn a few days previously. Finn had walked with him as the group separated after the midday break, and sat with him on a handy rock on the upland meadow to talk. It had been, they both agreed, nearly a half year since Bran had arrived, and Finn had gone on to quiz him about his time. Bran was able to say, with complete honesty, how well he felt that he settled in, and how much he enjoyed the work.

Finn had studied him carefully, as though weighing something in the balance, and then had nodded, approvingly. And then, to Bran's surprise, he had begun to ask his opinion on different matters. Did Bran think that Ty Caroc was the best place for the gang to live? If Prental and Roudhok came to blows, how would he deal with them both? Was there a better way to work with traders or the little sea-coast settlements to get their axes spread about wider? Was there a better way to attract new workers to join them?

Bran had few answers for most of these, and felt he had not been in The Valley nearly long enough to know one way or another, but he found the idea of grappling with the problems fascinating. This, presumably, was what took up Finn's time when he was not getting to grips with the seams of the true tuff. After a while the two had parted, and he had gone back to his little perch to carry on working.

Bran realised, too late, that he had forgotten to ask about Gan-Mor. Perhaps it was idle curiosity that made him want to ask. Perhaps, indeed, he should leave the whole matter well alone, and trust Finn's judgment.

That had been several days ago, perhaps a moon-phase, and it now seemed well behind him. It seemed, looking back, merely to be a thing of the moment. This climb, on the other hand, was a quest which he had been intending to take since he had first heard of the mountain and her fame. The elderwoman whose directions had guided him on that first journey had told him of it. She had said then, very directly, that the summit was not to be

## Part 1 – Melen

attempted too soon, and must be approached in the right way. But she had also said that a day would come which would be right for the climb; perhaps it was today.

She had not told him how to recognise such a day, but he hoped that now, finally, it had come. Previously, something had always held him back, but today was, he was sure, an auspicious day. He had settled properly in with the gang at Ty Caroc, he had found any number of small pieces of the true tuff to shape and polish. Just yesterday he had begun to loosen out a larger piece which, he hoped, would be transformed into his first complete axe. And the wild clear brightness of the sky today seemed to him to set a seal of approval on the endeavour. It was, he was convinced, the right time.

Mynyth Mam was not the highest of the nearby peaks, nor the most central, but she was the most renowned. From all that he had heard, she stood proud, looking out south over the great bay and west towards Innis Mon. She was the last of the great peaks in the region, set apart from the ridges which ran up towards her from the north, and attended by lesser hills to the south.

He would do her honour, by standing at her summit on this winter day and offering some gratitude gifts from out of his store. He wanted the challenge of the unknown, not the comforts of the familiar. And he would also be doing honour to the circumstances of his upbringing on Innis Mon, the men and women with whom he had grown up, but who could not be there in person with him.

The elderwoman had come to him before he left, up there on the eastern headland of Innis Mon. She had showed him then, clear against the distant skyline of hills, which of the hills was Mynyth Mam. So, he thought to himself, if he could see the mountain from his old home, then surely he could see back the other way, from the mountain westward towards his old home. It would be a fitting tribute.

Surely by now he had waited long enough in the way that the elderwoman had spoken of, by taking the time to be accepted in The Valley first. Surely it was time to climb the peak.

The ground litter of leaves crunched beneath his feet as he walked on. The blanket of chill air had come in quickly, and the frost had settled deep in the valley floor overnight. Lacework patterns of snow adorned the ridges where they climbed towards the peaks. The beck, in its winding course between the bare trees, wore a thin skin of ice, and he picked his way carefully across the stones there, using his ash stave like another limb to support himself. Then it was up from the valley floor, up and over the stubby head end of Drum Crog, and down again to the smaller valley beyond, The Valley's little sister, listening to the scolding chatter of wrens as he disturbed them.

His first goal was the summit of Pen-y-hal, and he had his first misgivings as he looked up at it. This close to the midwinter day, the northern slopes above him were all dark with shadow. Unlike the peaks of his own home, which enjoyed the heat of the sun every day that it shined, these rocks had not seen direct sunlight for a month or two. And with winter's grip so abruptly fierce upon the land, fingers of ice and powdered snow reached much lower down toward him. He had already slipped twice as he crossed the second beck, and the little tarn to his right was ice all over. But once at the summit, he reasoned, he would be in sunshine all the way along the ridge south to Mynyth Mam, and the short winter day would be plenty long enough for the rest of the journey.

The first half of the ascent was easy. The bracken was brown, shrivelled, and all but gone back into the ground, and there was no problem ascending through the hawthorn and juniper to a green knoll. From this point on, it was only scrubby grass and bare rock. He turned and looked back towards his home, and his workplace.

Ty Caroc was out of sight, hidden behind Drum Crog, but the peaks and crags where he climbed to work every day were in clear view off to his left. He had gazed across from there so often in the high days of summer, across at this very spot from the gullies under the great pinnacles. Now he was finally standing here, at their base. He turned away and considered the steep

## Part 1 – Melen

slope.

The top did not seem so far away, but the curve was against him, and it was hard to tell true summit from false hope. There was some good rock, here and there, but with a lot of mush and scree between. He shrugged, checked the lacings on his shoes and set off. The ice had settled into a thin layer over some of the surfaces, and had worked its way deep into the crevices. The folds of the terrain pushed him constantly towards his right. That was bad; the slope steepened on that side into sheer crags which he would be loath to tackle in summer, let alone in this dark pole of the year.

He frowned, reluctant to back off and lose the height he had gained. There was a bulge to his left, a swollen extrusion of harder stone. It looked sound from his vantage, and if he could work over that he would be back on track, heading once again directly towards the summit of Pen-y-hal. He started again, clambering up and over the nearer face of the swelling, tying his staff out of the way, behind his back. It was of no use on this part of the hillside.

The first section was easy, but then the scramble worsened. The bear-skin leather soles of his shoes were good for keeping his feet warm, but the grip on the stone was poor, and he was starting to regret the choice. Boar would have been better, or even doe, if only he had some, but bear was what he was wearing.

Then he was working his way up the bulge. He thought all would now be well, until he reached out with his left foot, and could find no grip. His breath went out of him in one panicky gasp. There was nothing there for his foot to settle on; the surface was icy, and rubbishy, all without any forewarning. He closed his eyes, tried to breathe normally, aware of his precarious position, but not knowing whether it was better to persevere or retreat.

He brought his left foot back to where it had rested; it had felt sound when he had reached it, but now it seemed woefully small and slippery. He paused, resting where he was, pressing himself against the rock, and feeling the chill seep from the hillside into him even through his winter clothes. He wanted to move back down again, retrace his steps and find another way around this outcrop. But he found that he could move neither hand, nor release the firm grip they had where they were.

He closed his eyes, trying to calm down his ragged breathing and regain control of himself. But his body would have nothing of it; it was locked up, closed in on itself, and only wanted to obey its own rules.

From somewhere overhead he could hear buzzards calling, their remote and unhuman cries doing nothing to help him relax. If he fell, would they cluster around his broken body as the life ebbed from it, and feed themselves on him? Fleetingly the thought crossed him that he would rather that crows ate him, so that his body remained, as it were, within the family.

His fingers were starting to tremble with the fierceness of his grip. It was foolishness, he knew; he clambered up amongst steeper crags than this little one every day of his life, and thought nothing of it. But those rocks were familiar, strong, reliable, whereas this slope was none of those. Besides, the ice it harboured was treacherous.

He opened his eyes again, looking to the side so as to see where he might move hands and feet. He had only just now clambered up, and surely he could work out how to back down the same way again. But even his eyes had blurred now, and he could no longer see the hand- and foot-holds he had used so readily on the way up. He thought, vaguely, of loosening his staff to help his balance, though he could not imagine how it would help. And, worse still, it would mean letting go of the rocks with one hand, and that he could not do.

He clung there, frozen, for what seemed a very long time. There was no chance of anybody being within earshot, and he had told none of the other gang members where he was going. In all likelihood, if once he fell, nobody would ever even find his body.

There was a sound of wings nearby. He shivered, wondering

*Part 1 – Melen*

if one of the buzzards had circled closer, curiosity calling it down from the high air. There was a scabble of bird feet above him, somewhere higher on the bulging rockface. He needed to look up, needed to face whatever it was that had landed near him.

He turned his head back again, slowly, not wanting to upset his fragile balance, and looked up. The bird was not a buzzard, but rather a raven, and a feeling of vast relief warmed him at the sight. The raven considered him steadily with one eye, then turned its head to look with the other. It croaked to him: a softer, more resonant call than the crow or the rook, and, as Bran knew very well, only one of the many calls the bird could make. He had been named by his parents for the raven – Bran – and so felt a connection of kinship with it.

This particular raven was old. He was reasonably sure that it was a female bird, but could not be entirely certain. Some of her wing feathers were tattered, the result, he suspected, of encounters with buzzards and eagles over the years. The black feathers on her head and neck were no longer single-toned and glossy as they must have been in youth, and age had given her a richer mix of shades and tones. She was entirely grand, majestic in appearance.

"Elder Raven, I need your help just now, if you will."

The bird hopped across the top of the rock, apparently finding no difficulty in moving over the icy surface. She considered him once again, head on one side, seeming for all the world as though she was weighing up his predicament.

"Look now, you can see that I'm stuck here, can neither go up nor down. It's a foolish place to be, and well I know it. But you see, I'm named for you; Bran map-Broch they call me, Raven son of Badger. So I'm like distant family, properly speaking. I'm Bran, you're bran. But you're an elder raven, lady of the skies and mistress of your kindred, and I'm just me on my own, stuck here, unless you choose to help me."

The bird took two careful steps to the side, clacked her beak, and turned around.

"Now see, I'll promise whatever you need, if you'll just show me how to get off here. I'll get food from Lanerc's farm and set it out for whoever of your kindred lives near Ty Caroc. Or up between the Ban and the Brig if you want. Wherever. And I'll make sure their nests are safe from wild beasts that might tear them down when I see them up where I work. Or if I find one of your kind who's lost their home and all, I'll see to it that they turn out alright. But I really need your help just now, mistress raven."

His fingers were starting to tremble from the strain of gripping the stone. But he kept his head up, and his gaze fixed on the old raven. She flapped her wings, took off briefly, and landed again on a tiny ledge just across from his right hand. She tapped the stone with her beak, then glanced sideways at him again, croaked one last time, and took flight. He struggled not to feel a pang of disappointment.

But then he looked at the place she had been. It was, he thought, just within reach, and had more substance than the flimsy grip he had at present. He pressed himself against the rock face, clenched his left hand still harder, and then, trying to effect an air of resolution, let go with his right hand and reached for the ledge.

It was firm, and good to grasp, and held his weight. He stayed exactly where he was for several long breaths. Now that his right hand had moved, he could move his left over in front of himself, and his feet would creep back along the ledge. The way out had been there all the time, but he had been unable to see it.

He crept, step by step and limb by limb, back down to the base of the bulge. Finally he was back where he had started, on safe ground. He slumped down, back against the rock, careless of the icy chill, and sat with closed eyes for what seemed a long time.

Eventually he heard a raven's croak on the high air and looked up again. A solitary bird was circling over the summit of Pen-y-hal, a long way above his head. He could not be sure that it was the Elder Raven, but it seemed altogether likely. He stood again, his legs still trembling a little from the exertion and the terror of

*Part 1 – Melen*

it all, waved an arm, and shouted up to her. She carried on her circling, marvellously indifferent to him.

He was starting to shiver, arms and body protesting the cold around him. He took a last, regretful look up the slope to the peak and then started back down into the valley. There was no possibility of carrying on towards Mynyth Mam today. It was time to retreat, to get himself back to Ty Caroc and burn a profligate fire to restore himself. He had some way still to go, up and over the low end of Drum Crog and across the beck close to Ty Caroc, and he needed to keep himself moving.

He was cold in his body, and felt defeated in his soul. He would have liked to have a sense of triumph at having survived the attempt, but he could not. He just felt miserable. The unfeeling heights of Pen-y-hal had got the better of him, and in all truth he knew himself lucky to be standing upright and close to home. It had not, after all, been time to assay the climb, and he had been wrong to attempt it. And now, after all that had happened, he had a promise that he would need to honour.

A moonphase later, he was back in Dolgolvan. He had coupled with Melen again. For his part, it had been a fervent and hasty business, though even when almost lost in the excitement of it all, he had not quite forgotten about her own needs. Now he was lying back, staring blankly up at the rough wood and straw ceiling of the plain little room that Bechan had allotted to them tonight.

All those days, ever since his failed ascent of Mynyth Mam and the experience of being stranded on the icy rockface, he had been preoccupied and mostly silent. He had kept himself away from the other members of the gang, even at the midday meal sessions beside Pwil Gesgod, and avoided any gatherings in the evenings.

Finn had sought him out once, enquiring in a solicitous but indirect way about his well-being. Bran had put him off with easy words, words that deliberately failed to skirt too close to his experience on the mountain, and Finn had wandered away again, dissatisfied but unable to decide what to do next. The other men in the group seemed unsure whether or not to follow his example, and ended up trying to carry on as though nothing had happened.

Lewenith had come the following evening as he sat in his doorway, paring down a new roughout. She sat just outside his hut, saying nothing, but weaving a new basket with practiced hands. The two had worked away at their different tasks, the reed and the stone taking their respective shapes. They had remained in companionable silence, and after she had gone, he realised that his spirit had lifted a little. She had left him the basket she had made, and when he finally went inside, he hung it from a peg wedged between two of the wall stones, and part-filled it with some dried leaves he had picked to drink as tea through the winter.

The bright dry frost of his climb had rapidly given way to dull clouds, but the chill in the air was now here to stay for the season. Tonight, the men walked briskly along the track east from Ty Caroc. Somewhat to his surprise, Bran found himself once again starting to warm to the company of the others, and he joined in with their jibe and crack as they dropped down the slopes towards Dolgolvan. Finn had an air of relief about him as he saw this.

In any case, the focus of humour was Roudhok tonight, who had a bandage around his upper left arm, with dried bloodstains showing through part of it. Prental kept asking him which of the girls would want to be with him when he was in that state, and Roudhok's normal good humour was wearing thin.

When they dropped down from Bryn Brith, the stark fields were as unkempt as ever, with uncleared piles of debris scattered here and there. The usual smell of burning hung in the air. But there was a new feature: wooden poles sharpened onto

## Part 1 – Melen

points and beaten into the ground, with a row of dead crows left to hang limply between them. Their beaks pointed downwards towards the earth, and their feet had been tied to a leather thong between the posts. He glanced at them once, shivered, and never looked in that direction again. He understood that the barn-and-byre folk were protective of their crops, but he found the whole spectacle revolting.

Once at Bechan's house, he had gone at once with Melen into one of the outhouses, ignoring the half-heard comments of his workmates. Despite his haste, which had taken her aback, she insisted on selecting trinkets from the supply he had brought with him before yielding to his urgent passion.

Now, afterwards, they were starting to become cold, and their mingled breath steamed up from them. The single coarse blanket had been pushed aside by their efforts, but he had resisted pulling it up again to cover them just yet. Despite the outward chill, though, he felt that the thaw which had begun while Lewenith sat with him outside his hut was starting to take proper root within him. He was returning again to his world.

So, relaxed and sated at least in part, he told her about his experience on the climb towards Pen-y-hal. In the telling, he departed once again from Ty Caroc, crossed the becks to the start of the ascent, reached the bulge of rock that had thwarted him, and, finally, made a solemn promise to the raven for her help. But the story he told her was simply descriptive, and he had said nothing about the sensations of body and mind which had gone along with the bare events.

She was, all too obviously, not following the story in any detail. The names and the locations meant nothing to her. She had never been there: had never set foot further west than the first slopes of Bryn Brith. Her world started and ended at the fields that bordered Dolgolvan, and The Valley was just a distant name.

She had seen a raven in flight – or so she thought, though it might have been a crow, or even a jackdaw, and she wasn't altogether convinced that there was any real difference between them. Weren't they all just black birds? Even so, she had never seen any of them closer than circling the heights of Bryn Brith. In truth, she had no particular interest in birds of any kind, unless they threatened the crops. Crows were bad for that, and good for nothing at all, she was quite sure.

She said at first that she had heard of the summit that he meant, but she became less certain the more he talked about it. The peaks, which were so individually personal to him, were to her, simply a group of forbidding heights. Certainly she would never have even started the journey up any of the slopes, still less attempt the summits.

Eventually he had finished the tale.

"I didn't think I'd be back here with you ever again, Melen."

She was on her side to his left, and glanced up at his face. She was still flushed with the heat of their exertion, and in the guttering, smoky candlelight, this deep in the winter's dark, the yellow cast of her skin hardly showed.

She reached out and picked up one of the little pieces he had brought her: carefully, so that the weakness of her left side was kept away from him. It was a habitual posture, he knew now, and nothing personal to him. She had chosen the duck, he noticed, and was tracing its contours with her fingers. She seemed to like those birds, he thought, so ever since that first time he had made sure to fashion something of its kind from one stone or another, and then bring it along to her.

"Don't be silly, Bran. You'll always be back here. I don't know why me, though. You should chop and change around like all the rest do. I told you last time; you'll get me into trouble if you carry on like this. Makes me uncomfortable, it does."

There was a melancholy note in her voice, an odd choice of emphasis in her speech, and he looked at her in surprise. But she added nothing to her words. He turned to face her more fully and caressed her cheek so that she turned her head towards him.

"Why so?"

She was silent for a while, as though considering whether to say more. Eventually she continued, but in a much lower voice,

## Part 1 – Melen

as though to ensure that none but the two of them could hear her.

"I've been with some of the other men. Before you were here, I mean. And I know sometimes they went with me because my body's odd." She swallowed, and then carried on before he could speak. "What with my skin being this colour, I mean, and this arm not working properly, and all. It was like a bit of fun for them, a bit of a laugh with the others when they got home. But they only did the once, and then they went back to the other girls. That's what Bechan wants. That's why she keeps me on, too, I'm sure of it."

He shook his head.

"That's not why I choose you. Look, Melen, I've been thinking. You don't have to stay here, nor keep working in Bechan's house and all that. All what you've just now been talking about. Why don't you leave Dolgolvan, and come out to live with me at Ty Caroc?"

She looked baffled, as though his words made no sense.

"Leave Dolgolvan? How would I live?"

"There's room in my hut. I'll set it out however you want. It would be yours to decide, so long as I have space for my tools and work in progress. There's enough space for two of us. It would be good for me to share the place with you."

She stared at him and frowned. As she continued to speak, her barn-and-byre accent became steadily stronger.

"I don't mean where would I live? I mean how would I live? See, I don't know how I'd manage there. And why would I want to? I've no family out there, cos they'd all be back here in Dolgolvan. I'd never see them no more. I couldn't bear that. Anyways, they'd never let me do such a thing."

He shook his head.

"The men I work with, they're more than family to me. I mean, my own folk that birthed me and raised me are all back on Innis Mon, but I left them all back there to join the stoneworkers. So the people here, they're family to me now. I reckon they might be that to you as well."

"Not to me they're not. Not never. And that's another thing. They'd all be looking at me all strange-like. All those men out there at your houses, I mean. They all know who I am, what I've done. With you now, and with some of them too, maybe, back in other days, when the other men wanted something to laugh about. It'd be shameful out there, it's not like being in Bechan's house where it's always been done. And most of them would just laugh at me, cos of what I look like. I know you don't, but all the rest would do, all the time like. I couldn't bear it."

"We'll manage. We will. And maybe I could teach you a few things about stone. We started last time, didn't we, with the names of types of rock. I mean, it wouldn't be everything, not all at once, I couldn't do that. There's just too much learning. And it wouldn't be right by the others. But I could do a bit, just enough to help out with the work."

"I suppose then you'd be making all those nasty marks in my skin? Bad enough that you men do it to yourselves. Worse with me being a woman. My family would never speak to me if they ever saw me looking like that."

She clutched at her arms, touched her breast, and wore a repugnant expression. He looked down at the tattoos on his own chest, the marks of his trade. The memory of the men and women of Innis Mon was bright in his mind: the pride of carrying in your body the evidence of skills hard-learned. It was part of the traveller way.

"They're proof of what we've done, who we are, what we've mastered. I'm proud of each and every one of them."

"But you cut them in women too? Not just in the skin of you men? Look now, I've seen them on Gan-Mor. You can't tell me you don't."

"Well, of course we do. A woman can learn her own skills, and so she'd have her own marks, put there by whoever trained her up. No difference."

She pulled a face and shuddered. He wondered, briefly, what Melen would think if she ever met Lewenith, with all the diverse insignia of a healer on her.

## Part 1 – Melen

"I think I know who I am without cuts and marks like that. Who my family is. What my place is here in Dolgolvan."

"Nobody would make the signs unless you wanted them to. And you could live out at Ty Caroc without having them."

"But why? Why would I leave everything here?"

He looked around at the hovel they were bedded in, remembered all those times when both her own people and his had mocked her for her limping shape, for the uncomfortable hue of her skin. He thought, briefly, but decided at the last minute not to say, that a few tattoos might well disguise some of her misfortune. It would not help, and so he tried to change the direction of his words.

"But what is there here for you?"

She stared at him in disbelief.

"Everything and everyone I've ever known. You only know Bechan's house, you don't know nothing about where I live all the rest of the time. All everything in Dolgolvan, the marketplace and the back ways. My home and my family are all right here." She paused, then rushed on. "I know what it's like here, and I know all there is to be known about living here. I even know where I am with Bechan and all. She's alright, a girl might do a lot worse than being here. And all of us girls too. We look after each other. Why would I leave my home and my family and all, only to go out there into them terrible wild places with you? Nobody would never come out there to see me, nobody that I know here, not out into the middle of nowhere like that. Not my family, not Tios, nobody. They'd hate it, and they'd hate me for it. I don't know your Ty Caroc, and I dare say I'll never know it. I have a place here that I know, and family, and friends and all, and I have nothing at all out there in those awful empty places. You have your place and I have mine. And I don't know I want to be with you every day like, not having to live the way you do out in the wild. This is my place."

"But my place is better. It could be better for us both."

"These are my family. Nobody can just leave their family, not without the proper ceremonies and with their parents giving agreement. And I don't believe that these men you work with can ever be the same to you as your kin. If they are, then truly it's a strange life you have. How can they be? They've not known you grow up with them."

"It's a good life. You should try it with me."

Something closed in her face, and her gaze moved away from him up towards the smoky roof.

"You need us more than we need you. If you all went away we'd not lose much, but if we all went away you'd have nothing. You should just go, all of you, leave us alone. This is our land now, not yours."

He blinked in surprise. The words sounded like something she had heard from others, perhaps many times. In her mouth they only seemed borrowed. And the words made no sense; how could land belong to anybody?

He looked up and down her body. As he'd thought often before, he could never confuse the stockiness of her frame, the fullness of her chest, or the width of her hips, with those same features in a traveller woman. But at the end of the day, those were trivial differences, and her woman's body had become familiar to him.

The divergence between them ran far deeper, though, than a few bodily changes. He remembered old stories from his childhood, of a people who lived in caves and were consumed with greed for wealth. Dolgolvan was made of houses, not caves, but that same spirit of acquisitiveness from the tales filled the streets and alleyways here. After all, he could not be angry with her, despite the feelings struggling inside him at her dismissal. He stayed silent for a long time, working out what to say.

"You'll not come, then?"

She shook her head once, with finality.

He took a long breath, drew back from the gulf they had almost crossed. He wondered if he would be ever able to go back to the idea with her, or whether he should simply abandon it for ever. She was still holding the stone duck, cradling it against her breast. He touched her cheek, still wanting her to acknowledge

*Part 1 – Melen*

his companionship.

"You must have a whole row of ducks in your room at home by now."

She opened her mouth but said nothing at first, and was suddenly very remote. He could not read her expression, but it seemed to reflect complete incomprehension, or perhaps disbelief. After a while she laughed, a short harsh noise that confused him even more. Her face had closed to him again.

"Something like that, I'm sure."

It had been the wrong thing to say, and he had no idea why that was. The silence fell between them once again. She pulled the blanket back up to cover herself.

"I suppose you'll be wanting to stay the whole night again?"

They had already talked about this, in the very brief time while Bechan was watching over the transaction, and deciding which of the huts to make available to them. But looking back, he could see that he had rushed everything about the whole evening, and so it was no surprise she was asking again.

"Always. You know that."

She nodded distantly, and covered him as well. Then she turned her head away a little and closed her eyes. It was clear she had no more desire to talk. For his own part, he still felt full of words he wanted to share with her, words of terror on the icy rockface, words of shivering anxiety as he had finally lowered himself to the ground, clothes wet and icy, words of gratitude to the elder raven which, he was convinced, had saved his life.

He wanted to tell her not just about what had happened, but to make her feel what it had been like to be there on the slopes of Pen-y-hal. And he wanted, too, to add words of affection to impress upon her that, after all of those things, he was glad to be back here with her once again. That just now he wanted to have her beside him in other ways than coupling in haste under Bechan's watchful arrangements. But she had turned away, and wanted none of the same things that he did.

It was the same in the morning. She gave in to his caresses, acquiesced to his ardour, and seemed on the surface to be with him in the coupling. But some other part of her was already outside the room and away elsewhere. She was like a seam of tuff that, after a brief show above the surrounding rocks, had hidden itself away again.

Afterwards he dressed quietly, while watching her cover her namesake skin with meagre barn-and-byre garb. He had no idea what had happened between them. They parted.

A voice called out from the track from the village; Nant was approaching. Bran concealed a little internal sigh. He had indeed arranged to meet with Nant again, but now that the day was here, he felt a great desire to be alone. But he stood, turning to greet the older man, who was obviously very excited about something.

"Did you see all those falling stars last night?"

Bran shook his head. He had become caught up with the next stage of shaping one of his recent pieces, and had lost track of the time until fatigue, and the deepening gloom in his hut, had overcome him. In the morning he felt unrested, and with a conviction that he had woken up with every owl call through the night. The dullness of the morning's clouds, resting in a heavy layer a little up from the valley floor, reflected his own feelings.

"A lot, were there?"

"Enough to notice. Not as many as I expect we'll have just after the next new moon, but pretty fair all the same. All across the southern sky, they were."

They wandered along the track towards the quarry. Bran was content to let Nant make the choice of path, just as much as the choice of conversation topic. But he said nothing for a while, and so far they were just following the regular track, a little up the valley wall to avoid the reedy area spawling across the valley bottom.

*Part 1 – Melen*

They branched up to their right shortly after, doubling back along a great shoulder of land that pushed out into The Valley. For a while they were facing back east, but then the path swung back again. At the top of a steep section, where the path flattened, they sat on a convenient rock. They had climbed through the low-lying layer of misty cloud, and were now in the spring sunshine. Bran's mood began to lighten. Nant took some cob nuts from his bag and shared them with him.

"By, these are good. They're from nearby? Or did you trade them?"

"Just here in The Valley. I found what I consider to be the best stand of hazels a year or two after I first came here, and they never disappoint." He pointed across the low ground to the lower slopes of Drum Crog. "Over there. I'll show you another time."

"That's kind."

"It's nothing. But anyway, see, I was thinking about those falling stars. Where they came from, like."

Bran shook his head, puzzled.

"The sky, surely?"

Nant laughed, shortly.

"Well, yes indeed. But where in the sky? I don't just mean the south. I mean where do they all come from? I was out there, on a crag just up from the village, where I could see all the southern sky. And there was all these falling stars, every once in a while, one after another, but there weren't any less of the fixed stars or the wandering ones. Not that I could make out, anyway. Which puzzled me. They have to come from somewhere."

Bran thought about it for a while.

"Does it matter?"

"I suppose not. But maybe it does. I mean, there's a lot more fixed ones than wandering, so you might say it doesn't matter so much if you lost some of them. But my feeling is that they're like wandering stars that came down here instead of staying up there."

He gestured vaguely into the sky. Bran looked up, as though

he might see some trace of the night's activity, but of course there was none. The time of the falling stars had long since gone, and in any case, he would not be able to see them in the day. He stayed silent for a while, turning the matter over in his mind, and eventually Nant spoke again.

"And you see, this is what I reckon. The fixed stars don't move except all together, alongside each other, I mean, all in their same paths. The wandering ones go to and fro, and my belief is we only know some of the ways they move. Like you said that other time, we know as how the morning star is gone for the better part of a year. But what's she doing all that time she's gone? Where's she moving when we can't see her? None of us know; there's secrets that the wanderers keep from us about how they move about. Like we keep secrets about our own training from those who haven't done it themselves. So far as I've heard, there's none of the great stone circles tell us about these falling stars, when they'll come and go, how many there's going to be on any day, any of it. And once they're fallen, I'm guessing they never rise up again."

He stopped, pursed his lips, looked across at the great peaks where they both worked, and then carried on.

"Anyway, it seems altogether likely to me that the falling ones are in fact wanderers, not fixed ones at all. But wanderers whose time is up, so to speak."

"I'm sorry, but I still can't really see how it matters?"

Nant frowned, and shifted into a more comfortable position on the rock.

"Well. I reckon that the fixed stars are like the barn-and-byre folk, and the wandering ones are like us travellers."

"That seems fair."

"And up there, there's a whole lot more fixed than wanderers. Nobody can deny that. And down here, there's a whole lot more barn-and-byre than travellers."

"Is there? How do you know?"

Nant shook his head. He looked glum, as though putting words to his thoughts was opening up a seam of melancholy.

## Part 1 – Melen

"They have more settlements than we do, and more people living in each one. Just think about comparing Dolgolvan with Ty Caroc. You could fit all of Ty Caroc many times over in Dolgolvan, especially as they pack their houses in so much closer together. And it's the same everywhere. Leastwise, it's been that way every place I've seen, and every place I've heard others talk about. You're right that I haven't counted each and every person, but I've no doubt that there's more of them than us. No doubt at all."

"Alright, I'll not argue."

"Well, see, I think that what happens down here is like, like, what's the word? Like a reflection in a tarn of what goes on up there in the sky. The water reflects the sun and the clouds: in the same way, what we people do follows the movements of the stars." He paused, and looked quite directly at Bran for the first time since they had sat down together. "So, if the sky is slowly losing wandering stars, while the fixed stars are staying the same..."

Bran shivered suddenly as the thought ran to completion inside him.

"Then the land is losing travellers, and one day there'll just be barn-and-byre."

Nant nodded, sombrely.

"I fear for the way we live our lives, Bran. I like what we do; it's a good life for us, and I wouldn't change it. But what if our time's running out? I got quite morose in the end last night, watching them stars fall down like that."

They were silent for a while together. Bran eventually shook his head, not in disagreement but, as it were, to clear away the remnants of gloom that he still felt. He wanted, very much, to talk about something else.

"All the lads are off to Dolgolvan in a few days. Me too. Will you be joining us?"

"Not me. Not this time. You'll have seen that I don't come along most times. Hardly ever, really. Just every so often when some of the other lads nag me too much. I said before, didn't

I? It's easier to go there once in a while rather than have all that badgering. But I don't, like, enjoy it very much when I go. I only follow along those times for a quiet life."

"I wasn't intending to nag."

Nant leaned back, pulled out another handful of cob nuts and offered them.

"Ah, but that wasn't my meaning. Not with you. It's the others, when they talk as though I was missing out on something. I don't like the way they keep on. But you now, you've just asked once, not over and over. But I do like it when the rest go off, it's quiet-like among our houses. Avank and Lewenith are still there, of course, and a few others, mostly older ones, but they leave me be by myself and don't interfere."

"So, what then? You just carry on working? Like it was any other day?"

The older man laughed, abruptly.

"Not exactly." He paused, then carried on in a quick slide of words. "You may as well know about it. I have a little supply of the mushroom for myself. Not the ones we eat: you know, the other ones. Very relaxing it is, just the right size pinch in some warm water. I wait until you've all gone, settle down by myself, and there I am, gone away into my own little dreamland. All very peaceful, and I get more reward out of it than going along the track to Dolgolvan and the women there."

He stopped, eyeing Bran to measure his reaction. Bran pursed his lips.

"You'll be careful, won't you? I knew a man on Innis Mon took too much, frightened himself something terrible. They had to get a healer woman from right across the island to work with him until he calmed down again. You've not had that yourself?"

"Never that bad. Once or twice the places I've gone, well, they've been dark. But so's waking life sometimes. Almost always it's good places I've been to. Restful and exciting both at the same time. Like this world, but brighter colours and all. Warmer sounds. Better for me than a night with Braith, or Tios, or whoever. I don't have to keep worrying about what they're

## Part 1 – Melen

thinking, or what they want. This is just for me. Sometimes I take a few crumbs on an evening, if it's been a bad day. Helps me sleep and all. But mostly I use it on those days when you all go off to the town." He laughed, more naturally this time. "Well, for all that, I suppose we should be moving on to the peaks. But if you ever want some of the other for yourself, I always have a little to spare."

They walked on westwards, the great peaks ahead of them, and after a while Bran decided on the best way to reply.

"Not just yet, but thank you. If ever I need some I'll know where to go."

Nant nodded.

"You enjoy all this about the heavens, how the sun and the moon and the wanderers go about. Not many of the lads do. Did you ever think of going to where they make the great circles?"

"I asked Morvin about that. Back on Innis Mon, I mean, before I came here. Someone who'd been an apprentice with me was going over the water to the great western island to do just that. But Morvin said no, he reckoned I'd do better here. With smaller stuff."

"It's heavy work, to be sure. I knew a man back where I come from, he had a fancy for that and went off to do that. There's none of the great circles out east, you see, so he had to go."

"None?"

"Not that I've ever heard of. Earth banks and wooden circles: no shortage of them. But no circles with more than, I don't know, six or seven stones at most. So you see he had to go far north of there, some islands up where the sea goes to ice sometimes in the winter. He came back one summer and told us about it. Big work. Hard. Clever, mind, and tricky, what with needing to know about the moonphases, and the long mooncycle, and the sun's dance, and the wanderers, and then being able to set out the stones rightly."

"And not just the stones in the ring: you have to get the ones right nearby too. Avenues or whatever up on hillsides nearby."

"That's what I hear. And long, too. I've heard it said that

it takes a family five generations to get all the alignments right when they go to a new place. So by the time your kin has got through all that, you're not going to let someone else do the finishing. Not however skilled they might be. I'd like that side of it all. But that aside, however interesting the work, what I wouldn't like is how you have someone telling you all what it has to be like, the whole thing start to end. Not like Finn, where what he does is to make sure we all work smoothly, and we don't get too deep into disputes with each other. No: from what I heard, the wise one in charge really is in charge, saying where each stone has to go, where to dig or heap up, what weight of little stones must be moved, everything. Seeing as how that's what his family has discerned. I know for a fact that wouldn't suit me, and from what I can tell I don't think it would suit you either. I reckon your Morvin knew you well. But it seems that it did suit this other man. I don't know where he was going after the work in the north-east. Maybe up again into the far north where they have all kinds of things already, or over to the great island beyond Mon. I suppose he goes about from place to place, going to wherever where they're fashioning something like that. You're happy here, though?"

"Yes, thanks. Seems like Morvin was right about me." He wanted to change the subject, and gestured to the long arch of the crags stretching north from the Ban. "Are Drus and Spink still working along there?"

"I haven't seen them lately. But I think so. If Drus gives up now, he'll think everyone would see it as failure. So he'll carry on until he has something to show."

"I don't believe it'll be the true tuff."

"No. It won't. It can't be, not at that elevation. But he'll find something to show, and then tell us all that was what he planned from the start. He's been up along there too long to just give up. That's why I chop and change around all the time, so I don't get locked into some place that's all show and no substance."

"All the same, it's a fine place to work over there. First time I saw it, I thought it was the ridged back of some great creature."

## Part 1 – Melen

Nant looked at the hump-backed ridge as it swelled away from the Ban.

"You did? I don't see it like that."

Bran tried to describe the vision he had had on that first day, by the little tarn on the way from Dolgolvan, of a great fiery beast descending on the land. Nant listened politely, but in the end shook his head again, staring at the towering peaks ahead of them.

"No, I can't see it. Sorry. My lack, not yours, I think."

Bran had the clear sense that in truth he was not in the least bit interested in this way of seeing the land. For all his knowledge of the layout and connections between the peaks, for all his careful learning of what could be found about the past occupancy of the quarry, this way of envisioning its remote origins was a mystery to him. Bran sighed and gave up, and they walked along the ridge together in companionable silence for a while. The winter light, though pale still and watery, was starting to dissipate the cloud bank, and parts of The Valley were beginning to show through the veil.

They were nearly to Pwil Gesgod when Bran spoke again.

"I've been meaning to say. I finished my first axe, and gave it over to Finn for him to inspect a couple of days ago. Plenty of little pieces before, of course, but this was my first finished axe."

"Oh, that's truly good news. Of course he accepted it. And now you're altogether one of us, I should think."

"I suppose so. Finn came over to my hut last night, and said he'd looked it over carefully, and that all was well. I think he'll tell everyone at the break today."

Nant nodded, obviously genuinely pleased for him.

"I'll say it again. I'm right pleased for you. Shows that there's purposes here for all of us, not just yourself."

Bran nodded.

"What you were saying about the traveller way diminishing like the falling stars. I'm not yet sure if I go along with that, but it did set me thinking about something else. We all keep to ourselves, with our own secrets. Us stoneworkers, to be sure, but then there's those who work in wood, or leather, or they're healers, or whatever."

"Of course. They have their training, and their own signs they make on their bodies, and we have ours."

"But maybe we'd do better to come together more. Stay in a place together."

"Like Dolgolvan?"

"No, that's not my meaning. Something traveller-like, not barn-and-byre, but somewhere where we'd be working together more. Right now if I want, I don't know, if I want something crafted from wood, there's nobody in Ty Caroc who has that skill. I wouldn't even know where to go to find someone."

"The far end of Lugh Laesach, so I heard. But I'm not certain."

"Well, anyway, for lack of that I hack it together myself, and maybe it does the job, but I know full well it's not good work."

Nant shrugged.

"It's not like we need that very often. If there was a woodsman living at Ty Caroc, what would he be doing most of the time?"

He walked a few more paces, and then, with a conspiratorial air, carried on speaking.

"But you know, back with you passing your axe to Finn, Cegit never did do that. Never has to this day." He grinned at Bran's look of surprise. "Oh, he'll talk about being one of us, and he'll go along to Dolgolvan and all the rest, and he'll fashion all kinds of stuff, but in truth he never passed his first axe over."

"But that first one's supposed to go out to trade. Once Finn's checked it, I mean."

"That's right. It marks the last stage of being a newcomer here, and the start of being a proper part of the crew. And it shares out some wealth to all of us. You might say it shows we're sharing the work of our hands, and that we give each to the others. And then every so often, some piece of ours goes the same way. I like doing one axe each year like that, but that's just me. Everyone has their own habit."

"But Cegit never did?"

## Part 1 – Melen

Nant shook his head.

"He never did. Not from that first time until now. But it goes further than that even. You can't have missed seeing that he holds a lot back from the rest of us."

Bran stared at him, uncomprehending for a moment. Nant nodded.

"It's true."

"But that's not right. Surely that's not right. Not for a traveller."

"No, it's not. I agree. I'll not say he's idle, but I will say he's quick to take and slow to give, and I will say he's never passed on any of his work over to Finn to be traded out. Just keeps hold of it for his own use and benefit."

"What does Finn say?"

"Ah well, that's the best question of all, isn't it now? Why doesn't Finn step in and insist on him doing it right? But he doesn't though. Too anxious about losing a man from the team, is my reckoning about that."

Bran shook his head, not knowing what he should say in reply, and Nant continued.

"There's less of us at Ty Caroc now than any time I can remember. Not enough new ones coming in, neither as apprentices, like Prental, nor properly trained, like you. Finn now, he's chary about saying something that would drive someone away. Look now, I reckon the last few people that have joined us have been good choices: you most of all. But with Finn being so short of pairs of hands, do you think he'd turn away someone that was a bit, shall we say, on the edge? I think he'd err towards taking a risk rather than making a stand. And my belief is that Cegit knows this full well, and he knows he can get away with what he does."

Bran stayed silent, but nodded in acceptance of the words. They parted soon after, to go to their respective working places.

The rest of the morning passed uneventfully, and Bran enjoyed, as he always did, the quiet groupishness of the midday break by Pwil Gesgod. Prental was his usual self, fooling around at the water's edge, but today it was entertaining rather than irritating. Finn sat beside him for a while, as he did with each of the men, making sure that all was well. Roudhok was surprisingly chatty.

Cegit started a story, all about his own birthplace considerably to the south, where sandstone and limestone mixed with shale, and people built great burial chambers for the dead from errant slabs of great grey rock. The tale seemed to be a long one, and Bran's appreciation of it was coloured by what Nant had said.

He glanced across at Finn from time to time, wondering for the first time how he felt about Cegit's behaviour. Would he step in as foreman of the gang, or leave things to sort themselves out? And although Finn was leaning in and nodding with the rest of them, Bran realised that in fact he was remote, detached from the show. His whole posture was entirely different from how he carried himself with the rest of the team.

Before too long he became weary of listening to the tale. He slipped away from the story, back to his high perch among the crags, and carried on working. The short afternoon wore on, and the light began to fade. The sky was clear of cloud, and a great hush descended all over the land.

And then, suddenly, a tap of hammerstone broke away a concealing piece of surface stone, and exposed a long stem of the true tuff. He stopped, rocked back on his heels, and looked at it carefully. Then he lay down, belly on the cold ground, and scrutinised it for a long time, as best he could without touching it. He felt a growing sense of real excitement. This was not just a fragment of the true tuff; this was a deep vein that would yield plenty of material, enough for several axes. So far as he could tell, it was flawless. All he had to do was prise sections as roughouts away from their bedding.

He leaned forward to begin the next stage, clearing away some loose bits of shale from in front of the piece. Then, antler and hammerstone poised, he stopped himself. He did not need to do this tonight. The rock would still be there in its niche in the morning, the light would be better, and he himself would

*Part 1 – Melen*

be fresh at the day's start. And, tucked beneath an overhang of rock as it was, the site would be shadowed very soon.

Very slowly and deliberately, he put his tools back in his bag and stood up. He was not going to be rushed into this. He turned away from the rockface, threaded a careful way down to the valley floor and, finally, strolled along the track back to Ty Caroc. By the time he was approaching his own little hut, the evening was closing in all around. He sat outside to heat through the bowl of stew he had left from the day before, and ate it as the stars shone with increasing brightness above him.

Tomorrow he would get to the site at first light, and spend as long as it took to gently ease the first piece away from its present home in the vein of tuff. Perhaps it would be out in a day, but equally it might spill over into a second. But the time taken was unimportant now; far more to the point was getting each rough-out intact, and safely into his hands.

However, there were other considerations. It was only a matter of days until he would see Melen again in Dolgolvan, and he planned to take the piece along with him. Not to give to her, of course – it was far too valuable a find for that – but, perhaps, it would inspire her to come out and live with him at Ty Caroc. She had never seen unworked tuff before, fresh from the mountain, and showing nothing yet of all the shaping and polishing work which would transform it. Perhaps this find had come at an auspicious time, and he would not neglect the opportunity.

"You're surely not going with Melen again?"

They had just passed the row of hanging crows, by now rank and rotten. Bran forced himself to look away from them, and grinned at Brogat.

"And why not?"

"You don't have to prove anything to us, not any more. Alright. That first time we, like, sprang her on you. You weren't to know. We've said before; it was just a bit of fun. But look, bud, take turn about with the others. It's only fair. I'd say Braith, except I have a fancy for her tonight myself."

"I like Melen."

Brogat shrugged, and they walked on. Before long they were turning down the last street before Bechan's house. Concealed from Brogat's sharp eyes, held in a separate pocket from his usual collection of trinkets, was Bran's latest find from up among the crags. It was the long, fine roughout of the true tuff which, he was sure, would in time become an axe.

He wanted to show it to Melen, and planned to bring it to Dolgolvan every month from now on. He would not give it to her as though it was just a pretty thing, but she would be able to see the different stages of his work. He would use it to show the difference between the trinkets that took a day or so to make, and his real work which took months.

Perhaps it would convince her to come out and live with him at Ty Caroc, if she could see the artefact growing and developing like a new child. But whether the attempt was destined to succeed or fail, Bran had no intention of revealing any of those plans to Brogat.

It was still winter, but well past the time of the shortest day, and the sky was lighter than it had been last time. In between last time and this, the men had gone as a group on the longest night up to Dronow Moar, to see in the new season. Bran had enjoyed the gathering at first, the excitement of seeing travellers assembling from all around the hill country, but he had soon found the sheer numbers of people oppressive, and had been glad when they came away again, back to the quiet Valley.

But although the light was returning, it was still dark inside. Bechan would never light tallow dip if there was no pressing need, so the inside was as gloomy as ever. The women were standing in a loose gaggle, half in and half out of the shadows, and he looked eagerly among them for Melen.

*Part 1 – Melen*

He could not see her. Perhaps she was hidden somewhere in the group. But the other men were pairing off with them under Bechan's watchful eye, and the group was thinning, and still he could not see her. He knew the faces of the others, but had never troubled to learn what each was called.

He was still standing there, looking around. Bechan nudged one of the young women to step forward. He couldn't remember her name.

"Melen's not here?"

"She's not. But you'll like Ehos here."

"Where is she?"

Bechan had half-turned away, and was stern as she glanced back at him.

"Not here. She's not yours for the asking whenever you please. You'll go with Ehos instead tonight."

His mood was souring, and his voice rising.

"I'll not go with Ehos, no. It's Melen I want to be with, not somebody else. Will she be back here again next time?"

Brogat had glanced back at the disturbance, but shrugged and left with Braith. Ehos was standing nearby, confused by the way Bran ignored her, upset by the anger in his voice.

"That's my business and not yours. I'll not have you treat my girls like this. Go with Ehos, and go with her now, or else get away from here until you've learned how to conduct yourself properly in my house."

He flushed, fists clenched, then turned towards the open door and strode out into the evening. He leaned against the wall outside, trying to decide what to do. Behind him, the door slammed shut. He almost went back in, but thought better of it.

Almost straight away, another woman came out from a side door and turned towards him. She was not Ehos, but one of the other women who had been left when the men from Ty Caroc had taken their choice. She stopped beside him and spoke to him, barely above a whisper.

"You're Bran, aren't you? Melen said you were always kind to her."

He looked at her, puzzled, trying to think who she was. She saw his confusion.

"They call me Tios. I'm Melen's friend." She hesitated, uncertain for a moment how to continue. "I'm just someone who didn't laugh at her. And we talked, and she told me you didn't make fun of her neither, and that you always treated her nicely when you were here."

Her name seemed familiar – perhaps Roudhok had talked about her, or even Nant – so he nodded, even though he couldn't recall seeing her before.

"Where is she tonight?"

"Look now, she won't be here again, not never. Her father gave her away just before the last full moon. She's in the new man's house now, and she'll not be back here again."

"Gave her away?"

He felt stupid, unable to comprehend what he was being told. That full moon must have coincided with his journey to Dronow Moar.

"Yes. It seems that her father had enough wealth to attract a man for her. Someone older than her, but not too old. And although he's from this town here, not somewhere else, so you could say he's a second choice, it's something for her. I've seen him; there are worse houses she could live in. But whether it's better or worse for her, she's under his roof now. She'll not never be back here with the rest of us. And he'll not let her have anything to do with me no more. Nor none of us. I miss her, but I'll not be able to talk with her now. I might see her in the street, but she's not allowed to talk to me no more. He'd have words with her."

He paced up and down.

"Why wouldn't Bechan tell me? I deserve to know something like that. For sure I do. She should have told me. Before it ever happened."

The woman looked away.

"I heard the mistress talking with Melen's father, and he said that you weren't to be told, not just you I mean, but none of you

## Part 1 – Melen

lot from out there, and that he'd have words with her as well if any of yous found out before and interfered. She'll not want to cross him, so she'll just keep to what he says."

He was silent. She turned back to him.

"I'm sorry. But I thought you should hear it. Better to know than not know, and ask the same thing again next month."

He groaned and squatted by the wall, his head in his hands. He still felt stupid, and was starting to resent the manipulations around him. She carefully touched his shoulder.

"Bran, look, I'm not her, I know that. But nobody chose me tonight, and we can still go inside if you've a mind to. Melen said you were always kind to her when you were with her, never cruel or anything. You made her feel good, and didn't just take for yourself."

He took a long breath, gripped her hand, and stood up.

"It's a kind thought, Tios, but I'll not be pleasant company tonight. Not any more."

She hesitated, touched him again. Her face was anxious, fragile, at his rejection.

"If nobody chooses me too many months in a row, I lose my place in Bechan's house. She kept Melen on cos she reckoned it was a bit of laughter like for all you men, gave you all something to have fun with. But she watches all the rest of us to make sure we're doing enough to keep our place in her house. She truly never thought anyone would actually come to like Melen, actually want to be with her over and over. Like what you did, I mean. That made things more tricky for her."

"I did like her, yes. I never cared what the other men thought about that."

"She told me that. Even when you said silly things to her, she knew you meant well, no matter how the words came out. Something about taking her away from Dolgolvan into the wild places. But Bechan kept her – and we all knew it – she kept her because most of you lot just reckon she was someone to make fun of. She was, like, entertaining for yous. But it's not like that for me. Bechan won't just keep me here if I get skipped too many times. Please take me back inside now."

Her words didn't quite make sense to him.

"I'm sure that'll not happen. But it's better I just leave here now, I think. I'm glad that you told me what you did."

She swallowed.

"Please don't tell Bechan we spoke. She'd take it badly, and I can't be ending up on the wrong side of her. Not this on top of the other."

He closed his eyes and nodded. She said something wordless, incoherent, painful. He almost took her in his arms to hug her, but he did not know if he was trying to comfort her or himself. He wanted to comfort her as a friend, and as Melen's friend, but had no actual desire for her, and no wish to give her false ideas. Instead he turned away down the little alleyway, leaving Tios by herself. He glanced back once, and she was still standing alone by the wall, looking bereft.

Then he stormed away from Dolgolvan, bright anger driving his steps. He almost stopped at his home in Ty Caroc, but changed his mind and pressed on up the valley, past where the workings stood high above him on the peaks. He did not stop until he arrived at Lanerc's farm, shadowed now under the row of great crags. Lanerc's dogs barked only twice at his arrival in the yard, before recognising the familiar footfall and coming to him, nosing softly around his hands and legs.

Lanerc opened the door to him.

"Bran! What brings you here? But come in, lad, come in. Yan, Tan, go on by now, get back in your place again. Leave him alone and go on by with you."

He shut the door on the dogs and led Bran further into the round room. Gwennol was beside the fire, turning flatbread rounds on the hot stones. The two children were nowhere in sight, and Bran assumed they were already asleep behind the barrier of piled up hides. He went further into the room, suddenly unsure why he had come here, of all places.

"Bread's ready, if you have a mind?"

He sat near Gwennol and took the bread round from her. She

## Part 1 – Melen

frowned at him abruptly.

"What's amiss, Bran? You look, you look, well, shrivelled."

"And angry," added Lanerc.

He avoided their gaze, turned the bread this way and that in his hands. Lanerc looked at him sharply and nodded.

"Maybe that'd go down better with some honey. I've a fair bit I gathered last year."

He pulled a pot over, half-full of honeycomb, and gestured for Bran to help himself.

"Wasn't it tonight that you lot all were going down to Dolgolvan?"

He nodded, jerkily, then, feeling foolish, told them about the three times he had gone with Melen, and about the numerous trinkets he had given her. Part-way through, a look of sudden realisation crossed Gwennol's face. Lanerc scratched his head.

"Melen? Isn't that the lopsided girl?"

Gwennol looked at him crossly, and he shrugged.

"Well, she is, isn't she?"

"Aye, that she is, and she has sallow skin along with it. What of it?"

He shook his head and held up his hands.

"Nothing, dearest, I'm just making sure I know who's talked about here."

She frowned at him again.

"Go on, Bran."

He told them how Melen had not been there, and that he'd heard from Tios how her father had given her away. Gwennol listened to it all before replying.

"When I was last in the village, a month or so back, there was talk of how Melen's family had come into a whole heap of wealth they'd never expected, all in the back end of the year. And that her father had right then arranged for her to be given away, into a matching he'd never expected. He'd said before, oh, so many times, as how she would just be just dead weight on his hands forever, and all of a sudden she'd brought him more than he'd ever seen before, more than all his other bairns if they were all put together. I mean, she was only given inside the town, not outside somewhere, so some folk are saying it's still a slight on the family. But he'd never thought anyone would have her at all, because of how she is. You know about that. So he like seized the moment and found this man for her, got them paired before the day was out. It must have been only a day or so after you lot went over there last time."

Bran stared at her, silent, and she carried on.

"And this surprises you?"

"Of course. Isn't it her own choice?"

She shook her head.

"Not among barn-and-byre folk, Bran, not if they want their kindred to ever acknowledge them again."

Her tone indicated that some personal history was caught up in that, but he had no desire to find out more.

"But I gave her all that stuff. That wealth. It was me who did that. That was my wealth that her father used. I wanted her to make her own life, her own choices."

"Oh, Bran, my love." Her voice was very soft, very gentle in the night air. "And how did you ever imagine that she could have held on to any of that?"

He stared at her.

"What do you mean?"

"Bechan would have taken her part of it all. Then whatever was left would have been taken by her family when she got home. She'd have nothing for her own self. Bechan does whatever she pleases for herself, to keep the wealth flowing into her own hands. She doesn't have a lot of interest in what the girls want."

Bran remembered, all too clearly, the look on Melen's features when he had talked about a row of ducks in her room. He flushed, profoundly embarrassed. Then the conversation with Tios just before he left Dolgolvan abruptly made sense. He groaned.

"And I think I was cruel to Tios as well. Not that I meant to, but that was how it all ended up. This has to be a ill-starred day."

*Part 1 – Melen*

He told them about his failure to grasp what Tios had meant behind her words. Lanerc shook his head.

"You cannot make it better, lad. That's their way."

"Then what can I do?"

"Nothing, lad. Not without spoiling everything that passes between your lot at Ty Caroc and the folk at Dolgolvan. Leave it be, lad. It is what it is. Let it go."

Gwennol nodded.

"Look on the best side for her, Bran. She's not under Bechan's hand any more, and she might get the chance to be a woman in her own house. She won't be staying like she was still a child, and an embarrassment to her parents."

"And on the worst side?"

The other two looked at each other.

"Her new husband might not be kind to her. It's the better part of a month, so likely he'll have got her with child already. She'll be that way over and over until the carrying wears her out. And those children will be living at Dolgolvan all the while, and I dare say that most of them won't live long enough to get grown up. They'll die of sickness or the blight, or the harshness of life there. It's a different world, Bran."

"I offered her a place out here once, you know. At Ty Caroc, I mean. She laughed at me, like I'd said something truly without sense."

Lanerc frowned.

"Of course she did, lad. There's precious few barn-and-byre folk who can leave where they've been brought up, and then to come and live out here. Outside the village borders. It's all a wild place to them, and something to be feared. Not to mention being cast out by their own family."

Gwennol leaned back on her stool.

"Did you ever think that could happen? Truly? Look at it from her side. She saw you a few times, once a month for a while, for a very particular reason. Then, every time, you were just gone again in the morning. And against that, every day, there's everyone she knows and has lived with all her life. Why would she choose you? I won't say it could never happen; maybe she could have left there and gone out to Ty Caroc. But it's a rare thing."

Lanerc was nodding, clearly swayed by some very strong emotion.

"If it had have happened, it would have been a very great thing. But it hardly ever comes about that a barn-and-byre woman leaves her place. More often the other way around: sometimes that's an easier change to make for the man. But it would still have been hard: harder, I think, than you guessed it might be."

Gwennol looked at him, hearing undertones in his words that Bran was missing.

"That's very true."

Bran was silent for a while.

"I never knew that. Any of it. Come to think of it, I knew very little about her: Melen, I mean. All what made her who she is. Nothing, really, though I thought I did."

"That's true enough; you didn't know. Better to find out this way than any other."

He sighed.

"What's the new husband's name? I'll find out what he's like."

She shook her head.

"No: you will not. Absolutely not. It's no use thinking that. No use to you, no use to Melen, no use to anyone at all. Do what my Lanerc says, Bran. Let her go. Leave it be. It can turn ugly very fast; only last year a traveller camp was broken up over at the southern end of Lugh Crum over some dispute about land."

Bran stared at her in disbelief, then looked at Lanerc, who nodded.

"Three travellers killed, there were, and more hurt bad. All over some land where you'd think there was plenty enough to go around everybody. Land! Can you believe it?"

Gwennol leaned forward urgently, tapped his leg.

"You have to protect Ty Caroc from anything like that. None

*Part 1 – Melen*

of us want that sort of thing happening in The Valley."

He looked down, turned the bread in his hands, over and over, aimlessly. Lanerc pushed the honey towards him.

"Eat it, lad. It's a remedy for all sorts. Don't just fiddle with it."

Bran shook his head, but after a moment he tore off some of the bread and ate it. It was good, and he thanked Gwennol for it. After a while he sighed and leaned back.

"You're both right, I'm sure of it. But I hate it all. Best I keep away. In fact, you'll be witness to my oath that I'll never go back there. Not ever."

"What if you need supplies and all? Don't say something rash that you can't keep to."

Bran nodded slowly and frowned.

"By, you're a difficult man to please. But fair enough. Let's say this. I'll never go back to Bechan and the girls. I'll never try to seek out Melen. But if I need aught from the town, I'll trade for it and fetch it just like I've done until now."

Lanerc thought about it.

"I can witness that with a clear heart. You keep that oath now, and it'll be good on you, lad. Gwennol?"

She smiled, leaned forward and patted Bran's hand.

"That's all settled, then. And for the best, I'm sure."

Lanerc got up.

"Let's split one of those new cheeses what was finished the other day."

He fetched the cheese and cut each of them a large piece. Bran was never sure that he liked Lanerc's various attempts, but he always felt unable to refuse the offer. This particular serving was, he thought, one of the better ones, though he had no idea which of the animals it had been taken from. But it was firm inside rather than slimy or dripping, and the taste was better than he had expected. He felt himself relaxing in their house, for the first time since leaving Dolgolvan.

"Y'll stay the night here, lad, won't you?"

"Oh. I wasn't going to. It's not far back to Ty Caroc."

"Nonsense. Better you stay here the night and get away with the morning. Y'll be fine here, we've plenty of room enough."

He wavered, but Gwennol put another bread round in his hands, and he found that he had no desire to go back to his empty little house in the village.

And later, alone on the bedroll they had set up for him near the door, after Lanerc and Gwennol had gone away together to their own bed, he felt very lonely. Earlier that evening, he had imagined himself lying beside Melen and talking with her about his discovery. But that would never happen again. He was full of sorrow, and frustration, and emptiness, and dismay at how little he had, in truth, known about her.

# Part 2 – Brannen

THE SPRING WAS SPREADING through The Valley, and the little yellow spring flowers were unfolding quickly under the trees before they came into leaf. Winter wolf's banes were there, and primroses, and little clumps of occasional daffodils. The garlic leaves were showing, but it would be a while yet before they bloomed.

Bran sat for a while at the edge of the glade of the foremen's rock, enjoying the sight. So far the year had been mixed, with plentiful rain in the lowlands leaving a layer of snow up on the fells. It was still there today – the crest of Drum Crog had a narrow fringe of white, and the taller ridge blocking the high peaks to the west was more thickly coated. His own working place, though high up on the Ban, was sheltered and had, so far, remained open.

The flowers were, however, a sign that the heat of the year could not be held back much longer. He looked again at the blooms where they spread close up to him. The celandines were starting, and it would not be long before lily of the valley appeared. Every pool was full of frogspawn, and the tadpoles would emerge before long.

But today was not a day for stopping here. With the winter weather behind, Bran had decided it was time to attempt Mynyth Mam once again. He was restless, like the flowers, and like them, he wanted to ascend, to get away from the ground.

He was acutely aware of his previous failure, and even looking back now, he still could not understand how it had happened. Perched up on his workplace, he had searched himself often for reasons why he had become cragfast. Even at the time he had known that his regular climbing was more challenging, but the knowledge had not helped him. The ascent was unfamiliar, but surely not beyond his skill. Perhaps he had simply tried the climb too early; the elderwoman had, after all, told him to be patient. But he was more inclined to think that it was simply because he had taken the wrong route. What, after all, could there be that he needed to wait for before succeeding at the climb?

This time, then, he would not go by way of Pen-y-hal. His

experience high up on its slopes near the tail end of the year had soured him against that peak. He had decided that he would go nowhere near it. One day, perhaps, when the weather was warmer later in the year he would try again, but not yet.

This time he intended to go first towards Lanerc's farm, past the tail end of Drum Crog, then across into The Valley's smaller sister. A steady ascent would bring him up to a middle-height pass, from which he would curve south, up onto a sinuous ridge. Pen-y-hal would be well off to his left, so he would be completely clear of it. Instead, he would trace the long slope of the ridge in a sweep, so as, finally, to reach the summit of Mynyth Mam.

He stood up and strode on. The days were still a little shorter than the nights, and if he was to get to the summit and back in a day, there was little enough time for looking at the flowers. Before long he had passed the track up to the workings, and then the rock of signs where Don's body had been laid out. It had long since been picked clean, and stood again solitary and empty.

Then it was up a short incline, and across towards Pwil Glas; he skirted the tarn and surrounding wetlands on the right, disturbing a heron. The bird flapped lazily away from him to the far side, and then settled again to wade, and to probe the shallow waters for food.

He was near Lanerc's farm, but it was no part of his plan to spend time with him and Gwennol just yet, so he kept away from it amongst the trees. Before long, he was working his way over the tumbled ground beyond. The tarn drained away from him, down into The Valley's sister, and for a while he kept roughly parallel to it before following the contours of the land more to his right. The blackthorn was in blossom in the more sheltered hollows of the land, and some of the tree buds were on the verge of breaking out into leaf.

A steady ascent brought him up to the top end of the little valley. Ahead of him the land levelled out; he had no idea what he might find if he persisted in that direction until he reached the sea. Cegit had talked vaguely about a long, dreary upland plain, culminating in a valley that dropped down steadily towards the coastal plain, and a little landing place for boats. He had said nothing about landmarks along the way, but Bran was fairly sure it was considerably south of the traveller settlement by the tarn that the gang had once traded with.

In any case, that was not his destination today. From his vantage point the fells rose up left and right, and he could ignore the plateau ahead.

Mynyth Mam was south from here, so he turned left and began picking his way up the slope. There were no real tracks here, only occasional false trails made by whichever animals lived up here. The surface, however, was sound. Pen-y-hal, with its steep crags and treachery, was well away to the east, and he was increasingly pleased with his choice of route.

The way led steadily upwards, easy by the standards he was used to, and so he had plenty of time to reflect on the winter's events. A season had passed since that last time he had been to Bechan's house, and since he had failed to see Melen. His workmates – most of them – had been three times to Dolgolvan since then, but he had not gone with them. Each time they had come to his door, wanting him to be with them, and each time he had refused without explanation. If any of them guessed the reason, they kept silent about it.

He had indeed been back to the town a few times in the daytime, trading trinkets for necessary supplies. But he had kept the promise he had made in front of Lanerc and Gwennol, and had made no enquiries about Melen. He had no idea where her new home was in the town, and did not want to know.

On his first visit, he had worried briefly about meeting her by chance at the market, and he had made sure to stay back in the shadows while he scanned around the open area. But he had gone there early in the morning, and the only women in sight were considerably older than any of those he had seen in Bechan's house.

He looked back, to realise that although the Ban and the Brig were still clear of cloud, the knuckles at the end of The Valley were now veiled in clouds, which had appeared since his de-

## Part 2 – Brannen

parture. So too was the higher ground behind them. He could not see ahead towards Mynyth Mam yet, not with the crest still rising ahead. But Pen-y-hal was still clear of cloud, so he was hopeful that his onward journey would remain fine.

He carried on. There was a short section where he needed hands as well as feet, scrambling up a little gully, but it was soon past, and the slope began to flatten out. His pace quickened again; he was eager to see the whole curve of the ridge ahead, and was convinced that before long he would catch the first glimpse of the day of Mynyth Mam.

He had spent considerable time up on the crags of the Ban, and at other high vantage points nearby, gazing across at this curving ridge, and the peak beyond which was his goal. It was all clear in his imagination, and he felt that he knew the whole journey already.

So when he got to the first of the high points along the ridge, and saw that the later ones were already crowned in wreaths of cloud, he was not unduly worried. He knew where he was going, and his route seemed straightforward.

He sat on a convenient rock and chewed on some dried venison. He had not stopped since The Valley, and deserved a break. He drank some handfuls of water from the beck flowing nearby, and rummaged through his pack. He had gifts to leave on the summit. He had brought some food, albeit dried, since not much was available at this time of the year. Then there was the pinion feather of a raven which he had found recently, a shell which he had picked up on the beach at Innis Mon and brought with him, and, most precious of all, a polished piece of the true tuff whose shape, even when first lifted from the seam, was so like the profile of Mynyth Mam that the two obviously belonged together.

He got up and set off along the ridge again. The cloud had come in more thickly during his brief rest, and he felt a slight unease. Back in The Valley, where he knew the shape of the land intimately, this would have been nothing. Here, in unknown territory, it was another matter. But surely his path was plain; certainly it had seemed so back when looking from the Ban. And the clouds might vanish as quickly as they had appeared. He pressed on.

He had been following little animal trails through the ling and the scrubby grass. There were no trees here along the ridge, where the soil was thin. Mynyth Mam herself was bare, clean in her lines, like a breast that the land offered to the sky, and he imagined his path would take him steadily further away from the things of men.

The cloud thickened, and his world narrowed to a small circle close by. He began to hear the calls of curlews, but the birds themselves were invisible to him. Only their ethereal voices indicated their presence. Perhaps they had been nearby all along, but he had not noticed them before, wrapped up in his own thoughts.

He walked on, trusting to his memory of the ridge curling gently southward. But then the vague track that he had been following dwindled to nothing. He stopped to look about. There were two faint ways branching away from each other, going each half right and half left, though neither were very promising.

The right-hand path dropped a little downwards, which he thought would be a waste of effort. The slightly better path was to his left, but Pen-y-hal was on that side, and he had no desire to end up there. And he was fairly sure that there were crags in that direction along the crest before ever reaching that summit. Perhaps the descent on his right was just one of the undulations along the crest. And with dropping down a little, he might regain some visibility.

He took a step or two to the right, and then several more. Looking back, the point at which he had branched off had already disappeared. In fact, even the minute track was barely to be seen. He hesitated, torn between caution and the desire to reach Mynyth Mam. He pressed on, and found that the path still descended, albeit very slowly.

He continued down for a while. The footing was good at first, though becoming slowly wetter underfoot. Perhaps there were tracts of moss and peat along the ridge. Craggy lumps rose up

## Part 2 – Brannen

on either side. They were never very large – shorter than his own height, in fact – but their presence bothered him. Every time he had looked across at this ridge it had appeared smooth, easy, inviting.

He stopped where the ground levelled out briefly and leaned against a great boulder while he considered. Several animal trails ran off in different directions. Ahead and right seemed to drop down too quickly. Sharp left was barely to be seen, and he was still concerned about the crags of Pen-y-hal. Ahead and left seemed the best, so he shrugged and went that way.

His clothes were becoming damp, bedewed in the thickening cloud. The path would across to a boggy hollow, which he skirted on the uphill side, and then, to his relief, started climbing again. The curlews still sounded around him, eerie and out of sight except for occasional quick shadows in the mist.

He had a sense that he was going into a gully, and then, became sure of that, as rocky walls to left and right narrowed beside him. He paced on, going more slowly with each step, and after a while the path stopped in a hollow. There was a gully ahead of him, steep and made of rubbishy rock that looked set to crumble if he put weight on it.

He shook his head. He was not about to go climbing or scrambling on unfamiliar land, not when the mists around him blocked off any sense of what was ahead. In any case, he was now convinced that he had never seen this part of the land before, not in any of his careful studies from the quarry. This shape was completely unfamiliar.

He leaned against the rock beside him and frowned. He might be close by the peak he sought, but he might not. It was frustrating to give up for a second time, but better to be frustrated than to get into difficulties once again. And he still had the unpaid debt of the promise that he had made to the Elder Raven. He had strayed away from what he knew, and it was time to back away.

Sighing, he turned back and set off back down the gully. The walls widened again, and he paused. He could no longer remember if he had kept to the left or the right as he had entered it. He tried going right, up the slope again, but it felt wrong, and the ground was slippery. So he retraced his steps as best he could recall and continued down the slope. He had thought that he would recognise the little level space with the boulder, but now, nothing was at all familiar.

The little paths had vanished, so he gave up trying to find them, and simply headed downhill, in an erratic course avoiding places that were too wet, or where the footing was poor. After a while he found himself beside a little beck, so for the lack of any other landmarks he followed it as it trickled downstream. The curlew sounds were fainter now, further away, and the air around him was very quiet.

The ground started to level off, and the beck was joined by others, so that the area became increasingly soggy to cross. Then in turn it joined a rather larger stream, running from right to left across his way. The cloud was still thick around him, but off to his right he could make out a darker shape. This proved to be a large, errant mass of stone, resting there quite out of place in all the wet. He pulled himself up onto it, considering his choices.

He was quite sure that by now he had lost all reckoning of the track that he had wanted to follow. That was somewhere up behind him, back up the slope, and he would not find it again today unless the fog vanished as quickly as it had appeared. But the frequent twists and turns of the tiny tracks he had followed meant that he had no real idea which way would take him back towards home. His only true guide was the little stream, and whatever larger watercourse it joined. Would it take him back down into the Valley's little sister, or would it trail off in some completely new direction, leading him ever further from the places that were familiar?

He thought back to his climb up from Lanerc's farm. He had crossed several becks on his way up, all tumbling downhill to join together, finishing in the tarn at the bottom. But there had been – surely there had been – a kind of lip he had gone over at the top. If so, then downstream would take him away from fa-

## Part 2 – Brannen

miliar territory, somewhere west or south. He would eventually come out at the coast, possibly quite near the place he had first landed all that time ago, but possibly far enough away that he would still not know anything. In any case, that was a very long way away, and he was not equipped for a journey of more than a day.

He sat for a long while, listening to the trickling water, hoping that the cloud would lift, but it never did. Eventually he got up and turned right. He was going to try upstream. The ground stayed very wet for some time, and he had to cross frequent inflows from the higher land on either side. But the main branch was clear, and he followed it with increasing optimism. The sound of curlews had returned, accompanied by their little shadowy ghost-shapes darkening the mist nearby. That felt good; it was as though little misty spirits were accompanying him, and he was glad to have them back again.

Finally, the stream dwindled, and the land started to dry out and become more stony underfoot. He reached a level stretch, then crossed the lip of the land and started downhill. He was convinced now that his choice had been right, and he was dropping down into the little sister valley. The clouds were still thick though, and he could not yet be entirely sure. Another stream was on his right, rushing faster down the steeper slope ahead.

And then, eventually, he saw something he recognised – a wet tract of land, with the path to Lanerc's farm following the drier ground uphill. He breathed a sigh of relief, realising just how little confidence he had had in his choice until now. He branched left, following the level ground around, and suddenly he was out of the cloud, and familiar territory was ahead.

The Ban and the Brig peered over the ridge that Lanerc's farm nestled beside, and their tops were still clear. But looking back, all the ridge behind him – probably all the ridge all the way around to Mynyth Mam – was still shrouded. The bank of cloud only covered what he had been aiming for. He would call in to the farm on his way through, talk to Lanerc and Gwennol, immerse himself in human company again. They would probably find this latest failure a source of entertainment, and he felt a great need to laugh at himself, after the ghost-curlews and the feeling of being lost in the clouds.

Once again he had been thwarted in his attempt. He shook his head, ruefully. He would have to leave the quest again for a while, and try to decide what day would be truly auspicious for his next attempt. The food he had kept with him would not last until then, but in truth it was quite meagre, and he had already had doubts as to whether it would have been sufficient. The other gifts he had set aside – the pinion, the shell, and the piece of the true tuff – would wait together in his house. Perhaps he should have taken more of everything, or better items, or ones that were more precious; maybe the mountain had simply found his offerings to be inadequate. That was something else to think about.

It was the start of summer, and before much longer it would be a whole year since he had arrived. The daily routine had become second nature – up early at first light, at least on a fine day, then along the valley track and over to the rock pinnacles where the true tuff lay hidden amongst the base rocks. A quiet day's work. Coming together with the other men at noon, swapping old stories alongside time and food. The high cries of the buzzards circling the fells and drifting on the wind. And, lately, the swoop and dive of swallows and swifts around the uplands, newly returned after their long absence.

He was often frustrated by the lack of constant, reliable success. The true tuff here was not like the veins of superficially similar rock he knew from Innis Mon. There, once you had found the trail of a sinuous thread, you could follow it systematically until it plunged too deep into the rock face.

## Part 2 – Brannen

Here, a promising start so often led to disappointment. Sometimes the band petered out almost before it had even started, but more often a roughout that seemed sound would prove to have flaws and cracks inside it. The land itself teased you, offering its goodness and then hiding it again. He was, slowly, coming to appreciate this as part of The Valley's dance of life, rather than a deliberate attempt to thwart him.

He had found all manner of small pieces, to be sure. He had shaped them a little, just enough to show the forms of animal or bird that lay concealed within them, then polished them to bring out the true colours and sheen that the tuff held underneath its rough shell. All of his earliest ones had gone to Melen in Dolgolvan in those few visits.

After she had been taken from him – nearly half a year ago now, when he had sworn that he would not go back to the women there – he had taken all of his made and half-made pieces, and offered them up to the waters of Pwil Gesgod, throwing each as far as he could into the still waters so they would be forever lost to everyone.

He had pondered for a long time exactly how and where he would devote the items. He had contemplated another trip to Mynyth Mam, but his twice-repeated failure had made him wary. Besides, he wanted these things out of his house quickly, and would not wait for an uncertain outcome. Then he thought of burying them in a grove of beech trees he passed on one of the routes from the base of the Ban towards Lanerc's farm. He had come to love the beeches, with their woodland mix of giant ancient trunks and small attendant sprites, and just now they were all putting on the bright lime green of their spring colours.

But in the end he had chosen Pwil Gesgod: water instead of wood or earth. It was closer to where he worked every day, and closer to where the rocks had come to the surface. So the rocks had gone back to the water, back to the mountain. That had been very early one morning, so he did not have to explain himself to the other men. Since then, starting again with empty hands, he had steadily built his collection back up, there in his little round hut in Ty Caroc. He was now completely separated from the days of imagining a life with Melen.

The latest of these finds was in his carryall today, so he could work on it a little more in the gaps between exploratory digs. But larger pieces – not just larger but also sound and true inside – had not often come his way. There had been some, to be sure, and he had taken a few proper-size axes right through from start to finish, with all the detailed and devotional work that had entailed. The first of those had gone to Finn for the benefit of the whole team, and he planned to do the same with the first completed item after his settling year was up. And there had been others, though never quite so many as he had wanted.

He had moved on many months ago from the first gully that Finn had showed him, but had never moved too far away from it. Instead, he had worked his way systematically around it, mostly from side to side but also up and down where the rock looked favourable. Nant's arguments about not staying in one place had persuaded him, at least in part, although every so often he wondered what Morvin would think.

His feelings about his chosen sites on the mountainside swung wildly from moonphase to moonphase, but he had chosen to move on from each place before the frustration built too much. Perhaps there truly was a good vein of tuff to be found in every place, a real vein with more of the bigger pieces he sought, but it was not for him to find. Better to let one of the other men discover it after he had given up.

So he moved from one site to the next quite frequently, and today was the day for another move. The summer was at hand, the longest day was not far away, and he felt as though a change was coming.

On this particular day he had passed Crug, sitting as he usually did in a slouching heap on his outcrop, and had wished him a good morning. Then, instead of following his usual path to the gully, he kept more to the left, closer to the quiet stream, further from the loud one, and worked his way up the fellside closer towards the crags that lay close to Brig, the second summit. He

## Part 2 – Brannen

had only been up here once before, on a clear spring day, but he had seen a cleft in the rock that seemed promising.

None of the other men were up in this area just now; he had looked out for the signs of someone else's working, listened out for the tap of hammer on rock face, and was now confident that he would interrupt nobody. He would go back to that cleft, and see if his intuition about it was correct.

But there was another sound up here, a strange one, and he stopped to listen. It was coming from a craggy ridge to his left, on the other side of the beck. High up on the ridge he could see the ragged rim of a raven's nest, and the sound was somewhere below it. He scrambled over the broken rocks towards it, and found himself looking down at the broken body of a wildcat. It was, just barely, alive, but its eyes were gone, pecked out. He looked up, considering the nest. The animal could have fallen from there, sightless, and tumbled down the unyielding rocks to end its life here.

The climb up to the nest was challenging, but it had to be done. Finally, with skin scraped on his arms and legs, he was up beside it. The sight was worse than he had anticipated. Both adult birds were claw-torn, bloody, lifeless. He was used to death, but what he saw affected him more suddenly than he had expected. The claws which had killed the birds pulled sharply at his own flesh, for all that he knew the wildcat itself had not survived. He was named for these birds, and felt their loss like a shard piercing his own body. He moaned a little, whispered out some words for the dead.

The female lay draped half in and half out of the nest, with the male close beside. There was blood on her beak. With them had been several young, fledged but not quite ready to leave the nest. It seemed as though the whole family had been killed.

A nearby crow-call sounded, and he turned to see a row of the ravens' smaller cousins perched nearby, drawn by the carrion, waiting for him to move away. He grimaced, and shouted out, angry, "Be off with you all. Have you no shame? These are your kin. Take the cat instead."

He picked up a splinter of rock and threw it at them. It fell well short, and they took no notice. He looked once more down into the nest. The adult birds had, no doubt, secured their revenge on the wildcat, but all he could see was death. He had come too late. Just for a moment, he had hoped that the promise he had made on the slopes of Pen-y-hal could be fulfilled here, but that hope was rapidly fading.

But then, the bundle of feathers twitched slightly, and from underneath the bodies he could hear a faint croak. Hardly daring to breathe, he gently pushed aside the bodies of the female, and two of her young.

A raven head, small but alert, and definitely alive, peered up at him. It turned its head, clacked its beak, croaked again. One bright eye stared solemnly up into Bran's face, met his gaze, and Bran found himself submerging in the intensity of that regard.

Then the bird turned its head and watched him for a while with the other eye before glancing away. Bran felt suddenly released from the grip of that look. He sighed with relief, nodded, and eased aside the dead birds, both parents and nestlings. He worked his hands underneath the living one, and lifted it carefully away from the nest.

It turned its head both ways again to look him over, made a little gurgling noise in its throat, then opened its bill wide. Bran laughed, filled with acute relief. His promise had come to life again.

"I suppose you're hungry. But that can wait: let's get you away from here first. And away from all those rotten crows over there. Nothing to be done for your parents and all, I'm truly sorry to say, but at least there's you to tell the tale."

He wrapped the bird in a fold of his tunic, briefly considered the precarious climb back down the way he had come up, and instead took a much longer circle around the top of the crag. When he was well away from both the nest and the waiting crows, he sat on a boulder and considered the juvenile bird again.

"Well, you're far too young for me to say if you're a boy raven or a girl, and it won't matter to you for a year or so yet, either

## Part 2 – Brannen

way. But I have to call you something, and I'm going to suppose that you're a little lady, like the Elder Raven who I met a while back. So your name shall be Brannen. As for feeding you right now, there's precious little save for the bit of bait in my bag. We can share that, I reckon. You see, I made a promise to an old lady relation of yours, and looking after you fits well and truly into that promise."

The bird hopped away from him, looked him up and down, then came back, rested her head on his arm, and opened her beak again.

"Make me work one-handed, do you?"

He rummaged awkwardly in the bag, pulled out the bundle of bannocks and dried fish and set it on the rock in front of them both. Brannen inspected the pile, seized one of the bannocks, then a second, separating them from the rest. Then she held one down with a clawed foot while breaking bits of the oat mixture off with her beak.

"Greedy little bugger, aren't you?" He frowned back across at the crag, where the crows had now gathered, noisy and busy around the bird's former home. "But fair enough, after all that you've seen today. If I'd been just a little later we'd never have met, and those crows there would have been gorging themselves on you as well as the rest."

Brannen took some of the fish, put it with the bannocks, and carried on eating. It was river fish, small and bony like all those in the becks and tarns here, but the raven did not seem to mind. Bran frowned at her.

"Look now: I need some for myself. Unless you're going to earn your keep by chipping out pieces of rock with me for the rest of the day. Maybe I'd better eat my share now."

The two of them picked at the food until there was nothing left. Brannen clacked her beak again, looked with each eye in turn at the empty food bag, then settled herself with her head on Bran's arm.

"What am I going to do with you?" The bird opened one eye, glanced at him briefly, then closed it again. "One of us has work to do, you see. But before that, let's take stock. You've got all your feathers, at least. So you're part-grown. And you seem to like the food I can give you, which is just as well, seeing as you're a great hungry gos, and I can't sick up food like your mam would have done not so very long ago. But I'm hoping you know how to fly, or else you can learn by yourself, since that's something I cannot teach you."

He got up, wrapped the empty bag loosely around Brannen so as to carry her more easily, and made his way carefully over to the base of the cleft he had originally been seeking. He stopped, frowning. The scramble up the rocks would be easy enough with both hands, but he wasn't nearly so sure he could manage it while carrying the bird in one arm.

"Well, I won't be doing that until you can fly up there beside me. And I cannot imagine you'll be happy waiting down here today till I finish. Not with those ravening crows still round about. So where shall we try for the time being, if I shan't be going there?"

The raven made a soft gurgle in her throat, looked around, and clacked her beak two or three times.

"Now, maybe that'd be a fine and useful thing if I spoke Ravenish. And if I thought you had the slightest idea what exactly it is I'm looking for. But I don't reckon you'll have had any use for the true tuff in your short life so far." He sat on a handy outcrop and studied his surroundings, inspecting the lie of the land, idly preening the bird's feathers as he did so. The ruff around her neck was oversized and fluffy compared to how it would develop as the raven grew up.

"I'm going to try over there. See it? That little gully, where it shows a gleam of white when the sun catches it. I can get there with you like this, and not be worried about the both of us taking a tumble. But I'm guessing now that you'll be hungry again before I will be, so let's move along with it."

He went to the mouth of the gully, and placed Brannen, still partly wrapped in the bag, on a boulder. The bird made a noise of mild protest that she was not still in immediate contact with

## Part 2 – Brannen

Bran's body, but settled after a while. Bran took out his tools and started investigating the crannies and crevices, looking for the intruding rocky veins that would yield the true tuff in sufficient size that he could work it into an axe. It was high time he proved to the other men that he could regularly find and fashion more than little toys and trinkets.

As the morning went by, his excitement grew. The interior of the gully was riddled with cracks and crevices, and as he probed into them he found what he had been looking for all this time. A vein of the true tuff ran across the gully, erupting to the surface in a couple of places, and veiled in between only by a thin skin of surface granite. He teased some of the crannies open a little, enough to confirm his first thought. Finally, he glanced up, to see the sun well on its path towards the crown of the sky.

"Brannen, I reckon this'll do us for now. There's months of working here, and if it's all as sound as those first signs show, there'll be plenty of good material to shape and polish. With good-sized lumps there too, if I'm patient and don't split it apart by rushing at it."

He sat down by the bird and, very gently, smoothed the feathers on her neck. Bran was acutely aware that his new companion had become increasingly restless as the morning had worn on.

"I'm going to say we've brought each other good fortune today, but with all that you've eaten we've nothing left to celebrate with. Which means that I'm taking you over to Lanerc's farm, and I'll trade some food for us now. He's a good man, and you mustn't hold his mixed blood against him. He's more traveller like us than he is barn-and-byre like the folk over at Dolgolvan. He's alright. But you should know that we're going to be spending a lot of time right here in this gully over the next few months, so don't you go getting fidgety. You can always fly about if you get bored, and that's more than I can."

He left his working mark at the bottom of the gully, clear so that the others would see it, picked Brannen up in his carryall, and set off back down the hillside. The little raven looked back once or twice towards his former home, made little crooning noises as they went, but made no real protest. Once, near the bottom, Bran heard Brogat's voice from above and to the side. He waved and carried on.

At the bottom of the slope, he turned right, up the long valley away from Ty Caroc. There was no point going back to his home, and Dolgolvan was too far away. In any case, just as he had told Brannen, the little farm in the clearing beside Pwil Glas was more to his taste. He would see what he could find there. Lanerc was in his debt just now, to a small degree, and besides, he and Gwennol knew him well, and would trust a promise that he made.

Much later in the afternoon he was back at the gully, a full bag of supplies swinging at his side. He now had some meat, a plentiful supply of bannocks, and a messy bundle of fish bait tied up on its own. Brannen had sampled all of them, and was happy again.

Finn scrambled up to him not long after his return.

"Missed you at the midday meal, Bran, we did." He looked at the raven, perched on a rock beside Bran, and nodded. "Oh yes, Brogat said you'd gone daft over a bird. I can see why; this little one's a smart boy, isn't he now? What happened then?"

Bran gestured across the hillside towards the empty nest.

"A girl, I think, not a boy, but yes. Wildcat got the rest of the brood, but this little one lived to be found by me before the crows took her."

"What'll you do with her then?"

"I have no idea just now. She's happy enough just here: certainly happy enough with the food I give her. Though she makes a right mess when it's gone through her, so I'm not at all sure she'll be living in my hut."

Finn laughed.

"And you're talking to each other about all this, I'm sure."

"Well." Bran paused, met Finn's eyes briefly and then turned away across the hillside. "I won't say that we have, like, a complete understanding. But I talk to her a lot already, and she talks to me in her own way."

*Part 2 – Brannen*

Finn laughed.

"Well, we all talk to the rocks, and the trees, and the sun and the rain, and pretty much everything else up here. Why not talk to a raven?"

"Fair point. And maybe there's some sense gets through to this here bird for all that. It's for certain that I struck lucky up this gully here, right after saving her from the wildcat and the crows, so I'm convinced that there's more than chance in the meeting between us."

He shrugged, glanced briefly again at Finn to see how the older man responded. But Finn just nodded absently, then looked up the gully.

"So just here's a better shout than back where you were? I've seen you working your way round about there this last little while. And there I was, convinced that that first place I set you up in would be good. Ah well, it is what it is, I suppose."

"Oh, no harm done, Finn. Perhaps there's good stuff hiding in there, but I'm just not the one who'll be finding it. Let it stay there for someone else another day."

Brannen rapidly settled into Bran's daily routine. In the mornings, on the way west towards the diggings, she would alternate between flying ahead and perching to wait on a handy rock or low branch. Flight had in fact come naturally and immediately to her, and Bran suspected that she had already been taking small fledgling flights before he found her. At the rock face she would stay close to Bran most of the time, making occasional little croaks or crooning noises, as counterpoint to the tapping of hammerstone on rock.

If she got bored with that, she would fly around nearby, never going out of sight or straying more than a very short flight away. And eventually, if Bran simply continued working, she would strut over to him, making little noises in her throat, and rest her head on Bran's leg or arm. That usually meant that it was time for food, and there would be no more work until that need was met.

Bran liked having the company. He talked almost endlessly to the raven, and listened intently to the stream of diverse noises that were made in reply. They were always, he convinced himself, on the verge of comprehension. He was mightily relieved that Brannen already knew how to fly, for that would have been a lesson far beyond his own skills to impart, but he did wonder what else the bird would normally learn from her own elder companions.

Sometimes the two of them sat, working their way through an oat bannock or some dried fish, and watching the other birds high above them. Most were buzzards, falcons, or crows, with the occasional eagle, and some were herons, geese, or other waterfowl. And every day now, the swallows and martins were in the sky, fully emerged from whatever mysterious place they hid during the colder months.

But some of the birds above them were ravens, and he always pointed them out to Brannen, in case the little bird should want to join her own kind. But Brannen would glance up at them for a while, then clack her beak once or twice, and settle again to rest against Bran's body. Sometimes the overhead flights became combative, as a pair of crows or ravens – sometimes a whole group – would drive away a buzzard on a speculative hunting foray. But Brannen was, as yet, too young to do anything other than watch the flashing wings and beaks far above.

Brannen would come along to the midday break while the men ate their bait, but would stay at a distance, watching carefully from a nearby perch as Bran met with the others. The bird was a continual source of entertainment to the crew.

"You know, Bran, some others of us are going to get our own birds. All to match our own names, just like yours."

"Is that so?"

"Indeed it is. I'm looking out for a woodpecker now. I've

## Part 2 – Brannen

heard the one I want enough times now, down towards the beck. I reckon it's only a matter of waiting a bit longer until he comes right over to me."

Bran nodded.

"Maybe he'll knock some sense into your head then."

Cegit laughed.

"Perhaps he will. Roudhok there, of course he's after a robin, and there's no shortage of them around."

"He'll need to share out some of his bait."

Roudhok put a protective arm around his bannock.

"Not likely, Bran. I reckon he'll come on his own. Just because he likes me. But Finn there, he's got a problem now."

Finn grunted and waved a hand at him.

"Cos there's no birds or anything that'll match his name. We reckon he'll go back to his dad's name and go looking for a mole. A mountain mole, that'll be."

"I'll team up with any beast that'll help me get the true tuff out of these hills."

Cegit took the chatter up again.

"And then Avank'll invite one of them beavers to help push out the wall of his house. But Prental there. Well." Prental looked up at him and scowled, but Cegit carried on. "He's got no hope, not with his own name nor his family."

Prental turned to Finn, but the older man said nothing.

"You leave my family out of all this. They're no business of yours." The men all heard the pressured tone in his voice. He stopped, forced himself to speak quietly again. "But what I don't know, Bran, is what exactly you're planning to do with that raven of yours? I mean, we all know as how Lanerc needs them dogs of his to keep stuff away. Foxes, wolfs, that kind of thing. Bears even, maybe. But that raven now: how do you think she's going to earn her keep with you?"

Bran watched Brannen where she perched nearby, and his face softened.

"Well, it's not like she has to. Earn anything, I mean. She's going to be my companion, going to and fro up there in the sky where I cannot get to. I reckon she'll show me things I'd never know just by walking about."

Nant nodded to him approvingly. Prental had shrivelled back into himself, as though he had used himself up by asking his question of Bran.

"We all need a companion. Of one sort or another, and well, if yours is a raven, who's to say that's not right?"

There was a little silence. Cegit glanced up at the sun and started to pack bits away in his bag. Brogat looked around the group and then, hesitantly, spoke up.

"You've not been coming with us to Dolgolvan lately, Bran." Someone laughed, but he pressed on. "I mean, isn't that where we find a companion? Most of us, I mean. Not just a bird, however clever it is."

Bran shook his head, wondering what, if anything, he should say. But before he could decide, Nant spoke up again.

"Lad, Dolgolvan's not real companionship. It's alright for a season or two, but it's not what some of us are needing. It's not what Bran's looking for. I mean, it's not like we all want the same thing as one another." He leaned back to speak to Gan-Mor, who had been ignoring the conversation up until this point. "Isn't that right?"

Gan-Mor shrugged.

"I suppose we're not all the same, are we now?"

Cegit stood up and laughed shortly. Brogat looked at him uncertainly, but Cegit tapped him on the shoulder.

"Take no notice of them. They're all just in a funny mood, I reckon. A bit of luck up at the quarry and they'll be back with us soon enough. You'll see."

The group started to break up. Prental sat alone for a moment, then ran after Finn as he started up the slope to his working area. Bran watched him catch the older man's attention, talk to him urgently, point back down the hillside. Finn stood listening, hands on hips, but at the end of it all made a dismissive gesture and carried on upwards. Prental stood there, disconsolate, and clearly at a loss what to do next. Finally he turned and trudged heavily

## Part 2 – Brannen

away towards his own workings.

Brannen, now that the other men had gone, hopped back to Bran and leaned against him where he sat. She clacked her beak impatiently, and Bran shook his head, sighed, and gently preened the soft feathers around the raven's neck.

"Well, Brannen, there's trouble brewing there, if I'm not mistaken. And Finn needs to come up with a better answer than what he's done so far." He sighed again and looked down at the bird. "Not our problem, though, is it now? Not yet, anyway. Right now we need to get back up to our own little quarry and dig out some more tuff."

They went back to their little crevice in the rocks, but the work was slow that day. Bran started to feel that his time would be better spent back in his hut, working away at the later stages of preparing the tuff.

"You see, Brannen, there's no point just hammering away at the surface, when it's a day that is just never going to go right for you. I'm not saying I'd go as far as Nant, for he'll chop and change every time the wind shifts. But if the day's not going with you, then I reckon there's no point trying to fight it. It's not as if I'm short of other jobs to do."

Brannen ruffled her feathers and clacked her beak. Bran laughed and stood up.

"Ah well, never mind. That lesson'll be for another day. Come on then you, let's first of all go to Lanerc's house and find out what he has to trade today. Then we'll just go back and work at Ty Caroc. It's just not my day up here, but it'll be my day for something, I'm sure."

They dropped down to the valley floor, then up and over the ridge that separated Lanerc's area from the main branch of The Valley. As they crossed the neck of land that straddled the gap between Drum Crog and the knuckled ridge to their right, they came out of the trees and onto the open scrub. Larks startled up, their music sounding all around.

Brannen made a cheerful noise and set off hunting their eggs where they nestled among the tussocks, but came back close to

Bran as they came over the crest and skirted the marshy ground that led up to the little tarn. Creeping thyme coated the drier patches purple.

He sat with Gwennol while Lanerc rummaged through some baskets for the things he needed. She had a fine eye for the true tuff, and picked out several of his pieces as a fair exchange. Brannen, meanwhile, perched on a low tree branch and dropped fir cones for Yan and Tan to chase in a flurry of excited barks.

Finally, considerably later, they were back at Ty Caroc. Bran had picked several pieces from his unfinished pile, and was sitting outside with them, shaping and polishing each in turn. He had a mind to be properly systematic about finishing more pieces. It was all too easy to sit up on the crags of the Ban and chip away at the rock, teasing more roughouts from their seating. It was always – especially in these summer months – much harder to turn the roughouts into properly finished items.

He considered the handful of items he had brought outside, and glanced in at the larger pile still on his bench. He frowned; not many of them had any chance of becoming an axe. Perhaps two or three. Most would be smaller pieces, and while they were still good to trade, he needed to make sure they did not become his main focus. He needed to concentrate his work on the larger pieces, and not let himself be satisfied with whatever came easily to hand.

Brannen was watching him, a little pile of bannock grits just below her perch on the adjacent rock. Bran picked up the shaper he was using; it was like a smaller, more precise version of his hammerstone. He showed it to Brannen.

"So you see, lass, you've got to use this just right. You can't just bash at the piece you're working, nor not even press too hard neither. Just little taps at just the right angle. Like this: watch me now."

He worked his way along the length of the stone he was holding. Little flakes dropped at his feet like crumbs as they split away from the main core.

"Then when it's done right with this, we'll switch to an antler

## Part 2 – Brannen

tine and do some really fine work. And eventually it'll be cloth and my own spittle rubbed in, which'll bring out the shine no end. When we're done it'll be truly splendid."

He sat back and looked at the raven, who put her head on one side and gazed back.

"But you know, I can't help thinking that there should be something else we can use to quicken it up. Some kind of stuff to use instead of spit. You know, like sap from a plant, or water from a tarn, or something. I don't know, you see, 'cos Morvin never taught me that, and I don't see any of the others in the gang doing that either. It'll need somebody who knows other secrets than what I do. But right now it's back to this."

He tapped gently away with the shaper, a quiet pok, pok sound that, he well knew, would scarcely be heard outside the ring of houses. It was quite unlike the bold clatter of a hammerstone up on the main rockface. He worked his way down one of the long sides of the stone and then held it up at eye level, frowning critically at the curve it still showed.

Bran carried on working, becoming ever more engrossed in the work as the late afternoon wore on. Brannen grew bored and began flying in an experimental way further away from the houses. Suddenly a shadow fell across Bran's lap, and he started, blinking up into the sun.

"Oh, Finn, it's you. You quite startled me."

"Didn't harm the stones, I hope?"

"No, they're alright."

Finn nodded and squatted down beside Bran.

"Missed you this afternoon, up there. You left early, I think?"

Bran nodded and carefully put the stone he had been working to one side.

"Nothing was going for me up there, so I've been back here catching up on the finishing work on all this."

He gestured to the neat row of partly-worked stones arrayed beside him.

"They're looking good now. I've got a whole heap myself that I need to get around to. It's altogether too easy to just keep pulling from the tops, day after day while the weather's fine, and never get around to finishing them."

Bran nodded, ruefully.

"True enough." He paused, then looked quizzically at Finn. "Nant told me that our group always used to send the roughouts away. To some group over west by the coast, I mean, and they'd finish them off for us. Is that right?"

"Yes it is. We've not done that for a while now. I mean, think about it. If we pass on the roughouts then they get the credit for the axe. But if we finish them, why, then everyone knows it's our work, start to end. And there was a few times when they reckoned the roughouts weren't no good inside, cracks and flaws like, but we all knew here that they were sound right the way through. So I talked with Avank and we pulled back." He shrugged. "Made sense at the time, but most of the lads don't have the patience they need to take it all the way. Not properly, not like you're doing now, careful-like, steady as you go. So every once in a while I get to wondering if we should go back to the older way. What do you think?"

Bran leaned back against the wall of his hut, realising as he did so just how stiff he had become from sitting in the same position.

"Not rightly sure it's for me to say."

"Go on. Suppose it was for you to say."

He put the antler down beside the stone he had last been working.

"Well, seeing as you insist. I like taking it the whole way. For sure it takes time away from the crags, from the seams of the true tuff, but there's nothing like the feeling when the thing is done, right to the last polishing. And you know it was just you what did it. Not some other person in some other place who you don't know, who maybe didn't do it right. But when it's all you: well, there's nothing like that feeling now, is there?"

Finn chuckled.

"Can't say there is. But you forget, in between times, how good it is, and you only remember all the time it took."

## Part 2 – Brannen

"But that's just it. I'm not telling you what to do now, but I reckon that sometimes the younger lads need a bit more, well, a bit more direction. They need to be reminded what it feels like to get the whole thing done, start to end. The slow finish as well as the quick find at the rockface. If we're not going to send roughouts out to someone else, why then we've got to do them ourselves, and enjoy the doing of it." He looked up at Finn, his eloquence faltered, and he concluded more hesitantly. "But it's your call, you know. I'm just saying. And you did ask me."

"That's alright, lad. I did ask you. What would you do then about that?"

Bran shook his head.

"I don't rightly know."

"Well, help me out here. Should I be getting us all to send the roughouts out west to Pwil Gwo again? That was the place Nant talked about. Or should I be getting us all spending more time on the finishing. Or should each of us make that choice separate like?"

"It's your shout, surely?"

"It is, but I'm asking what you would do."

Bran frowned down at his pieces of stone. This wasn't anything that he had learned from Morvin, and he found himself lost for words. The silence dragged out. Finn sighed.

"Well, lad, if you get any ideas, just talk to me. Doesn't matter if your first thought isn't the right one."

He got up again, but Bran stopped him from going.

"No, there is something else I wanted to ask you. Not about this. About Prental. He didn't like what Cegit said."

"That's true enough."

Bran waited, but Finn did not continue.

"Well, maybe you could say something, I thought."

"To Cegit? Or to Prental?"

"Cegit."

Finn pursed his lips and turned to look back up the valley to where the Ban and the Brig towered in their majesty.

"Who do you think is the better stoneworker?"

"Cegit is. Just now, anyway. Maybe Prental will catch him up one day."

"Not likely. The lad hasn't got the feel for it. Oh, he's alright at what he does, but there's a spark that's missing in his guts. Cegit, now, he has it. On a good day, leastwise."

"But Cegit never gives his portion to the rest of us. Does he now?"

Finn took a deep breath.

"You've been listening to what's said."

"I have. But I've been watching too."

"Well." Finn remained standing, his shrewd eyes closely fixed on Bran. "That's as may be. But if it came down to choice, and one of them had to walk, then right now, Prental's the one I'd miss less. You see, there's not so many of us that I can risk the better people going."

Bran stared at him. Finn nodded.

"Think about it, lad. One day you might be making choices like that."

He walked away. Bran watched him for a few paces, then turned to Brannen.

"Lesson's over for today, I think. Let's get some food going."

Bran scrambled up one of the several gullies between the Ban and the Brig. He rarely came up here, and the sight always came as a fresh surprise. He was standing in a broad shallow bowl. The edges of the bowl were ragged, where little peaks and promontories lifted above the rim. The Ban was the highest of them all, but the Brig, and the part-ring of crags attached to both peaks, were not far behind. Ahead of him the land was flatter, less distinguished.

He was still holding the roughout that was today's prize, but he did not want to stay at the quarry any more. He had become

## Part 2 – Brannen

restless, and the only way he knew to assuage that was to move about.

He walked on, cresting a rock-strewn raise, avoiding the peat and boggy tracts that were scattered across the upland. From the top he could see all around. Northwards, beyond a patchwork of ridges and valleys, sprawled a much higher peak.

The great stone circle of Dronow Moar was somewhere on its lower slopes, but it was lost in distance, and in any case he was unsure exactly where to look. Beyond that, another arm of the sea reached far inland, and beyond that again was a haze of hills. He had asked the other stoneworkers, but none of them had been that far north.

"Don would have known," was all their answer.

Brannen took flight across the bowl, swift wingbeats taking her farther away than was her custom. Bran nodded to himself; eventually the raven would leave him and settle once again with her own kind. That would be right and proper, but difficult, and he felt a sudden wishful pang, hoping that today was not that day.

Larks and pipits were taking flight across the moorland, and he watched as Brannen stooped down from time to time to raid the nests that her high soaring exposed. He walked right across the bowl to where the land dropped down northwards. Even Nant could tell him little about the land that lay that way.

To his right a long ridge extended, and he could hear the cry of buzzards there. Ty Caroc was in that direction, down in the hazel groves of The Valley, and he supposed that he could follow the ridge along there. Perhaps even to Dolgolvan, should he have a wish to go back there again. Certainly to Alt Ariannaith and the small lakes below that peak. To his left was a belt of higher ground, bordered on the north by a great rounded lump of rocky hillside.

He wasn't sure exactly why he had come up here today. There had been no plan in his mind, no great quest that needed to be accomplished. He was, simply, curious about this arena, so close to his daily place of work, and yet so little trodden. He picked up some of the rocks as he passed them, but there were few enough at the surface, and they were uniformly of no interest to him. It was the regular rock of the land, and he could find no seams of anything more striking, neither the true tuff nor anything else he could shape into a thing of beauty.

He shook his head and circled half-right, then down a long valley and back, eventually, to Pwil Gesgod. He had wondered, at first, how far Brannen would stray, but the bird never let him go beyond sight, always wheeling in vast airy circles to come back overhead. From the pool, the two dropped down a grassy shoulder of land to head back homewards.

The sun, which had been shifting behind high clouds all day, finally settled below them all as it descended towards the knuckles. Golden light filled The Valley like a trough full of oil, and the little becks falling down the great walls on either side sparkled. Summer was a-walking, he thought, walking proud across the land. It would be a good end to the day, if only he did not have to continue working. Perhaps that was why he had ventured into that northerly bowl, to prolong his time up on the sunlit heights today, and correspondingly delay the tail end of work back at his little hut.

He walked slowly back to Ty Caroc, relishing the warmth lingering through this late into the afternoon. His slowness was partly that of satisfaction, but also because he kept seeing, wherever the shade of the hazels and the rowans was deeper, little groups of froglets migrating uphill, away from the beck.

There was a strange restlessness in him tonight, a sensation of dissatisfaction, but he could not pin down what caused this. The day was splendid, his work had gone well, he had no lingering wish to find Melen, and his colleagues seemed to have accepted that he would not be going back with them at the half waning moon. But the urge to do something different remained. Indeed, now that he thought about it, he realised that it had been steadily growing, moon after moon through the year.

He pushed open the door, fetched the stones he was working on, and sat on the rounded rock just outside his door. He wanted

## Part 2 – Brannen

to get the first shaping done on the roughout he had brought out of the rock today. That done, he would carry on with the fine detail on the earlier pieces. He would be using the hammerstone first, then the antler, then a rough cloth, ending up with the finest rag that he could find. There was a pleasing completeness in that; by the time he stopped in the late evening, he would have used all of his various tools, one after another. Tonight, he would finish two of the pieces at least, maybe more, and then he could put them away in his keepsake bag for later use.

He frowned and leamed back against the stones of the hut wall. On reflection, it would be best that one of the two finished works should go to Finn, to add to the communal supply of trading goods. It had been a while since he had passed anything on, and the memory of Nant's words about Cegit pressed down on him. It would be best not to gain a reputation for meanness, nor reluctance to give.

He picked up the hammerstone and began working his way around the roughout, taking little slivers off to make the shape more regular. It was slow work, necessarily slow in order to avoid the reckless stroke that would ruin the piece. He turned it in his hands between each little sequence of taps, gauging each time the best angle to strike at next.

"So you see, Brannen, it's little by little. None of your quick bash and dash work, not if this little beauty is going to end up as an axe. And I'll be right disappointed if she don't, seeing as how she's plenty the right size, and the grain is just right in her." He paused and waved a finger at the raven. "But you never can tell, not until the last moment. Maybe there's a split or a flaw just lurking there, awaiting for me to do something foolish."

Brannen hopped towards him and peered closely at the roughout. Then she looked up at Bran and tapped her beak on the seat beside him. Bran laughed.

"All right. No need to be impatient. Let's have another go."

He turned the roughout in his hand, choosing the next place to strike, and then tapped gently once, twice. Another flake came away and fell to the floor. Brannen shook her wings and bobbed her head up and down.

"Oh, you like that, do you? Well, there's more to show at this stage than later on. When I get to polishing with a rag there'll be nothing to see except for a bit of dust. But the stone itself will come to life then. It's truly the best time of all, when it really comes to birth from out of this lump here. Even if it seems like I'm not doing so much. You'll see."

Brannen studied both the roughout and the hammerstone. She opened her beak, once, twice, but no sound came out of it. Bran tapped again, gently, and another flake split away and tumbled down onto the ground. Then he paused, turning the rock over again in his hands while he decided the best way to proceed. Brannen stepped forward and stretched her neck out, her beak almost touching the surface of the roughout. Bran became very still, suddenly anxious at what the bird might do.

"Careful now, lass."

Brannen put her head on one side, and then slowly and very distinctly, made a noise in her gullet.

"Pok, pok."

Bran stared at her, still not moving. Brannen repeated herself.

"Pok, pok."

Bran turned the stone a little and tapped it gently, twice, then waited for the reply.

"Pok, pok."

The raven peered up at him and clacked her beak. She had an air of triumph about her.

"Well, lass, that's something special. If only I could get you to learn to do the shaping as well as make the noise, we'd be well away now, wouldn't we? We should tell someone about this. But who? Most of the lads wouldn't care. Finn would wonder what all the fuss was about and tell me to just get on with the work. Nant, maybe? No, Avank would be better. He'll want to hear all about this, and he'll actually listen."

He stood up, stretched, and put both his tools and the unfinished roughout in the carryall which was just inside the door to his hut.

## Part 2 – Brannen

"Come on, lass, we'll take these and go to Avank, see what he has to say about this."

Brannen stepped a few paces, then flew up onto a nearby tree. But before either of them could move further, they heard shouting from the track that led east towards Dolgolvan. Bran frowned.

"We'd better see what that is first, I reckon."

He set off towards the track, and soon saw Prental there, a couple of the other stoneworkers beside him. Prental was holding his left arm in his right, and his clothes were disarrayed. One sleeve was torn, and his left leg grazed, though none of his scrapes looked to be truly serious.

So far as Bran could tell as he approached, Prental was more shaken than he expected, despite not really being injured. He assumed that the younger man had just slipped while working, and then made his way back to Ty Caroc. The direction was odd, though, if he'd been working. Finn was striding up from the far side of the village to join the rest of the group, and arrived with the little group at almost the same time as Bran.

"What happened, lad?"

He eased Prental's right arm away from its hold and ran practiced hands up and down the left arm.

"Looks nothing bad, at least." He glanced down at his leg. "Just a bit messed up by the looks of it, aren't you now, nothing serious. Where did it happen? Near up at where you've been working?"

Prental swallowed.

"No, it wasn't up on the Ban. Nowhere near that."

"Alright then, but where?"

"Well, I was going over to Dolgolvan. Needed some supplies there. Nothing much, just some bits and pieces that Lanerc never has."

He fell silent. Finn waited only a short while, and began to sound impatient.

"Well? That didn't happen while you were getting salt, or roots, or whatever."

"No. It did not."

He looked at Finn with a curious mixture of hopefulness and defiance.

"Well, I did get to the town, did my bargaining as usual. All that was fine. But then, not long after I'd left again, I was still in the fields at the edge, three men stopped me, told me that my kind weren't welcome there."

Finn stared at him.

"Did you know them?"

"Never set eyes on them ever before."

"So they weren't from Dolgolvan?"

"Don't reckon so. They were barn-and-byre, though. Leastwise, they talked like that, and dressed like that, and said horrible things about us travellers."

"But from the looks of you they didn't stop at words."

Prental shook his head, slowly.

"I tried to back away from them, get back into the town to the trading hut there. I didn't want anything to do with them at all. Anyways, I was sure they'd nothing to do with the town itself, and I hadn't got very away far from the first houses, so I thought it'd be best just to go back again and wait for them to move on. But then..."

He stopped, abruptly.

"But then you're going to tell me they had other ideas."

"They did. One of them tripped me and pushed me over, another grabbed my arms so I couldn't do else, the third one grabbed the keepsafe bag I had with me. Then they stood around laughing, and said again as how I wasn't welcome. I wasn't putting up with that, so I said that we all came here for trade things, and how it was good for both sides. And the actual folk in the village, the ones that mattered, they were right happy to see us."

"And then?"

"Then one of them, the one in charge, I suppose, tore the bag in half, tossed the contents all around, all what I'd traded, and told me that it wouldn't be long before they'd drive all us lot away somewhere away from here, he didn't care where."

Finn nodded, slowly, then looked around at the others.

"Well, seems like no real harm was done." Prental moved, restlessly, and Finn frowned at him. "Unless else happened that you've not yet told us."

Prental muttered something that nobody could hear, and then, seeing Finn's impatient scowl, spoke more clearly.

"I picked up what I could, left the flour and some seeds, and ran on back. But before I left, they said that they'd let me off lightly because I was only a boy, and if they'd found someone of proper age they'd have done worse. They told me to say that to the lot of you."

He stared round the group belligerently, as though daring anyone to reply. Roudhok laughed, but he was looking east down the valley, not at Prental, and his laughter was not from amusement. Cegit started to say something, but Finn interrupted him.

"I'll not have anyone thinking to go after them. That'll be just what they're wanting. That's why we'll not chase after them now, nor never. And for now, nobody goes over to Dolgolvan on their own. I want pairs or more. If you're going elsewhere then fine, that's on you, but if you're going to Dolgolvan, y'll do as I say and keep in a group."

Brogat spoke up.

"It's not long before the half waning moon. We'll still be going there, yes? I don't want to miss that just because of whoever this lot was that Prental met. Otherwise it'll be two moons between times, and I don't want that. Besides, I said to..."

He broke off, suddenly, not wanting to carry on. Finn paused and then continued.

"That'll be fine; we'll all be together on the track there. Just make sure you're with someone else on the way home. Bechan'll not want anyone at all interfering with her trade with us. Whoever this lot might be, she'll not be with them. And Prental spoke truly, our business is good for Dolgolvan too. I reckon this was some outsiders, nothing to do with those we know."

"But they're all barn-and-byre; won't they stick together? We might, if it was another traveller group asked for our help."

Finn stared at Nant, who had spoken just after arriving at the edges of the group.

"No, I'm entirely sure we wouldn't. Not if it upset our own trade, and it wasn't a right thing to ask in the first place."

Nant started to say something else, but Finn shook his head.

"No, it'll be as I say. None of us goes to Dolgolvan on our own, none of us goes looking to get payment back for Prental's misfortune. We treat it like it never happened."

He glanced around the group, and seemed happy with the nods and approving noises that the other men were making. But Prental spoke up again.

"But they said I wasn't properly one of you, that I was too young. That's not true, is it now? You're not taking their side on that?"

Finn pursed his lips.

"Well, you are the youngest here, can't argue against that. But y've had the marks made in your body to show you're one of us, all barring a few you're still working at. But those others out there don't know how to read all that, it's only for us travellers, and just travellers who are also stoneworkers too. Just forget it, lad."

"Don't know that I can."

Finn shrugged.

"You have to. I'll not support anything more than what I've just said. You show you're one of us by keeping my word."

"It's not right that they just get away with it. You'd not do the same if it was Cegit. Or any of the others. You'd go after them. It's just because it's me."

Finn turned away and started back towards his own hut. Prental stared after him, then looked in despair around the group as, one by one, the others all started to scatter.

"What about me? Won't none of you take my part in this? It's not fair."

Nant wavered.

*Part 2 – Brannen*

"Come on, Prental. You know there's no point trying to change Finn's mind when he's declared it. Come on back to your house now. I've got some flour you can have."

"I don't want the flour. It was never about flour. I just want Finn to take me seriously. He just always walks away and calls me 'lad'. But I'm one of the gang here, aren't I?"

"Of course you are. Finn knows that too. I'm sure he does. He'll stand by you when it matters. And look now, he calls everyone 'lad', not just you. He calls me 'lad', and I'm proper old compared to you."

"Easy for you to say. He doesn't treat you like he does me."

He shook Nant's hand away and trudged away to his own house, hunched over and looking down at the ground.

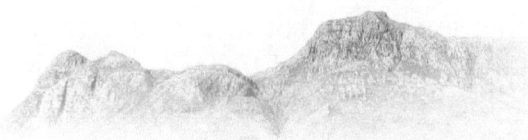

It was a reduced group that sat beside the tarn, eating their bait. It was a blowy day – not so much as to make working up in the crags dangerous, but enough that the clouds scudded by, and few birds were aloft. Bran had spotted a pair of eagles during the morning, circling high on the gusts over the western end of The Valley, but most of the other birds were staying low, out of sight. Even here at the tarn, only a pair of ducks bobbed on the choppy water, where normally they would see ten times that number.

Several days ago now, Finn had sent Cegit and Prental with some of the gang's recent work out west. They were to pass by one of the stone circles which sat well beyond any of the ridges that Bran knew, and then, beyond that, to track down and then rebuild links with a traveller group living by a tarn close to the coast. Pwil Gwo was that tarn's name, because it was small in size.

This was the place where, some years previously, there had been the mutual trade links that Nant had mentioned. The Valley had supplied roughouts for the tarn dwellers, and they had done all the finishing and polishing work over there, before sending the completed axes across the water.

Bran still thought it strange that any of the gang would contemplate another person finishing their work, with never a sight of the final product. For his own part, he would never do that, regardless of what the rest of the gang chose. But Finn had turned the matter over in his mind for more than a month, talked the matter over with Avank, and in the end had made his decision.

The trading link had faded with the years, while Finn's team had done their own finishing work. Thinking back, Bran had realised that regret over the lost connection with Pwil Gwo had been nagging at Finn since the dark of the year. Indeed, perhaps more importantly to his mind than the settlement itself, was the fact that the crew in The Valley had also lost access to the little sea-landing that lay on the coast just beyond it. The group at Pwil Gwo didn't have boats of their own, but they stood in the track between the hill country and the coast.

Landing stages were useful, in Finn's mind; they gave access to all of the wide water beyond, and to the lands in every direction across that water. Little boats, like the one that had carried Bran to the land on his first day, would use the place as a regular staging-point as they crossed the sea to other settlements. And that in turn meant that The Valley axes, and by association the men's fame, would spread far and wide. So Finn had a mind to rekindle the relationship.

To Bran, without knowing the full background, it all sounded very much like what Nant had told him about other traveller communities in the area. And, indeed, of what he remembered from Innis Mon. The quarry where Morvin had trained him kept close links with sea-landings around that great island, and some of the work done had been shipped away, following the great sea-routes that ran with the tides and the currents. The sea was, despite its wildness and the constant risk of turmoil, a more reliable route for trading than the little tracks that ran here and there across the land.

He had not heard of this particular landing place before, but

## Part 2 – Brannen

he knew of others, like the little sea-landing near where he had first landed to the south. He supposed the one near Pwil Gwo was just like it; how much difference could there be, other than the minor accommodations needed because of the shape of the land there? In former years there had been more transfer of goods and skills, more links and more contacts between traveller groups scattered here and there, but in recent years – at least, according to Nant – these had mostly faded away. Old friendships had decayed, even though the trade routes were the lifeblood of the wealth of them all, and Finn felt keenly the loss of this particular one.

So they had talked about it as a gang many times over at the midday meals, and then afterwards with Avank and Cowann of an evening. When Finn had finally suggested that Cegit and Prental were the best suited, they had shrugged and agreed. Bran took a secret pleasure in the choice, for it seemed to him that Finn had taken notice of his concerns about the bickering of the two men. Prental might well feel himself to be a more central part of the whole group.

But the reasons aired openly were more prosaic. Cegit had been there before, when he first approached the Valley from the west. He needed a travelling companion, and Prental was keen to be away for a few days. It would show something of the life of the team to this other place – a young man and an older one showing off the different stages of the work.

So they had left, and today was, according to Finn, about the time for their return. Any earlier, and it would mean that they had been turned away out of hand, or perhaps that the community at Pwil Gwo had disbanded and scattered in all directions.

Bran had asked Nant about their route, but to his surprise Nant knew little about it, other than the parts that Bran had already walked, along the full length of The Valley and then up the higher ridges beyond. Apparently there was a long lake, dark in its craggy valley, over there beyond the high land.

"It runs north-east to south-west, with sheer sides. The southern shore gets hardly any sunlight in the winter half of the year.

Gloomy, dark. Keeps itself to itself. You get a lot of seabirds coming up from the coast, and there's no shortage of deer and foxes and such like all round. Bears, boars. But there's nobody lives down there. On a day with low cloud it sits too heavy on you, pushes you out like it doesn't want you there. Something has its home there, I've no doubt, but not people. No barn-and-byre settlements either – they want to go there even less than us – and travellers pass quickly through it on the way somewhere else. There's a couple of gathering places in the next valley south, but beyond that there's just wild moorland stretching south from there, on and on. All that land round about there makes this part where we live look busy."

But Nant knew nothing about Pwil Gwo itself. He could – and had started to – tell Bran about other times, when there had been real commerce and cooperation between the two groups, but Bran had heard all about that from Avank already.

The midday bait was nearly over when there was a call from the western ridge behind them. Cegit had just crested the high shoulder and was coming down to them, and Prental was close behind him. The gusting wind took his words away, so they all waited until the two had come down to the water's edge.

They sat in the middle of the group and, for a while, said nothing. Bran frowned; there was something awry here, since neither of the two was silent by nature. But as he had come to learn, the men of the gang had developed to a fine degree the art of avoiding a subject they did not want to tackle. And if today signified an early return, they had come back quickly, and surely that was no good thing.

Finn watched them, puzzled, waiting for them to volunteer some news, but they avoided it, talking idly of other things. Cegit was fiddling with something in his carryall, while Prental plucked springs of stonecrop from the gaps in the rocks, and scattered the white petals here and there. It was Brogat who first broached the subject openly.

"Well? Did you find Pwil Gwo? Do the gang still work out there?"

## Part 2 – Brannen

"Oh yes." Cegit looked at Prental, but the younger man leaned back and waited for Cegit to explain. "Ah, well then. They are there still. And still doing what they did, smoothing and shaping roughouts. The tarn is just how I recollect it. About the same number of houses, maybe a few more. No less, certainly. Men and women both, a proper encampment. Well set out, you know, like they knew what they was doing. Nicely done. I reckon some folk are there just for a season, whereas others stay all through. Real traveller like. A pack of kids running here and there. I wasn't expecting to recognise anyone there, seeing as it was all that time ago. Back then I was only passing through."

Prental nudged him.

"You spent a fair time talking to those two men. Like you still knew each other."

"I suppose. Maybe."

He nodded, thought about it a while, and then carried on.

"Well, getting there was easy, just like you said. Over the ridges at the back end of The Valley, past a couple of little tarns, then down again the other side. That track along the tops is bleak – you're under a great wall of rock part of the way, and it's wild there. There's good stone amongst it all, but you couldn't live there the way we do here. But truly that was the best part to look at, when we were looking down at how the sunlight caught along the length of the valley and the lake what nearly filled it." He paused, lost in his memories for a little while, and then nodded. "A real golden light it was, filling the whole valley below us. That was the finest part of that whole journey, for the clouds came in fast afterwards, and the rain followed, and we got very wet. It was all the way along that long dark lake – I didn't like that much, it was too closed in for my taste. Better in these summer months than it would be in the middle of winter, but even now the light doesn't ever reach much of the southern shore. Anyway, then the track goes mostly west but north a little. We came out of the fells onto the flatter stretch before the seashore. Easy as anything it was, although the rain was still coming down something fearful. The tracks turned a lot better going on towards the coast, where the little boat landing is. We didn't get to see the landing-stage or anything, too far away for that. Nor anyone that might be a seaman. But we could see how you'd get to all that, easy enough. And the paths north and south were clear and sound, for that matter. It was just coming from the dark lake that was a bit tricky. Like it hadn't been used for a while."

He stopped again, but Finn was clearly unsatisfied with what had been said so far.

"And are they working there still? With stone, I mean."

Cegit nodded, pushed a little rock around with his feet.

"That too, aye. There's a few older men in charge, like, and about as many apprentices alongside them. Different stages of training, you know. My guess is they'll be making the marks on the lads under their own name, not sending them outside to learn. I mean, where would they send them? Looking about, as we did, we could see roughouts from a fair few different rocks, not just tuff. We saw a lot of different colours and textures there, a lot of stone to be brought in, so it all must have been gathered together from a big scrap of land. It couldn't all come from round about there. And there was some pretty decent finishing and polishing work going on. But..."

He stopped again.

"Come on, lad. Tell us all."

Cegit sighed.

"Well, like I said, they've got all kinds of stone there. But not ours. I didn't see anything that might be from near us. Some of what they got's alright, some not so much. But..." He hesitated, then went on in a decisive rush. "They say they're not interested in us. Not now any more. I mean, we talked with them for hours, those who seemed to be in charge of it all. And they recognised the quality of it, too, it wasn't like a quick glance and forget it. They were polite enough and all, listened to what we had to say, looked at what we'd brought along. But after it all, they told us as how there's others as have worked with them closer in the last while than we have. Asked where we'd been all this time."

"But you showed them what you had?"

## Part 2 – Brannen

Prental nodded, feeling able to speak now Cegit had given the heart of the news.

"Of course we did. Mostly the axes, the finished one and the roughouts too. But as well as that we showed around other bits and pieces that we had, so they could see we wasn't just doing a single thing. And what we had was better than what they were using. I could see it, and I reckon they could too. I mean, anyone who worked in stone would see it, and they weren't blind or stupid."

"Is this right?"

Cegit nodded.

"Oh yes. Prental's told it right. They examined all what we had with us, the finished and the rough. Knew what they were looking for alright. They could tell it was sound. And we both saw the stone they had lying all about there. It was mountain stone alright, decent enough, it wasn't rubbish, but for sure it wasn't not like ours for quality. They knew it too. I'd guess most it came from north of here, that big area west and north of Lin Tios. We've seen the like up at Dronow Moar before."

Roudhok shook his head.

"I know that stone. It's not bad, but it's nothing like what we get from the Ban and the Brig here. Or the knuckle ridge on the west, for that matter. And a few other places. Why'd anyone choose that other stuff when they could have ours?"

"Well. I reckon they know full well that what they've got is second-rate at best. But they'll tell you that the lads up that way have been bringing them stone like that for, I don't know, maybe ten years. Year in year out without fail. Seems those who bring that stone don't live at the quarry like we do here; they pass by in the summer and camp there up in the northern valleys, pull out what they can just in a season and then move on again. Right traveller life, it must be. But they don't even try to finish anything off. What they do is take all the roughouts down to Pwil Gwo for finishing, and when they're there they pick up whatever they're owed for the last season's lot, food, supplies, whatever. Then they're off again."

He fell silent. Finn thought for a while.

"Then will they start up again with us? You said they know that what we've got is better than that northern rock."

Cegit pursed his lips, looked away across Pwil Gesgod, then shook his head.

"I don't think so, Finn. They were, like, clear about how they reckon that this other lot are reliable. And, by way of opposite, we're not. Not reliable, I mean."

Prental nodded.

"He's right. It's like they think they can't depend on us now. They know that our rock is better, but that's not enough for them. One of them told me, right to my face, that he'd rather have second quality stone that he knew was coming on time, than a promise of first-rate which never so much as appeared. Said that was no more than damp in the air when you really want proper rain. They think that we're..."

He stopped, seeing the look on Finn's face. Cegit finished for him.

"They think we can't be trusted any more."

A murmur ran around the little group, of surprise, anger, and disbelief. Roudhok flushed red, and his face was grim.

"And you let them say this about us? Without any comeback?"

Cegit spread his hands.

"There's not a lot you can say, bud, when they're sitting working with a whole heap of roughouts, and not one of them is ours. Kind of puts you in a bad place before you ever open your mouth. Anyway, they're a decent enough crew, if you get past that. I wasn't going to get angry with them when I could see as what they meant."

Roudhok snorted in disgust. Nant leaned forward.

"If you see it from their point of view..."

Finn interrupted him.

"I don't want to hear it. Not right now. Let's just take time about all this. Think on it tonight and we'll talk again this time tomorrow. But as for me, I don't like it being said that I'm not

## Part 2 – Brannen

reliable. I don't know what yous all think, but that's a heavy blow for me."

He got up before anyone else could say anything, and stumped off away towards the portion of the quarry he was working. Cegit reached out towards him, but Finn shook him off and kept walking. The others looked at one other, struck abruptly silent by Finn's reaction. In the end they scattered, each to his own place.

Bran got up slowly and worked his way across to his perch. Brannen had been circling in the still air above the Brig, but tilted her wings and dropped back down to a little crag on a level with Bran's head.

"Well now, I wonder what you'd have made of all that, if you hadn't been skiving off on those splendid wings of yours?"

Brannen clacked her beak and preened some feathers. Bran leaned back and considered her thoughtfully.

"I wonder if you ravens have your own disputes and such like? Where some groups take a liking or a disliking to others, I mean? What would you have done if you've been with Cegit and Prental on that particular journey, I wonder?"

Brannen finished adjusting her plumage, picked up a little stone and dropped it close to Bran, clacking her beak. Bran sighed.

"Yes, I kept back a little bit of bait for you." He opened up the draw-string bag, found the morsels of bannock and dried rabbit he had left over, and put them on a flat outcrop so Brannen could pick over them as she chose.

"At least you don't have to try and trade what you've done with your days with somebody else. Someone you've never met, who's made a choice without ever seeing you." He shook his head. "Finn was right upset, you see, and he'll be bothering away at what's been said all the rest of the day. Then again this evening with Avank. And maybe Gwovan too. And maybe he'll want us all there to listen, when we could all be doing some polishing or whatever."

Brannen carefully scrutinised the stone – now picked clean –

where the food had been set out, then stretched her wings out and shook them. Bran laughed.

"Go on with you, then. You go off up there and fly about while I finish here. We'll be going home by way of Lanerc's house for some more supplies, so don't go too far off."

Brannen tapped the rock gently with her beak, croaked a little, and was away. Bran watched her soar halfway across the great sweep of open space, before turning back to the rockface again. If all went well, by the end of the day he'd have eased the latest piece away from where it sat wedged.

The wind had become fierce during the night, and Bran had stayed in his hut rather than risk the gusts at the high places. The clouds had settled, low and dark, and erratic rainstorms rattled the roof and walls of his home. He had moved across to the doorway to get enough light to carry on with the roughwork on his latest piece.

Brannen had settled herself just inside the door, avoiding the rain. She alternated between gazing at Bran as he worked, and glancing around the floor of the hut at the little fragments of rock accumulating there. Bran, as usual, was chatting to her about the stonework as he tapped gently at the roughout.

He carried on working the stone for a while, before stopping to stretch. The raven croaked once and put her head on one side, before suddenly shaking her head and making the pok-pok sound in her gullet. Bran leaned back and laughed.

"Still trying to work stone yourself, are you now? It sounds good enough, though by rights you should be making that noise on the stone here."

Brannen preened her wing feathers, shook her head again, and pok-pok-pok-pok sounded through the hut.

"Well, lass, I suppose I'd better teach you some more. Look

## Part 2 – Brannen

here now, if I was to strike the stone on that side, angled down, I'd risk the whole thing falling into pieces. There'd be no more pok pok, and it'd be just rubbish, even though it's true tuff by its nature just now. You can guess I'll not be doing that." He turned the stone thoughtfully around in his hand, and peered at it from different angles. "But maybe just here?"

Brannen took two steps across the doorway, then hopped to pick up a little stone sliver in her beak, an offcut from the main piece. She dropped it in front of Bran and looked sidelong at him. She opened her beak once, twice, with no sound coming from it, and then, clear as anything, spoke one word, "rubbish".

Bran beamed and laughed.

"Aye, lass, that's rubbish, truly. And I suppose you reckon that's a good imitation of my own voice. Look now, I knew you were bright."

He rubbed his head, tossed the bird a chunk of his bannock.

"Well then, what else can you do?"

Brannen gobbled the morsel, then stepped round and picked up another shard. She dropped it carefully in front of Bran and spoke again.

"True tuff."

Bran laughed.

"That's well spoken. But it's not true tuff, lass. That's rubbish again."

Brannen looked at both stones, nudged one and the other, then dropped the first on top of the second and said, "Rubbish. True tuff."

"Alright, then. I see we've a little way to go before you can go out on the slopes and pick up decent stone for yourself. Those two you're working with there are both rubbish. Now, this one here..." and he held up the stone he was still working on. "This one here is true tuff, and if I don't mess it up in the making, it won't end up as rubbish. You see, it's not just what it is at the start, but how it comes along in the making, and if I go wrong in that piece of work, well, true tuff turns into rubbish. Except maybe for razors or needles, or whatever. But if the grain is funny inside, it'll never be an axe, no matter how much care I take over it. And it is axes we're after now, not just little bits and pieces."

He carried on smoothing the stone, with a careful hand. He was deep in concentration, and for a while didn't notice Brannen's fidgeting. Eventually he looked up. The raven was close by the door, looking out through the rain as it wetted the feathers on her head. From somewhere outside a noise of crows could be heard. There was nothing strange about that, except that one of the calls ended in a strange upward squeak. Every so often, amongst all the harmonious rest, the high discordant note sounded. Each time it happened, Brannen clacked her beak as though in annoyance.

"What is it, lass? You don't like the way that one talks?"

He put down the shaper and the hammerstone and came over to the door.

"What's he saying, then? I'm sure I don't know, but perhaps you do. Do crows and ravens speak the same as each other? And if you don't like that one being different, what do all them other crows make of it, I wonder?" He thought, suddenly, of Melen, for the first time in a few months. "Do crows make fun of each other for being different like people do? You never met Melen, did you now? I don't think she'd have known what to make of you, for her knowledge of birds – indeed of anything outside her village – was very limited. And she would never come out here to find out for herself what it was like. That's all gone, of course, all well behind me now, but I do wonder what her life's like these days."

They both stared out into the showers for a while, until the chatter of the crows died down again. He regretted bringing Melen back to mind, but it was done now. If Gwennol was right – and she probably was – then she would most likely be big with child by now, and not many moons away from labour. He shook his head. Barn-and-byre women died in childbirth far too often. He had sworn never to seek her out, but thinking of the possibility of her death was still profoundly disturbing.

## Part 2 – Brannen

He tried to set all that away from his mind, so that the death-thoughts would not make their way into the stone. Anything like that would show itself somehow in the finished piece. He got up, walked around the stone hut in one direction and then the other for a while, feeling the drizzle soaking into his clothes, looking up at the uneven ridge in the west.

When he felt steady again, securely rooted in the timeless stone of The Valley, he carried on. After that, he worked a little bit longer, entertained by Brannen's occasional interjections, until the rain finally eased to a halt. He looked out, and although the wind was just as strong, the day had turned dry as the clouds were pushed away eastward.

"Come on out, lass, it's overdue time we were out in the air. I need a break from all that shaping, and it won't do you any harm to get out either."

They set off east, not heading anywhere particular – certainly not Dolgolvan, though the track would ultimately go to the village. Before long they drew level with the crags that lined the north wall of the valley here. They were astir with birds wheeling about. Crows and ravens vied with hawks and buzzards, and the air was full of noise and feathers. Brannen settled on a nearby rock, gazing at the tumult, then glanced back at Bran.

"Go on, lass. Go join in the fuss and see what you can do. They're your own kind, after all, and they'll be glad of however you can help out."

Brannen took off in a flurry, flapping hard to gain height before diving down again to join another pair of ravens circling around a buzzard. Bran squatted down near the path to watch, trying to keep sight of Brannen in the whirl of jostling birds. It was too difficult, though, and after a while he just tried to get a sense of which side was in the ascendant.

Eventually it all settled down. Birds of both factions landed beside each other along the crags and scrubby bushes, and the raucous noise subsided. Brannen flew back and settled beside Bran. Her normal soft croaks had become fierce and martial, and there was a wild light in her eyes. Her feathers were disarrayed, but so far as Bran could tell, once they were all smoothed down again, they were still all intact and sleek.

"Sorted them out, did you now?"

Brannen took flight again, circling rapidly around Bran as he crossed the beck and climbed up to a crag at the base of Drum Crog. She was still full of the eager excitement of the conflict. From this vantage point, Ty Caroc stood out clearly, a little to the west. He couldn't make out the foremen's rock, hidden as it was amongst the hazels and ash trees, but in his mind's eye the track threading along from there to the quarry itself was clear. The Ban and the Brig stood proud beyond all that, lofted high above the sea of trees below.

As he watched, a break in the clouds let a shaft of sunlight down onto the great craggy wall beside the Ban. It was the time of year when directions were reversed, when sunrise first showed itself by reflection on the ridges to the west, and sunset on the eastern hills. A great wedge of geese was far above, and he could just hear their distant discordant calling as they flew north. He sighed.

"That's why we're here, Brannen. Where else would you see a sight like that?"

He sat in silence for a while, watching as Brannen slowly settled back to her normal calm self. After what seemed to him a very long time, the raven stopped fidgeting and flying erratically from ground to branch to crag. Bran nodded.

"Well done, lass. Not easy, coming down from that, I dare say. But it all makes me think that before too long you need to be back with your own kind. There's lots I can give you, and lots more I can teach you to say than just rubbish and true tuff, but you'll learn most from other ravens. And truth be told, I can't imagine you'll ever be able to get the tuff out from the vein in the rock. Your wings just weren't made for that."

He stayed there a bit longer, and then after a time stood up again.

"Come on, lass, we'll get on back now. Let's go along the way a little bit, so we don't mix up with all those hawks again.

## Part 2 – Brannen

Enough excitement for one day, I think."

They followed a rough track west, keeping part-way up the hillside and well away from the beck. After a while they crossed where the firmer ground came close either side of the water, and turned back towards Ty Caroc. A call came from behind: Nant was coming along the track, a bag of supplies slung over one shoulder. Bran waited until he caught up.

"Been up at Lanerc's?"

"Indeed I have. Got some nice stuff from him too; Gwennol's been bartering bits and pieces half way down Lugh Crum. You should get yourself along there tomorrow or the next day, before it's all gone. Better quality than what they show at Dolgolvan, and at more favourable exchange as well." He gestured to Brannen who was circling around them just above the tops of the hazel stands. "Been out and about with your raven now, have you?"

Bran laughed.

"I think she's her own raven now more than she's mine. But yes, we've been along the valley here and there."

He told Nant about the squabble, and the enthusiasm with which Brannen had greeted it and joined in.

"I reckon she'll want more of that before long. Just coming along with me to the workings won't be sufficient any more."

"Stands to reason that she'd want to be with her own."

Bran was abruptly smitten with a sharp pang.

"I suppose it does. But you know, I'll miss her if she's not with me through the days. She's, like, someone to talk with. As well as the stone itself, of course, which we all chat to as we work away. And look now, see this."

He stopped, called to Brannen and set two small flakes of stone beside the path. The raven, obligingly, declared that the first was rubbish and the second true tuff. Nant first grinned, then laughed aloud.

"But that's wonderful, Bran. Who'd have thought a raven could do that?"

"It'd be better if she knew, truly knew, I mean, which piece was which quality. Not just the words. Just now she only knows to say those two things."

"Ah, but that'll come later. There's plenty of people who cannot tell the good apart from the bad, never mind ravens. And travellers too, not just barn-and-byre. That's what we have the training for. Give her a few years and who knows where she'll be? Maybe taking over from Finn and making her own marks on the foremen's rock."

"Maybe she will, at that."

Nant laughed again.

"Can you imagine Finn trying to make the trademarks in her body? Where'd you think he'd put the very first of them, the hammerstone-and-antler that goes on a person's wrist? And would your Brannen sit still and let him do it?"

"I don't know that ravens have any of that business."

They walked along together for some time. Bran had the feeling that Nant wanted to say something else, so he held his peace and let the moment come by itself. Eventually, when only a few bends of the track were left before Ty Caroc, Nant sighed and sat on a boulder beside the track, gesturing that Bran should do the same.

"Bran, I know we were both just joking about Brannen getting the trademarks. Finn making them and all. But there's a serious side to all that. It's not just whether a raven or anyone else can learn the trade; it's whether the rest of the gang would accept something that's outside what they expect."

Bran nodded and looked at him thoughtfully for a long moment.

"You're not talking about Brannen taking Finn's job now, are you? We both know that that will never happen."

"I'm not, no. I'm really talking about the girl you used to see in Dolgolvan at the half waning moon."

"Melen. Her name was Melen."

"If you say so. I don't know all their names along there. It's that long since I've been regular-like. But I do remember her, because of, well, because of her appearance. But never mind that. I'm not talking about that, but rather this. I listened to some of what the others said, back in the winter, and I know you were thinking of bringing her out here."

"At one time I was, yes. But that all got pushed aside by her own people. I went along there to Bechan's house one day, and she was just gone. Disappeared. Her own family had just taken her away."

He stared down the track, blankly.

"Of course they did. Sooner or later it would have happened just the same."

"Look, Nant, I talked about all this with Lanerc and Gwennol. I heard it all from them, how the barn-and-byre families would never have given their approval."

"That's so, and I'm right sure Gwennol will have told you better than I ever could. But I don't much care what the Dolgolvan lot might say. I did hear as much from one of the girls there, Tios I think it was; I saw her in the market one day and we talked a bit. But no: it's your own people that I'm thinking of just now. What I'm saying is this. Even if them folk in Dolgolvan would have kept quiet and let it happen, the lads out here would never have stood back. It's too far from what they understand. It'd be like letting a raven be foreman, only much more so. They'd laugh about it like it was a big joke, and have a crack about it to tease you, but if they ever saw it starting to happen, they'd have made sure it didn't."

"How?"

Nant shook his head, sombrely.

"I have no idea. But I've seen it before, how they can be just difficult about something they have no feeling for. And then it never happens, however sound an idea it is in the first place. And travellers, I mean, not them other lot."

Bran was silent for a long time.

"You know, Melen herself didn't want it either. Looking back, I'm sure of it. Towards the end we just couldn't agree about all manner of things. I didn't know what to make of it at the time, but it was like she would argue about whatever I said. Even if what I was saying a good thing and I was sure of its rightness. I just didn't see it at the time."

"I dare say." He looked at Bran hesitantly. "You don't mind me saying this?"

"No, I'm grateful to you. I always thought the lads here were just joshing her because of how she was, what her skin was like and all. I hated that, you know. But you're saying there was something more behind it."

"Oh, there was. There still is. I don't know that barn-and-byre and traveller can mix. We all have to choose one or the other."

"Lanerc and Gwennol managed it."

"That's true. But they've done so by becoming mostly traveller. The barn-and-byre side of Lanerc's family won't acknowledge them, and Gwennol's people have never been easy with the whole thing. The two of them have done it by not being part of either side. But truthfully, if you look at the way they live, they're more traveller than the other. Living out here in the middle of the land, I mean, not in one of the towns. Even if they do live just in the one place all the time."

They sat together for a while longer, letting the words sink in. Suddenly Bran looked at him and stood up.

"We live in the same place all the time too. This is why you keep out of some of the gatherings, isn't it though? Because you're at odds with some of the ways we do things. You reckon that us lot out here are just as set in our ways as they are down there in Dolgolvan."

Nant nodded.

"Don't get me wrong. I love the work. And this is the best place for me to live. I'm never going to change it for anything else. And I've got some good friends here, those I can talk to about all this every now and again. But I'm not going to say that it's all fine, when clearly it's not. I worry, Bran, I worry about what'll happen to us out here in The Valley as time goes by and the barn-and-byre way fills the land. It gets into us all, you know. Even living out here, away from the towns and the fields, their way works itself inside us no matter what. So yes, I worry about

*Part 2 – Brannen*

what we'll become."

"You've said the like before."

"I have. To you, at least, and a few others. Gan-Mor, for one. Avank. Lewenith. But I've long since stopped saying it too much in front of the rest. By and large, they just don't want to hear it."

Bran nodded, and they walked the last stretch back to the stone huts.

Bran came back from the peaks a little earlier one day. He had teased out a biggish lump of tuff, and wanted to do some preliminary preparation the same day. Better that, than leave it for the morrow and lose the sense of how it had come into his hands. The whole process, the whole history of the rock mattered, not just the shape in itself.

But when he arrived at Ty Caroc, there was a newcomer sitting there, on the very same rock that Bran had perched on when he had first come to the village.

The young man – shorter than Bran, younger even than Prental, with untidy reddish hair – brightened, and came over to him. Words bubbled out of him in a jumbled rush.

"Are you Finn? Finn map-Gwath? I was told to see him when I got here. I'm Tresklenn map-Deru. I finished my apprenticing at a stone working place away up north from here. Half a moon it's taken me, but I'm right glad of every step."

He pointed north, and would have carried on, except that Bran shook his head and held up a hand to stop him.

"Finn'll be here soon, and he'll see you then. I'm Bran, and I was the last one here, arrived a little over a year ago now. But you must wait for him; he has the final word. I won't speak for him, for he's the foreman of us all, but my belief is that he'll be glad to see you. He'll want to know how you've been trained, and he'll want to check the trademarks on you, but if you've got that proof of learning I don't suppose there'll be any hindrance to you being here."

Tresklenn nodded eagerly, not sure whether to keep facing towards Bran or westward down the track that Finn would come along. Bran grinned.

"Finn will call us all together when he gets here. I'll leave you alone if you like, but if you'd rather talk that's fine."

Brannen swept in at that point, flying low over the two men's heads and settling neatly on a nearby branch. Tresklenn flinched at the abrupt approach of such a large bird, with such a large and cruel-looking beak. Once he had recovered himself, he gazed at the raven in open-mouthed surprise.

"He's very close in to the houses, isn't he? They don't come anything near like that back where I come from. Are they all like that?"

"Oh no, this here is Brannen; I rescued her when she was young, and she's stayed beside me ever since. Comes up to the workings with me and all, she does."

Tresklenn started to stretch out a hand towards Brannen and then stopped, looking again at her beak, and the slightly wicked look on the bird's face.

"I'm not sure..."

"Well, neither am I some of the time. She's a right trickster when she wants to be, and she's given me some sharp nips if I've guessed wrongly what she wants. Better safe than sorry, maybe. But she loves imitating things. All kinds of things. I've listened to her perched up on a crag imitating crow noises. She lures them down, you know, to get them to play with her when she's a bit bored. Right confused, they get, when they look at her and try to work out what's happening."

He decided not to tell the newcomer about how she equally often lured pigeons down from the trees, by lying perfectly still on her side until they approached close enough that she could turn on them, dispatch them with a single snap of that ferocious beak, and then feast noisily, messily on the remains.

"Oh, she's bright, then. Can she copy other things?"

*Part 2 – Brannen*

Brannen strutted closer, picked up a little pebble and dropped it at Bran's feet, and then made her "pok-pok" noise followed by "rubbish".

Tresklenn laughed.

"I see you're training her to work stone."

"If only I could get her to know the true tuff when she sees it."

He picked the pebble up, said, "Thank you, Brannen; this one truly is rubbish," and then leaned back and turned again to Tresklenn.

"So do you have tuff up where you came from? What's the stone like? What kinds of things have you been making?"

Tresklenn pulled a polished fish-carving from his bag and eagerly showed it to Bran.

"We have tuff, but it's not what you call the true tuff. Like a cousin. What you have here is truly special, it's the only thing like it in the whole land. Everyone knows that. I've seen little bits of it, and worked a tiny sliver, just for practice. What we have has a coarser grain, and the colour's not the same. But it's decent enough for making both pretty things and tools. Besides, it's what there is, and you have to use what you've got, don't you now?"

"That's nice work. Show that to Finn when he gets here. I like the way you've got the fish shape matching the colour-swirls in the stone. There's places near here where that would get you a decent amount in trade promises. When Finn's seen you and given the nod, the rest of us can tell you what's what and who's who."

The younger man put the fish away again and looked around at the village, with its irregular grouping of houses loosely clustered around the open centre.

"Do you do your own finishing work here? Back north we set aside part of the camp as a tool area and worked there together if we weren't out at the seams."

"Well, Finn'll tell you about that, so I'll just say it's a topic for conversation just now. For a long time we've done all that ourselves, but back in the previous foreman's day..." he paused to gesture towards Avank's home, "back then we sent the rough-outs to a settlement west of here, beyond those big mountains at the head of The Valley. Finn had an idea to maybe bring that back again, and he sent a couple of us over there to talk with them. But it didn't go well; seems they didn't want us any more. But that might change again, if we've a mind to persevere with them and try again. Some of the lads want to go back to that way of working, while others are happy keeping it here."

"What do you think?"

"Me? I'm happy doing it myself. I like the idea of doing it all from start to finish, and I don't much like the idea of giving it over to someone I don't know. Not that there were complaints about the job they did, not so far as I've heard, though other things got in the way. It's not that: it's just I just want to keep my own hand on it. But as for where we work, well, just in our own houses mostly. We don't have anywhere we all get together to do that. Not that it's a bad idea, mind, just that it hasn't been our habit up until now. Maybe it should be. What else are you used to that we don't do?"

Tresklenn scratched his head and glanced around the village.

"Well, I don't exactly know yet. What about – I don't know – what about a place to sharpen tools? We had two great rocks half-sunk in the ground that we used those for." He laughed to himself, lost in the memory for a moment. "All of us went over to them as often as there was need, and did the sharpening in that one place. Those rocks got great gouge-marks in them, what with all the use they'd had over the years. I don't see their like hereabouts."

"No, nothing like that. There's enough hard stone around here we just pick up what we need where it lies. Hammerstones, sharpeners, whatever. Once Finn's said aye to you, any of us will show you where to find everything, but most of it's easy to find."

Not long after that, Finn came back, with the others together in a loose gaggle just ahead of him. Bran beckoned him over.

"Finn, this is Tresklenn, just arrived from up north somewhere, couple of moonphases away. He heard about us and wants to join us."

Finn checked him over, talked with him about his training, studied the trademarks in his body, and announced his acceptance. Just as Bran had been the previous year, Tresklenn seemed perplexed by the informality of it all. The others clustered around him then, mobbing him with questions and conversation.

Bran watched as Finn showed him his hut, over near where Prental lived. Then he waved all the others away, scattering them so Tresklenn had a chance to breathe, and to settle himself in. It was all very familiar, all completely reminiscent of his own arrival. Only Drus was missing from that day.

Bran had become, all of a sudden, impatient with everything. He still wanted to get those first stages of preparation done on the rock he had extracted today, but he couldn't face the thought of doing it right now. Later would be fine. For now, he wanted to get away from Ty Caroc and its occupants. He felt a restlessness that he did not understand.

He splashed across the beck in the bottom of The Valley and zigzagged up the tadpole head end of Drum Crog, working his way then along the crest. The heather and the ling were fading now, with only patches of purple left amongst all the blooms which had gone over. It had been a good year along the ridge, but it was waning.

Brannen circled around him in great wide circles, sometimes keeping quite close, but more often far across the empty spaces either side of the ridge. Bran stopped on the crag, at the very crest of the ridge. Almost directly opposite were the two great spires of rock that governed his days, and he felt the surge of passion, of heady delight that the sight always gave him.

Surely, if anywhere could be called home, it was this place. Why, then, did he feel this dissatisfaction?

Brannen was over in The Valley's little sister, a small dark speck against the great flank of Pen-y-hal. Bran remembered his time there last winter, the sudden terror of it all, and thought how his promise had led him to Brannen. He had no idea if the great Elder Raven would still be alive or not, but surely if she had passed beyond his knowing, then another would have taken her place. Either way, he felt that the debt had been settled.

If Brannen wasn't with him every day, at Ty Caroc or up on the crags of the quarry, he would miss her, for sure. But it was right that her circling would take her ever further away, further out from human society, back into her own kind. Her orbit should grow ever larger, not be constrained to his own life.

Before he could reconsider, before his anxieties and aloneness could unravel the decision which had formed within him, he stood and faced south. He was looking towards Pen-y-hal and towards Mynyth Mam, though the great mother mountain was entirely hidden from him just now. Mostly, he was looking towards the place where he had made his vow.

"Elder Raven, lady of the skies and mistress of your kindred, today I give Brannen back to you." His voice faltered for a moment, and then he continued. "I rescued her from the wildcat and the crows when you showed her to me, and I have reared and raised her as best I know how. I have taught her what I can about the true tuff, and the life of the traveller. But I cannot teach her all that she needs to know when she lives with you."

He swallowed, watching Brannen turn above the cross-valley where Lanerc's farm lay hidden and head back again.

"Today I give her back to you. She is yours, and she is of you, and she should be with you as she flies. And I'd be right proud if one day she turned out to be an Elder Raven herself. But that's years away, and even if you can see that far, I certainly cannot. And if I'm wrong, and she's a he raven after all, then it'll be different again. But never mind that. Right now, today, I give her back to you."

He sat down again, feeling proud of himself, and at the same time bereft. Brannen flew straight and level back towards him, then turned to fly on her back for a while before rolling over and coming down to settle beside him.

Bran laughed and stroked the soft feathers on the raven's neck. Just now they were young, and pure black, gleaming like jet, but

## Part 2 – Brannen

as they aged, they would turn to different shades, a mix that baffled the eye with tones and shimmers of slight colour and tint, dark blues and purples all together.

"Showing off now, aren't you. Another year, and you'll be doing that for real to catch the eye of some young boy raven. Unless I've got it all wrong, and you're the boy raven who'll be looking for a girl. Either way, I reckon you're still too young for that. But there's never any harm in looking for a companion, is there now?"

Brannen clacked her beak and stared up at Bran, turning her head so she could do so with each eye in turn. Bran laughed.

"Well, you're not wrong. It's both of us could use company, I reckon. We've fitted well together this last little while, you and I, but maybe you'd fit better with your own kind, and me with mine." He bent down so that his head was on the same level as the bird's. "When you want to go, you can, you know. I reckon I've fulfilled the promise I made to the elder mistress raven, now that we've been partnered-like for these last months."

He paused and swallowed.

"Now, I shall be sorry to see you go, whenever you decide that it's right to, but it's right that you do. Go out there and be with your own kinfolk; defend your territory against them buzzards now, fly well with the other youngsters this year. Then when next year comes around, you think about doing that upside-down trick to catch someone's eye. And y'll be welcome anyday to see me, back at the village, or more likely up on the Ban or the Brig."

Brannen rubbed her head absently against Bran's hand, then hopped down to pick up a pebble from the ground and fluttered back beside Bran. She dropped the pebble into Bran's lap, croaked gently, and then said, "true tuff"."

Bran looked at the pebble. Of course, it wasn't the true tuff, not here along the sinuous ridge of Drum Crog – the vein of that precious stone was far higher up the levels of rock than anywhere that might be reached along this crest. But in another, better sense, the true tuff was exactly what it was.

"Aye, lass, you're entirely right."

He stood up and walked along the rest of the crest, almost to the high rock thorn at the western end, before descending to the tarn that lay beside Lanerc's farm. He thought about going to see them, but it was getting late in the evening, and the owls were beginning to sound amongst the nearby trees.

So instead, he came down into the main branch of The Valley, near to the rock where Don's body had been laid out all those months ago, and ambled slowly back along the track home to Ty Caroc. Brannen stayed close above and around him, moving like a shadow in the gathering gloom.

Then as he crossed the open centre of the village, and glanced across to see Prental talking with Tresklenn, Brannen lifted effortlessly higher, and soared off into the darkening evening sky. Almost at once her black feathers faded into the shadows.

Bran worked on into the late evening, getting the first shaping done on the roughout until the light faded and he could no longer see what he was doing. Brannen did not come back that evening, and Bran felt a peculiar mixture of pride and sorrow at the loss.

Then the next morning, as he scrambled up to the gully where he was working, there was a familiar sound of wings, and there was Brannen again. She stayed with him for a little while, and then took flight again into the great void.

After that, Brannen's visits became more erratic. She would be there at the quarry for a short while for a few days in a row, then away for a moonphase or more.

How far, Bran wondered, did she let her wings take her? Was she always within a few minutes' flight, or did her exploration take her much further away, up to Dronow Moar or over to the coast? When she left the valleys, did she soar over the highest peaks in the land? Did she, perhaps, make her own pilgrimage to the peak of Mynyth Mam, or was that just a human thing to do?

Bran decided that the stone that he had worked on that first evening, the time when he had restored his pledge to the elder

*Part 2 – Brannen*

mistress raven, and the day that Brannen had left, would be one of his gifts to Mynyth Mam. That was, he considered ruefully, assuming that he would finally make the ascent successfully and reach the summit.

He would add it to the other items he had set aside for that journey – the raven pinion, the shell, some dried berries and other foods. It would replace the older fragment of the true tuff, the one which was shaped like the mountain herself. That fragment reflected his earlier self, and it no longer seemed appropriate.

But in any case, the time was not yet right. He often looked south to Mynyth Mam from the gullies he worked in, or when the gang were gathering for bait at Pwil Gesgod, and every time he looked, he knew it was too soon. It had been too soon on both those occasions before, but he had not realised it then. He had thought himself ready, and he had been thwarted. This time he would wait, and wait with proper patience, and – eventually – his third time would be rewarded. But as yet, he had no idea what he was waiting for.

*Richard Abbott*

# Part 3 – Lindirgel

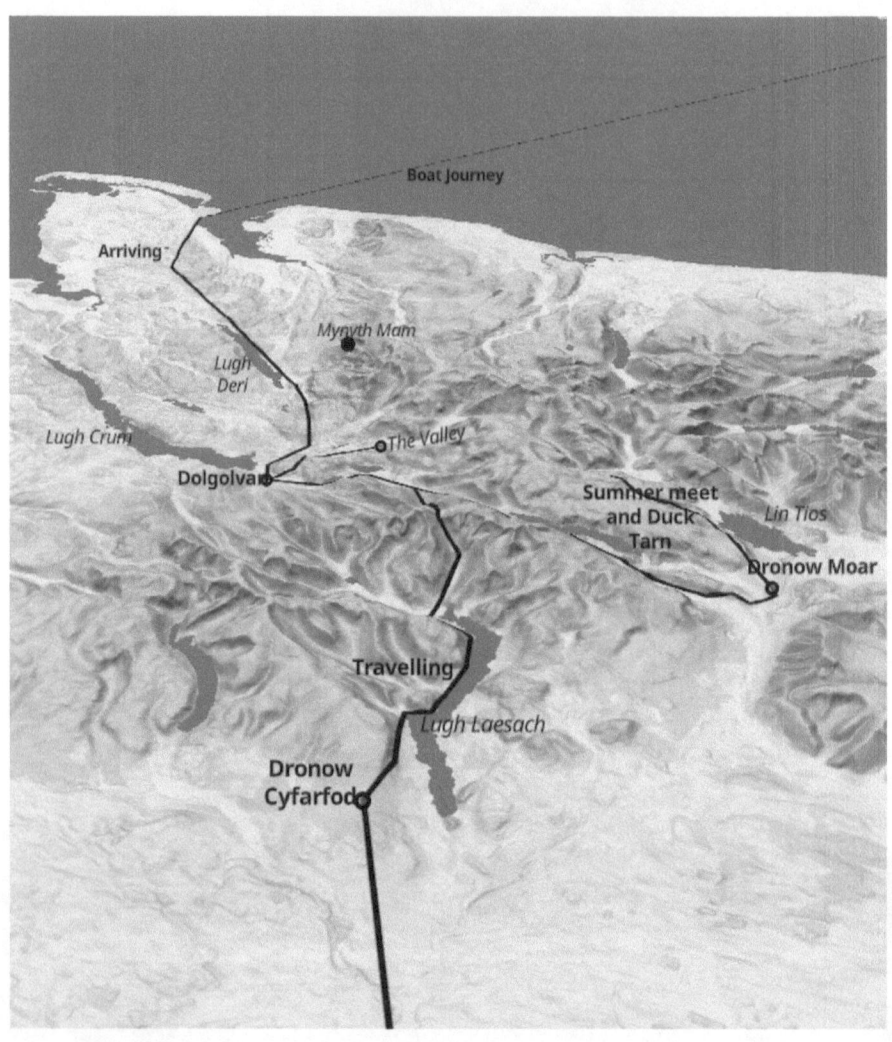

## Part 3 – Lindirgel

THERE WAS NOISE IN THE HEART of Ty Caroc, the open place at the centre towards which all the little huts faced. Bran was working at the first rough polish on one of yesterday's finds; it was coming along, but even this initial buff would take half the morning. He laid the stone down. It would not do to hurry this stage, and he was both bored and curious, lured out by the early autumn day. Through the open door he could see that the men were gathering, clustering around some focus that he could not quite make out. He got up, went across to join them. The beech trees in their loose ring around the stone buildings still held their leaves, with some still green, and others already turning yellow or brown with the autumn. A moon had passed since Tresklenn had arrived, and Brannen had increasingly withdrawn into her own life. The distraction outside was good.

At the hollow centre of the group was Gavur map-Ymelud, the trader, beside the little handcart he brought just after a full moon every so often. He was watching the stoneworkers pull at this and that, arguing, speculating, negotiating. But Bran's eye caught not the familiar, but the strange. A woman was beside the cart, her posture making clear that she was entirely separate from Gavur. She remained silent, aloof, and there was a thinly-veiled hostility that clung around her. She was not constrained in any way, and he was as yet unsure why she was there. The men were carefully, studiously ignoring her, apart from quick glances when they thought the others would not notice.

He looked more carefully at her. She was tall, dark-haired, dark-eyed, and reminded him of the women of his own island. She wore outer layers of doe-skin leather, and a rim of squirrel fur bordered the neck of her smock. A shell necklace showed over the smock, and she had set a clutch of cormorant feathers in the bun of her hair where a leather tie held it up.

And in the outdoor-darkened skin up her arms, in little pin-pricks and ink all the way from wrist to shoulder, were signs and symbols whose significance he understood, at least in a general manner. A few he could see plainly; others disappeared below the fringes of her smock and skirt. She had been taught some kind of skill, and she had been taught by somebody who signalled the training with a similar style of marks to those used by the stoneworkers. He didn't recognise any of the particular signs she bore, but there was no reason that he would, since every trade had its own signs. Possibilities circled around him.

Lewenith had just joined the group. She exchanged some trinkets of rock for some salt, and then turned a little to face the newcomer. The two women studied each other briefly, then Lewenith nodded without speaking, and went back into her hut. Gavur took a step towards Bran.

"Bran! Join us, my friend. See what I have for you today."

Gavur was affable, confident. Bran glanced in the cart but saw nothing that he needed.

"No rope?"

"Not this time. Next, perhaps. How much were you looking for?"

He pointed to the side of his house.

"At least twice that height. More if you can."

Gavur nodded.

"I'll do what I can."

"And who is this? No apprentice of yours, to be sure."

The trader laughed shortly.

"She's not mine. I let her travel with me as a favour to an old friend living near Mon. She is on her own journey. She goes as and when she pleases, except that I shall need recompense for the food of mine she's eaten, and the time she's taken."

Prental, on the other side of the cart, straightened and laughed.

"Don't take your chances there, Bran. Come on back with us to the women at Dolgolvan; it's been far too long. I know Melen's not there who you favoured, though I could never think why, but there's others. And this one here looks too much like hard work. Not worth it."

Gavur shook his head.

"She could be a nugget of gold in a mountain of scree for one of you. Lindirgel is what she calls herself, but, just as true as I'm standing in front of you, my honest belief from my journey

## Part 3 – Lindirgel

here alongside her is that she should be named Bronwen. Who's interested in her?"

The woman looked scornfully around the little group.

"Who's interested in me? Don't any of you think that I'm an easy take. The man who lays his finger on me unasked will regret it ever after. I'll so freeze the manhood within him that he'll never lie with a woman again. His heart will fail at the sight of a breast, and the thought of a thigh will make his pride go weak. Whether by day or by night, whether in the hills or the valley, whether this year or the next, my curse will follow at his heels, and my words shall never be away from his side. And even my far-away half-sisters in this place Dolgolvan will mock him if ever he goes to them again."

They drew a little away from her. One or two turned their backs. Brogat shook his head.

"She should be called Bron-suraf, not Bron-wen. I'll have nothing to do with her. None of us should. You keep her, Gavur, and try your luck with her over at Lugh Laesach. Anywhere away from here."

There was a murmur of agreement, a hardening of attitude, but Bran walked across to her. Having not so very long ago joined the men of Ty Caroc, and after all that had happened at Dolgolvan, his sense of community with them had never fully settled. The exchange had scattered it again. Moreover, he admired her solitary defiance, and the clear signs of wit and training that she showed.

"I'll chance it."

Some of the men murmured behind him, but he ignored that. She considered him distantly, head slightly to one side. She was only very slightly shorter than him, and her bearing was proud. It would, he thought, be easy to feel dismissed by her. He nodded his head in greeting to her.

"I am Bran map-Broch of Innis Mon." She seemed sceptical, having listened to the way he used his words, the lilt of his voice. At a guess, her home was close to the other island called Mon, the one that almost joined the mainland. Mon Mewn was about as far south of Mon Allan as his journey east here to the mainland, perhaps a little further. "Innis Mon Allan, I mean, not Mon Mewn. Carn Pennau is where I lived. Is Lindirgel your given name?"

"Lindirgel merch-Raeadra. From the encampment near the grove and stone circle on Mon Mewn, looking across the straits at the mainland."

He nodded. He did not know the settlements of her island at all, but he could imagine where it was from travellers' descriptions.

"I know where you mean."

He turned to Gavur.

"I accept responsibility for her, if you will."

Gavur leaned on his cart and ran a hand through his hair.

"If she's what you're looking for, then that's good enough for me. But it's as I said; I need trade goods in return. She's not a gift, my friend, neither from me nor anyone else. We have yet to agree a fair exchange for what I have given up during her travels with me."

Finn stepped forward, clearing his throat.

"Bran, let's you and I have a crack about this. Before anything's done that's not so easily undone."

He took Bran's arm and led him away from the group. Gavur watched them go, his eyes thoughtful, and then busied himself with items that the other men wanted from his cart. Bran let himself be taken behind the nearest hut, out of sight of the others.

"You're a good lad, Bran, and I'd not like to see you do something that would divide the men. I'll not have them all set against one another because of some stranger coming in."

"That's why you're our foreman, Finn. I'm content with that, and I'll do nothing to upset it all."

Finn looked at him, steadily, and said nothing for a long time before shaking his head.

"Then why do this? It's too long since you came with us at the half waning moon. You know that most of us don't have women living out here at Ty Caroc. Dolgolvan's the place for that."

## Part 3 – Lindirgel

"Finn: look now, it's not how it was on Innis Mon. And even here, it's not altogether true, is it now? Lewenith lives with Avank. Cowann has Salis to help. Why should this be any different?"

"To be sure. And Cornigil beds at Gwovan's house. But those are not the same at all, and you know it. Gwovan's leg was crushed in that rockslide. Avank is easily old enough to be your father, and has earned respect and an easy life, not least by being foreman before me. And Cowann, though I'll grant that he's a fine stoneworker, would mislay his own fingers if he didn't have somebody alongside him. You know all that."

"Lewenith has been with Avank a long time. Years. Long before Avank stood down so you could take his place. I've heard the tale from Nant. Look, I'm not objecting to that. It's a good thing – good for Avank, and good for Lewenith, so far as any of us can tell. It's how it should be for them. You go along to Dolgolvan every month with the others, and I'm not saying anything against that. But I'll make my own choices about this."

"It's something to do with that Melen, isn't it? Whatever happened between the two of you. You just have to get past all that."

Bran grimaced.

"Go back to the numbers you talked about now. That's nearly one man in four of us that you named."

Finn frowned.

"It's the older men I'm talking about here. You're nothing like their age. Think about what you're doing, Bran. You know you're not in the same place at all. You owe nothing to this woman, and you have no debt with Gavur. Tell me why you do this."

Bran paused, marshalling his thoughts.

"I think she may have a talent I can use. I'm sure of it."

The older man shook his head again, then leaned close in to Bran, his shrewd eyes bright in the afternoon sun.

"It's a talent for making division that she has, that's what it'll be. Of that, I feel sure. I don't understand why you're set on this. Let go of her again, and come back to Dolgolvan to satisfy yourself."

"I'm not interested in her for that, and you know full well that I won't be back there with you at the half waning moon. But tell me straight now; do you forbid it? If you do, I'll maybe challenge your word."

Finn sighed.

"No, lad. You've heard what I have to say about it. If you're set on this, I'll not forbid it; it's just not that important to us all. It is what it is."

"But you don't like it?"

"I can't say that I do. And you've seen how the men look at her after that little speech of hers. What if they turn against you because of her? And listen now; if that happens, I'll not hesitate to put you away from us. Outside Ty Caroc. Are you sure she's worth that?"

He studied Bran again, then sighed slowly and released him. They went back to the cart. Most of the other men had dispersed by now, and Finn followed them, striding away towards his own hut. Gavur beamed when he saw that Bran remained. He glanced this way and that, and seeing that nobody had stayed to dispute the matter, gestured to the woman, who stepped away from him after one last, dismissive glance.

"I release any claim over her. You'll not regret this, Bran, not at all. Take your time, and we can settle the exchange next time I come by. You're an honest man; you'll not forget there's a debt owing."

He turned and left with rather unseemly haste, pulling the cart away down the track that hugged the valley side. Bran half-turned to the woman and gestured towards his hut. Her dark hair formed a contrast in shadow with the bright mix of colour of the nearby beeches.

She went ahead of him, ducking under the low door-lintel. She turned this way and that, in a quick, thorough glance which, he felt, absorbed all there was to know about his habit of living. She gave a long, curious glance at the alcove where he kept his devotional pieces, but touched none of them. Then she turned

## Part 3 – Lindirgel

back and looked very directly at him.

"If you're thinking that what I said to the others applies any the less to you, you're entirely wrong. You with your honeyed words about knowing where my home is. Anybody might say that, and until I'm convinced you mean well, I'll do the same to you. Don't use me badly, if you have any care for your own future."

He shook his head.

"You'll get no demands from me."

"So why take me into your home?"

He picked up the rock that he had begun to fashion earlier. It was the right size – about half the length of his forearm, elbow to wrist – and not far from its final shape, but otherwise it was scarcely begun. It was still dull, rough, and betrayed all too clearly how recently it had lain half-buried in the other rocks.

"You see this? When I'm done with this it'll be polished quite smooth, and have a rare shine on it. You'll near enough see your own face in it. Like this little piece here. But it takes longer than I'd like to prepare – much too long, in fact. That little princess there will take me well past the shortest day, mixed in as she is with other jobs. Maybe longer. Just now she's as unformed as a newly caught baby, hidden inside its mother while its true shape comes upon it." He put the embryonic axe down again. "Now, this'ns right at the start. I've done the prayers and the chants, and given thanks for taking her from the mountain, but I've not even found out what her name is. Look now: you've got skill and you've had training. I don't exactly know what talents you've learned, or what it is you can help me with just yet, but as soon as I saw you, I began thinking that you and I could find a quicker way to turn it out."

"And you want me to work for you on these bits of rock. Just to turn them into axes. Just to cut things down. And what's wrong with the men all around you? Can they not already do this for you?"

He grinned.

"It's not just axes. We make all kinds here, depending what

lies already hidden in the stone. There's a skill there as well, knowing what's inside."

She looked at him, around at some of the other pieces of stone that lay round about, picked a couple of them to study them, placed them down carefully again. When she spoke again, she sounded perplexed.

"So why do you need to go up into the high crags for this? Aren't there rocks enough you can find in the valleys without doing all that?"

"Well, yes and no. If all you want is one rock to pound on another, then by all means you pick up whatever's to hand. But that's not what's done here. We go up where we know the true tuff comes up out of the ground, just here and there like a spring of fresh water, and we know the features of the land all about. That's what our learning is for, so we know the best stone from the ordinary, and how to work it so all of its true qualities come out. You've had training; you know as how the important things aren't always on the surface."

She touched the rock fragments again and nodded, but remained silent.

"But then, you asked about the men here. To be sure, they're good men, most of them, but they won't change from the ways they were taught, that they have always used. But I have a fancy that you and I could work together to change some of that. You with your talent and me with mine. You've learned things that maybe we can use together. When once you've seen one of these little things truly finished, you'll see why we do this. These axes are worth more than jewels, and they're better than any other precious thing. People up and down the land, people who live beside the other seas, west and east and south, they all want these. Not to cut down trees, and not to cut down their enemies. They want them because they are rare things of great beauty. They join the sky and the earth, the earth and what's below the earth, and they take up the qualities of all of them. Some of them will get used for work, to be sure, but others will go as gifts at springs of pure water, or as parting gifts for the dead, or at wed-

## Part 3 – Lindirgel

dings, or as goodwill gifts between one clan and another. You'll see. I'll show you every single step of what I do. We'll start with the naming tomorrow. But look now, it's slow work, do you see? Help me do the work faster, better, and together we can get more of these bits of rock out to where they're wanted."

She turned again and looked at him curiously.

"You sound quite eloquent about it all." She paused, swung her gaze all around the room again, assessing the full places and the empty, the tidy parts and the untidy, and gave a last lingering glance at the special pieces he kept in the alcove. "Swear to me that I'll be safe here in your home, and I'll work on this with you. We'll see where it goes. But our first job will be to change the way you organise your house."

He picked up one of his tools, nicked a finger with the sharp edge so that a drop of blood welled out onto the table.

"I do so swear. And yes, change the house however you like. If you're to be living here, it's right that you add your own special things into the alcove there. And after all you said today out there in front of everyone, I'll invite you to share my house, and my table, and my tools, and my plans, and my food. Even the care of my raven Brannen whenever she drops by, though that's rare enough these days. But I'll not be asking you to share my bed, and in return I'll come and go as I please without asking you first."

A shadow of a smile crossed her face. She took the tool from him, drew blood from her own finger, and let it drip onto the little puddle of his.

"Then let it be so. And besides that..." She stood, took the longest of the feathers from its place in her hair, and laid it in the alcove beside his own trinkets. "Let this be the first thing I put in the corner you've set aside for such things."

He sat down on one of the wooden stumps he had dragged in all those months ago, and gestured for her to do likewise, across from him.

"I'm thinking that you travelled with Gavur by your own choice, and not because he compelled you in any way."

She snorted dismissively.

"I could have left the journey whenever I wanted. Until now I had not felt that the time was right. My elderwoman, back on Mon Mewn, she sent me out to learn what was needful. It was never anything to do with that man's opinion."

"My fortune as well as yours, then."

She looked at him warily but said nothing. He waited for a while, and then continued.

"Look now, I'm not asking you to tell me the secrets of your training. But I don't know the meaning of the marks made on your body."

He gestured to where the tattoos showed on her arms. She ran her hands along the marks and signs, tracing out the pattern of ink here and there. She looked away, abruptly uncertain of herself.

"Well." She hesitated again, then lifted her head, full of pride. "I can't tell you all of it; it wouldn't be right. But in brief, you see, one day, if things go aright, I shall be an elderwoman myself."

He blinked in surprise and leaned back against the rough stone of the wall.

"It's a long training, surely? It makes mine look like a brief thing. How long..."

He paused, unsure how far it was suitable to follow the line of thought. She laughed.

"You are right. Just now I am far too young. The training is only a part; I must become familiar with all the stages of being a woman before I am accepted. Some of those stages I have already come to; others I do not yet know. This journey is part of the learning. Until I am prepared in every way, I make myself useful however seems best."

"Then one day you'll settle with a traveller group? Keep the memories and the journeys and all alive from one generation to the next?"

"I will. But don't ask me where, because that I don't know yet, nor will I for a long time to come."

He nodded, remembering Nant's words: *'they're self-willed by*

## Part 3 – Lindirgel

nature, and won't go where they don't feel it's right for them.'

"Meanwhile, I'm to learn all that I need out on the journey, stopping when I please for as long as I please. And for now, that appears to be with you, here in Nant-y-Laesach. And, it seems, out of all the things that I never would have guessed, to be spending a while helping you to make these axes."

He laughed with her.

"Since you're living here now, you can just call the place er-Nant. The Valley. We should celebrate now with something more than water. And although I have neither mead nor fruit cider, I have some good rose hips here that we could use for tea."

In the first moon cycle after that meeting, they established a routine. Every fine day, at first light before the sun had risen above Bryn Brith, Bran continued to go west from Ty Caroc along to the quarry. He returned in the afternoon with whatever stone roughout he had teased from its home, and then started to show her the many stages of preparation that followed on from there. He had examples, all set out in a row, of every stage – the first blocking, the smoothing, the fine shaping, the polishing. Those working days were growing shorter all the time, and he was beginning to enjoy their conversation in the house.

At first he simply described all that he did, the way he had been taught by Morvin to do it. Later, as her understanding grew, they would make changes together by blending his skills with hers, but that would all come in time. In the meantime, she told him in general terms of how plant saps and fibres might be used to work with wood and cloth; she had no idea yet how they could be used with stone.

Neither had asked the other yet about the trademarks they each bore, though some were openly visible to each other, and indeed to anyone. Bran's own hammerstone-and-antler was one such, being it was the first he had ever had cut into him. There was a similar mark on her lower arm, blurred with time and the constant rub of her sleeves, so that he could not quite make out the shape properly. One day he would enquire, but both trades had their secrets, and neither wanted to be the first to ask what the signs meant.

Bran had taken her to see Lewenith the first morning after she arrived, guessing correctly that they would share a lot in common. The two women said nothing about their training or experience while Bran or Avank were near, but could often be seen together a little way away from the building. There, they were deep in conversation, or else inspecting some sprig of vegetation together.

It was, perhaps, the first time that Bran had seen Lewenith living up to her namesake, and he became gradually used to hearing the sound of her laughter. In consequence, Avank was also happy. He limped over to sit with Bran outside his house often in these afternoons, picking up this stone and that, tracing the outside curves and the inwards grain while the two of them discussed how best to approach the fine work.

Lindirgel rearranged his rows of clay pots, throwing out some of the contents where she deemed them to have lost whatever virtue they once held. Some of the pots could be refilled even this late in the year, but others would have to wait until their proper season.

"You have a decent quantity of self-heal, but you picked it at the wrong time and in the wrong way, so it's lost most of its virtue now. But this meadowsweet is excellent. And this bedstraw likewise," and she picked up another receptacle and moved it between two others, "this is good, and properly collected, but there isn't nearly enough of it for what I'll need. I'm guessing you didn't use it very much?"

And thus the conversation went on. Bran's knowledge of the various plants had only ever been practical – this one would restore an aching limb, or heal a cut, or ease a pain in the guts, while that one was simply a pleasant flavour to drink. What he

## Part 3 – Lindirgel

knew, he had learned by listening to other stoneworkers. Lindirgel was hugely more familiar with the proper use of each in its season. But even at that, she reckoned that Lewenith's training had been much deeper and more comprehensive than her own.

"She was properly trained, you see, while I only need a few bits and pieces. Most of what I learned was piecemeal. I can follow what she says at a distance like, but she knows it through and through, close as touching."

She bartered for another dozen of the small empty pots from Dolgolvan one day, and placed them alongside the others, waiting for the right season to come around before they would be filled with this herb or that. Most would stay unfilled until then, and she recited through a list of all that she wanted to fill them.

Some of the names she mentioned were familiar – though he had never known any reason to gather the plants – but others were new. Hedgenettle, for example, which she insisted was quite different to the common nettle. Or Shepherd's Knap. Both of these would be collected next summer, in their season.

Lindirgel got to know the other two older women soon after – Cornigil and Salis – but it was with Lewenith that she became by far the closest. She spent hardly any time at all with any of the stoneworkers other than Bran, who had been quietly curious as to whether she would start to associate with Gan-Mor.

He did not take her up to the workings, as he was unsure how the other men would react, and he did not want to provoke them. But they walked along the track below it on their way to Lanerc's farm several times, hearing the distant plink of stone striking stone. Once on their way back from Pwil Glas, they sat at the top of the steep descent and looked across at where he worked, day after day. It was the season of rainbows, and as they sat down with the sun at their backs, a particularly fine one had shone out across the valley.

"The other men won't mind me looking?"

He shook his head.

"This whole place, the Ban and the Brig and all the crags besides, that's not secret, not as such. I mean, the particular nooks and crannies where each of us looks for the true tuff are personal, and none of us would interfere with another's workings, but there's no secret in you looking up at the hillside like this. It only means something deeper to those who've had the training. We're not sitting here because you're not allowed over there. It's just that after how they all were when you arrived, it's best for a while we look from a distance."

She shook her head.

"It's no hardship. I can see all I want to from here, and I don't want to actually dig stone out of a hillside. But I am curious about this; have they said anything else about the fact that I'm in your home?"

"Not a word." He laughed, shortly. "Though two nights ago was the first time at the half waning moon – when they all go off to Dolgolvan, as I'm sure you know by now – the first time ever that nobody's dropped by to see if I was going along with them for the night. They always used to. I don't know what they think we're about in the hut. They've become mightily incurious. I mean, I see them for the midday bait, and we talk up on the crags as much as we ever did. About work things. But not so much beyond that. Nant's alright, it's like he scarcely notices any change at all. Well, maybe he hasn't noticed; you know by now what he's like. But the rest?"

He shrugged, and then continued after a pause.

"Would you consider being elderwoman here at Ty Caroc? I reckon we feel the lack of it, and life would be better if we had one living in the village. Although to be fair, I don't know if the lads agree with me."

She frowned and looked at him.

"That's a great many years away yet, and I cannot say I've given it much thought. But unless Finn and the others change their minds about me, it doesn't seem very likely that they'll want me here, does it? I'd not settle like that in a place that didn't want me."

They sat silently for a little while before she spoke again.

"In a few days, it will be the dark of the moon. I shall be away

## Part 3 – Lindirgel

for two or three nights, perhaps four. You mustn't ask where I go, and you must not try to follow."

He glanced across at her, curious, but not quite knowing what to say.

"But you'll be safe?"

"As safe as anybody can be when they're alone in the land." She paused, frowned, and then continued hesitantly. "I can say this much to you. This will happen every moon cycle. The dark of the moon is a time for retreat. Away from the hearth and the home. There's no reason you would have known about this, so I am saying it for you to understand that it's not just a whim, but an observance. One that I cannot tell you much about. But you reminded me with your talk of the half waning moon – my retreats away from Ty Caroc will happen each month, always a few days after that, as the moon comes to its dark."

"I'm not asking where you're going or what you'll be doing there. But I will ask how you know where to go, seeing as how you've not lived here before."

"I asked Lewenith, and took her advice. She knows this land, and she understood exactly what I was looking for. Not that she needs it herself any more: that's all in the past for her. So, if there should be some overpowering need, she knows where I can be found. But you must not ask her just out of curiosity. This is my time."

"You'll take food?"

She laughed.

"Of course. It's a time of retreat, not of fasting. That oat porridge you made yesterday; I simmered half of it until it hardened, and I've cut it up to take as bannocks. And I have some dried fish, a few apples, and some berries; I'll be fine. You can see I have good food supplies, as well as also the makings of a fire and all, and I'm not going to starve. You'll see me again when I'm back. I'll tell you what I can afterwards, and not a word more than I should."

She left in the late afternoon on the third day from then, a carryall on her back with supplies. The day was set fair for her, with clear skies and a crisp air. She set off away down the track towards Dolgolvan, but Bran felt sure that that was not her destination.

He looked around the little hut, which abruptly felt empty. Lindirgel had bundled all her few belongings into neat piles, and had taken back the cormorant feather from its place beside his own special things. She had tied it again in with the other feathers, tucked the whole clutch back into her hair with habitual dexterity, taken one last swift glance around the room, and had gone. The bend in the track had hidden her.

He went to the door and searched the sky, but Brannen was not in sight. Far up The Valley there were birds circling, Perhaps they were ravens, but they were too far away to tell for sure. He sighed and went back inside, pushing the wooden door closed and banking up the fire. At least he would keep himself warm and busy.

The night was quiet, and he worked far too long into it, using fingers to tell the rough from the smooth when even the candle's tallow light was too dim for his eyes, and the room was full of pungency. Eventually he straightened and stretched. He was very stiff, and knew that Morvin would have chided him for working without regard for his own well-being. He had, so very rapidly, become unused to his home being silent.

He woke early the next morning, before the day's light was properly showing through the windows; he had forgotten to pull the loose drapes across them. The little house was still silent, and in the half-light he looked across the little gap, the two handswidths that divided his own bedroll from the place where Lindirgel slept. They had never talked about this separation, but since the very first night they had diligently maintained it. Lindirgel had, of course, taken her own bedroll with her when she walked away earlier in the day, but it would never occur to Bran to encroach on the reserved space.

He arose, got himself ready, and walked along to the quarry. He was there first of the whole crew, even before Roudhok and Prental. Only the natural sounds of The Valley could be heard,

## Part 3 – Lindirgel

the running waters, the wind in the junipers, the birdcalls, and there was not a single sound of human activity. He went on up to his working place, and to his great delight Brannen landed beside him in a flurry of wingbeats.

"I'm right glad to see you, lass. Could have done with talking with you last night after she left the house, talking about all the stonework we did together. She's gone off for a few days, not sure where but no more than a few hours' travel." He laughed and tossed a piece of bannock to the bird. "I know less about where she is now than where you go."

He tapped his hammerstone gently on a nearby rock, and Brannen obligingly made her "pok, pok" sound in response.

"And I'll be after the true tuff again today, none of your rubbish now." He looked west, where the clouds had already started to look threatening. "Though reckon I'll not be here very much of the day, if that lot comes in hard. Maybe it'll go south and miss us here."

He worked, and talked to the stone, and talked with Brannen, and after a while the other workers arrived, and the sound of the stoneworking echoed around the uplands. At some stage Brannen flew away again, leaving Bran to concentrate on the work. He carried on at the quarry for half the day, then when the rain set in, he went back to his little home in Ty Caroc to carry on the later stages of the work.

Each day was much the same, except that Brannen hardly came after that first day. Finally, in the early evening of the fourth day Lindirgel returned again, looking weary but pleased. He set down the antler and rubbing-cloth and set water to boil, saying nothing about the enormous sense of relief that her return had triggered in him. As she shrugged off her carryall and flopped down onto one of the wooden stumps that they used for seats, he reached for the pot of dried mint leaves. She shook her head.

"Have whatever you like for yourself. But for me, would you make it half-and-half from yarrow and dandelion root? I brought back a bagful of beech mast, but that'll need preparation before I can use it."

He found the pot of dandelion root easily enough, and then looked blankly along the extra pots she had added since arriving.

"Next to last at the far end. Beside the willow bark and the raspberry leaf I brought with me, there in those two smaller pots."

He took down the pot in question, sniffed the contents, and then mixed the two ingredients as she had asked. They went outside and sat in the late autumn sunshine at the door of the hut. The wind was light, but chill, and the hot tea was welcome. Lewenith appeared at her own door, nodded to Lindirgel, and went back inside again. He spoke cautiously, not wanting to encroach on her secrets.

"Did it go well for you?"

She beamed.

"It did, thank you. I found the place Lewenith told me about easily enough. I will not tell you where it is, but I can say that it's a little grove of mixed yew and holly trees. Very old, in the mouth of a gully, and it has a most special feel. And it's almost a perfect circle. It even has a little beck running across the centre." She waved vaguely eastward. "On the slopes of Bryn Brith, well away from the track towards Dolgolvan. Nobody would stumble across it unless they knew where to go. It was exactly what I wanted. I'll go back there each month around the dark of the moon for a few days. It's just perfect."

She nodded, decisively, and stopped speaking, and he knew better than to ask any more about the place. So instead, he talked about his own work over those few days, and the occasions when Brannen had soared back in to keep him company. He did not mention how empty the times had seemed, back here at the village after his times at the quarry, nor how he had simply carried on working far too late into the evenings, with far too little light to do a proper job, all through having no better choice.

He also did not mention how the reaction of the other men had bothered him. Even Finn, it seemed to him, hardly ever spoke to him now outside the bait sessions beside Pwil Gesgod, and that omission tugged on Bran more than the others.

## Part 3 – Lindirgel

Nant had indeed dropped by on one of his alone mornings, and walked with him to the workings. They had taken the path beside the dead men's markers, and talked in much the same way as they always had done. But even Nant did not touch on the subject of Lindirgel's presence in the village, and Bran did not know how to understand this.

"How has your time been while I was away?"

Her voice brought him back into the hut from the place of his distraction. She had been unpacking her bag, and the cormorant feather was back in its place in the alcove. He got up, brought over to her the roughouts that he had been working with.

"I got a bit further with each of these. Nothing you haven't seen before, and I just used all my familiar techniques. I thought it best to wait until you were back before experimenting with anything else." She nodded, and seemed pleased. "And up in my little gully on the Ban, I've nearly loosened out what I think is going to be a particularly splendid piece. It's large, and as far as I can tell up to now it's very sound. I've not come across a flaw yet. Nice colours too. It'll be a good one for us to work on together."

"How long until you've fished it out?"

"Maybe tomorrow. I don't want to rush it. Better to take an extra day now, than to spoil what might be an exceptional piece of the true tuff."

"Fair enough. I can wait to see this."

She half got up, then sat down again and sighed.

"I'm weary, Bran. And hungry: my food ran out yesterday, and for all my words before setting off, I ended up fasting for a while anyway. Do you have a spare bannock to hand?"

He found one easily enough and brought it to her, together with an apple and a handful of cob nuts.

"I can go to Lanerc's farm and fetch some cheese if you want. If he has any such that's fit to eat, that is. You know how it is with him. Or tell you what: Gan-Mor went out on the hunt this morning, and maybe has something to spare?"

"Do you know, I have a fancy for rabbit. If we have roots and herbs to go with it?"

He nodded, and started to get up again, but she shook her head.

"No, you stay and start cooking the roots. I need to talk with Lewenith first, and after that I'll go across to Gan-Mor's house and see what I can barter."

Bran came into their hut in the middle afternoon. Two moons had waxed and waned since Lindirgel had arrived. The sun in his own journey had continued to decline, and the days were now very short this close to the winter turning day. Heavy clouds hung over the crags on the north side of The Valley, and obscured the higher parts of the crest of Drum Crog. He had been working in the fringes of the cloud all day, and was damp with mist and droplets. So far, however, there had been neither proper rain nor snow, and he was pleased to have got home comparatively dry. Other things, however, were not so good.

He tossed his hood, with its rabbit fur lining, onto his sleeping roll. One of the ties unravelled onto Lindirgel's roll, separated from his in that narrower end of the room by the two careful handswidths they maintained between them. He shook his head, moved it off her part of the sleeping area, and carefully coiled it up again. He sat, heavily, on one of the wooden stump seats. She frowned at him, taking in his strained expression.

"Well, what's the matter?"

He looked up at her.

"Cegit's gone."

"Gone? Gone where?"

"Told Prental he was going back to that lot at Pwil Gwo. Reckoned he'd had enough of the mountain life and was looking to be out there near the coast for a while."

"Today?"

*Part 3 – Lindirgel*

He nodded.

"Seems that he stopped at the far end of The Valley, just below the main way up to the quarry. Went there with Prental just like usual, talked to him a bit in ways that upset the lad, and then sent him off up to the Ban. But the lad waited down there until Finn arrived – which was a surprisingly sensible thing to do – and then he told Finn right away what had happened, and that Cegit had just left. Heading out west, it seems, following just the same way that he and Prental went in their summer journey."

She sat down opposite him.

"Didn't you tell me as how he'd known about them from before?"

"He had indeed. Though when he told us about the trip last season, he made out it was only casual-like, and nothing lasting. And that it was only one other man he knew, someone about his own age. Whereas now from what he said to Prental, it was a fair few people, men and women both, and different ages. Seems in fact that he spent some time while they were both over there in the summer, talking, making plans and all. All this without Prental knowing anything about it. Mind, it wouldn't be difficult to distract Prental, get him interested in something else I mean, while Cegit got on with whatever he wanted to."

She nodded slowly.

"And what did Finn say about this?"

"He's not yet spoken a word to the rest of us, barring a quick announcement to the rest of us at the midday bait time. He hasn't yet let us all talk it through, nor given his own mind about it. But his face showed a lot for him. He's taken it bad, I feel sure, even if he's said nothing. My guess is that right now he regrets asking Cegit to be one of those who went. Easy to say that, though, after it's turned out like this. I don't think he could have known at the time."

"And Prental? It was just the two of them on that trip, wasn't it? Will he follow on as well, do you think?"

He shook his head.

"No, he's alright. So far as I can tell, anyway. Says he's got no mind to go anywhere just now. And I believe him too; he's not yet finished getting all the marks from Gwovan, and if he left now he'd have to spend time looking for another person to train him up. And maybe repeat some of what he's already done. It's not good if you chop and change around, and you have to persuade someone else that you've truly mastered all that's gone before, and that your reasons for moving on were sound. And besides, he's become close with Tresklenn, more comfortable in himself than I've seen him for a long time, and I can't see him moving off." He paused, and grinned. "Turns out that Tresklenn is quite the trickster himself, knows all kinds of odd moves and sleight of hand that entirely fool the rest of us. Prental likes that; it goes with his own temperament."

She leaned back against the wall.

"It's not just what Finn thinks, you know; it's all of you. What side do you think the others will take on it?"

He thought about it for a while.

"Well, I don't reckon they'll follow him out there. For one thing, not one of the rest of us has ever had any connection with that group. And for another..." He hesitated for a long moment, and then shrugged. "Well, you might as well hear it from me as from another. Cegit had something of a reputation for being lazy amongst us."

He told her what he'd heard from Nant, how Cegit had never passed over to Finn the first finished work he'd done in The Valley, nor anything since.

"I don't know the truth about that original piece – of course I wasn't here back then when he first came – but it's certainly true that I've never seen him give any other pieces, not even once. The rest of us do, a couple of times a year, so Finn has goods to trade with if he needs to, or if there's a thing we all need to get as a group. But Cegit never did."

"And none of you asked why?"

"If Finn never did, then the rest of us wouldn't. It was Finn's shout to make, first and foremost, and all of us others would take his lead on it. He's foreman. So no, nobody took Cegit up about

## Part 3 – Lindirgel

all that, not so far as I've heard. But we all knew."

"Did that make him lazy? It didn't seem to me he did less work than the rest of you. He was up on the fells just as much."

"Perhaps lazy's not the right word, then. It made us think less of him, that he wasn't really bothered about the rest of us. I mean, if he wouldn't give things in to trade that would benefit all of us, then how far was he part of the group anyway? Now, since Finn wouldn't make anything of it, the rest of us didn't either. Except Nant, I suppose, who told me and, for all I know, talked to everyone else in his own time. But as a group we just let the matter drop, or we told ourselves that on the hunt he brought back more than his share. Which he did. Or that he was a good singer – which he was all right. That maybe he made up in other ways. But now he's left, perhaps the lads will forget all that, and all they'll remember about him is that he didn't share his work with us all as he should. So when I say lazy, I suppose what I mean is that he didn't care about the whole lot of us as a group together."

There was a little pause for a while.

"Did you like him?"

Bran frowned.

"I didn't ever know him as much as some of the others. It wasn't to do with like or dislike, but he and I never had much to do with each other."

"Then you won't miss him?"

"I won't, no. But I'm bothered about what it'll do to Finn's mood, and for sure it'll leave us all not feeling quite so secure. Like when it's breezy up on the tops. You're not really worried, but you hang on just that little bit more in case."

"Finn's mood? What do you mean?"

"Well now, he's anxious about the team working together. It's like he feels it's his fault whenever something happens that's difficult." He shrugged. "I suppose, since he's foreman, maybe it is his fault. I don't know about that. At any rate, he feels it like a great lump of stone, poised up above him, hard and unforgiving, and all ready to drop. And I told you before what Nant said, that Finn worries about how few of us there are. How few join us now, whether fully-trained or as apprentices. The way Avank and Gwovan talk, there used to be a lot more youngsters come along each year. So you see, Finn will hate the idea of someone just leaving, even if it doesn't lead to someone else doing the same. But all that aside, the main thing it'll mean for now is that Finn wants us all to gather in Avank's house tonight so we can have it out together, talk about it as a group."

"That's all right. It's easy enough for me to invite Lewenith over here so we can talk. She and I will have a good time while you lot can decide what you're going to do next."

He laughed.

"I'm not sure there is anything to be done. Cegit will be halfway to the sea by now, and I can't see what kind of plan Finn might make to stop him, even if he wanted to. None of us would set off today to try to catch up, not this late on, not with the days as short as they are now. He has a long start on the rest of us."

She thought about it for a while.

"You're right; Finn can't stop him. Not now. And considering the way he up and left, I can't imagine that he would ever want him back. But maybe he'll want to be sure the rest of you won't up and go too."

"There is that."

He busied himself for a while, unpacking the contents of his carryall and arranging them as he saw fit in the working area. Lindirgel picked out some of the pieces, and they decided together which they would tackle first. She had placed a sprig of beech in their combined alcove for special things; the leaves were dry and brown now, but still clinging to the branch. She had also been gathering in some of the fern and bracken as it died down, and wanted to see if the plant fibres could help the smoothing. Neither of them was sure how best to combine her skills and his, and it was early days still.

After a while she stopped and looked at him.

"You know, there's no shame on Finn, or any of you – or all of you together even – no shame at all in Cegit journeying on after

## Part 3 – Lindirgel

a while. He's traveller-bred, after all. He was born to move on, when the time was right."

"I suppose that's true. I think what Finn won't like is him not saying anything beforehand, just being there one night and gone the next morning. Finn doesn't like things happening sudden-like. He certainly won't agree that the time was right."

She made a dismissive noise, but before he could reply, Lewenith called from outside and then came in. She was holding one of her wicker baskets.

"Finn's over there now, wants the lot of yous to get together now and talk about Cegit going. And Avank says would you mind going round the other huts and fetching out all t'others? And you and I, dear," and she was looking now at Lindirgel, "we'll have some time together here while they're having their little chat. I brought a whole heap of sloes – from those blackthorn bushes I told you about t'other side of the beck – and also some juniper berries Roudhok gathered up for me. Reckon we could do something with them this evening."

Lindirgel took the basket, looked inside and sniffed appreciatively. She glanced at Bran, who nodded.

"I'll be going, then."

He scanned around the room vaguely, wondering if he should take anything, but decided soon enough that nothing was necessary. Lewenith was settling herself on one of the seats, and as he slipped past her, he noticed once again the tattoo marks, all blurred and faded on her aged skin. What did each of those mean, he wondered? And did she and Lindirgel share some of the same marks? And if Lindirgel mastered some other facet of all that was necessary in becoming an elderwoman, then could Lewenith make the proper marks on her? It seemed altogether more likely that she would need to find someone else, someone who had mastered her own training to do that. Perhaps she'd have to travel back to Innis Mon Mewn. There was no knowing, and he certainly could not ask, so he went out into the drizzle to collect the other stoneworkers.

Much later he trudged back to the hut. It was fully dark

by now, with clouds covering the quarter moon, and he made the journey more by memory than sight. At least the rain had stopped, though he still splashed through the occasional puddle.

The two women were sitting inside when he got there. Lewenith was laughing at something Lindirgel had said, but he did not catch the words. They both looked up at him as he pulled both the door and the internal drape aside.

"Bran, help my friend get back to her home, would you?"

He took Lewenith's arm, and they set off slowly, carefully, back again through the shadowed night across the village. He tried to keep them away from the wet patches he had found last time, but she didn't seem bothered.

"By the feel of'y, it was a serious discussion with no real outcome."

"That's fair. I expect you two had a much better time than we did."

"I think we did. I'll let Avank pass on anything he deems useful. But I won't hold my breath, and I'll not pressure him to speak if he don't want to."

"There's not a lot for him to tell, really. Finn started with how disappointed he was, and he'd much rather hear someone say as how they wanted to leave directly from them, and beforehand, not find out afterwards from someone else. Everyone agreed. Prental said a lot about how he didn't know anything as to what was happening, kept saying it to make sure we all knew, especially Finn. And we all said yes, that was fine, he wasn't to know. Then we all just went round and round for a long time not saying anything new."

She chuckled.

"That sounds entirely normal. But Finn had to call y'll together like that. Wouldn't be right not to. But I'm sure y'll all have reckoned the time might have been better spent on the stones y've all got."

He nodded, ruefully, then wondered if she could see the gesture in the dark. But her arm tightened on his.

"Finn's alright. Knows what's best to do, though he don't

always do it comfortably. But see now, behind that front of his, he has a deep worry about what'll happen here. He doesn't like what he hasn't planned for. Y'need to remember that when you hear what he says. We're all going into a time when there'll be a lot of changes. That'll sit heavier on Finn than on some others I could mention."

"Nant says the like, every now and again."

"Yes, indeed he does. He's a man who thinks a lot while he's up there among the stones of a day. Now, he's a mite too fond of the mushroom to make me feel altogether easy about him, but even so I've a great deal of time for what he says about things. Finn don't always like it, mind, but that don't mean Nant's wrong."

He looked at her, not sure how or even if to reply. She laughed shortly.

"Now look, Bran, here's my door, and Avank's too. Thanks for your kindness, but I reckon I can get inside from here alright, and you can get yourself back to Lindirgel now."

But she held onto him for a moment longer.

"I'm right glad you put your heels in so she stayed. Good for me she's here, and maybe it's good for the both of you as well."

He hesitated.

"We're learning to work together well, is all. There's no more than that." He frowned at her shadowy figure. "I'm not asking to find out what each of you was taught by whoever apprenticed you. But I've wondered how much the two of you learned the same things?"

He felt her amusement through the physical contact between them.

"You're mightily keen to find out what training others have had." She shook her head as he started to protest. "Nothing wrong with that. More of yous all should be asking, I reckon. But look now, her training's got plenty to go still, while I finished mine long since. No more room for any more marks on this old skin, but hers could have a few more here and there as she moves on. And you could ask her that same question, y'know. If y'had a mind to, that is. Up to you. But for now, I'll just say that some of what I know joins up with her, and same t'other way around. It's a long time since there was someone at Ty Caroc I could talk to about such things. I'm right glad of it."

She paused, and he thought briefly that she had finished. But as he was about to leave, she suddenly added, in a lower voice.

"You should go with her up to one of the meets at Dronow Moar, now. Spring might be alright, but t'summer much better. More useful for you both work-wise, too, for what that's worth. There's always lots of stoneworkers there, and woodsmen, and the like. As well as those who's training the same way like she is. Not that the work's the only reason, mind. But see now, she wouldn't find nearly so many folk there she could talk with about her own trade until at the mid-year. There'll not be nearly so many afore then."

Bran hadn't thought before about the great circle being a place where workers from all different trades might meet.

"Midsummer's when the elderwomen go along there?"

"Well, in truth there's always one or two there, proper ones who've finished it all off, if you see. But in midsummer there'll be more like that she'll be familiar with. Now, I used to go up there every season, me and Avank both. Mind, I cannot make that trip now, nor Avank, more's the pity for us. We had good times there, good times with other people and good times for ourselves. Be nice for us to know that you two were picking that up."

He looked at her in mild surprise. It was, so far as he could recall, the first time she had said anything to him that sounded like advice, other than when she was talking about some of the green plants and fungi that they had seen in The Valley.

"Maybe we will. I'll say what I can. Not that I'm all that familiar myself. I went last winter solstice, as I'm sure you remember. I wish now I'd gone there last summer, but I was too taken up with what was going on here in The Valley just then. But I'll tell her about it. What I know, at least."

"No need, I've told her all what happens at the season meets.

## Part 3 – Lindirgel

It's just for the both of you to decide when to go. Like I say, summer'd have more there that's useful, but better that you choose for yourselves together."

It was the cold pole of the year, and winter stalked around Ty Caroc and The Valley. Most days there was a dusting of frost around the stone houses, deepening into snow along the ridges above. Although the days were growing longer again, both days and nights kept a bitter chill. Bran swaddled himself in warm wraps whenever he went up to the quarry, but through this moon cycle those visits had amounted to hardly one day in four. The mornings stayed so dark, and the evenings closed in so quickly with the misery of the weather, that some days it seemed scarcely worth taking the walk through the trees towards the peaks above them.

He kept away when the cloud level refused to lift above the ridge of Drum Crog, or when the rain drove hard against the buttresses, or when the wind was gusting and fierce, or when the ice filled the crevices so that any grip for hands and feet was treacherous. The memory of his time on Pen-y-hal was still painfully close to him.

There was, however, plenty to do, and he felt fully vindicated in the decisions he had made over the summer and autumn months to accumulate a considerable number of roughouts without actually finishing any of them. So now, with the inclement weather upon them, he was able to progress steadily through part-completed pieces.

He also had time to work with Lindirgel on mixtures of extracts from plants that might speed the smoothing process. They had not yet achieved anything other than minor improvements, but she was optimistic that they would find better success as the passing year brought more fresh green stuff out of the ground.

For he could tell that the year was turning, despite the recent weather. Hazel catkins dangled from branches, and there was a little more bird-noise every morning. Nevertheless it was clear that for all that, full winter had not yet passed. The beech leaves were still brown on their bare branches, and none of the buds were opening to displace them with greenery. The ridge crests were still often fringed with frost or snow, even when the floor of The Valley remained clear.

Lindirgel had set off on her monthly withdrawal as usual, on a rare day when warmer air washed up from the south. He had become used to her absences now, and did not feel the same anxiety or aimlessness as he had on the first occasion.

The second day reverted to northerly winds, and the third brought snow down with it, to form a thick dusting half-way down the ridges, as well as a thick crust of ice all the way across the beck. That night was grim and fearful, with heavy rain that froze as it touched the ground, and gusty winds that pushed their way through every imperfection in the stone walls of the house.

He slept badly and woke often. Sometimes it was the wind-noise that disturbed him, but other times it was the thought of Lindirgel out in all this ferocity that nudged him awake. He had no idea what shelter she had, and no idea whereabouts he might try to find her on all the lumpy mass of Bryn Brith. Lewenith would know where to look, but in all likelihood she would not tell him. He was not, yet, prepared to ask her and face refusal.

The morning was dark, silent, and still bitterly cold. He had made sure there was plenty of wood for the fire, though, and banked it up to keep the house warm. He fiddled at one task and another for most of the morning, picking up one stone after another restlessly, without really working on any of them properly. He heated water for tea and let it cool again without applying it to any of the many leaves he had. He started making a soup, using some rabbit and roots he had in store, but then kept it slowly simmering without eating any of it.

Finally, with freezing rain once again rattling the stone walls

## Part 3 – Lindirgel

around him, when the unseen sun beyond the clouds was well past its zenith and would be not that far above the western ridge, the door opened and Lindirgel came in. She was wet through, and the skin on her face and hands was white beneath her hood and sleeves. She was shivering, her body quivering with great shakes.

She pushed the door closed again to keep out the elements, and stood, dripping, just inside, apparently unable to move further in. He jumped up, put another couple of pieces of wood on the fire, and without stopping to think, went over to her and put his arms round her, not caring that the wetness of her clothes was soaking into him.

She stood there, wordless for a while, her head against his shoulder, the hard tension in her body slowly relaxing as the shivers that racked her body gradually quietened. It took a long time, but eventually she looked up at him and pulled back a little, and something of her normal humour was back in her face.

"I think you can let go of me now. I'll be fine. Truly, I'm all right now, you needn't be worried about me."

He sighed, relieved beyond measure. He brushed his hand across the damp patches which marked his own clothing. Then, suddenly struck by a stray thought, he frowned at her.

"I'd have done the same for any of the lads, you know. Contact with another person's what you want when you're cold. It's just what anybody would have needed then."

She nodded.

"I know. And I know also that I need to change out of this wet stuff, and eat whatever's in that soup you've made."

He glanced at the clay pot and nodded.

"It's about ready. It'll take hardly any time to finish heating through. Then we can sit together, and you can tell me whatever you can."

He pushed the pot back closer to the fire, stirred it, found a bannock each from their supply, listening all the time as she moved about the hut. She was silent for all that time, focused on the immediate tasks, until after a considerable while she spoke.

"You haven't eaten either?"

He shook his head as she sat beside him. He ladled out most of the soup into shallow bowls, put the bannock on top of each. She had changed her clothes, and glancing around he saw the pile of wet things draped over a wooden rack near the door.

"Didn't seem right to. Not until I knew you were back safely."

"You didn't need to do that. I was fine. I can't have you worrying each time I go off at the dark of the moon. It's just as much part of what I do as you going up in the crags. I trust you to take care of yourself up there, and you need to do the same for me each month when I go out there."

"I don't go up when it's like this. I stay here and work on other jobs."

"Oh, Bran, it wasn't bad out there, not until the last little bit. The holly and the yew sheltered me most of the time, and I've made a little bower for when I'm sleeping. It's very comfortable. Well, most of the time. It was only this last day was so bad, and I was on the journey back then anyway. Exposed all out in the open against that storm." She paused, put the soup down for a moment, and touched his arm. "But I am grateful you'd made this. And that you were here when I got back. I did keep wondering what I'd do if you were away up on the Ban or the Brig, and I'd just be getting back to a cold house and nothing to eat. So truly it was a great relief to come through that door and find you here with a nice fire alight, and the smell of good food just waiting for me."

He sighed, and relaxed a little more.

"Like I said, I'd do it for any of the crew."

There was a mischievous light in her eye as she took up the food again.

"Of course you would." There was a little silence, comfortable between them. "And in any case, the winter is passing. By the next dark of the moon, spring will be properly here. I'll not have that same particular challenge, and you'll not have to help me in that particular way. Not until next winter, at least."

He did not have an answer to that, and for a while they sat

## Part 3 – Lindirgel

together in silence, eating the soup. Bran put the bowls to one side and fetched them another bannock each, together with some of Lanerc's cheese.

"Is there anything else you'd like?"

"Well, what I'd really like is fruit. Berries or something. Maybe a little wild pear. Or better yet, a handful of tart wild cherries. But it's altogether the wrong time of the year and we've got none. I won't be getting that until the summer for the berries, and the early autumn for the rest, so properly speaking I shouldn't even talk about it. But in the absence of all those things, you could make me some rose hip tea for second-best, really strong like, so I get the goodness from it."

He fetched the correct clay pot down and started to boil water. She sighed, rearranged the empty bowls, and then settled herself back again on the stool, wrapping a corner of deerskin around herself.

"And now, while we're waiting for that to be ready, you can tell me all what has happened here while I've been gone."

He frowned.

"Well, the main thing is that Tresklenn went and hurt himself. Slipped in a gully, bashed his head and his left arm. He said he couldn't see right, and his words came out all stupid for a while. They were all jumbled up, I mean, no sense to them."

She looked sharply at him, and started to say something, but he held up his hand.

"It's nothing too serious, or so Lewenith says. She made up a poultice for his arm, gave him some sort of herbal mix to drink morning noon and night, and told him to stay lying down for two days. She doesn't seem worried. Well, most of us have followed her lead. Finn's got us all going to see him in turn at his hut, each leaving some food or whatever for him; it was my turn to do that yesterday. And we're cheering him up when he feels particularly stupid for getting himself into trouble like that." He laughed. "But Prental's all worked up about it and has hardly left his side since it happened."

"That's no surprise."

"I suppose not."

"He's not been here long, has he? Didn't he get here just before I did?"

"That's right. Less than a month. And now Finn is all wondering if he did the right thing by letting him join the crew. Whether he's got the head for it, the balance and all. Said once to me, when we were on our own like, as to whether he'd been too quick to take him on, and maybe should have thought about it some more." He looked at her quizzically. "I don't suppose there's anything you can do for him that Lewenith might have missed?"

"Nothing at all. That's neither my gifting nor my training. If it's healing that Tresklenn needs, then she knows far more than I have ever learned."

"Fair enough. I don't think he'll be up at the quarry for a little while yet, but the main thing he kept asking her was whether he'd be fit for the next trip to Dolgolvan. And she would not say one way or the other to that. I reckon she wasn't all that impressed that it was the main thing on his mind."

She nodded, and was silent for a while.

"And how's Brannen?"

He grinned.

"Seen her a couple of times while you were away. Here at Ty Caroc, I mean. Maybe she was out at the quarry, but she'd have soon found out I wasn't up there in all this."

She sipped at her tea with real pleasure, then set it down again. There was a different, determined air about her.

"Now, there's a camp I heard about that I want to travel out to this month. Out west of here, towards the coast down a long valley."

He frowned, considering what he knew in that direction.

"Prental and Cegit went along a valley west of here, with a great deep lake in it. But I don't recall them speaking of any settlement there, not until they got right out to the coast. The way they told it, it was all empty of people. They went west along The Valley, then up past the great high peaks and steep

## Part 3 – Lindirgel

down again. Pretty much due west all the way."

"That'll not be it, then. This is a long valley with just a stream running down it, no lake, just little tarns here and there. And it's a bit more south. You start from The Valley's little sister, not The Valley itself, so it has to be more south than what they did."

"That sounds like the way I started on my second trip towards Mynyth Mam, when the cloud all came down and there was nothing I could see. I told you, didn't I, how I got completely turned around and had to give up. But never mind that. Gwennol has often talked as how you go over some flat uplands, then across another rim of the land and then drop down from there towards the sea coast. Steep at first but levelling out before long, as soon as you get into the trees. I've never been there, but it sounds easy enough to find."

"It was Gwennol told me about this place. It must be the same. The only trick is not to be lured into heading south along a beck there, through thick woodland. You have to keep that on your left and go over that lip of the land you mentioned. Anyway, it seems there's a wise woman there who I should meet and talk with. Well, so she thinks, anyway. Not an elderwoman, not in the strict sense that I mean the word, but close enough that we'll perhaps have something in common to speak of. Maybe."

"How far down that valley is it? From what Nant has told me, it's more than a day's walk to get all the way down to the coast, what with the steep bits and all."

She shook her head.

"Not that far, not nearly so. The camp I'm looking for is past the big peaks, but well before the hills stop, up on the ridge north of the river. Near a couple of small tarns, but before you get up to a much bigger one. She told me the signs to look out for so as to know when to turn right and left. It'll not take a day to get there. I was thinking to travel out one day, stay the next, and come back here on the third. I mean, Gwennol means well, but in all truth she doesn't really know me, nor what an elderwoman is, and for all I know it'll be a wasted journey. But I think I have to make the effort. Getting to know who there is to be known around here is time well spent, and it's all part of the training."

He nodded.

"Of course." He hesitated. "But maybe set out on a day that's warmer than today?"

She laughed.

"You can be sure I'll get myself properly warm before I go off again. I was thinking of next moonphase, no sooner than that. And I'll wait for a proper fine day."

He thought for a while.

"I wonder how many others there are nearby? Other people you might want to see, I mean. I just don't know how you'd find out, except by asking here and there."

"Before I went away this time, Lewenith said again about going to one of the summer festivals at the stone ring north of here. She keeps on about how she used to go with Avank, and how much they liked it there."

"At Dronow Moar, you mean? Yes, she's often said as much to me. I've only been there once before, in the winter, but I had a mind to go in the early summer this year. I was thinking of a meet that's happening more than a month before the big solstice gather, a month and a half before, maybe. And a different lot of people there, so Lewenith says. I'd like it if you came along with me."

"You'd like that, would you?"

He glanced at her, and reddened slightly at the quizzical look she gave him.

"I would. For trading, you know. And meeting people. It'd be useful for us both. Finn went last year, and some of the others go at the spring and autumn meets. It's not the great midsummer festival, it's more for exchange and the like. I've a fair collection of bits and pieces to take there. And yes, I should like you there with me. You know more than enough about all this to stand by me when I'm negotiating. You'd be a real help, for sure. And besides, there'd be folk there who truly are training the same as you. Makes sense to go to where they're all gathering, instead of wandering all about the land trying to find them."

## Part 3 – Lindirgel

She stood and tidied away their bowls, half-turning away from him and rearranging some pottery vessels before replying.

"If it's at all like the festivals at the circles where I come from there'll be dancing and all going on there, long into the evening. Even if it's not one of the great days of midsummer. And oftentimes trading truly isn't the main thing people go there for. You wouldn't know anything about that, I suppose?"

"If you don't want to come, just say as much. I'm going anyway, whatever. But for sure there will be trading, and last year there were healers and herb dealers there. So I heard from Lewenith, anyway. All sorts. I thought you might like the chance to spend some time with those who've got skills just like yours. If you're going over towards the coast for three days to talk to someone who might not be the least use to you, it might be worth the same time to go north to the festival."

He paused, and decided it was better to acknowledge what she had said.

"But I suppose there might be some dancing as the sun goes down."

He was aware that she was studying his face, but he kept looking down, crumbling the last piece of bannock in his fingers.

"Do you know, I think that I will go with you."

He took a long breath, and finally met her eyes.

"It'll be good, I'm sure."

"And if there was some dancing there, I'm not saying that I'd mind. Not necessarily, providing it's with you. I reckon it's been overly long since I last did anything of that sort. But I'm not interested in some stranger who I've never met before and don't know."

Bran scrambled down the steep track from the hut where Drus lived. Ever since Finn had first told him about the man, Bran had made periodic efforts to cultivate the beginnings of a working relationship with him. But it always failed. Drus was rude, arrogant, and consistently unhelpful. In his own eyes he was the best worker in The Valley, and he never missed an opportunity to remind his listeners of it.

He made no secret of the fact that he still did not believe that the training Bran had received on Innis Mon should count for anything, and that if he had his way, he would be apprenticed all over again. The only minor consolation he offered was that in his view, Tresklenn was even worse.

Bran decided – as he did every time he met the man – that he should try no longer to treat him as a possible colleague, and should never again climb up to his isolated home. So far, he had always gone back on that decision after only a few moons, hoping that time would effect a change. He still believed what Finn had told him, that the man was talented, despite all the difficulties of being near him.

This time Lindirgel had gone with him, not so far as Drus's house, but keeping him company up onto the plateau. She had stopped at the last rounded crest before the land dipped in the approach to his house, backed up as it was against a sheer upright wall of rock. Then she had met with him again as he had left, and seeing his mood, kept silent until they had descended most of the way into the valley, and the ground started to level out.

"I suppose he was unhelpful?"

"In the extreme. Not just unhelpful: positively unpleasant. Wouldn't say anything that might be a clue."

He had been trying to learn more about a particular abrasive mud that Drus used to smooth the stone that he found. Bran had heard about it from Avank, who remembered Drus saying some time ago that he had located a secret source of this mud, not in The Valley but somewhere nearby. In Bran's mind, it might serve as the local equivalent of the rocks that Tresklenn had talked about: The Valley's variation on the great grinding place that filled the centre of his old encampment. Drus denied nothing

## Part 3 – Lindirgel

about the mud – indeed, he boasted about it, even showing Bran a small dollop on his finger – but would reveal nothing about where it came from.

"If I hadn't heard about it from Avank, and seen some of the stuff on Drus's finger just now, I would be convinced it was just a tale he made up to sound clever. But although I know now that it's real enough, I'm no further forward with actually finding it."

She put her hand on his arm.

"I found out something. From that lad Spink that Drus keeps around."

Bran frowned.

"Spink's not right in the head, you know. He's strange. He might have said anything. Finn always says he's got a natural talent, but I've never been close enough to him to see it. I can never make out why Drus lets him stay there. Except maybe that he always does exactly what Drus tells him to."

"I know all that. But he did talk about how he and Drus went every full moon to a particular place north of Dolgolvan, two small lakes side by side, and told me how he collected something that he called paste from there. They always go at night, so nobody sees exactly where it is that they go. As far as I could tell, it was close by where a beck flows into the northernmost of those lakes, out from trees into a reedy area."

Bran stopped, overcome with surprise.

"He told you that? And it all made sense as he told it?"

"He did. And yes, it did. Clear as anything. I don't suppose that Drus would be happy at the telling, but there you go. If we're lucky, he'll never get to hear about it."

He turned back east, then glanced briefly up and south to where the sun had long since left behind the uneven humps of Bryn Brith.

"If you don't mind, why don't we go there now, see what there is? It means back across the ridge again, but it'll be worth it if we find it. And I don't want to go too close to Drus again, so we'll head this way a while before going up."

They went along the track a short part of the journey to Dolgolvan before branching left, working their way up and over the ridge, just before the crags where kestrel and raven vied for the high places. Bran looked around for Brannen, but she was nowhere in sight.

They had come a good distance along the plateau, and Drus's hut was far out of sight by the time they reached the crest. Above them on their left rose the cloven rounded summit of Alt Ariannaith, but their focus was downhill. Below, on their right, were the two small oval lakes. They were joined by a little river that, later on, flowed beside Dolgolvan. The second lake lay behind the first, following the low ground as it skirted Bryn Brith.

Ahead of them, the crease of the land which they had been using as a rough track wound between the low trees. The junipers sent twisted trunks and branches low across the ground, and the hawthorns were bright with flowers now, having taken over from the earlier blackthorn. A great many bulbs had pushed through, seeking the laughing face of spring as it glanced across the land. On the other side of the lake a long ridge stretched away to the north further than they could see.

Bran's heart jumped a little as he suddenly recognised the notch in that ridge, the one which he had first seen from the stone circle on that first journey after arriving on the mainland. They sat to share a barley bannock between them, and to drink from a noisy little beck. They were shaded by an ancient holly tree, set on an outcrop that swelled abruptly from the slope of the hillside. A rowan in full glorious flower was a little down the slope from them, and behind them, unnoticed, a steep gully ran up to split the summit. Their way led in the opposite direction. He pointed across the broad valley to the break in the ridge.

"I saw that from the south, when I first came into this land. Our elderwoman did not tell me anything about it, or what lay beyond it, but it called to me. It still does."

She looked at him.

"Have you gone there yet?"

"Not yet. The men in the gang only know it as the way over to Lugh Laesach. A couple of them have been there: most haven't.

*Part 3 – Lindirgel*

One day, I want to take that path."

"I know a little of it; our elderwoman had heard more than yours, perhaps, or maybe she simply wanted to make sure that I'd learned something of it. Let me tell you some of what happens after you go through that gap and find the valley on the other side. After a time you drop down to the southern end, the uphill end, of Lugh Laesach, and you make your way across marshy ground. Then you climb back up onto another ridge. It runs north and south, and you turn north."

She had taken on the sing-song cadence that everyone used when recalling a route. He leaned back against the rock, enjoying the musicality of her voice.

"At the north end of the ridge is a broad stone circle. From there you turn to the east and look at the great backbone ridge of the land, there away on the far side of a broad valley. You have two choices. The first is to go up and over the Summer Road across the spine of the land, steep and short. But that way is bad after the leaves have fallen, and the autumn winds have come in. The second is to go further south, on the Winter Road; this is longer but not so high, and you can pass that way in all except the worst storms or the deepest snowfall."

She stopped, hid her eyes from both him and the distant pass. After a short pause she began again, this time in her normal speech.

"Well, there was a little more than that, wasn't there now? Waymarks to tell you when to turn left or right, stone rings and standing stones, that sort of thing. Paths to follow and paths to leave well alone. The signs to look for to lead you to the Summer or Winter Roads. There's a whole lot of places across that way, single stones and avenues and circles and all. But as to what lay away beyond the tops of the Winter and Summer Roads, she did not know. Or, at least, she did not tell me."

A great longing welled up in him.

"Would you go with me there, one day? When we're all done here?"

She grinned, her eyes still averted.

"I might. If I do, I want to go on the Summer Road, not the Winter one, so we'll have to plan it right. But we have business here first, don't we?"

They looked down again into the valley below them, ignoring for the moment the encircling hills and their possibilities.

Around most of the margins of the two lakes, trees clustered in to lean over the water and nod at their reflections, but here and there the ground was damp and marshy. To north and south, larger stands of reeds stretched a little along the valley floor. Lindirgel pointed downhill to the closer lake.

"That one, he meant, I'm sure. Lin Gwair, he called it."

"That's what Nant calls it, too. And I've heard the lads calling that other one Lin Gwo, which seems right for it."

"And we should go to where that beck flows into the northern end. Look, there are the trees and the wet land Spink talked about, easy as anything to see."

They followed a series of animal tracks slanting diagonally down the ridge, avoiding the boggy ground along the edge by staying amongst the alder trees. Finally they waded the beck at a shallow place and followed the bank back down towards the lake. Dragonflies flitted over the stream, and quick flashes of blue showed where kingfishers hunted. From the woods on the eastern side of the lake a cuckoo was calling.

The beck settled into the lake, and a long spur of damp gravelly clay followed it out on one side into the deeper water. Great flocks of geese and swans swam in noisy rafts further out, and called to each other from the shores of the island. A pair of oystercatchers, black and white with an orange flash of beak, called plaintively each to the other as they skimmed the water. Bran felt a great wave of longing wash over him, an unexpected pang for the sea-coasts and sea-birds of his island home.

He looked down, squatted in the mud, scooped up some of it in his hands to thwart the prickle of tears.

"Do you think this is it? I've never seen it close to, only a little glob that Drus showed me in his hand at a distance."

She leaned over him and inspected it.

## Part 3 – Lindirgel

"What do you want from it?"

"I'll be using it to polish the tuff. Along with the sap and such like you've been getting me from your plants. The two together will bring out the shine once I've shaped the stone into its final form."

"Then it has to be a bit rough, doesn't it? Gritty, like. That looks too smooth to do anything to the stone."

He nodded, pulling out a flake of rock from his bag and rubbing the mud along the surface with his finger. He hesitated.

"I can't tell just with a quick test here. But..." He frowned and shook his head. "But I think you're right; this'll never do enough to make a real difference."

They carried on searching. The spur was made of much the same substance along its whole length, but the lakeshore further away from the beck, just before a large stand of reeds, seemed more promising. He picked some up, rubbed it in his fingers, tasted it, before again trying it on the stone.

"This might be better. Look now, you can see it start to abrade that rough bit there, even with just this little effort. I reckon this might do. Maybe. I just wish I knew exactly where Drus gathers his stuff from."

He stayed kneeling close to the shoreline.

"You don't sound sure at all. Why not get little bits from a few places nearby, test them out to see what works? It's no distance to come back here when you've found the right one, but it would be a shame to miss the place you need and think there's none at all."

They worked their way back several hundred steps from the water's edge, gathering little quantities of the soil as it changed and storing them away in little pouches. Bran marked each with some of his trade marks to remember which was which. The ground was flat, here in the lake's margin, and occasional deposits of pebbles and gravel showed how far up across the valley floor the water had risen or the beck washed down in storms and floods.

The last sample was from where the little bushy trees, hawthorn and blackthorn, hazel and willow, gave way to those of a proper height, oak and beech. Badger sett entrances loomed between the larger roots. Inquisitive robins peered at them from low branches, and little flocks of finches darted away into the bushes. A great mob of jackdaws took off nearby, and circled briefly, noisily, before alighting again among the taller trees like great dark leaves.

"Come on, let's get back so I can try them out on some pieces of true tuff."

She had been kneeling beside the trunk of a great beech. He stopped, held out his hand to help her up. She seemed mildly surprised, but accepted the offer. When she was on her feet again he ran his hand over the smooth bark of the tree.

"You know, I always think of you alongside beech trees."

"And why is that?"

"It's how I first saw you, back last autumn when the beeches near Ty Caroc were beginning to turn. And besides, the oak and the beech..." he gestured to the two largest examples nearby, "they're like the chiefs of the forest, man and woman. The oak's the foreman of them all, you could say, maybe, and the beech is the elderwoman. It's like the other trees all circle around them as the centre."

She laughed.

"I'm not an elderwoman yet. Nor you a foreman."

"Nor is the beech sapling over there fully grown. But one day it will be."

She turned away, still amused at the thought, and they started off on their homeward journey again. Bran was thinking about their day, and putting the thoughts together with others he had been having. They climbed half-way back up the sloping track, turned to take a last look at the twinned lakes, and then pressed on back to Ty Caroc.

Once back at their home, he found an offcut of tuff that was no use for real work, and tried some of the contents of each of the pouches in turn on it. He turned the soil into paste with some spittle and rubbed it on with his fingers, then polished it away

## Part 3 – Lindirgel

again with a spare piece of antler and some rags. The last one, the sample from beside the badger setts, was the best, and they could both see how the stone was starting to pick up a better shine after only a short treatment. He ran a hand through his hair, streaking it accidentally with soil.

"I think this is it. Spink told you truly, which I had never expected. I'd thank him, if I didn't think it would give him trouble with Drus. So now, I can get any amount that we need from there. Or we both can, whatever, now we know where to go."

She took the stone from him, turned it over in her hand.

"I'll try a little of it with some nettle sap tomorrow, see if that helps."

He nodded, and a great smile spread across his face.

"This is exactly what I hoped for when I saw you arrive here with Gavur. Finn and the rest didn't see it, but I knew we'd make something work together."

He hesitated before going on.

"Have you decided about the festival at Dronow Moar yet?"

She considered the question.

"Well, we've missed the spring meet; that must have happened nearly a month ago, while I was away at the dark of the moon. You know I'll be away again in a few days?"

He nodded, familiar now with her habits.

"Well, the moon phase would have been quite wrong for me for that time, anyway, so whether or not you went, we couldn't have gone there together." She wrinkled her brow in thought. "You said that the early summer one was about a month and a half-month before the solstice?"

"That's what Lewenith told me."

"So that would make it almost a full moon cycle from now." She paused a little longer, than nodded slowly. "I think that would be fine. Yes. Yes, we'll go together."

He grinned, feeling a sudden wash of surprise that the decision had been made. She said nothing more about it, while he cleared away the stone from his working area and arranged the pouches of mud in a neat row, with the successful – and so important – one pulled forward out of the line. When everything was tidy once more, she took the cormorant feather from her hair and considered it.

"This won't last many more moons. I shall need a new one before this becomes too scrappy. I shall need to find an obliging bird, or else trade for a new feather."

"They say there are cormorants on Lin Gwo. I've not been there to look, but it would be worth finding out for sure. But if they're there, then they'll be on Lin Gwair as well; it's no distance to fly between the two, and not much further to walk. I'd be happy to help you find an obliging cormorant. We can look next time we go for this mud, unless it's something you have to do alone?"

"Oh no. There's nothing that would forbid us looking together. Or even, if worst came to worst, me getting one from a trader if there were no birds near to hand. The reason for the cormorant is a secret, but not the getting of the feather. Let's go together when I get back from my time away."

"I don't suppose..." He stopped, awkwardly, and then carried on when she turned to look at him. "I don't suppose we could get an oyster-catcher feather as well?"

"No reason why not. Is that bird important to stoneworkers?"

"Not to the others, not so far as I know, anyway. But it's important to me. I remember them from Innis Mon, and when I heard them when we were over at Lin Gwair, the sound quite took me back there. So I thought maybe if I found a feather or two of them, they could go in the alcove there and join your cormorant. Then maybe I wouldn't miss them so much when I hear them one day here."

She shrugged.

"You can put whatever you want there. It's for you to know why you'd have such a thing in the special place."

*Part 3 – Lindirgel*

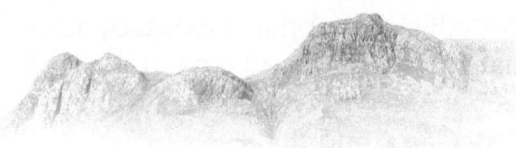

The time had come for them to go up to Dronow Moar. They had stopped briefly at Dolgolvan for food and supplies, and then headed north, taking a well-trodden track east of Lin Gwo. It climbed slowly from the town, so as to keep well above the course of the beck as it threaded the narrow gap between the fells on either side. The human tracks had been covered up by a whole mess of animal prints, where goats and small cattle had been driven.

After a little while the track climbed again, up over a spur jutting from the heights to their right. The land opened to their left, and they looked down on Lin Gwair. Opposite them Alt Ariannaith rose into the sky, blocking out the plateau behind it and the way across to the quarry. They could not see the path they had followed on the day when they had first found the mud there, but the stands of juniper and birch were clear enough. Each time they came to a branching point, or could see across to some distant landmark, Lindirgel stared at it for a short while. Bran supposed that she was fixing the route in her mind.

They carried on past the northern end of the lake, where the track with the animal prints petered out and scattered in different directions. The beck was still vigorous, and was still their guide along their way north, and they were well away from the hills and slopes that fringed the valley. They found an open glade, and sat for food and drink on a ledge on the side of a large rock there. Bran tapped it.

"Not bad stone, this. Not pretty, and it wouldn't take much of a shine, but it's good and solid."

Lindirgel finished a handful of berries.

"Do you think people will ever live up here? Or will they stay in a heap at Dolgolvan?"

He glanced here and there, and then shook his head.

"It's a bit closed in. Better than what we passed by at Lin Gwo, though. Perhaps it'll only ever be a journey halt, unless there's something people one day want to come and see. Like the great rock between Ty Caroc and the true tuff."

"Where you lot all make your marks?"

"Not all of us: just whoever's the foreman. Finn just now, Avank before him, and so on and back. But yes, that place."

"Well, why don't you put your marks just here?"

He frowned.

"I don't have marks of my own that I could put there. I won't unless I ever get chosen for foreman myself."

"You could be foreman here. Even if not over at Ty Caroc." He looked at her, surprised. She had a challenging, mischievous air about her, and she carried on. "I mean, I suppose you do have some tools with you?"

"Always." He leaned back, thought about it, and laughed with her. "Well, why not? It's not as if Finn or the lads will ever come along here to see it."

He scrambled up onto the flat top of the rock, moved here and there across it, swept aside some loose leaves and twigs, and pulled out his tools. She watched him, quiet, curious. He leaned forward, tapped the stone with his fingers, then rubbed at it, tracing the lines of the grain in the rock. Then he squatted back on his heels to think for a while before finally nodding to himself. The air was full of tapping and hammering for a while, much to the annoyance of the local sparrows and finches, who flitted restlessly among the nearby bushes.

Eventually he brushed and blew away the dust and loose rock fragments that littered the surface, and grinned down at her.

"Well, you might as well witness it."

She followed him up to the top. He had fashioned a little group of dimpled holes, with a few larger, deeper ones off to one side. Between the cups, he had worked to enlarge some natural cracks in the rock to form dividing lines, and that part looked like a waterfall with boulders splitting the flow.

"What do you think?"

## Part 3 – Lindirgel

"I like it. So those are your marks?"

"I've never had my own marks like this before, only the working marks we all make below our own patch on the cragside. And sometimes they're not marks cut in, but the same pattern set out in stones placed where the others can see. But if I ever got to make a foreman's marks, I reckon they'd look like this. Now that I've chosen them, I mean."

She touched each of the cup marks, traced the lines with her fingers as though running her hands through water, and finally nodded.

"What do they signify?"

He shook his head.

"It's not like that. Not like the marks we make in our bodies to show learning. They're just marks that seem to fit me. These here..." and he gestured to the pattern of little cups, "they look a bit like the working marks I always make. I just now added the long strokes to make it different. Which if ever I was foreman I'd be wanting to."

"It's like water falling into a deep lake: this, look here. Which, naturally, I like to see because of how I'm called. But I'm curious as to why you fashioned it that way."

He blinked, realised that she was right, and that the pattern he had fashioned made echoes with her given name.

"Oh. I see it now. Secret Lake, daughter of Waterfall. But that wasn't my plan at first. Not so's I knew it, anyway. Really, it wasn't. I hadn't seen it until you said."

She traced the marks again with her fingers.

"Well, they look good enough to me. Do you think they'll last?"

"It's good stonework that I do; of course they'll last. Though as the years go by, the moss will fill them in, and the water will run into them when it rains, and the ice will wear them away somewhat, and maybe some other folk will make marks beside them without knowing what it is they do. I don't suppose anyone will ever know what it is that this collection of signs truly means."

They stood up together, and considered the signs he had made one last time.

"So, Raven son of Badger, foreman of the great rock in the glade beside the beck that flows into Lin Gwair, shall we carry on together towards Dronow Moar now?"

He nodded, and laughed again at the marks he had made, and they scrambled down, leaving the sparrows and finches to their own squabbles as they headed north.

Although the animal drove had now vanished, the steady climb up the valley was clear to follow. Long before they reached the high point of the raise, the trees had thinned out to bushes and low scrub. At the top, they were overshadowed to east and west by higher peaks, which they glimpsed through the trees standing like great rock door pillars. How, Bran wondered idly, could you ever make a lintel to bridge the span between them both?

They took one last look back at Lin Gwair, nestling in the bosom of the hills, and then turned to see the next valley. Bran realised that, without knowing when, they had passed the notch in the hills, somewhere off to their right along the way. Walking amidst the trees, he had missed the turn-off point.

Ahead they could see two more little lakes, blue under the blue sky, but thin and elongated rather than round. A ribbon of land crossed the valley from east to west to divide them. At the far end the land rose into a low ridge, and beyond that several high peaks blocked the land beyond from their sight. Lindirgel pointed to the higher one, which stood up into a point, like the Brig back home. Its pair, beside it to the east, was flat, like the Ban.

"They say that from the top of that tall one you can see Innis Mon Allan on a clear day, and again from that ridge there. But not my own land: that's beyond any person's sight."

She sounded a little plaintive.

"I hadn't heard that." He gazed at the peak with new interest, wondering what it would be like to climb up to the summit. It was nowhere near so fierce and rugged as the heights he scaled daily, though he thought it seemed higher. "But I do know that we stop well short of the peak. Dronow Moar is on a flat open space before it."

She nodded and they stared down the hill, and she spoke abruptly again.

"Do you want to be foreman at Ty Caroc?"

He shrugged.

"Never thought about it much. Finn's there just now, and he's not likely to shift. I suppose like any of us he might miss his footing, or something. Not be able to do the work any more, I mean. But I wouldn't wish that on him. Avank only stood down when he couldn't rely on his legs to carry him up to the quarry every day. Finn will be there a long time yet."

"That's just not right. How can it be right that he stays there as long as he chooses?"

"Well, if any of us didn't like how he does things, we could take issue with him. Leave, or else challenge a decision. It's happened before in other places, and it hardly ever turns out well. Roudhok sometimes talks about a time that happened back where he learned, and he had to choose whether to stay with his friends, or leave in order to go with the man he was learning the trade with. And I suppose you could say that that's what Drus has done, and nobody praises him for it. Or Cegit."

He walked on for a while without speaking. She walked close beside him, keeping the silence with him. The slope descended into the valley more steeply than the climb up from Lin Gwair, and the footing was not nearly so good. Indeed, the whole valley was steeper-sided, more forbidding. It wasn't grim and dark, the way that Cegit and Prental had described the ribbon of lake on the way to Pwil Gwo, but there was still a remote emptiness about it, a kind of wildness expressed in water, rock and tree. It did not feel the kind of place where their kindred might want to live; it was a corridor route, not a home.

Ahead of them, after the valley forked into two limbs, sheer crags rose up on the right, guarding a long series of rounded hilltops. The bird calls were quieter, more distant. Along the valley walls, the gorse and broom flowered like fire on the slopes above the treeline. Finally, as they skirted the northernmost of the lakes, he spoke again.

"I know what you're saying. And maybe I'm not comfortable about it all. But, you see, The Valley is not like any other place in the land. I mean, of course the stone is different, to be sure, better than anywhere else. But the life there is different too, quite different. Once you're there, you don't want to leave. Maybe you'll feel the same when you've been there a whole year. But then again..." he walked on for a while, brooding on the matter. "Then again I do believe there's something in what you say, and you're right when you say that I'm not altogether easy with it all."

"I think it bothers you that the folk at Ty Caroc are not real travellers. Not any longer, anyway. It nags at you."

"What do you mean, not real travellers?"

"Oh, they're not like the barn-and-byre lot at Dolgolvan. I don't mean that. But look at them, Bran. How many of them have moved on in the last, oh, I don't know, ten years? Now, Cegit left, to be sure, but he's moved straight to that other place, Pwil Gwo, and he's just settled down there instead of here. He's not travelling, not even for a season. And what did people say? Everyone thought less of him for doing it, for stepping out. Can you think of anybody else who has left? Ever? How many of them have gone out even for a few months to walk the land before coming back again? None, I'll warrant. Most of them came in like you did, or towards the end of their apprenticing like Tresklenn, or like Prental before him. And they've all stayed just there ever since. You see, they're not travellers, not real ones."

He frowned, but what she said was correct. She looked at him, saw the uncertainty that made his foot slip on a tree root, and put her hand out to steady him.

"Careful now, the land's not so good here as what we're used to."

He nodded and squeezed her arm in thanks.

"It's a lot to think about. But I feel in myself that you're right,

## Part 3 – Lindirgel

and I don't know why I didn't see it until now." He stopped, and faced directly towards her. "I'm right glad you've said all this, but I don't exactly know what to do next."

"Bran, look, let's not talk about it while we're going up to the festival. Leave it for now, and we'll do what we came here to do. The trading and all. And the dancing too, since I'm entirely sure they'll have music like you said. I've a fancy I shall enjoy dancing with you. And we'll pick this talk up another time. Tell me now, which way do we go to Dronow Moar?"

He pointed ahead, describing how they would follow the outflow stream along the right limb where the valley forked, under the loom of the crags and avoiding the marshy ground to the left. He was certain that she knew these things all along, and was just trying to distract him from the pressure of her earlier words. The thought that she was concerned for him filled him with a new sense of warmth.

They crossed the river – which flowed in a busy, gurgling rush but was not difficult – just below a prominent rise that stood proud of the valley wall. Bran thought, looking up at it, that there might be good stone there, but that he was not the man who would quarry it. After all, there was good stone along Drum Crog, and good stone in the valleys down to Lugh Deri, and no doubt good stone pretty much everywhere nearby, and no one person could work it all, however long they worked.

Once on the western bank, they followed a diagonal route ascending steadily into a fold in the ridge. Once there, he felt that they should now be in sight of Dronow Moar, so they scrambled up the side of an outcrop that pushed above the birches and rowans. Across the lower land in front of them, on the other side of a waving sea of branches and leaves, a broad glade had been cleared along a flat bridge of land. A great ring of stones stood there, the entranceway pointing almost directly towards them. People were thronging the circle, which was itself surrounded by a ring of bright awnings. Further out, at the edge of the encircling trees, tents and bustle showed where all the crowd had camped.

Lindirgel drew in a long breath.

"There are so many people."

Bran nodded, himself surprised at the crowds.

"More than I thought there would be. Many more even than last time I was here, back in the midwinter, and I thought there was too many then. They must have travelled from all over everywhere to get here, spent ages on the journeys." He took another look. "Well, I suppose that does mean that there'll be a few people we can talk to and trade with. It's not like we'll be lacking in that. Which is one reason we came here, after all."

The bottom of the slope ahead, on the direct path to the stone circle, was sure to be boggy, so they approached in a great loop to the north. They passed a little tarn where ducks bobbed with the ripples. And then, quite unexpectedly, all of a sudden they passed through a great stand of bluebells, and Lindirgel laughed with delight at the sight and the scent.

But when they finally neared the stone circle, they had left all that behind, and found themselves in the midst of a dense gaggle of camps, where children played, adults cooked, and heaps of belongings stood patiently beside makeshift lean-to shelters.

"There's too many folk for me here. Is there anywhere else we can pitch our camp? We might as well be staying in Dolgolvan as here."

They worked their way around the west side of the camp, finding that the occupation became less intense as they continued to the south. It was as though everyone who had travelled from north, west, and east – which because of the directions of the approaching tracks made up the great majority of the total – had settled at the first part of the temporary settlement, and not many had carried on around the ring.

They were satisfied in the end at a place a little way into the woods that extended like a spur from the long ridge above Lin Tios. Their rain cover nicely spanned the gap between two rowans, and could be weighted down with some handy stones on the windward side. Their two bedrolls went below it, along with the remnants of their belongings left after taking the trade goods

## Part 3 – Lindirgel

out.

A little track opened back towards the stones, so they could see the focus of the meeting-place, without feeling that they were becoming lost in the midst of a town. Bran took a deep breath. A buzz of noisy chatter came from that direction, and further away, the sound of several kinds of music being played all at the same time.

"Time for us to do some work, I think. Let's see if we can forget just how busy this all is, and meet up with just those few we came here for."

They walked the short distance back to the stones. All around the perimeter they could see little groups of people, collected together by the skills they shared – leathersmiths, woodworkers, ropemakers, crafters of clay, and so on. A little further out were stalls with food and drink on offer. Meanwhile, the open hollow of the ring was clear of people, and in the very centre a yew and holly twined around each other, reaching higher together than Bran's shoulder. They walked around the edge, looking at each group in turn. They discovered the stoneworkers in a close-knit gaggle on the side facing towards the tall peak that they had seen earlier in the day.

Bran took a step towards them, then stopped. He looked back at Lindirgel, who shook her head and made to move on again.

"You go with them. I need to find the people here of my own kind. I think they'll be back a little way from the ring, probably on the north-west side over there, on a line between those two ridges. But wherever they are, I'll find them. And we'll meet up with each other again later, I'm sure. Even though there's so many people, it's not like the place is so huge that we'll get truly lost."

They separated, and Bran went over to the group of stoneworkers – a larger group, he realised, than the entire team he worked with in The Valley – and introduced himself. There were voices and accents of all kinds there. Some people sounded like Don or Tresklenn, some like Nant, others came from the great island out to the west, and there were others still whose voices echoed Lindirgel's own intonations. Only one person came from the deep south, like Prental, having trained in the flint-and-chalk lands there.

It was an easy, comfortable group, with men and women sharing what they'd learned recently, and willing to listen to the others around them. He realised before long that there would be no trading here; they had met to exchange knowledge and ideas, not goods. They soon found out that he worked in The Valley, and questioned him eagerly on what it was like to work every day up at the heights. In turn, he learned about quarrying in other places, chiefly the northern parts of the land.

He stayed for a while, long enough to realise that while he was happy to meet people who shared his own set of skills, he also needed to spend time looking for the tools he needed. And moreover, he spoke with similar-minded people all day up at the quarry, and he wanted something different out of this journey. Lindirgel's earlier words had stirred up a restlessness in him which, he was starting to think, was an integral part of being a traveller. He wanted to look around the whole ring of stones, and meet with those whose skills he did not know.

He found first a trader who had exactly what he was looking for: an antler tine to replace his current one, which had begun to split apart. He walked away with two tines instead of one, being a matched pair, or so the trader told him, from a stag in a remote valley on the eastern side of Lugh Laesach. He had a nagging doubt about the literal truth of the source of the antlers – they didn't look as symmetrical as he might have expected – but in any event the pieces were good enough for his needs. His carryall was a little lighter, but he had passed on only trinkets, of the kind which once he would have given away at Dolgolvan. He was content with the trade.

## Part 3 – Lindirgel

He walked back towards the great circle, and wandered up to the group of skilled workers nearest to him. They worked with wood, he found, in so many different ways – some carved or whittled it, some turned and shaped it with heat or water, others built boxes or houses or boats with it.

They fell silent and regarded him oddly as he approached, as though concerned that he wanted to listen in on their secrets. They knew at first glance, of course, that his skill was not the same as theirs. But the mood relaxed as he talked about how the stoneworkers sometimes had need of wood-craft for all kinds of purposes, and how they lacked the skill to do the work properly. They had only the most basic of skills for making a haft for an axe, and when they set up a simple prop to bear weight, it was surely much thicker and heavier than it needed to be to do the job in hand. They nodded then, and brought him into their own circle, quizzing him in ways that he couldn't really answer about the kinds of things he needed.

Like his own fellow workers, they came from all over the land, mostly much too far away to be interested in a collaboration. But there was one who lived at the southern end of Lugh Deri, Lefant by name, and they made a half-agreement to meet up later in the year. Bran must have passed quite near to his home on that first few days' journeying to Ty Caroc, all without realising it. Lefant was, it seemed, the most northerly member of a loose group of like-skilled people, spread out in a broad scatter around the shores of the great bay there. He was short and stocky, with mousy hair. He would fit in without attracting notice at Dolgolvan or any other barn-and-byre settlement, but he said that his family had always been travellers, as far back as any could remember.

Bran had no clear idea in his mind just then exactly what he wanted from the exchange, but it seemed important to be making these connections. The diversity of people at Dronow Moar, and the sheer numbers who had travelled to be here, was daunting. It had made him realise just how isolated life could become in The Valley, tucked away from the broad sweep of events occurring on a wider scale. He thought back to Lewenith's eagerness that he come here, and all that she and Avank must have gained from their times at the circle. It wasn't just the trading or the journeying – it was the meeting between those of different skills and habits which was exhilarating.

After a while he wandered away again, finding a stall where he could swap another trinket for some drink and a promise of food later. Then he settled himself to listen to a little group playing music for a time on horns and a bodhran. It felt good to be here, for a while at least, but he also realised that he missed Lindirgel being beside him.

As the sun touched the ridge north and west from the circle, and the half waning moon lifted over the eastern ridge, Lindirgel found him again. He watched her walking towards him, filled all of a sudden with a great lightness of spirit. The glow of warmth and affection he had felt earlier in the day washed through him again. She seemed happy herself, and she touched his hand lightly as they met.

"I've just spent time with another woman, going about the land as part of her apprenticeship just like me. And she's training much like I am. Averick, they call her. But she's a few years ahead of me, and she passed on all kinds of things about the trackways round here. And I gifted her back with knowledge she might one day need of Innis Mon Mewn, so we're both happy. And what have you been up to?"

They sat together, on a stump of wood just outside the main circle, and shared some berries and a flatbread filled with venison while they spoke. The musicians had stopped, and there was only the noise of the crowd of people nearby. They told each other of their time apart and their meetings. He showed her the new antler tines he had bartered for, talked about the stoneworkers and wood-crafters, and felt himself relaxing into the simplicity of their shared time together.

"When do you think you'll actually meet up with this woodsman?"

"I'm not sure. I don't exactly know what we might do to-

## Part 3 – Lindirgel

gether, but it seems to me that there has to be some advantage in sharing skills, rather than staying separate."

"That may well be true. And I hope you do meet him down near Lugh Deri. It must be less than a day's walk to get there." She paused, and shook her head. "But as for this place here, there's altogether too many people pressed all close in for my liking, you know. There surely must be as many as at Dolgolvan."

He looked around at the busy confusion all around. People were milling in groups around the stones and the food fires. It was altogether strange to him as well.

In the centre of the stones two men were wrestling, gripped tightly onto each other as they each tried to throw the other. There had been a whole long series of individual bouts, and Bran guessed that the contest was nearing its end. There was only a handful of competitors still standing in a little group to one side, surrounded by a much larger group cheering them on. One of the stoneworkers he had met earlier seemed about to defeat a younger man. Bran thought he recognised some of the trademarks on his skin as showing his membership of the leathersmiths. He was small and wiry, and the stoneworker could not quite achieve success, despite strenuous efforts.

"I can't tell. But maybe not. Hugely more than Ty Caroc, to be sure. Why, just taking the stoneworkers on their own, there's more gathered here than in the whole of Finn's crew. But I'm sure there's not nearly as many people here as are living at Dolgolvan. That just keeps getting bigger and bigger. I don't know when it will stop." He shook his head, remembering. "Nant once told me that he thinks that the barn-and-byre lot will just keep increasing, and us travellers will dwindle away. I don't like the idea of that, but when you see Dolgolvan, you can't help wondering. He counts the houses there, you know, each year, and given half a chance he'll tell you how much he thinks it's enlarged these last few years. I expect he's right about that, for he's good with those sorts of ideas. I can't quite imagine the town just growing on and on, but if he's right, that's exactly what's happening. But whatever the truth of that, I don't believe there's as many people as that here at Dronow Moar. Even if it does look like it to you and I."

She frowned, considering.

"Perhaps. It's seeing them all in one place with no houses keeping them hidden from each other. But also, what I mean is it's not just the numbers. It's the life. And I think we travellers'll end up becoming just like barn-and-byre. There'll come a time when you can't tell the difference. Living in one place all the time, I mean, pushing away whatever doesn't agree with what we first thought, never stopping to go out and walk the land for a season and then coming back. The rhythm of it." She paused slightly and glanced at him. "That's more or less what I was talking about on the journey here."

A cheer went up nearby, and they saw that the wiry man had won, probably by cunning rather than sheer strength. But cunning was all part of the challenge, and it might easily prevail in such a match. The two contestants helped each other out of the ring and two others went in. Further away, a group of people were racing dogs up and down the lower slopes of the fell just to the north, and the sound of the baying hounds carried over the gulf of air between them.

"We have the circles, and the great monuments."

"Just now we do. But maybe they'll start to copy us, or maybe they'll make their own things to build in their own fashion. They already make places out of wooden stakes, you know, and some of them are a fair size. And they make huge great chambers and mounds for their own dead. With stones, and soil banked up, and all."

He pulled a face.

"That's only so they can say that some piece of land is theirs, telling everyone as how some ancestor lived there. As if anyone could say that the land belongs to them."

"Well, that aside, it's not what we shape or build that makes us; it's how we live, and how it's not like them. And how we see to our dead. They build these great heaps of earth and stone,

## Part 3 – Lindirgel

while we give the body back to the land from which it sprang, and all the other life that's there upon it. But what if we begin to live their way? What will there be to tell us apart?"

She shrugged eloquently. He sat for a while, his thoughts sombre, reflecting again on what she had said in the early afternoon as they walked here. He got some more berries and they shared them as the wrestling drew to its eventual close, and the younger children ran off into the nearby trees.

Then the sun began to dip behind the western hills, leaving the sky aflame with evening colour. As the shadow of the land crossed the ring of stones, a horn sounded off to one side, followed by a roll of drum beats, heavy sticks pounding on a hollow log, with lighter taps resounding on a tambour alongside them. She laughed.

"There's some music after all. For us all, I mean, not just a little group. Would you believe it? And look there, there's even people starting to dance."

He grinned at her.

"So would you like to dance with me tonight, Lindirgel merch-Raeadra of the settlement by the grove and stone circle on Innis Mon Mewn?"

"I think I would, Bran map-Broch of Carn Pennau of Innis Mon Allan. But for now, I think we're both of Ty Caroc in Nant-y-Laesach, and I have to say I'm content to be there with you for a time."

He took her hand, and they led each other into the circle. There were more drummers now, some joining the original one by pounding the main beat on the log, and others keeping a faster rhythm on lighter frames.

Drum-making, he thought idly, must be another trade with its own secrets. You would have to know what size of log to use, what kind of wood, how to fashion a striker and then wield it to best effect. Someone else was blowing a ram's horn, and another player had a set of reed pipes driven by a skin bag under her arm. He had no idea how to make any of the instruments, and reflected again on how separate all these skills were. But he pushed the thought aside as the music became fast, loud, exciting.

Bonfires leapt up in flame around the edges of the circle as the fire in the sky started to darken. The circle was now full of people between the stones, perhaps half of the people who were at the meet, people dancing in couples and groups. Bran had lost any interest in the numbers, for his whole attention was fixed on Lindirgel as they touched and separated, joined hands and released each other, turned away and then came together.

The music eventually paused, and the crowd split in a buzz of excitement to drink. As well as water from the nearby beck, there were skins of a potent cider brew made from crab apples and some berries. Lindirgel sniffed at the clay bowl someone handed to her, pulled a face, and declined it.

"That's not for me tonight, I'm thinking. I want to remember it all in the morning."

The music started again, slower this time, and she pulled him back into the ring. Her eyes were bright in the firelight, and this time around they held onto each other's hands and did not let go.

The first rush of the bonfires' flames had gone down when they next paused, and the larger logs glowed with a slower, fiercer heat. A man stood at the entranceway to the stone ring, facing back across the circle to where the sun had set. A singer and teller of tales, Bran mused: another separate skill all on its own, about which he knew almost nothing.

The dancing had stopped, and there was an air of expectancy as the people gathered closer. The pipes and the lighter drums had stopped, and there was only the principal drummer and the ram's horn still playing, sounding out the wayfaring beat for them all, the rhythmic act of walking across the land.

The man sang a lay of the traveller's life in his deep voice, forever moving on to the next hills and valleys, filled with all the wealth and poverty of the long walk of life. And as sign and symbol of that, he led them all in procession around and between the stones in the circle. They all came out of the entrance

## Part 3 – Lindirgel

passageway from the circle, born from the womb of life, weaving to and fro past every stone until all had finished, and in the end they were back at their starting point. But this time when they emerged from the gap between the stones, it meant death, and exposure to the wild things of the world.

They joined together in the repeated chorus between verses, men, women and children all walking in the circle, all travelling on the journey together. The land, and the movement they shared, was everybody's and nobody's.

Lindirgel leaned back against Bran after they had finished the circle, as they stood with the others and listened and sang, and he put his arms around her waist, feeling the rhythm of her breath as she leaned against him.

Then the music of pipes and horns began again, and all the drums were once more beating with the pulse of their blood. He held her close, holding her back from going with the rest into the circle. She turned to face him and meet his gaze– she was almost the same height as him, and the deep brown of her eyes was on a level with his own. He moved a little towards her, hesitantly, but she leaned in to him and they kissed.

The kiss carried on for a while, and the music, the dancing, and the bustle of people went unheeded around them. Finally they paused, their faces still very close.

"We could dance again, if you like."

She took a long breath, and gripped his hands tightly.

"I'm thinking we could go back to our own little camp. Away from here, from all these others. Then we could have ourselves a different kind of dance together."

He hesitated again, wanting to be certain.

"You're sure?"

She nodded.

"I am. Completely."

They walked away from the stones, the bonfires, the music and the crowds of people, walked into the moonlit area around, and they found their camp among the dancing shadows of the leaves of that first ring of trees to the south. She was nearly a shadow herself to him, dark eyes, dark hair and dark clothing, until the clothing slipped away. But they were still only shape and curve and touch to each other in the warm darkness, and that was enough for tonight. They lay together and coupled, with their heartbeats stronger than the pulse of the drums, and their breaths louder than the high melody of the pipe and horns nearby.

After a while they were done, and they held each other tightly, with the woollen wrap around them as covering. The sounds of the nearby night creatures had become louder than the ebbing noise from the circle. Her mouth was very close to his ear as she spoke.

"Are you planning on staying here tomorrow?"

"I'm not sure. I've met who I wanted, done what I needed to. What about you? Do you want to stay? To see that apprentice elderwoman again? Averick, you called her."

"I don't, no. What I want is to be away from here. Like I said before, the crowd's too much for me. Let's leave with the first light."

He leaned back a little so he could see her shadowed face, and nodded.

"For sure then, let's be away."

"But can we not go straight back to Ty Caroc? They won't miss us for a day or two."

He thought about it, then hugged her into his body.

"I've heard of a place we might like: a little tarn up on the ridge south of here. Nobody goes there from one season to the next. It'll be the opposite of Dronow Moar and all of its busy crowds. Nobody except us."

"Good. Take me there when the sun rises tomorrow."

"Truly?"

"If it wasn't so dark now, I'd want us to leave tonight. But first light will do for me."

## Part 3 – Lindirgel

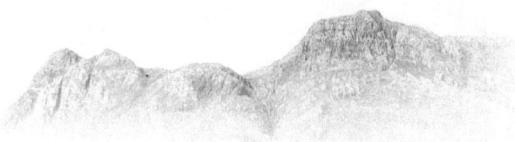

They did indeed leave as the sky started to grow light, well before the sun had climbed over the ridge, and well before anybody else was stirring. Instead of dropping back down and east into yesterday's valley route, they followed the ridge more nearly south, following a crest of crags standing high above Lin Tios. Both shores of the lake were thick with trees cladding the slopes, but their own path was above them all, across open country.

Lin Tios finished in the south with a wide swathe of boggy ground. They kept high, and branched away up a long valley, splashing across the frequent becks that ran down from the higher ground to their left. The ridges either side of them were wild and empty, with rolling upland that looked quite different from the bold crags and screes that Bran knew best, but below them the floor of the valley they were following was thick with hazel and alder.

The valley narrowed and came to an end, and a large tarn rippled in the light breeze, its clear waters mirroring the bright blue of the sky. A rough wooden building stood close to one shore. It showed signs of care and occasional use, but just now it was deserted. It might be a place to stay while animals were pasturing, or it might be a place where travellers came to fish the plentiful waters.

"Is this the tarn you meant?"

"No, but this is a sign that we've been going the right way. We circle around the western side. Starting by that single holly bush." He gestured to the right. "And then we go over that ridge, just along there where the crest dips down a bit. Not far now."

They skirted the marshy ground bordering the water, and made their way through another stand of low trees, climbing slowly across a wet and messy stretch of land until a last scramble over a ridge. On the other side of the lip, they passed a single standing stone.

"Who do you think set this up?"

He shook his head.

"Nobody I ever heard of. There's no markings on it, cups or spirals or the like. I can't even tell if it was put here by people like us, or whether the land simply threw it here in its tumult one day."

She looked around.

"It's here at the edge between one bowl and the next. And those junipers might have been set there on purpose. I think it was put here with thought and devotion. But I suppose we'll never know."

They stood silent beside it for a short while, but the rock continued to hide its secrets from them. They both touched the rocky surface as they passed. Lindirgel, he noticed, was still acutely observant of the signs and marks of their route.

Ahead of them, the land opened into an oval bowl, drier than the slope they had just crossed, with rocky outcrops walling it in on three sides. It had been a short day's journey, and the sun was still high. A small tarn nestled in its base, rimmed by a thin belt of alders and willows. Ducks swam among the white lilies on the far side from them, the usual local mix of mallard and merganser.

"Here you are; this is the place."

She nodded at it with approval, then pointed a little to their left.

"And we'll stop there, I think. Give me the net now, and I'll fetch us one of those ducks while you make up the camp."

He took her pack and set off with them both, while she stalked a cautious route among the little trees and undergrowth to the right. He set the camp, gazing round at the delights of the secret bowl they were in. Celandine and violets were everywhere, and the first of the harebells were blooming. Heather grew along the ridges to either side, budding but not yet in flower. Butterflies were everywhere.

He realised abruptly that while he had been lost in the sur-

## Part 3 – Lindirgel

roundings, he had set the bedrolls separated by the two handwidths they had always kept back at Ty Caroc. A complaint of disturbed ducks sounded from the other side of the tarn. He grinned, reconsidered, and pushed the mats together. He left their leather rain-cover rolled away, off to one side. The evening was fine, calm, and there was little likelihood of any change overnight. He banked up the little fire, and soaked some of the dried pea mash while waiting.

Shortly after, Lindirgel came back. He walked over to meet her by the water's edge. She was carrying the net, folded again in one hand, and a limp duck dangled from the other. He was pleased to see that it was one of the mallards.

"I always reckon they taste better than the others."

"Maybe so. I've heard others say the same. It doesn't make much difference to me, but I've noticed you pick these when you can. Anyway, there were more of the mallards over there, so one less won't matter so much."

They scooped out wet soil from the tarn's edge and slathered it in a thick layer all around the duck. Then they put the whole package in the centre of the fire and banked up more wood on all sides.

Lindergel dried her hands while considering where and how he had set up the camp. She laughed as she saw the bedrolls.

"I can move them apart again if you want?"

"As it happens, I don't want that. Nor when we're back at Ty Caroc, neither. But listen, Bran." She took his hands and looked very directly into his face. "We'll have the bedrolls together from now on, and keep each other warm whenever it gets cold. I remember it getting very cold last winter at Ty Caroc, and that won't change."

"To be sure."

"Fine. Then we'll share each other's warmth every night. But we'll couple when I say, and not when I don't. I'm not barn-and-byre, to push out a dozen babs and be worn out before my time. And then lose half of them to sickness or the blight. I'm quite as serious about this as I was back on that first day in the village."

He nodded, keeping her gaze.

"I'll swear on it again if that's what you want?"

"No: you've kept your word so far, and I'm sure you'll do the same from now on. But you have to hear this from me now."

She waited until he nodded again.

"Now, that duck's going to be a while getting ready for us, so I'm going to bathe in the tarn. There was altogether too much woodsmoke at Dronow Moar, and anyway I need to clean myself. It wouldn't do you any harm to do the same."

She waited while he checked the fire again, and made sure that the logs were not going to roll anywhere.

"Does this tarn have a name?"

"If it does, I never heard tell of it."

"Then I name it Pwil Hoyat."

He laughed.

"Duck Tarn?"

"And why not? What would you call it then? Lovers' Water? Pool of Delight?"

"Pwil Hoyat will do nicely."

They bathed, in leisurely manner, in water that only seemed chilly when they first set foot in it. Lindirgel set the little bunch of cormorant feathers carefully to one side. Then she unbound her hair and washed it, and Bran enjoyed watching it fall and splash, dark against her body.

Then they took each other back to the bedrolls at the camp and coupled again. Afterwards, as they lay side by side, Bran traced with a finger some of the tattoo marks of her training, where they had previously been hidden by clothing.

"Are these secret? Or can you tell me?"

She shrugged.

"Some and some. Much like yours, I suppose."

He nodded, and pointed to what was obviously an old mark, without a doubt her first, visible on her lower right arm. It depicted a circular path looping around a simple peaked mountain. He showed her his own first mark, the hammerstone-and-antler made when he began his apprenticeship.

## Part 3 – Lindirgel

"This was made by Morvin when I started with him, to show that I had begun my apprenticeship with him."

"The same for me, by Alarch who taught me." She laughed, and traced her finger around the marked-out path. "I was so young at the time, and I felt so proud of myself, when I really hadn't done anything yet."

"What others can you tell me?"

She rolled half-over to show a mark on her left hip, looking for all the world like a drop of inked blood.

"This was to mark when I had my first monthly flow. The same place on the other hip is empty just yet, and will be filled when I deliver my first living child. The place here on the left below this one: that is for when I have gone a whole year with no more flow. To be an elderwoman I need all three. Until then I am still only an apprentice, no matter how many routes I learn or skills I master."

"What if you have no child?"

"No child, no elderwoman. There was a woman out on Mon Mewn who could never get the sign on her right hip. A child never caught in her, though they say it wasn't for want of trying." She chuckled. "But in all seriousness, it was a very deep anguish for her. But my own teacher said that the rules were quite strict, and that she would never serve as elderwoman, regardless of what she learned or did with her life."

They talked of each other's marks, finding the signs that could be spoken of, and the ones that were secrets. Before then, Bran had only had a vague idea of the training that other people went through, and it was as though whole new parts of the world were opening up.

Eventually their talk lapsed. Bran poked at the fire to hasten it a little, waiting with little patience for its heat to bake the duck in its clay wrapping. Hot sparks crackled and sizzled in response. Quietly, in the distance, he could hear where the tarn's outflow chuckled between stones on its way down into the valley below. Lindirgel went back down again to the tarn to fill the two waterskins.

"Which way do we take when we go?"
He pointed.
"Along there, to where the beck goes down through the woodland. Then we have a choice; follow it all the way down the slope to the valley floor, then trail along the whole length of Strath Gors to the pass which comes down beyond the quarry. Then follow our own valley eastward to get home to Ty Caroc. Or else stay up along the ridge here, and come across the ridge of high ground between Alt Ariannaith and our own peaks, this side of where Drus has his hut. Then we come down at the last, onto the track a little way towards Dolgolvan from our house. Either way, we'll be home before nightfall."
She sighed.
"And we have to go there tomorrow?"
He prodded the fire again, watching her curiously.
"You're not in a hurry to get back there."
She looked away, up and right at the great crags standing up to their west, hard-edged against the afternoon sky.
"There are worse places to spend a night, to be sure, and no, I'm not in a hurry. I know it's your home – well, our home for the time being – but if the journey back there took another day, I wouldn't mind. Indeed, I could stay just here and be happy while the seasons turn."
"And where would you be living?"
She gazed around.
"There are plenty of rocks just here. Couldn't you use them for something?"
"I certainly couldn't make an axe out of these." He reached out with a foot, nudged a rock about the size of his head towards her. "Some of it's not bad walling stone, but you'd not be making anything of great beauty from it. There's no true tuff here."
"But you could make us a house here? There's enough of what you need?"
There was a look of challenge in her eyes, and he grinned in response.
"Well now, I learned a bit more while I was going through my

## Part 3 – Lindirgel

apprenticeship than just how to make a decent axe. Let's look around here. There's no wood of any size close by, but plenty of stone, if you don't mind a house like the ones at Ty Caroc. And I reckon I'd be better at fashioning a stone house than a wooden one. We could get what wood we need from back down by that first tarn, or the stand of trees we passed through on the way over here. How big do you want it?"

"About the same as our house back in The Valley. Built in a circle, the same way. I've come to like that shape, rather than the oblongs we used back on Mon Mewn. Then there has to be a door, and a hearthplace inside."

"All right. I'd be looking for a dozen or so big squared-off blocks to run up the sides of the door, criss-cross overlapping each other." He gestured with his hands. "To be quoins, you know. I can't see any handy, so we'll have to cast about for them. Maybe at the base of those crags across the tarn. And then a big lintel to go across the top. That's a big job just in itself, moving it here and lifting it. I'll show you how we raise it with ropes, one side after the other, resting on slabs all the way. Then after that, we need a whole heap of salmons."

He looked at her, assessed the quizzical look she wore. He reached out to pick up a stone from nearby, where it was half-buried in the soil.

"Like this one here. Two flat sides, about as long as my forearm, and easy enough for just me to lug around on my own. I'll be doing that, and you'll be getting together plenty of little bits to plug the gaps, stone flakes and brushwood mostly, with mud from the tarn. As well as the salmons, we need a fair bit of just general walling stone."

"You'll set them in rows?"

He shook his head.

"Not exactly. They have to be regular-like, but not uniform. Certainly not in lines. It's not just that they look bad; they don't carry weight properly, and the whole thing'll sag before long at all. No: I'll arrange them so there's a careful variation in size and shape and colour. When I'm done it'll look natural, like it's a proper piece of the land here." He laughed, remembering Ty Caroc. "Prental, you know, he always does his walls too even, all the blocks the same. He gets stuck in matching in a kind of simple way and not seeing it like it was a living thing. I don't know how many times we've all told him. Anyway, forget him. Mine'll be better than that. After the walls, of course we'll need a roof. Like I say, there's no big trees up here for timber, so we'll use little ones and prepare some skins to stretch between."

He stood up, pointed off to one side.

"I'd put it on that flat bit over there. It looks good enough as a hard stand. Close enough to the tarn to get water, and catch the occasional duck, but not so close I'd be worried about the winter storms."

"Would it stay dry inside?"

"No reason why not. It's away from any flow of water, to be sure, And if you're thinking about rain, there's a trick we have of putting a layer of flat slates at an angle, a little way down from the eaves. It angles the water away from the walls, makes it flow out rather than in. We'll keep dry enough. You'll see."

She nodded with satisfaction.

"So that's done then. And I can get leaves from that open stretch of land we just crossed, before coming up this last little slope. Nuts and berries in season. There's plenty of hazels over there. Maybe I'd keep a goat as well."

She stopped. He was laughing.

"You're wanting to keep animals? You'll be growing crops next. And wanting me to build you a barn alongside the house."

She grinned in response.

"It's just one animal, not a whole heap of them. Not a cow in sight. I should have got a little goat at the meet at Dronow Moar while we were there. But we weren't thinking about livestock just then. No matter: there'll be another day for that. We'll take a trip every month or so down to the village at the head of the lake down there."

"Lin Tios? Yes, why not? And what will you have me doing all the while?"

## Part 3 – Lindirgel

"Oh, I'll keep you busy enough building this and that." Her face fell a little. "But you'd miss all that proper stone work. I know that."

"Well, it's only in The Valley that the true tuff rises up, only there in the whole land."

His voice was full of pride, and she waited a few moments before carrying on.

"But you could do the fine work here?"

He was silent for a long while, looking around at the bright fierce sky, the blue of the secret tarn, the rocks, the trees. The quiet beauty of the place pressed around them both.

"Well, yes, of course I could, it's just me working with my tools. I could bring the roughouts and just work at them here. But I don't know what the other lads would think. Just now they're used to having us do all the work in The Valley – the rough cuts and the polishing, all of it, you see. I don't know that they'd approve. Nor what Finn might think."

"And does that matter?"

He thought about it again, rolling the stone at his feet this way and that. Up to their right, two crows were chasing a buzzard away. He watched them, his face softening, as a man might watch his younger cousins at play. None of the three birds were very serious about the conflict. The two crows were casual in their mobbing approach, and the buzzard barely twitched and jinked, and only at the very last moment. It was just a bit of practice fun for them all, anticipating something more determined on another day.

"I just don't yet know. I've heard that the lads can make things difficult if they don't like something they see happening. Not just Finn: it's all of the group together. I've never seen this myself, but Nant told me so."

She leaned back and looked at him for a while.

"I see. Is this why I get the feeling that you're not altogether happy there either?"

He avoided her gaze, tapped the layer of hardened clay surrounding the duck.

"Your duck's done now, surely; let's eat some of it. I need to think some more before I talk about that."

They cracked open the clay wrapper and peeled the shards away from the duck, taking the feathers with it. It was indeed ready, and they shared it, along with the pea mash and some of the barley bread they had bartered for at the stone circle. A few handfuls of early berries rounded out the meal. She mopped up some of the cooking liquid with her bread, leaned back, and after waiting for his answer, eventually spoke again.

"That's fair. Tonight's not for that. I propose we spend one more day and night here, and go back the next day, all along the ridge paths you talked about. Averick told me yesterday about the long valley route, so I'd like to learn something new along the way."

The next day dawned fair, with only a gentle breeze stirring a clump of willows along the bank of the tarn, and the heather sprawling up the sides of the bowl that contained it. They did little during the morning, except that Bran showed her how and where he would start to build a house for them, and rummaged around for examples of each of the kinds of stone he would need. It was an easy, entertaining make-believe that neither of them thought would ever truly happen.

When the sun was at its zenith, they scrambled up to the crags which bordered the southern side of the tarn. Their shadows stretched in front of them across the rippled water. A heron stood motionless at the far end of the tarn where the ducks had been swimming on the previous day.

She touched his arm, hesitantly, and he looked at her curiously, surprised at the unexpected lack of confidence.

"We talked yesterday about how you needed the stone from The Valley. And how there's a choice where you get the rough

## Part 3 – Lindirgel

bits, the raw tuff, and bring them back here to do the shaping and the fine work. But then you said how the others in the gang might make life difficult for us. But why? Who says it has to be done at Ty Caroc?"

"Well now. It hasn't always been done like that, remember? It is now, but when Avank was just starting they would send the raw tuff roughouts up to Butaintal, at the north end of Lin Tios. And there's another settlement that they've used as well, closer to Dronow Moar. And you already know about that other place, Pwil Gwo, where Cegit and Prental went. Where Cegit went when he left. People there used to do some of the fine work to polish the stone up, even if they'd no decent stone of their own thereabouts to begin with."

"And that all stopped?"

"Well, there was some kind of falling out, and long before Finn became foreman they'd ended it. I've never heard the whole story from anyone. There was a tale that at Butaintal they'd been cheating on us, saying that some of the stone we'd taken was rubbish, but then keeping it for themselves. Whether that's true I don't know, but I can't believe that the crew here would do that sort of thing. Avank told me once it goes this way and that every few years, and that's why we switched once to near here, and then again to Pwil Gwo. Whoever it is, we give it to them for a while, some years go by, then we fall out and take it back, after a bit we make up again, and so it goes. That's why Finn sent Cegit and Prental there last year, to see if they could rekindle the old connection. But as you know, they weren't having any of it, and Finn was right upset about that. And that was long before the whole thing about Cegit joining them."

"Why was he bothered?"

Bran shook his head.

"Truly, I'm not sure. We've done without them for much longer than I've been here. It's not like we'd miss them. My guess is that he wanted to be remembered for something grand. Not just being a good foreman – which he is – but to have some bigger deed against his name for after he's gone."

She shook her head, then shrugged.

"And what happens to the stone next?"

"Whoever does the finishing work takes it to traders, and they carry the axes away here and there. We've never trusted Gavur with that, him what you travelled with to get here, but he's not the only trader, not by a long way. Nor the best, nor most reliable. But whoever it is, maybe we meet them at Ty Caroc, or maybe we travel a bit to deal with them. There's a sea-landing about a day south from here, near where I first came in after the journey from Innis Mon all that time ago. Our axes travel all over, some by land and some by sea. When people see them, they surely want to have one, whether it be for actual use, or as part of a treaty, or maybe a devotion gift. Whatever."

There was pride in his voice, and she waited for it to pass by. After a few moments he shook his head and grinned.

"But that's not what you're asking, not really. Let's go back to what you said between Lin Gwair and Dronow Moar. Is it right, what we do at Ty Caroc and the way we live?"

She nodded, and he settled himself more comfortably, wriggling down against a flat end of rock and taking her hand in his.

"Well, first off, it's been going on a long time. More generations than anyone knows, I reckon. The true tuff has been there for ever, and stoneworkers have been digging it out for as long as they've known it was there. But I don't know as how the life is the same now as it used to be. Nant reckons that before our time, in ages past, people just came and made summer camps to take the stone, and then moved on after a season. Those little stone huts further along The Valley than us, and like where Drus lives; Nant says they're much older than Ty Caroc and that they show as how people came and went. I don't know for sure, but that seems right."

"That would be of a piece with how we travellers live in other places."

"It would. Though The Valley's not like other places. It has a, a..." he paused, casting about for the right words. "It has a charm, or a glamour maybe, something that draws you in and

## Part 3 – Lindirgel

keeps you there. Like the selkies that'll take you in to the sea and keep you there for years and years, so's you forget what life was like where you were before. But this isn't just one kind of creature; it's everything, in the air and the stone, the trees and the birds and all. Like it's all alive in a different way, and it calls to you to stay. You must have felt something like this already, though it's not yet a year since you first came here."

She nodded slowly, reluctantly, unwilling to abandon her line of thought.

"But if we give up our way of life, we're no different to barn-and-byre, and we might as well just settle down in their great huge towns. Forget who we are, forget all what we've made of the land in times before."

"I know. And you're right. But I think there's more."

They sat for a while, looking out across the little tarn. After a while, the heron flew off, and he stood up.

"Let me show you our choice of routes onward from here. I'm sure you'll learn them both, soon as anything, whichever way we go tomorrow."

He led her up over the crest, to a little outcrop, from where they could see both the ridge curling southward, and the joined valleys below them to the west. Just visible, as scarcely more than little moving flecks, little groups of deer grazed across the upland ridge. They were moving slowly in the open ground between the low clumps of trees, with no apparent thought of haste. She looked at each way in turn for a long time after he had described them both, eyes shaded against the sun.

"Let's go down, and follow the two valleys. That way will be across new ground, for me at least. I can easily imagine how this top way goes, so in truth there's little to learn there. Seeing it now has quite changed my mind from what I thought yesterday. Show me how we start off."

He pointed to where the outflow from their tarn gurgled over the brink of the slope and then tumbled into the trees on the hillside.

"Along that way at first, then crosswise down the slope so we come to the beck just above that broken up stretch. Beside the stream all along the valley you see over there, almost to the end but not quite. The way curls a little to the left, and the valley wall dips down; that's where we cross into The Valley, a little bit further along from The Brig."

They walked a little further along the ridge, with no particular goal in mind, and after a while sat together and shared another piece of the flatbread they had obtained at Dronow Moar. She leaned against him.

"So what more is there to say, that you keep on stepping around?"

He took a long breath.

"I was thinking, while we were up at the circle, while you were talking with Averick, how many different talents we have. There's yours and mine, of course, but all kinds of others besides that. Like woodworkers. Musicmakers. And so on. Boat builders and crew, like what I travelled in from Innis Mon. Each with our own skills, each with our own special marks in our bodies." He traced one of the tattoos on her lower arm with a finger. "All not really knowing what each other's work is like."

"Of course. How could we know about a skill, without living it day after day?"

"But how can we stay in the land, if all we know is our own skill? If I build a house, then I can make it of stone, to be sure. But if I want some wooden bits in it, say in the roof or the door, then I make it as a stoneworker, not as someone who truly knows wood. I wouldn't know whether it's best to use rowan or ash or beech or oak for a particular job. I don't know what size to use, not really, so I might make it too heavy or too light. I dare say if a real woodsman saw what I'd done, he'd be entertained at best, and horrified at worst, all by my lack of true skill with wood."

She was still puzzled.

"And this is why you talked to the woodworkers? You want to join up with them?"

He nodded.

"Yes. Well, no, not exactly. That is to say, I don't want to be-

## Part 3 – Lindirgel

gin all over again and learn wood, all what different kinds there are and their uses. Or any other trade other than stoneworking. I like working with stone. But I do want to work alongside a true woodworker, them doing their bits and me mine, and you yours. And whoever else the task needs, all doing their own bit. Working traveller-like to make a good job for whoever wants it, whether they be barn-and-byre or one of us. Think about how it was at the circle, now, how we were all in our own little groups for the most part, until the time that the music brought us into a single people. All on the journey, all joined together, whatever our skills or training."

"How would that work?"

"I don't exactly know. I mean, Finn's our foreman because we all reckon he's best. Maybe not the best stoneworker amongst us, but the best all round. The one we all listen to. So we do listen, and then we get on with it. By and large, anyhow."

She laughed, though not unkindly.

"Except for Drus. And Cegit. And Prental doesn't always like what he says. Neither do you, for that matter."

"Well, that's true. But most of the time we go with what he says, and none of us would want it otherwise. That wasn't what I was saying. We listen to Finn because he knows our trade; he's done all what we're doing, works hard, understands what won't work, and can help us when things don't go right for us. Now, how would it be if a woodworker tried to be our foreman? He wouldn't have the first idea what's right and wrong with stone. I dare say he'd be like Brannen and not know the true tuff from rubbishy bits. No more than I'd know the proper wood for some job from useless lengths. How are we going to follow him, or him us?"

There was a long silence between them. She sighed.

"And yet you think it has to be done? Somehow."

"I do. If us travellers just stay in our little camps, stoneworkers here, woodsmen there, leather crafters somewhere else, whatever: if that happens then the barn-and-byre people, and their whole way of life, it'll just squeeze us out. I don't know how it's to work, but I do think that it has to. You must think that as well." She frowned, puzzled, and he carried on. "You left the woman who trained you, to be away, up here, and travelled to be part of some other group of people you'd never known. Now, to my great delight that happened to be here in The Valley with us, but it had to be somewhere. You said as much on that first day in Ty Caroc."

She nodded, her eyes distant as she thought back to the day.

"This journey is all part of the training. Yes, I did say that. And I meant it, too, though I hadn't thought through where that notion would end up, or what it would signify that I'd be living in a group of other-skilled people. Lewenith is the closest, as you know, but she's not trained like me, and nobody is, of all those living out in The Valley." She frowned again. "But then, I don't have to listen to what any of you might expect of me. I do my part of the work, hunting or gathering or whatever, but none of you tells me what to do and where to go. Same as I don't tell any of you. It's different."

"It is. And I don't see how it might work to have different trades working together. Not just yet, anyhow."

"The barn-and-byre lot do it by having one of them whose voice counts more than the others. A chief. I don't exactly know how someone gets to be chief, but I don't think it's because everyone agrees he's the best. And with them it's always a he, not a she. But however it happens, if the rest want something done, they go to their chief and try to persuade him. Or he might call one of them out to do some job that he reckons needs doing. The chief can make something happen in the town, even if some folk don't want it, just because he thinks it has to get done anyhow."

"But we don't have chiefs like that. Finn's foreman because we respect him. If that ever stops, he loses any prospect of getting us to do jobs. I work up at The Quarry because I like it, and I've got the talent and the training, not because he says so. Same for the rest of us. He can't just tell us where to cut stone, make us do it even if we don't want to. There'd be more of us than just Cegit leaving if that ever happened."

## Part 3 – Lindirgel

"So how's it going to work, then, this traveller mixed group idea of yours?"

He shook his head.

"I just don't know yet. But I feel more and more that it has to work, if we're going to keep a place in the land for ourselves. We've got to make our own bands with a mixture of skills so we can tackle jobs rightly. Not just stay forever in our own separate groups, for if we do then the barn-and-byre lot will displace us, just as soon as they can." He grinned suddenly. "But enough of this for now. Let's enjoy Duck Tarn and its surrounds, until tomorrow, and then make the journey back to Ty Caroc and see what we make of that."

They completed a circuit of the little crest that surrounded the tarn on all sides except where the outflow gurgled amongst moss and reeds, and then as they settled back at their camp he paused, looked quizzically at her, and picked up the subject again.

"But something that'll happen for sure, is that it's time for a break from the Quarry. A short break, I mean: two or three moons, perhaps even a couple of seasons. Time for moving about the land. Maybe across to the coastline on the east, near where Nant came from. I've never been there, and I don't believe you have either. I'd like it if we could travel together on that trip."

They left the next day, in the middle of the morning. The beck that left Duck Tarn tumbled far too steeply to follow, so they zigzagged down the steep slope, holding on to trees and finding animal trails as they went. The noise of the broken stretch of water they had seen from the crest grew steadily louder as they went down into the valley, and they ended their descent with a little rush of feet almost to the water's edge.

Then it was a matter of the long walk up the flat valley floor of Strath Gors, keeping to the southern wall in order to avoid the reedy puddles and marsh either side of the beck. The valley was considerably wetter than their own, but also straighter, and only curled a little to the right at the very point that they turned at an angle up the slope in order to cross over the pass. Before long they were at the summit, and paused to share some fruit while looking across at the steep pinnacle of The Brig.

It was odd to approach the crown of peaks from the opposite direction – all their expectations of the shape of the land were backwards. But as the path across to Lanerc's farm branched away from them non the right, and they came to the stone where the dead were exposed, and to the steep series of tracks heading up to the Quarry itself, everything became familiar. Bran was not sure whether he was making a happy return to what he knew, or was simply falling back into long-standing habit.

Brannen came to them then, spiralling down from the ridge of Drum Crog to settle on a nearby tree. She allowed them both to speak with her, and to pet the sleek feathers of her head and neck for a short time. But then, all too quickly, she launched off again into the great spaces of the sky. It felt, Bran thought, almost like a farewell visit from the raven. He would, he was convinced, see her again, but their former closeness was gone.

The gang had gathered for the midday bait at Pwil Gesgod. As always, Bran took the time to face towards the distant summit of Mynyth Mam and to recommit himself to his future ascent, bringing to mind his two failures so far. It was a warm day, and Prental had stripped off and thrown himself in the water at the margin of the pool. It was still cold from the peaks nearby, even this far into the summer months, but he was not deterred. Roudhok was sitting off to one side, looking pensive amidst the conversation. Finn nudged him.

"What's troubling you, bud?"

Roudhok frowned.

"I heard something, and I don't know what to make of it."

Nant looked at him.

"While you were at Dolgolvan?"

## Part 3 – Lindirgel

Prental laughed; he had climbed out again, but his feet still dabbled in the water.

"You were with Colomenn, weren't you? Couldn't you get her off this time?"

Finn stared at him, and Prental subsided. He was sitting on a nearby rock beside Tresklenn, who was strong enough now to get up to the quarry, but not for a full day's work there. He would take stone from the heights in the morning, and then walk back to Ty Caroc in the early afternoon to carry on with fine work back at his house.

"Go on, lad. Tell us."

"I'm not exactly sure what there is to tell. It was nothing to do with the girls. It was before then, when I went down to the market circle. There was a little group of men there – little pale men was the thing I thought first off, with pale hair and all, looking for all the world like they were never out in the wind and the sun properly. Well, they were showing anyone who was nearby a different kind of axe."

"Not made of tuff? What was it?"

"I don't think it was any kind of stone at all. But I don't know for sure. They had some pieces of rock with them, light brown it was, much too pale for tuff, and with kind of reddish veins and blobs in it. Some bits had turned a kind of green colour. I'd not seen the like before, not ever while I was learning. For sure not around our peaks here."

"And they worked it into an axe?"

"No. Not the separate pieces. The stone was too weak for that. I took it in my hands, and any of us would know that it would never polish up, nor yet take an edge that would last. It made no sense to me."

"Did you ask them?"

"One of the barn-and-byre folk did. But I was listening close-like. They saw me, and laughed at me, told me that all my stone learning wouldn't be worth a handful of shale once they got going properly."

Prental shrugged, nudged Tresklenn and grinned.

"I suppose some of us have got it and others haven't."

Roudhok made a little jerky movement with his hands, but ignored him and carried on with his story.

"They told me that their way was better, and I should just pack up."

There was a pause. The others in the group glanced uncertainly at each other. Eventually Finn spoke again.

"Look now, folk have said this sort of thing before. Every few years someone says they can make a better axe than us. It never comes to anything. They can't keep the quality like we do. They have a lucky find, and they think that's it for ever. But it never is. Don't worry about it, lad. I've seen all this before."

Roudhok shook his head.

"I know what you're talking about. I remember one group a few years back. Just before Brogat here joined us, it was. They'd come over the valley road from the east, must have been somewhere near where you come from, Nant. They had some kind of stone they thought was better. From an outcrop they'd found, on some islands just off the shoreline. And you're quite right, it didn't last. But this wasn't the same at all."

He stopped.

"Go on, lad, tell us."

"Well, they wouldn't say much about how it worked. Said it was their secret, and you had to learn with them from scratch before they'd tell you. Well, that much made sense. We'd say just the same ourselves if someone just turned up one day with none of the marks in their body. But I watched carefully what they did, so we can all think about it together." Several of the men nodded. "Well, they had some sort of little fire, and they put rocks, just ordinary stones they picked up from the ground, all round the flame so the heat went where they wanted it to – that also meant that you couldn't really see exactly what they were doing. They had little pieces of that brown stone, and they put them into a funny bowl thing on top, with a lid fitted on it. The bowl itself was made of clay, baked really hard, and I saw inside while they were packing it, and they'd made like an in-

## Part 3 – Lindirgel

side layer of quartz, small flat pieces bedded down on crushed powder of some sort. Maybe more quartz, but I couldn't see it clearly. I don't think they wanted anyone to see that, and the barn-and-byre lot wouldn't know what they were looking at anyway. But I did." He grinned with satisfaction, and then his expression turned puzzled again. "Then they added something else that I didn't recognise, a kind of coarse granular stuff that they kept in a bag. I don't exactly know what that was. Not regular clay, for sure, but something from a rock. That bowl and that grain stuff, that was definitely one of their close secrets. And they blew into it from below somehow, using a kind of pipe thing, I'm not sure how that worked, but I don't think it'd be hard to work out, since all it did was to make the flames hotter. Then all that red and green stuff came out of the rock into a kind of puddle. They poured the puddle out of the clay bowl – you could see the quartz real clear then, if you knew to look for it – into a mould they had handy. Like an axe shape, but small, no more than a finger or so across."

"They poured it?"

Roudhok nodded, his eyes distant as he thought back to what he had seen.

"Aye, they did. And it looked for all the world like honey as it came out of the hot bowl into that mould..."

Prental laughed again.

"Honey! They saw you coming."

Roudhok half-stood, abruptly angry.

"I'm saying something that matters, and all you do is piss around."

Finn lifted a hand.

"Easy, lads. Let him tell it, Prental. I want to hear it, even if you don't. You were saying they poured it like honey."

Roudhok sat again, turning himself ostentatiously half-away from Prental, who moved off and started skimming little stones across the tarn.

"Aye, truly they did. Like honey, really hot honey that you couldn't touch. Most of them had burn marks on their arms and hands, and scorched clothes, just like we have cuts and bruises. One of them had lost an eye and had a great mark across his cheek. So I reckon it's not an easy life, nor a comfortable one. Well, anyway, that aside, they put that axe shape that they'd just poured off to one side while it cooled, somewhere away under cover so you couldn't really see what it was like any more. Then they got out a complete axe from another bag. A different one. They told us they'd made it earlier, though of course none of us saw them doing it. I mean, there wasn't nearly enough of the honey stuff to make a proper size axe. You'd need a whole lot more of the honey, and so you'd need a whole lot more of the green rock too."

"And this finished axe was made of this honey stuff too?"

Roudhok shrugged.

"I said it looked like honey. Poured like it when it was really hot. But it wasn't actual honey. The axe they passed round, the proper-size one I mean; well, that was set hard. You could touch it however you wanted. And it was solid, not soft like the one they'd just poured out. They handed it around to anyone that wanted to hold it. Some did, some didn't. I did. I wanted to see what I could find out. It was cold by then, real cold, not hot any more at all, and the blade felt cold to the touch too, nasty feeling, not like our stone ones. Now, they hadn't bothered to polish it up, so the surface was terrible, like it wasn't properly finished off. But they said you could do that yourself if you wanted. Indeed, that anyone could just in their own home, that you didn't need proper skill or training in their secrets to do it."

"And was it any good?"

"The edge wasn't that bad. They showed us how it could chop up some little bits of twigs, nothing of any size, and they were careful to have a bigger bit of wood underneath. I think you might blunt it if you weren't really careful, you know, turn the edge over on itself, but they wouldn't talk about that. But whatever this honey stuff is, when it cools it leaves a kind of edge that can be made blunt by folding. It doesn't chip away like ours. I don't exactly know if you could unfold it again, or

## Part 3 – Lindirgel

if you'd need to do something else to get the edge back. Maybe you could rub it with a rock of the right hardness."

He paused, and frowned at the memory.

"But you know, the oddest thing about it was not the pouring or any of that. It was that the haft went through the blunt end of the blade. The blade had like a socket in it, opposite to the working side, and the haft went through the socket."

Brogat shook his head.

"That'll never work. You have to put the head through the haft, not the other way round; we all know that. The blade won't take it; it'll split in no time at all."

Finn nodded.

"That's why all these other ideas never come to anything. They don't last under any sort of real use. Folk have tried, and to be sure I've seen a few axes done like that. But they come apart before long, and you're left with nothing much. They're for show, not for use."

"Well now, that's certainly true for tuff and other proper stone, but for this other I just don't know. What with the honey stuff pouring and then going off hard, it wasn't like there was any kind of grain in the blade. Not like ours, where you have to know its shape inside, and get everything fashioned to match. And they had yet another axe they got out then, which they said had been used for three months, day after day, and it was still just as good, so long as you put a new edge on it every few days. Well, that's what they said; anybody might say that, and their whole show was like full of cunning and easy words. And they still didn't show you properly how you might put a new edge on it."

Brogat snorted.

"Sounds like tricks and sleight of hand to me."

Roudhok frowned again.

"Well, it's true I don't know that I'd exactly trust what they said. There were too many gaps in the telling. But you can't argue with the fact they'd made something, and not at all the way we fashion them." He paused briefly. "Anyway, to finish the story, they told us that you could make an axe quick like, if only you had the right rock and the other things, all their proper bits of kit. Much quicker than we could turn one out."

There was a little silence again.

"This bothered you, lad?"

"It did. Mostly I just kept quiet and watched, but they knew who I was. I mean, you can't hide the trade marks we all wear in our bodies, and besides, none of us would want to. So even though I said nothing, I could tell they were watching me close like, seeing what I made of it, and poking fun at me every now and again. What do you think, Finn? Could they have hit on some other way of doing axes? Something that means the barn-and-byre folk don't need us after all? I know we could still do pretty things, like the animals and other things that Bran does. Well, all of us do, I know, but I reckon his work's the neatest of us all. But look, I don't want a life of just making pretty trinkets; I want to be making things that have a real use for people. Even if they're not travellers."

There was an awkward pause. The rest all stared at him. Finn stood up.

"Well, my belief is that it's nothing to worry about. Folk will find these little tricks every once in a while, but the novelty will wear off and they'll all come back to stone before long. I mean, you know where you are with stone, proper stone that's come out of the ground and hasn't needed heating up or whatever."

Gan-Mor was standing, leaning against a rock.

"Where'd they come from, this lot?"

"Different places, I reckon. The one who I reckoned was the foreman, he was a big man, the palest skin of the lot of them. When he did speak, it was hard to follow his words, like he hadn't properly learned them. He didn't say much. The one who did most of the talking, he sounded like Brogat here. And another one, seemed like his mate from the way they talked with each other, well, Gan-Mor, he sounded a lot like you. Over on the east side, I mean, whereas the talker was from our side of the land, but further south in all that mess of mountains. Most

## Part 3 – Lindirgel

of them seemed like travellers, the way they dressed and all, not barn-and-byre for sure. Except for the foreman and one other – they looked and sounded different, like I said just now. It felt like they'd gone about a lot together though; they were easy with each other like you get when you've worked side by side a few years."

Nant was curious.

"You come across them before, Gan-Mor?"

"No, never. Just wondered how far they'd come."

They all looked again at Roudhok.

"Well, I've already said. None of them was barn-and-byre, most were traveller, though from all different places, and I don't know about the two what I mentioned. Whoever they are, they certainly knew how to win over a crowd. Their crack was sharp-like, how they talked about it all. I don't know I believed all that they had to say, for it felt all half-truths and hands placed over your eyes, but they talked like they had something real to trade with. And there was clearly some in the crowd who were persuaded."

Finn was losing patience with the chatter.

"Look now, time's wearing on. Let's get back to work for now. Roudhok, let's you and I, and anyone else who has a mind to, talk with Avank and Gwovan about this later. When we're back at Ty Caroc, I mean, this evening. Not now. Between the two of them they've seen just about everything there is to see about this trade, and they may well have heard all about this before. I don't think there's any need to pack up working and find something else to do just yet, and our regular rock's waiting for us up there."

They set off, with some reluctance, back towards their working areas. There was a sense of the group scattering with nothing having been resolved, dispersing in a fashion not entirely comfortable. Bran sat a little longer, watching the rest go off in pairs. Finn turned away and led Roudhok off. His shoulders were hunched over; he was clearly still unhappy, perhaps feeling that he had more to say that had not been heard. Gan-Mor and

Nant were deep in their own conversation as they started the climb back up towards the veins of the true tuff. Prental dried his feet, pulled his clothes back on, and set off beside Tresklenn, taking a different route from everyone else.

Bran thought of going back up to the heights of the Ban, but decided against it. He turned back along the ridge, went halfway back to Ty Caroc and then dropped down into the valley using a steep descent beside one of the many becks.

Lindirgel looked up in surprise at his early return. She had arranged a neat row of about a dozen clay bowls on a low wooden bench, and was squatting in front of it. Each of the bowls had a different mixture of plant fibres and the paste from Lin Gwair. About half of them had some of the mix rubbed onto slivers of stone from a roughout, and her hand, smudged and grubby with the various pastes, was poised over the next in line.

"Don't let me stop you."

She grinned at his words, and carried on.

"Yet I'm sure you've come back here for a reason, and not just to watch me work."

He sat, and told her all about Roudhok's news. She carried on scooping some of the mixture from each bowl and working along the line of stone fragments.

"Is it important, do you think?"

"I don't know."

She rubbed her hands on a rag and gave him the first piece to test.

"Here, try this one first, then each in turn and tell me which one's best."

He worked with the paste, abrading the stone first with his thumb, and soon after with the antler tine from his carryall. Then he picked up the second.

"We're all gathering with Avank and Gwovan later this evening. Finn wants them to give their own view on the matter."

"He thinks they'll have heard about this before?"

He shrugged and moved on to the next stone.

"None of the rest of us have. Not exactly like it, anyhow. Finn

## Part 3 – Lindirgel

wants us all to think nothing of it, like it was just another little trick by people who wanted to make believe they've got something. But I'm not sure. The way Roudhok spoke, it sounded something more than that: more serious-like. But none of us know just what it is or what it means. We all trust Avank and Gwovan to approach it right, and to speak honestly of what they conclude. But maybe they don't know either."

He shrugged and picked up the fourth sliver. Some of the paste slid off the side and fell to the floor. He picked it up, tested it, shook his head, and picked the next one.

"What exactly is this honey rock? And why do they heat it up? Sounds more like cooking than stonework."

"I don't know. We ought to know of it, seeing as how it comes from rock, but yet we don't, none of us." He frowned, moving to the next piece. "There are plenty of things you find in stone, or alongside it, which are not really stone at all. Morvin told me that people far to the south of here, someplace he'd never been, they pick up little pebbles of something shiny, yellow in colour, which they roll out to be very thin and make ornaments from it. Little sheets you wrap round things, or tiny buttons. Heat helps with that as well, so he said. It's an important part of turning it into the shape you want. Now, he'd never actually seen any of this stuff himself, but seems it was very soft. You couldn't make an axe from it, nor any kind of tool to do real work with. It just looks particularly beautiful, and if you ever find some you can trade a lot for it. And apparently this yellow stuff can be found in seams in certain kinds of rock. Just like the true tuff appears amidst other kinds of rock. Now, if there's a use to it, and it's not just a striking colour or pattern in the rock, then, why, we should be learning that too. Making use of it for its true properties and not just to make a trinket look pretty."

He paused to inspect the stone sliver in his hand; he had been working the slurry into the grooves and rough places while he had been speaking.

"This one's good. Very good, in fact. Much better than the others so far."

She nodded.

"That's exactly what I thought. But you must finish all of them before you decide."

In the evening Bran went to join the little group in Gwovan's hut, leaving Lindirgel crushing several seeds and herbs together, intending to make another abrasive slurry to add to the latest batch of grit from Lin Gwair. Finn had not yet arrived, but stumped in shortly after, with Roudhok behind him. Prental, conspicuously, was not there, though Tresklenn was sitting in a corner. Gwovan glanced up at Finn, who shook his head.

"Well, I stopped the fight between them this time, before it got quite out of hand. But I've told them both, that next time they're on their own. They can sort themselves out. I'm their foreman, true enough, but I'll not tell them how to behave. If they have to fight, they should just get it out of themselves. But I won't have it affect the work, and I won't have it spill over to others taking sides."

Roudhok looked away from them all and remained standing.

"Well, sit down and tell us, lad. Tell us two old men here what you said at the noon break to the others."

Roudhok sat carefully, and then repeated his story for them, this time without interruptions. Afterwards, the two quizzed him for a while. Eventually they sat back. Finn turned from one to the other.

"Well? What do you make of it?"

Gwovan sighed, stood up and limped twice around the room, leaning awkwardly on his stave. They all watched him.

"Cannot sit for too long, you know. Old bones. But look now, I'd like to see one of them axes. It's hard to get a true sense of them, just from hearing you say all this, even though you spoke right clearly about it all. Did they tell you where that special rock

## Part 3 – Lindirgel

came from?"

"Not that I recall, not so's you could find it yourself, I mean. They reckoned there were special places where you'd fetch it, and they knew just where they were."

"Where'd they come from, then? Near or far?"

Roudhok shook his head.

"I don't know for sure. Seems to me from how he spoke, that the main talker came from well south and a bit west of here, like Brogat, in those hills where the land juts out into the searoad. Like us, though, they were mostly traveller, and didn't all sound the same when they spoke, so I guess they'd come together from a few places here and there. Then there were the couple of really pale men; I'd never seen folk like them before, neither traveller nor barn-and-byre. As to where their main workplace was, or where the coloured stone came from, well, they didn't talk about that. But one of them said as how there was most likely the same kind of stone around here, and that maybe they'd set up a camp somewhere nearby. An older one shut him up straight away, but that's what he said. That's fair, though; we wouldn't tell just anyone where to pull the true tuff."

Avank nodded.

"It's that thing with the haft is what interests me."

"Brogat said it earlier; the blade would split if you did it like that."

"The way we do it, yes. But the haft is always the weakest part of the whole, where the blade goes through it. Whatever wood you pick, whatever means you have of binding the blade to the haft, it's still the weak point. The wood splits apart where you've had to open it up. And it's not like we know enough about different kinds of wood to make the best choice. We all just go on what we were taught, and maybe a proper woodsman would say something else."

"The resin helps hold it together."

"It does indeed. And maybe we can mix different kinds of resin, make something that's a bit stronger-like. Bran, maybe you could talk to Lindirgel about that."

There was a sudden silence in the room. Avank glanced at the others, curious.

"What, you didn't know that the two of them have been working together on that sort of thing? Mixing up pastes from different plants and soil?" Nobody replied, and after another pause he carried on. "Any of us might learn from that, if we had a mind to. I'm just saying. But regardless, using resin the way we do is just trying to hide the problem away, so people don't see it. Not what you might call a real answer at all, is it?"

Finn was still pursuing the main topic.

"Resin or no, a new piece of wood to make a haft is a lot easier to come by than a new blade. Less work, less time, less skill involved."

Avank shook his head.

"That's so, as far as it goes. But put yourself in the place of the barn-and-byre folk. They get their new axe from us, and very beautiful it is, to be sure. But it's like Roudhok said, we don't make things just to be pretty – not unless we're making them to get one of the girls at Dolgolvan to hold onto us for a little while." Lewenith frowned, and he grinned. "Not for me, naturally, and that's for certain sure. But to finish what I was saying, we make things that are tools."

Gwovan sat, heavily, and picked up the thread of conversation again.

"And if a tool fails because the haft splits open on them, then yes, for sure they can make a new haft for themselves. And get us to apply some more resin at the same time. Bind some leather thong around it, whatever. But maybe instead of that they complain at us, and maybe we have to make them a whole new blade. Or they get another one somewhere else from a different group. Either way they feel cheated about something. If we could only get those hafts to be better, more reliable, I'd feel a lot better about what we did. And the best way to make the haft stronger is never to have to split it."

Finn frowned.

"But it is what it is. That's how we get the blade on the haft.

## Part 3 – Lindirgel

We can't open a hole in the blade, for it'd split open along the grain. The grain in the stone's more fragile than that of the wood, unless you get it just right. Like Brogat said. You know as well as I do that although a few folk have tried, it's never come to anything much. And it's the blade that takes the time, and takes the real skill too. I'd rather lose a haft than a blade."

"There it is. You're not wrong, Finn. But see, if it happens too much, it might mean that they stop getting our axes for everyday use. They'll still have them for gifts, and for making treaties maybe, or for devotion, but they'll not have them for cutting trees, or making buildings, or whatever. And we make the barter value of a really well finished axe, one for devotion, we make sure we get more trade goods for it. That axe costs them more of their crops, or whatever it is we want from them. Some of them will start to look elsewhere."

Gwovan nodded.

"I've seen people in some of the barn-and-byre places using something that's not even as good as we would call a roughout. That was a few years back, mind, when I could travel about better. But my surmise is that it still happens. One way we could quicken it up is not to spend so much time on the finishing. But none of us wants to do that."

There was a chorus of repudiation around the little hut. Gwovan shrugged, obviously unsurprised at their response.

"I know, the polishing and all helps the axe to work better and longer. We all know why it is we spend the time. But if we won't lessen the quality – and I'm not seriously suggesting that we do – then maybe they'll switch to using our work just for the rare things, like in their devotions, or for something to negotiate with an outsider."

Tresklenn was puzzled.

"So long as they still have them from us, what's it matter?"

"They don't need nearly so many of the one as the other. If they turn away from using our axes every day, they don't need us so much. And once they stop using our axes for one thing, maybe they'll think about stopping using them for anything.

And if they start getting axes from someone else, or worse yet muddle through with making their own, what'll we do?"

"They'll never have the patience for that. That's not their skill." He looked around at the others. "I don't exactly know what their skill is, but it's not with stone."

There was a muted scatter of laughter. Avank carried on.

"Well, there's levels of skill, isn't there? We all know that. They won't take the trouble to learn all what we do, but maybe they'll learn just enough to make something good enough for what they want. And there's the other thought I have. Like I said just now, they might just turn away from us and towards someone else. If these people with their honey rock have found out how to make a hole for their haft without the blade splitting open on them, well, I reckon they're onto something."

Nant leaned forwards.

"What are you saying here? That if we don't drop the quality, they'll drop us?"

"I'm saying that if they find they can get a good enough axe for everyday work from some other place, in enough quantity for what they want, then they might not need us."

Nant nodded, but Roudhok spoke before he could continue.

"You said you thought the honey rock people might truly be onto something. You mean something that might affect all of us?"

"Oh aye, in time. But chances are we've all got a while before that happens. I'll be dead and gone long before it's a real concern to the trade we've built up here. And look, lad, it's not like we're the only people making axes in the whole land. There's folk down south as have used flint for just as long as we've used tuff. Where Prental come up from. Those are good axes that they make, too, even though they're nothing like tuff. And then there's other gangs using inferior stone, but I'm not talking about them."

Roudhok shook his head, but Gwovan took over before he could say anything.

"Now, if all you want is an axe to cut down a tree, you don't

## Part 3 – Lindirgel

need something made of the true tuff, and you don't need it all polished and finished, right? I mean, it works a lot better when polished, but it'll do the job without. Yes? And any of us could make something quick and easy, right? If we didn't care about doing it properly? But we do care. We use the best stone in the whole land, and we treat it rightly, and we take our time over it, and we end up with something truly fine. We've always known that our work is the best, but maybe the barn-and-byre folk don't always want the best. They just want what's good enough for their daily work. If these honey rock people can give them that, why then Dolgolvan will switch to them, and most likely every other barn-and-byre settlement in the land will follow."

"But why would they use something they know is second-best? Where's the sense in them doing that?"

"I'm not saying it'll happen all in a day. But like Avank said, maybe second-best is all they want most of the time. They'll maybe stick with the best for negotiating with other towns, or for whatever ceremonies they have, but maybe not for everyday use."

Roudhok laughed nervously.

"So I'm alright in the stone trade still? I don't know that I can start over so as to apprentice again with these strangers. I couldn't leave all what I've known, all those people I've joined in working together. You're more than family to me, and I won't up and leave because of some trick show."

"You're fine, lad. But maybe those who are children now will need to find a new way to get apprenticed. Or the children after them. Who's to say? I don't know how long it'll be, but stands to reason that some day someone clever will come up with a better way to fashion an axe. It is what it is. We will have to change. And look now, axes is only one thing we can do. I mean, look now, there's good quarry stone up and down the whole Valley here. When the barn-and-byre folk decide they need to live in stone houses like us, we'll be here as long as we want getting blocks out for them and putting them together."

"What? Just build houses? Every day?"

"There's no shame in that: plenty of skill making a good house that'll stand up in all seasons in these parts. Walls and a roof too, we've the skill to do both. Fancy buildings to gather in as well as homes. There's a living in that for any of us who've learned the trade. We can already make a decent wall, but the roof's a tricky one still, seeing as how we don't really know how to use wood. But we'll learn how to make a stone roof that holds its own weight up, and then we'll build houses that'll stand up in any storm we might have. Maybe houses that are taller than what we have here, so you'd go up some steps inside."

"I don't want to start over and learn how to use wood."

"No, but we'll team up with them who can. Maybe make ourselves agreements with wood workers and turners. Find those what have those particular skills and secrets."

Roudhok shook his head, slowly, but Bran was following the words closely; what Avank was saying was all of a piece with the thoughts that he had been having lately.

"I just don't know that I want to pull ordinary stone as a living."

"There'll be other things too. Treasure hidden in the land that we don't even recognise just yet. Just think – when we work the true tuff, or any other rock for that matter, then along with what we want to see, there's all those other veins besides. Each one has its own colour and texture. Its own grain. They'll be good for something, but we don't yet know what, and just now we're maybe missing out by not knowing. What was it you said, Roudhok, about the colours in the stone they used?"

"Reddish flecks and veins mostly. And some parts had turned like a green colour."

"That's what I remembered. Now, we've all seen stone with those colours in, and more besides. I'm certain sure that the colours don't all mean one thing. We'll have to learn to know what colour means what. Which bits are just decoration we can bring out with the shine, and which bits are maybe something more. Like the true tuff, these other qualities'll not show themselves unless you understand where to look. Yes?"

*Part 3 – Lindirgel*

Brogat stirred.

"I heard of something like that close by the western shore of Lin Tios. But never thought anything of it as it wasn't the tuff."

Gan-Mor nodded.

"There's something like it in the hills beside Lugh Deri, as well."

"Well, there's a start. And when we've found it, we have to work out how to tease it out of the stone. Perhaps we can find good use for all these new things – right now we just have no idea what they're good for, and we'll have to learn. Maybe we've lost out on something with not seeing this honey stuff before, but now we know, we can work with that too if we want. If these honey people think that stuff is right here in this land, then we can find it too, and we can find it quicker than they can. There's nobody in the land that knows the stone of these parts better than us. Stone in all its moods, I mean, not just axes." He paused, shook his head, scanned around the morose group. "But yes, lad. I know what you're saying. It'll be a change alright, and it won't be comfortable for us, not while we're going through it."

A brief silence engulfed them all. Nant had said nothing for some time, but after a little pause he leaned forward again.

"There's more than that. Time'll come when we can't make enough axes for them, doing it the way we are."

Finn frowned.

"We can always make more axes, lad, and the true tuff's not going anywhere."

Nant shook his head and stumbled over his words in his haste to speak now.

"No, no, no. What I mean is this. Answer me now. Any of you. How many people are in Dolgolvan today compared to five years ago?"

There was an uncertain murmur around the group, and nobody answered.

"I'll tell you, then. Nearly twice as many. I counted my way round the lanes when I first came, and I do that every year at the end of summer."

He looked at the others, at their baffled expression, but they were all silent. He continued, obviously frustrated at their lack of response.

"So, one thing and another, they need twice as many axes. You see?"

"But that's good for us, surely?"

"There aren't twice as many of us. Just about the same number, in fact. And we don't make axes any faster than we used to. It takes us a season for any of us to turn the fresh stone into an axe."

"That's right: it takes as long as it takes."

"But the actual work, the finding and the cutting and the shaping and the polishing and all, if you left out everything we say and do through the whole thing, that would only take, what, a single moon-phase? If you worked on nothing else, I mean. But we take a season, 'cos we don't want to skimp on any of it, the words and the devotions just as much as the shaping and all."

"Of course: you can't rush the work. Not if you want it done rightly."

"And this is my very point. Go forward another five years, and let's say that Dolgolvan has twice the number again. Maybe they will, and maybe they won't; maybe they'll all get sick or something. But suppose it does happen. We'll not be able to keep up. They'll be getting their axes from someone else whether we like it or not, if that other gang can turn them out faster than us."

"But it's not about speed. It's about doing the job right."

Nant shook his head.

"That's not their way. If they want an axe to take down a few more trees to make their fields to grow their food to feed their bairns, they want it quick-like. We'll not be keeping up with them, not if we still take a season like we do now. Look around this room at us – if we all made one axe a season for the next year, that's still only a couple of dozen axes. That's nowhere near enough for them, let alone all those other folk who want what we make. All over everywhere that the traders take for us. Up and down the whole land. But let's stay with Dolgolvan just now. If

*Part 3 – Lindirgel*

we can't keep up, then for sure they'll find someone who'll trade them what they want. Maybe these honey rock people if they can turn out faster than us. Or maybe another lot working with stone like we do, even if it is less good. But someone else to be sure: not us. If we can't or won't keep up, we'll be pushed out of the whole thing."

Finn was shaking his head.

"Lad, you and I need to talk about this, just us on our own sometime without worrying the rest of the gang. It's not something to just bring into the open like this."

But Bran had been watching Avank, and saw how he had nodded his head soberly at Nant's words, even though he said nothing. At that point the meeting broke up, with the men going back, doubtful and uncertain, to their own homes. And Bran talked with Lindirgel about the whole thing, from start to end.

Bran studied the completed axehead carefully, from every angle. Finally he nodded, happy with the result. He and Lindirgel had worked away at the finishing stages with rags, slivers of antler, gritty mud from Lin Gwair, and sap from several different plants. He had first teased the infant stone from the vein of tuff nearly a season ago, and they had passed the piece each to the other many times since. Now it lay between them on the work-stone, polished smooth and gleaming. It was beautiful. He sighed.

"It's done, Lindirgel, and I'm right glad of all your help."

"It's the first we've finished together, isn't it now?"

"The very first all the way from start to end, rock-face to finishing. The first, but not the last. Indeed, the first of many, I'm hoping."

"Yes, but this one is the very first. We should celebrate somehow."

He leaned back against the rough wall, feeling the muscles in his shoulders loosen. Then an idea struck him.

"There's a thing I've been wanting to do for a long time. I've failed twice already, but I'm hoping that this is the third time when it'll go right."

"And what is it?"

He took a deep breath.

"I want to climb to the summit of Mynyth Mam."

He told her about the two failed attempts, and ended by saying, "So, did your elderwoman tell you how to go about it properly?"

She shook her head.

"She never mentioned it at all. Perhaps she knew, perhaps not. But I'm sure you'll remember the time we went to Dronow Moar, to dance and all? Where among other things I traded tales with that woman Averick from up north? Well, she told me one part of the journey." She closed her eyes so as to concentrate better. "Yes. Her telling started from a patch of wetlands south of The Valley's little sister, with a set of little tarns and mushy ground around them. We drop down from there to Lugh Deri. There's a settlement there, Ty Derwenn, mostly barn-and-byre but some traveller places too. You keep behind the settlement, away from the water's edge a little distance until you've got south of Mynyth Mam herself. Then you curl around west into a valley with a little tarn below steep crags. Follow to the wall-end behind the tarn, go steep up it and then follow it back south to the peak. And we don't come down the same way, but start down the side of the peak facing Lugh Deri, then after a short time turn a little right and drop down her flank to the lakeshore south of Ty Derwenn. There's more detail in the telling, of course, pointers and guidestones and all. But that's the heart of it."

He shook his head, full of admiration.

"Why did I not know this before?"

She shrugged and grinned.

"You just didn't talk to the right people, did you now? So will

## Part 3 – Lindirgel

you try Mynyth Mam a third time? Following this path I've told you? If you know where to pick up the start, I mean."

"Oh, that's easy. We go through the little sister valley, then up and over a ridge the other side, keeping well east of Pen-y-hal. That takes us down to those wetlands you spoke of. And it'll not be me alone trying it, but both of us together. I'd like us to go side by side and pay our respects together at the top. If you're willing, that is?"

She was, and they began preparing for the journey. Some food and spare belongings were easy to pack; they spent most time deciding exactly what goods they should take to leave as an act of devotion at the summit. By mutual consent, the new axehead was the first item to be chosen, and they then each separately picked out a handful of other things. Bran thought back to his two previous attempts, and how his selection of gifts had changed with time.

The next day, soon after the sun had lifted over Bryn Brith, they set off with a small pack and an ash-staff each. The first part of their journey was along the same paths as Bran's first attempt, but after that they stayed well away east of the slopes of Pen-y-hal. At some point they must have crossed the path he had taken to come into the land on his first arrival, but he recognised nothing except for the overall shape of the land.

By late morning they were skirting the wetlands, avoiding the boggy tracks around the cluster of little tarns by keeping to a circle of higher ground. To their right the outflow from the tarns tumbled down a noisy cascade into a rocky valley. Beyond that, the ridge south from Pen-y-hal marched towards the summit of Mynyth Mam, joining with the other crest he had tried to follow from Lanerc's farm. He could see both of his previous failed attempts from this place.

They pressed on, dropping down again through thick woods which suddenly opened out for them to show the whole ribbon of Lugh Deri, stretching for half a day's walk away from them to the south. Across to their right, a smudge of woodsmoke betrayed the location of Ty Derwenn, and behind it, the slopes of

Mynyth Mam reached up into the heavens.

"I've no mind to go there tonight. What better than to stay here?"

He agreed: whilst it was still early in the day, it was not so early that they could scale the mountain in good light and get down again comfortably. In any case, a cap of cloud clung closely to the peak just now, and he had a great desire to have clear sight in all directions when they reached the summit. It would be well worth delaying for clear skies, having waited so long for an auspicious day.

He went off to forage while she set up their overnight camp. This far into the summer, there were plenty of berries to find, and he filled a handbasket before long. That done, he went down to where a small beck flowed into the lake and filled a waterskin. He stood there for a while, looking down the length of the lake, remembering his first journey into the land. Back then he had walked north along this lake's western shore, all without knowing where his path would take him. Eventually he smiled to himself, and then set off back to the camp.

He was most of the way back when he heard a great heavy rustling in the scrubby trees to his right. It was moving away from him, away from the lake, away from where he had left Lindirgel, and struck by a sudden sense of alarm, he began to run. He burst into the glade and saw the half-finished awning slung between two trees, and Lindirgel standing beside it, mouth open, a look of awe on her face. Off to one side lay their two backpacks, torn open and with their contents spilled around.

"What was it? What happened?"

She turned towards him, still full of wonder.

"It was a bear, Bran. A brown one. Right here in the camp. I've never seen one so close, not ever. Some of the hunters back on Mon Mewn said as how they were a few up in the high hills, even there on the island still, not just on the mainland, but they never came down near where we all lived. The very oldest people living there said that they used to hear stories of the bears nearby, but only long ago. But this one: she was right here, Bran,

## Part 3 – Lindirgel

right here just close to me."

He crossed over to her, seeing the small tracks that the bear had come and gone along in its passage past the camp, the signs of passage like bent twigs and crumpled leaves.

"You're not hurt?"

"Oh no. I just stayed quite still and she took no notice." She glanced around, saw the shredded packs, went to pick one up. "Oh. I didn't realise she'd done this. Looks like the food is altogether gone, all what we brought with us."

Bran rescued the other one; it was in the same condition.

"Food doesn't matter. Nor these bags, not really, though I'm right glad she had no interest in the gifts we're planning to leave on Mynyth Mam. I suppose that feathers and shells, carved things and pieces of stone aren't so attractive to a bear. They cannot be eaten. But you're sure you're not harmed?"

She shook her head.

"I wouldn't have minded if she had taken me." She frowned, thought about it, and then shivered a little, clutching her hands together. "Well, I say that now, but perhaps it wouldn't be so good if it actually happened. Her teeth and claws were fierce-like. Would be terrible in your flesh, I'm sure of it. But for all that, I've always been taught that bears are special. They stand up like people when they want to. Their families and clans are like ours. A sow will nurse her cubs like women do, sitting upright with the little one across her lap, not from paps like other animals. And they're really clever: a different kind of clever from your raven, maybe, but something like the same. They're more like us than any other animal in the land." She stopped, shrugged, and seemed slightly embarrassed by her own excitement. "Look now, anyway, that's how it is for us."

He took her hands in his, stilling their restless energy. He waited a few heartbeats before he trusted himself to reply.

"Well, I for one am glad she didn't take you. I suppose we should move the camp?"

"I think so. Even though the food's all gone, and she may be on the forage somewhere else entirely, this might be a regular track she goes down."

He showed her the berries he had gathered, and they ate them together. They had seemed plentiful as he had collected them, but without anything else besides, it amounted only to a rather meagre meal. Then they took down the awning down and moved their belongings a hundred paces or so towards the lake, away from any apparent animal trails.

"Should we go back to Ty Caroc, get some more food and try again another time?"

"Absolutely not. I've been thwarted twice already; I'm not going to let a bit of hunger put me off the third time. Providing you're agreeable, that is. We'll maybe stop at Ty Derwenn when we've been up and come down again, but not before. We surely can get some bannocks there, or something like, and we'll gather some more berries along the way." He laughed and tied off the last tether. "Anyway, a day's fasting before we attempt the mountain would be a small price to pay if it gets us there."

The rest of the night passed without event, and they found some more berries in the morning before heading down towards the lakeshore. Lindirgel looked back towards their original camp with some regret.

"I'd have liked to see the bear one last time, you know. Took me quite by surprise, she did, that one time, and I was struck quite dumb. Do you think she'd have answered if I'd brought myself to say anything to her?"

"It took Brannen a couple of seasons before she said anything apart from her own wild noises, and that was when she was with me day and night, and me chattering away to her when I wasn't talking to the rocks and the trees, and whatever else was around. So maybe your bear would have needed longer to get used to you."

She sighed.

"I think you're right. But I wish now I'd at least tried it."

They worked their way around the head of the ribbon of lake, and then down the western shore, keeping some way back from the water's edge, screened from the nearest houses, and from the

## Part 3 – Lindirgel

scrappy ribbon of adjoining fields, by the first rows of trees that hadn't been cut down or burned. The barn-and-byre settlement of Ty Derwenn ran right down to the shore, where small boats were tied to a few wooden posts. He pointed towards it and shook his head.

"I don't want to go into the town."

"We'll need more supplies afterwards."

"We will. But let's ascend Mynyth Mam first. I have a great eagerness now to make the climb; I've waited a long time for this, and gone astray twice before. This time – especially now that you're with me – this time I want to reach the summit, pay our respects and leave our gifts, and see all what there is to be seen from there. We can get a bit of food when we come back down again."

They walked on, carrying south well past the barn-and-byre settlement, following an easy ridge of land which slowly took them away from the lakeshore. Bran kept glancing up to his right, up the slope, trying without success to consider where the green-veined rock that Gan-Mor had talked about might lie. Perhaps in future years there would be a different stoneworker crew based here, specialising in the honey rock rather than the true tuff.

He was also starting to wonder how far south they needed to go, when Lindirgel nodded with satisfaction. Two great upright stones stood beside the track, pointing towards the west, away from the lake and around the southern flank of Mynyth Mam.

They turned to follow the guidestones, finding one and then another, and then another, leading them always towards the centre. The land everywhere was alive with signs of traveller devotion, for those with the training and knowledge to find it.

He thought back to conversations with Nant about the landscape all around them, how the deliberate placement of stones complemented the natural architecture. Some person, or more likely a lot of people over a span of years, had set out all the individual rocks and the stone patterns that surrounded Mynyth Mam. Nobody had ever erected a circle at her summit – she needed none, for she was sufficiently monumental in herself to disdain any such embellishment – but on every side there were signs and pointers to help those wanting to approach her. It was, he realised, only his own ignorance of all this which had caused him to fail twice before.

Eventually they turned north into a valley with sheer walls on either side. A tarn nestled in the valley, blue where the sun struck it, but dark in the shadow of the crags. They walked steadily along its rim, and then up the steep wall behind it. A single stone stood at the crest of that rise, and they paused to rest there briefly. The aspect on all sides was already impressive, but he decided that he was not going to look properly until they had reached the top and presented their offerings.

After that the remaining ascent was easy. They continued to curl around, in the spiral shape that they had started low down on the hillside looking across at Ty Derwenn. The crest rose steadily, first eastward, and then south to the summit. The guidestones had stopped – there was no more need for them – and the way was clear. There were no more obstacles. They had ascended Mynyth Mam.

He was filled with a sense of rightness, of completion. Mynyth Mam was not, he decided, a difficult peak to ascend, not when compared with those he scaled daily. At least, she was not difficult once the conditions were auspicious and the weather generous.

It was not the hardship of challenge that gave this peak her pre-eminence amongst all of the peaks of this land; it was her setting, and her mystery, and the ancientry of the trappings around her. It was the weight of the past devotions presented by travellers who had made this journey before.

He was full of gratitude and wonder, feeling most deeply the fulfilment of his long-held desire to stand here. It was time, now, to turn that gratitude into tangible offerings.

Before anything else, they took their gifts from the bear-torn and roughly-retied bags, and decided where to place them. The axehead, naturally, had to go as close to the summit as they could

## Part 3 – Lindirgel

manage. Bran built a small plinth out of nearby rocks, and together they placed the thing they had fashioned together on top of it.

Then they stood in silence, each considering their own part in it. There had been hours of joint labour that had brought this into being, from the initial roughout through all of the intermediate stages, to the polished thing of beauty that they had birthed together. Their wordlessness was remembrance, and devotion, and prayer, all in a single shared act.

The other offerings they had brought – flowers, feathers, a few shells, some other shaped stones, and a little bag of the mud from Lin Gwair which was transforming their work – went in a series of circles around the central place. Some would last only a matter of days or months, while others might still be there for generations to come.

Bran felt himself awash with a sense of pride and accomplishment. He had failed twice at this climb, but this third attempt, when he had made the journey with Lindirgel, had been different. This one had ended in success.

They had each left their gifts there, both the ones that were personal and the ones that represented their shared life and work. He wished, briefly, that the elderwoman back on Innis Mon who had taught him how to make that first journey might, somehow, know that he had at last been able to pay his respects to Mynyth Mam.

And so, finally, they turned to look at what they could see. Southwards the land dropped steadily down to a huge expanse of open water, beyond which the land swept out in a great arc, low and featureless in the distance. The land fell in gentle sweeping waves to the shores of the bay, and glistening tracts of sand made a broad band between land and sea.

Northwards the crest of the ridge ran along in gentle curves, threaded between a string of peaks. None of them reached so high as Mynyth Mam; the great peaks of the land formed a cluster further to the west, separated from where they stood by a flat stretch of uplands.

Somewhere along that sinuous northerly ridge was the path he had failed to find on his second attempt. A little to the right was the more solitary peak of Pen-y-hal, the site of his first failure. And between those two angles they could see the distinctive, familiar shape of the Ban, from which he had so often gazed south at exactly this point. Perhaps his workmates were looking out from there even now.

Further right again, just visible as a break in the ridgeline, was the notch he had seen right at the beginning of his journey through the land here. He pointed to it, wordless, and Lindirgel leaned in to him. On that same side, immediately below them was Lugh Deri, rendered small by their present height.

Then they turned west, to where the long ridge of Innis Mon Allan rested between sky and sea, far out in the bay. It was blurred by distance, shadowed and hazy, but was nevertheless familiar to him.

It was clear from here that the bay that lay southward was only one part of a huge sweep of water, cradled in the embrace of the land. The long arms to north and south stretched out as though to grasp Innis Mon, but could not reach the island where he had learned his trade. Bran thought back to his journey in the little boat across that water, and marvelled at how far that journey must have been in such an exposed craft.

"That's where I came from. That's where my journey began."

She nodded.

"But it is as I thought; we cannot see my Innis Mon Mewn. It must be twice, thrice as far as yours, and nobody can see that far."

She was silent for a time, looking southwest to the place that she could not see.

"And perhaps one day I shall go back there, but that may not be before I have done all that I can to finish my training."

He let her look for a while, then they both turned again to the northeast, to the gap in the hills which had always beckoned to him.

"For now, can we journey that way for a while? Head across

## Part 3 – Lindirgel

the backbone of the land to the eastern shore? Go together to see what is to be found there? Go a-travelling together beyond where we can see?"

She glanced briefly at him before looking back across the ridges and the wooded valleys between them.

"Is that what you want now? For sure? To walk the land for a time?"

"I'll walk it for a time, if I can walk it with you."

He was, at last, sure of this decision; the mountain had made herself clear to him, and he was now certain of what he wanted for the couple of seasons ahead. They stood there in the sun and the wind together for a long time, looking in every direction, until eventually it was time to go. They approached the highest point once more, knelt together at the peak of the great mother mountain, and then stood again and began going down the hillside.

They did not retrace their path up, nor drop down directly towards Ty Derwenn, but rather came over the side of the mountain facing towards the ribbon of Lugh Deri, far below them, and followed the folds of the land back towards the valley bottom.

They walked in silence at first, still caught up in the spell of the high ground, but once they descended past the junipers, the hollies and the birches to the first of the great trees, the ordinary things of life pressed in around them again.

"We still have no food for tonight."

"There'll be berries."

"Ah. More berries. But maybe there'll be fish in the lake. It'll be proper to eat again, now that we've done what we came to do. But your bear took all our grain and made-up things."

She nodded.

"We can stop at Ty Derwenn. Someone there will trade us bannocks with the bits and pieces we have left over to trade." She gripped his hand and squeezed it, her eyes alight with a sudden idea. "Or even a stottie. Oh, I could eat a whole one."

He laughed.

"Then we'd best trade for two."

And then later, at their camp in the oaks of the foreshore of Lugh Deri, they sat together beneath the sighing branches, and beside the singing waters, and a great contentment filled them both.

# Epilogue – Travelling

After the bait at midday, as the men were scattering to their own places to begin the afternoon's quest for the true tuff, Bran followed Finn for a short distance so they could talk away from the others.

"Something bothered you, has it now?"

"I was wanting to say as how I'll be away for a season."

Finn looked at him sharply.

"Away where?"

"Not rightly sure yet, in all truth. I need to be on the paths for a while. Travelling across the land. I've not been this long in one place ever before. East, I'm thinking, over to where Nant used to live. I've never travelled that way."

Finn frowned at him.

"This is too sudden; I'm not sure about it, leaving like this. What's brought this on? You were never flighty before. Not while you've been here, and not before, from what I heard. You were apprenticed to Morvin map-Deru. You stuck with him all through. That wasn't a thing of a few seasons."

"No, it was not. But neither was it all in one stretch, one thing after another. I'd do a piece of the learning, then be walking about the land for a season. Then I'd go back to Morvin for the next piece. Sometimes he'd be out on the travelling himself. But he always came back, and so did I to him. And just the same, I'll come back to you, to the lads here and to Ty Caroc and the quarry. I've been with you two years now, summer and winter; it's time to be on the way for a month or two."

"And the rest, I'll warrant. Y'll be more than a couple of moons away, I've no doubt about it. Why, just getting across to the east and back will take a whole piece of time, let alone whatever y'see that y'fancy getting involved with there. Not back until the spring, if ever y'do come back, that's my belief."

"Well. Perhaps the walk over to that eastern shore will take longer than I'm reckoning at the moment. But I will be back for sure. The spring's a good time to aim to be here again. And look now, the winter's a fallow time anyway; oftentimes we spend it here at Ty Caroc and not up at the quarry anyway."

## Epilogue – Travelling

"That's beside the point, where we spend it. And indeed, all the more important you're with the lads here in the village, if we cannot be up on the crags. They'll be needing help, some of them, and all of them will want companionship." He shook his head. "I'd thought to give over to you some of my jobs. That maybe I could train you up in all that's needful to be foreman so you could work alongside me. So that I could make those particular final marks on your body myself to show you were completely done. Then I could step back a bit and let you choose how to take it forward."

He paused and stared at Bran, who said nothing.

"But I cannot do that if you're not going to be here. I need a man who I can rely on. I thought that was you, Bran, but you've shaken me with this talk of flitting off for a season. And I'm guessing that when you come back – if you come back, that is – then y'll be saying the same thing in another year or so."

He turned away and walked jerkily up and down.

"Look now, Finn..."

"And the men'll not stand for it, neither. They want someone who'll be there for them whenever they need it. Not someone who ups and goes whenever he pleases."

"For sure I'll come back, but for sure as well, I'll need to be away from here every now and again. I'm not barn-and-byre, look now; I'm traveller. So are all of us. So are you, come to that, though I don't think you've done much travelling these last few years."

"Don't you tell me what I should be doing. What do you know of it? Do you know how I've thought about leaving when the times are hard? When there's been bad years, or bad words among the lads? Oh, but I know where my commitment is. And so should you as well. Your life should be settled here, right here, here with all what we're doing together. Here in The Valley's the best place in all the land, the only place you should ever want to be, now that we've given you a place among us."

Bran stiffened.

"Like I just said, I'm traveller, Finn, not barn-and-byre. I'll not stop forever in any one place every day of my life: neither Ty Caroc, nor Dolgolvan, nor Innis Mon for that matter. Not however good a place it is. Now, I'll work with yous all, and I'll work hard. And my work's good, as well you know. But there are times I'll need to be on the journey, and this is one of them. I'll go, but I'll come back again."

Finn shook his head.

"I can't say I'm not disappointed, Bran. Indeed I am just that: disappointed. And I can't say this won't affect how you stand among the crew. I'll have to start all over again finding someone as might take on my part. I'd thought it would be you."

He took a step away.

"And I thought you'd be more grateful about getting your place here. I wonder what Morvin would have to say about this. And to think I trusted his recommendation and all when you first turned up."

"He'd tell me to go on my journey for a time and then come back when I'd done. I just now told you that: we worked together in bits and pieces, not all the time without spaces. There was whole seasons when he was away himself. I didn't just learn stonework from him; I learned how to be a traveller as well. And look now, I've kept my place here on the grounds of my own skill, not his. And you need good workers to be here with you."

Finn half-turned, then swung back.

"And that's it, to be sure. I need the good workers here, not disappearing somewhere else when they choose." He stared at Bran, and a sudden realisation lit up his features. "It's that woman, isn't it now? I knew she'd be a cause of trouble."

Bran stared at him, abruptly angry.

"Lindirgel will be on the way with me, for sure. She'll not want to stay here alone, not the way she's been treated. But I'd be on the way by myself from time to time whether she had stayed or no. She's with me, but she's not the only cause. I've had plenty of time to make my own mind up about this."

"We've never laid a hand on her."

"You've never taken her in, neither, nor warmed to her, nor

## Epilogue – Travelling

made her welcome. None of yous, saving Avank and Lewenith, who've always been right kind." He shook his head. "She's good for me, Finn, and good for the work. What she's brought in with her own training, the way we're working in different ways with the stone; you ought to show an interest there. You ought to be coming to us both and asking what's good about it. Deciding for yourself what's worth taking on and what's not for you. Like Avank said to us all a while back."

Finn sat down on a nearby rock. He looked suddenly deflated, and remained silent for a long while.

"Look now, Bran, I shouldn't have said that about her. About Lindirgel, I mean. Let me take those words back as if they'd never been said. But, you see, all this, it's all pressing up against me. It's all getting too much for me, lad. I had it all worked out in my thinking. I'm not getting younger, see, and there you were, come along to us here at just the right time. You've got the native skills to bring on the younger ones in their trade, you've got respect with the older men, and you're young enough still to keep this all going for years to come. And now look, I'm worried about this honey rock stuff that Roudhok saw down at Dolgolvan, I've got a bad feeling about it all. More so than those other things I talked about. And the folk at Pwil Gwo turning against us, poaching Cegit away the way they did. Seems like it'll be the end of us, or at least the start of a big change. But you mustn't say that to the lads, you know."

He waited for Bran to shake his head.

"See, I'm not the man to be leading the lads if what I fear comes true. I know the rocks here, the true tuff, the way the land lies and all. But I can't see myself keeping the lads on course if it all changes. I'm not one who can manage much change, you see. You're right what you said about that."

He fell silent again briefly, then carried on.

"And it's not only that. I've seen the difference in how the Dolgolvan lot treat us, you know. Time was they gave us respect for what we did. Now they look at us sideways, and if they could do without us they surely would. Year by year it worsens, and I don't rightly know what to do about it all. I thought you would take that on. But you can't if you're not here. Stay with us, lad, and take us all through this. Don't go away like this."

Bran slowly shook his head.

"I hear you, Finn, but I'm just doing what travellers have always done, and what maybe we should all be doing still. And I'm coming back. But if you can't wait for that, then train someone up to work beside you like you say. Just pick one of the other men."

"But who, lad? You tell me. Put your own mind to it. There's some of them too old now, they don't have the desire to take it on. And of the young ones – well, you know the men almost as well as I do. Prental is entirely wrong for the job. Tresklenn still doesn't know the Ban from the Brig. And he had that fall, and he's never been right since then, not properly right. In truth, I'm wondering if I did the right thing, taking him on so easy-like when he came here. But I need all the workers I can get, there's few enough of us as it is. Gan-Mor's not interested in being foreman, never has been. Brogat's a nice lad, but he hasn't got what this needs. Cegit left, as you know. Roudhok, well, he's too unsure about himself, despite all his skill. He couldn't keep the lads going on in the way it calls for. And I'm not thinking of Drus, not after all he's looked down on us these last few years. So you tell me, Bran: who should I choose to carry this work on?"

Bran thought for a moment.

"Nant? You've not mentioned him."

Finn laughed, and his voice was brittle.

"Nant knows his stuff alright. And he'll tell you night and day all about where things have come from and how they've been. But you know as well as I do that he's not a man to lead the others. I'm right glad I have him at my back, to be sure. When I've forgotten something that I should have remembered, he'll know it, and he'll remind me sure enough. But come on, lad, can you really see him as foreman?"

Bran was silent. He sat opposite Finn and shook his head.

## Epilogue – Travelling

"I don't rightly know. I like him, more than some of the others. But I understand what you're saying about him. But look, Finn, I can't not be off for a spell. I'll come back after I've been on the journey for a while. If that's not good enough for you then I don't see that I can help you with all this. You're wanting me to be something I'm not."

Finn stood up, looking much older than he had at the start of their talk.

"Then it is what is it, I suppose. But I don't know what'll happen to us all here in The Valley. I'm afraid for us all, and I needed all of us to be standing together. Now, if you go away on a journey, then fine, you can work with us again when you get back. I've got nothing against your work: nothing at all. But what I'm saying about you working alongside me; well, if you go now then that goes too. I can't be chasing things one way and another. If you go, then you'll not be foreman after me even when you get back. I don't know who it'll be, but not you. It won't be your marks on the great rock. Think about it, lad, and maybe you'll change your mind before you go. Stay here with us, and keep the trade going for another generation. Just think about it for me. This is not a good time for you to go."

He strode away, his steps swift and jerky. Bran called out after him.

"I'll be back in the spring at latest, when the bluebells are out."

But Finn said nothing more, and Bran had nothing more to say to him. He sighed, looked up at the sun, and considered going back to the place where he had been working, teasing out the true tuff from where it rested in secret. But he had no heart for it just then, and instead went back down to the valley floor.

He passed by the ragged Crug, sitting as always on the rock shelf beside the steep beck where it tumbled into a broad pool, the broken stones scattered all around him.

"Y'alright, Crug? What would you do, hey? Would you move on, if those legs of yours had more substance than a few old rags?"

But Crug said nothing, and Bran turned and went along the

track back to the house at Ty Caroc. When he arrived at the village, Brogat was just leaving his house. He was surprised to see Bran, and then glanced around furtively, first one way and another, and then behind Bran up the track to the quarry to see if anyone was following.

"I was just... well, I wanted to hear about what the two of you have been doing with plants and such. Mud, whatever. What Avank said about." He hesitated. "Lindirgel promised not to say anything to Finn just now, in case he takes it bad-like."

Bran grinned.

"It'll be our secret. She have time to teach you much?"

"It's a start. I've got a few things to try out. She said the best way is to find out for myself what works best for the way I work, and told me what plants I have to look for." Seeing Bran's acceptance, he warmed to the topic. "Who'd have thought that nettles would have a use like that? I've never thought of them as good for anything except soup. And I'm going to look round the shores of Pwil Brith for some speckly mud like what you have. If I can't find none maybe I could come with you one day to the place you go?"

Lindirgel, hearing them talk, had come to the door.

"That's one person who's keen to find out more."

Brogat looked from one to the other.

"You don't mind? I mean, I didn't know if it was a secret thing that I wasn't supposed to learn about."

"No secrets between us, I think. Not as regards this. Take your time and look around Pwil Brith, and if you can't find anything that works right, we'll take you next spring to the place we found." He nodded to Lindirgel. "I think we might be away for a little time until then."

Lindirgel took a deep breath.

"Tell me what he said, then."

Brogat shrugged and started to move off.

"Best I'm away back to work, I reckon. But I'm grateful for the tip. I'll let you know how it goes for me."

They went back inside and sat down.

## Epilogue – Travelling

"Well?"

Bran repeated the conversation to her.

"And does this change your mind?"

"Not in the least. He's never talked about this before." He stopped, thinking back through the months to reconsider some of Finn's comments. "Leastwise, not in a way that I could follow what he meant. It feels altogether too much like something he'd say to make me reconsider it all. But I'm not minded to do that. Let's you and I carry on the way we intended to, over the Summer Road to the eastern side of the land. When we're ready we'll come back, and I'll work here again."

"If there's truly nobody else here that can second him, he'll have to take all those words back again anyway."

"Maybe so, but I'm not doing it for that. I've never done any of this with the thought of being foreman. I do stone work because I love it, and I'm good at it. That's enough for me. His notion that I'd be doing it just to be his second, well, it's... it's..." He paused to think about what it was like, and eventually decided. "It's even less traveller-like than living in The Valley the year round."

She grinned, and nodded.

"Fair enough. When are we leaving? If we're going on the Summer Road, we shouldn't leave it too long. We're almost at the time when days and nights are equal."

"Let's go soon as we can, now it's decided. We should visit Lanerc and Gwennol at their farm today, to stock up. Fill a large pack each and start away early tomorrow. And say our goodbyes to the lads tonight as well."

"And Lewenith."

Her voice caught a little, and he looked quizzically at her.

"She'll tell me that if I'm gone too long, she might not be here when I get back." She made a little jerky movement of her hands. "I don't believe her, of course. But that's what she'll say anyway, regardless of how much nonsense it is."

He nodded sombrely.

"The same might be said of any of the lads. A slip of concentration, a gust of wind that catches someone wrong, a patch of mangy ground underfoot, a handhold that isn't what it should be, and that's it: one less of us. As happened to Don, not long after I got here." He saw the tense look on her face. "I know she's not young, but she's not so old that a couple of seasons will make so much difference."

"I hope not."

He took her hands.

"Go to her this evening, tell her and Avank both what it is that we plan. My belief is that she'll be pleased for us. But either way she should hear from you directly, not by hearsay from someone else. But for now, let's go over to Lanerc's farm and lay in some supplies for the journey."

Later that day they had gone over to see Lanerc and Gwennol, to trade for supplies and exchange what all four of them anticipated would be a temporary farewell. Bran realised as he took their hands at the time of parting just how much he would miss the steadiness of their presence. They had been, by and large, just on the edge of his experiences in The Valley, but they had always welcomed him and been kind. As he left, he took time to fix the place in his mind: the little wooden hut with the stone-faced walls that Avank had put in place for them, the animals in their little stockade, the crop strips running down towards the tarn, and, finally, the noisy, friendly dogs.

Brannen had flown over them as they came back towards Ty Caroc. But she had landed beside them only briefly to let them ruffle her feathers and speak to her, before she was called away by another raven, soaring on the upwinds that swept over Drum Crog.

"I wish I knew how far she roams from here." They watched the pair of birds as they swept eastwards and then away north

## Epilogue – Travelling

over the valley wall. "I mean, might she fly as far as Lugh Laesach? Or beyond that across to see us leave on the Summer Road? I used to wonder if ravens flew out to the coast, so that they'd see the sea and the little boats on it. But now I'm thinking inland. Or maybe her domain is just The Valley and nothing more. But I don't believe that. Who knows?"

Lindirgel shook her head.

"I have no idea. But I think she'll be here when we get back in the spring. Will she be having her own chicks by then?"

"I don't think so; she'll still be too young for that. Maybe the year after? I suppose we'll find out in due course."

Once they had got back to the village, Bran had made the circuit of the huts, making sure that all of the crew knew that he would be leaving the next morning, and that he would return in a couple of seasons. He was anxious to avoid any suggestion that he was slipping away in secret as Cegit had done. Finn was still morose about the matter, was short with his words, and kept himself busy with smoothing a roughout, rather than setting it down so that they could talk more easily.

Of the others, Nant was pleased, and told them of traveller encampments in the coastlands east and north of the paths they would tread to reach there. He said several times that he had no intention of going back eastward himself, but wanted them to find places where they would be made welcome. Brogat was disappointed, especially because of the previous day's conversation about new tricks of the trade, and said that he would be eager for their return. Most of the rest were casual in their words and manner, and Bran found it hard to weigh their mood. Was Finn right that this would inevitably worsen the way they thought of him? Meanwhile, Lindirgel had stayed until late in the evening with Lewenith.

The next day, early in the morning, they had left Ty Caroc, cut over the shoulder of Alt Ariannaith, and rounded the northern shore of Lin Gwair. With the turning of the year, the light shone first on the slopes to their west, and the track to the east they followed at first was still in shadow. From there, their route had started exactly the same as on the journey to Dronow Moar. But instead of following the path steadily north up and over to the quiet valley with the two lakes, they branched off to the right soon after the rock in the glade where Bran had left his markings. It would be a long time before they saw them again.

Now they were working a steady way up the long valley that would lead them directly to the notch in the hills that Bran had so often seen, so often wondered about. A little stream ran down the sloping valley bottom, fed by a series of smaller becks from either side, but their own path was well above the damper strip around that. So far, the only part of the journey that had needed care was where several valleys met, and the streams they held had fused into a reedy, messy tract. Otherwise it was an easy way to go.

As the last of the little trees dwindled away, the ground became less regular. Little waterfalls interrupted their route, and at one point a whole rocky outcrop glistened where the water from above coated the whole surface before sinking into moss below. They scrambled around and over a few boulders, and then, quite suddenly, they were at the crest of the long rise, and the land fell away ahead of them into a bowl.

Bran blinked with the suddenness of it. Ever since he had first come into the land, from his first sight of the notch in the hills, he had wondered what it would be like to pass through it. Now, finally, here he was, poised on the outermost edge of what he had been able to see before, and ready, at last, to go into the unknown lands beyond.

They turned to look behind them. There, the land rose and fell in a series of ridges – Alt Ariannaith, Drum Crog, Pen-y-hal, becoming increasingly vague with distance despite the efforts of the late morning sun. Mynyth Mam was hidden from sight behind Pen-y-hal, but he knew exactly which direction she lay in.

But over to their right, the Ban was no longer visible, nor the side of the Brig peeping from behind it. Both were obscured by the swell of the hillside close at hand. He felt a sudden, over-

## Epilogue – Travelling

whelming sense of parting. He had wanted to mark the moment when the Ban would disappear from view, to have some kind of inward ceremony to bid farewell, but he had missed the opportunity. It would have to wait until they returned, and would see the peak again.

"For two years those ridges, and the valleys between them, have been my home and my workplace. Seems strange to look back at them looking so small like this."

She shrugged.

"I've not been there nearly so long, so it doesn't affect me the same."

"And I suppose this move is taking you even further away from your original home?"

"You and me both: we'll not be able to see Innis Mon Allan from anywhere after this." She paused, and frowned. "We both committed to this when we set off. It's part of the traveller life, surely? To be leaving things behind all the time."

"Indeed it is. And I'm not changing my mind. But surely it's part of the traveller life to also feel sorrow about the places and people you leave behind?"

She nodded, wearing an unfathomable expression.

Ahead, over the lip they had been climbing towards, the land dropped away a short distance down to a tarn, noticeably bigger than Pwil Gesgod. To left and right there were steep slopes, leading up to rounded tops, but they had no need to scale them. On the far side of the tarn, directly opposite their viewpoint, the ridge rose up again, and Bran knew that a little distance along that ridge lay the summit of Uchelvelen. Their own way led off at an angle to the right of that, down another long valley which led at last to Lugh Laesach, a distant strip of blue only partly visible from where they sat.

They paused and shared a bannock while admiring the view, and then skirted the side of the tarn until they splashed across its outflow. They halted briefly so Lindirgel could point out the long line of the ridge standing sheer beyond the lake, and then they set off again down the long valley. It was easier than the climb, with bare rocks at first, then scrubby bushes before the little trees started to fill in the slopes, and then finally, much lower down where the soil was deeper, the great trees. And as they descended, they began to come across guidestones and little cairns that led on, one to the next.

The first of these was a great rock to their right. A natural split had been carefully widened by hand, to form a broad crevice that directed them to cross the beck. They did that, and from then on kept to the southern side of that valley. The noisy beck was always on their left, growing steadily as smaller outflows from one ridge or another fed into it, and occasional standing stones confirmed their choice of route. They caught another glimpse of the southern limb of Lugh Laesach before it was blocked from view by a wooded hillock, and then, quite suddenly, they were out of the trees and into the broad marshland that straddled the upstream end of the lake. Alder trees and willows stood tall amongst the waving grasses.

Lindirgel had stopped for a while beside the most recent fingerstone, looking carefully across the valley and up along the ridge. She had expected to have to navigate by noticing and heading towards landmarks among the rocks and crags opposite. But when they came down among the reeds their way ahead was obvious. A wooden causeway gathered their own track into others coming from north and south, and led across the wetlands. Here and there the wooden boards were cracked or split, but the path was unbroken, and before long they had crossed over to the eastern side, and stood once again on solid ground.

Lindirgel pointed towards a faint path that turned a little south as it wound up the steep slope between stony outcrops.

"That way goes up and over the high ridge, but it is not for us. We will go along the lakeshore at first, and then, once we're past the high promontory that you see there, we go up the ridge at a shallow angle, not steep like this."

"And that leads to the Summer Road?"

"Well, yes, eventually, but not yet, not for some while. The path takes us north of the high places on this ridge, and meets

## Epilogue – Travelling

other paths at a stone circle. Dronow Cyfarfod, it's called. Not so great as Dronow Moar, and from what I have learned, not used so much through the year. But we will use it as a waypoint, since from there we will be able to see the land's backbone across a broad valley. From there we will see the way that we must take. We will camp tonight beside that circle, and press on tomorrow. We should finish our fresh supplies tonight, and hunt tomorrow as we cross the lowlands beyond. We will need the dried meat for the drag over the hills."

They walked on. The path along the lakeshore was difficult at first, as the ground was broken and craggy, and the trees dense, all the way down to the waterline. But they made steady progress nevertheless, and once they had gone past the great promontory, the track became easier. The diagonal track up the hillside led them progressively further away from the water, and the ridge to their right dropped lower.

The oaks and beeches were well behind them, and they were walking amongst holly and birch, when they reached their overnight stay. Just as at Dronow Moar, the stones themselves were surrounded by a broad clearing, within which only a few ancient yews and hollies had been left standing. Bran suspected that they marked out where the sun or moon would rise and set at different times, but he was acutely aware that he lacked the knowledge to understand the pattern properly. It was another trade, with its own secrets and mysteries.

The ring of stones had a neatly laid kerb of flat stones as its perimeter, separating inside from outside, earth from sky, life from death. He wondered why this circle had been erected with the kerb – as also had some of the dead men's markers up near the Ban and the Brig – but Dronow Moar had not. Neither of them knew.

The setting sun still gave them plenty of light to make camp just outside the kerbed perimeter, and for a while they were busy with that. The land around them was empty of people, open, and several paths intersected nearby. In and around the circle they found a few signs of the last meeting here; a broken button, a sliver of rock with sharp edge, a little cluster of feathers tucked into the crevice at the base of one of the standing stones. It was easy to imagine travellers gathering here, assembling along the trackways from every direction to hold a feast or a festival.

Their fire did little to dispel the darkness of the night, and seemed very small amidst all the greatness of the plateau. But the autumn stars were bright above them, and the great wanderer was well above the horizon to the south. Lindirgel leaned against the nearest of the upright stones and sighed.

"Tomorrow we leave these hills and move towards places that neither of us know."

She was looking east, although the backbone ridge of the land was hidden in shadow. For a moment he was unsure of her mood.

"That's a good thing, surely?"

"Oh yes. It's what we began talking of at Pwil Hoyat, or even before that, and I'm right glad we're on the way now. That was in the summer, and now the days and the nights are nearly equal. It's as well we started now – if we'd waited too long it'd have to be the Winter Road and a much longer circle back north to reach the places Nant told us about. As it is we'll cross by the Summer Road and be more direct. And besides that, it's a journey I've wanted to do for a long while now."

"I wonder how we'll find The Valley when we come back?"

She turned her head to look very directly at him, and then hesitated for a little while before replying.

"Are you worried about what Finn said?"

He frowned.

"Both no and yes. No, because some of his words were just to try to make me change my mind, and not to come away at all. But yes, because I feel there's at least a morsel of truth in his fears. Some of them, at any rate. What if we stoneworkers are indeed heading for hard times and changes?"

"You mean this honey rock stuff that Roudhok saw?"

"Yes, that, but also the other things. The camp that Cegit went away to join, and no doubt there'll be others like it too. Local

## Epilogue – Travelling

traveller groups that want to take some of the work we've been doing, whether with the true tuff or some other rock." He looked sideways at her, and she nodded. "Or the way the barn-and-byre people are losing respect for what we do. I feel sometimes they'd push us out soon as anything if we were in their way, and what stops them is that The Valley seems wild and remote to them. They just can't be bothered to step out that way and learn how to live out there. Not that they care about the tuff: it's land they crave, of course. Perhaps one day they'll be clearing the trees, grazing animals, and planting fields all along The Valley. I don't know. Nant's best for talking about all this, and maybe I'm not saying it right."

"So do you want to stay after all? To turn around and go back to Ty Caroc?"

"No, not at all. It's like you said; we can't say we're travellers and not be on the journey every so often. Otherwise we might as well move to Dolgolvan today. But I wonder what we'll find when we get back. If not this time, then the next, or the next. If Finn's right, then all what we've been doing in The Valley for all that time – generation after generation – might not go on for very much longer." He shook his head. "Avank thinks we have a lot longer, several more generations at least. Leastwise that's what he says when we're all together. But maybe he's just trying to reassure us, and in truth he fears the same as Finn."

They were silent together for a while. The sky was darkening quite rapidly now, and the western sky above the fells was bright with the promise of fine weather tomorrow. Eventually Lindirgel spoke again.

"I've not been so long in The Valley as you, so I don't know what that might mean. But I like the travelling life, and I'd be sorry if the barn-and-byre habit swept it all away. And Ty Caroc is part of all that still, for all that your friends don't go on the journey much."

Bran nodded.

"This time away will be good. There'll be time to decide what comes next. And I'm convinced it's to do with all us different traveller groups coming together instead of keeping our secrets separate. When we get back, I want to go and speak with the woodsman down near Lugh Deri, and whoever else he knows, to team up somehow with us in The Valley. And anyone else that wants. Else we'll all be in our separate camps, as Dolgolvan and the other places like it just get bigger and bigger."

She leaned into him as a breath of autumn wind sent a chill over the stone circle and the moorland around it. He wrapped a corner of the blanket around them both.

"How long will it take to cross the Summer Road?"

She considered.

"I don't know all the proper ways on the other side. I mean, Nant gave me some ideas, but he's not trained properly to tell me in the manner that I am used to hearing a way told, so that much is guess. But I think ten days, perhaps a little more, until we get to the camps that he talked about. The crest of the backbone ridge is nearer the west side than the east, so we'll be over the highest point in three, maybe four days. There's a broad valley to cross first, and like I said before, we'll need to take time to hunt and gather as we go. But we're in autumn; the food will be easy enough to find. There's three ways we might choose when we're at the top, and I favour the middle way, unless the track looks poor when we get there. That heads northeast, down a winding valley. Southeast would be second choice. But whichever way we go, there's a great river to cross. We can do it higher upstream by wading, and if we go too far east, we'll have to find a boatman to carry us. But all those places that Nant told us about are north of that river, and that's where we want to go."

The night was fresh, and the next morning dawned bright and clear. Once their camp at Dronow Cyfarfod was packed away, Lindirgel led them both up a little raised patch of land and gazed eastward. She turned a little way towards the south and pointed to a dip in the hills.

"That's where the Winter Road goes through the ridge." She paused and turned slowly round to the north, her lips moving as though counting her way along the ups and downs of the crest.

## Epilogue – Travelling

Finally she pointed to a place almost due north-east. "And the Summer Road lies there. Do you see? Between that rounded peak and that jagged one. That's where we shall go over to the east of the land."

They stood and looked at the way ahead, leading off into places they did not know. A buzzard called from the higher ground to their right. It was the call of the Rising Land, the song of the journey, the song of moving on once again across the land to see what was beyond the horizon.

# Author's Note

QUARRY IS SET IN the overlap period between the Neolithic (Late Stone) and the Copper / Early Bronze Ages. It is located in what is now Cumbria, in northwest England. The Neolithic saw the widespread displacement of hunter-gatherer lifestyles by settled farming villages and towns. This not only meant changes in how tools were made, or food sourced, but also included a whole range of social shifts towards more structured and hierarchical organisations. One such change concerned attitudes to family life, with a shift from small numbers of children, with lower infant and maternal death rates, towards much bigger families with very much higher risks. From a social and historical point of view the second strategy was extremely successful – the settled farming communities with their fixed houses and claims on land rapidly outgrew and displaced the travelling hunter-gatherers, who steadily dwindled in numbers and influence – but the human cost, especially to women, was huge. Traveller groups in the British Isles and across the world now form a tiny minority of the population, and are still frequently regarded with suspicion and antipathy by the settled majority.

It used to be thought that the stone axe factory perched high on the Langdale Pikes thrived only for a few decades, but this has been progressively extended as more research has been carried out. It now seems clear that it was a source of high-quality stone axes for centuries, perhaps over a thousand years during the late Neolithic period. Langdale axes have been found all across the British Isles, from northern Scotland south to the Isles of Scilly. There are particularly high concentrations in the

North York Moors and Lincolnshire as well as more local sites in Cumbria and around the Solway Firth. They account for over a quarter of all native stone axes. Presumably they were originally intended as tools for everyday work, but they soon attained a much higher status as gifts, trophies, or parts of dowries.

In *Quarry*, the stoneworkers of Ty Caroc, the "House of Rock", think of themselves as travellers, but in fact live a life almost as sedentary as the barn-and-byre people of nearby Dolgolvan. Their way of life is being threatened by multiple factors, both social and technological. Instead of being valued for their skill and craftsmanship, they are starting to be regarded with suspicion and hostility by the settled communities nearby. However, by and large they still deny the possibility of change, and even more so that an end may be drawing into sight.

For those wanting to follow events and journeys on a map, Ty Caroc is modern Chapel Stile. A short walk brings you to the carved rock art at Copt Howe, west of the village. Nobody today knows how to interpret the signs on this rock or many others in the vicinity. Similar rock markings can be found elsewhere in England and Ireland. Whatever they originally meant, you can look from there along and up at the Ban and the Brig – Harrison Stickle and Pike o'Stickle – and contemplate what that would be like as your daily commute to work. Lanerc's farm is beside Blea Tarn, between the Great and Little Langdale Valleys, and ground surveys do indeed show signs that there was an isolated farmstead around this time.

Today, Dolgolvan is Ambleside. Mynyth Mam is now called the Old Man of Coniston, and around the more modern mining endeavours, all manner of much older relics can be explored in a considerable area surrounding the mountain. The summit is the focal point of a great many prehistoric stone monuments of various sizes, and overlooks the broad sweep of Morecambe Bay to the south, as well as westward out to sea towards the Isle of Man (Innis Mon Allan). Turning north, Dronow Moar is the great stone circle at Castlerigg. All the places named have modern counterparts, and it is comparatively easy to follow all the

## Author's note

journeys on a map. Better yet is to walk them on the ground, though Bran and his companions were used to longer and more demanding journeys than most fellwalkers tackle today.

Temperatures around that time were a little higher than is typical today, and as a result some settlements can be found in places that now seem very bleak. It's common for people to visit ancient sites and wonder why on earth our remote ancestors chose such a place to live and work; the simple answer is that at the time they were more pleasant locations.

However, the major difference between then and now is neither the shape of the land, nor its climate, but rather its covering. Today's Cumbria is vastly denuded of trees compared to the terrain that Bran knew, and the valley bottoms used to be much wetter. The process of deforestation began in the Neolithic Age, as the barn-and-byre groups cleared land for farming. Stone axes, whether of the superior Langdale type, or those made from more ordinary rock, were instrumental in people's ability to clear trees for grazing and cultivation. More recently, the widespread introduction of sheep across the fells has severely hampered the land's ability to regenerate woodland, though extensive tree planting has been carried out in many places. The open views along valleys that we enjoy today would have looked entirely different some five thousand years ago.

Meanwhile, to hugely extend the arable area, streams and becks were straightened and walled in to dry out the valleys. Look along the banks of almost any stream here in England's Lake District, and you will see that it now runs in a prescribed channel. Some recent environmental work has focused on "re-wiggling" these streams in order to restore some wetlands and reduce the consequential flooding downstream, but this has only been done in a tiny handful of places. All in all, only small patches of the land retain anything like their original appearance, although such places can still be found here and there.

Another consequence of these differences in woodland and river routes concerns where tracks and pathways were located. These were tiny in number compared to the modern network of roads and footpaths. They were largely located at the mid-level of hillsides, rather than along ridges or in valleys. Following a ridge necessarily means tackling every rise and fall, and every rough and craggy section. Following a valley bottom means constantly tackling streams and the boggy ground beside them. Mid-level routes are better. To get a good idea of where the old paths would lie, you can look at familiar routes like the Coffin Trail or Loughrigg Terrace in the Grasmere area, or the terrace path along the side of Cat Bells beside Derwentwater.

We have no idea what language the inhabitants living here in the British Isles spoke around this time, as it is long before anybody was writing about the history of the region. I have assumed that the common Brythonic tongue, with multiple close dialects, was being used then. Solid evidence for the use of this language is from very much later in history, and its actual advent in these islands is unknown.

Brythonic's legacy survives today in modern Welsh, Cornish, Manx, Irish, Gaelic, and Breton. The particular variant which was spoken in Cumbria is known as Cumbric. It is not a living language, and it survives only in a handful of placenames and similar fragments. The name Cumbraek refers to a modern attempt to revitalise this dialect, but so far this has had limited success.

In *Quarry*, the names of people and places are based on what we know of Brythonic, but simplified in order to help casual readers with pronunciation. I trust that readers who are familiar with Welsh, or indeed Cumbric, will forgive these simplifications. Most personal names are based on either animal, bird, or other nature-based names, or else are descriptive words such as "yellow", "happy", and so on.

I hope you enjoy this exploration of a long-vanished culture, whose material remains can still be found with ease in the hills and valleys of England's Lake District.

Finally, particular thanks are due to a number of people:

- Family members and friends have encouraged with great

## Author's note

patience the slow progress of *Quarry* amongst the demands of a busy family business. Especial thanks to Ruth for comments on an early draft.

- David Frauenfelder has also been a constant source of both friendship and encouragement: he has also given a great deal of practical assistance by way of insightful comments over a long period of time.

- On a more specialised note, mention should be made of NAMHO (the National Association of Mining History Organisations) whose conference *5000 Years of Mining and Quarrying in the Lake District* was held at Grasmere in July 2023, organised by CATMHS (Cumbria Amenity Trust Mining History Society). This included an informative walk up to part of the axe factory site on the Langdale Pikes, led by James Archer of CATMHS and the National Trust.

- The Threlkeld Quarry and Mining Museum, though mainly focused on much more recent mining and its equipment, has on display some Langdale stone, and some good information about the wider geology of Cumbria.

- The fact that ancient sites such as stone circles and rock markings are accessible and still cared for today, is largely thanks to national organisations such as English Heritage and the National Trust. However, a great many private landowners, local volunteers and enthusiasts also play a crucial part. All of these work together to ensure that the history of the land is protected and remains available.

- Finally, mention must be made of all those people who are still carrying on the tradition of working with stone and slate here in Cumbria. The numbers have dwindled over the years, and many sites are now at rest rather than active, but there are still people working to make things both practical and beautiful from the stone that lies both on and below the surface.

## About the author

RICHARD ABBOTT spends a great deal of time exploring the hills and valleys of England's Lake District.

The Langdale Valley, which features so prominently in Quarry, is one of his favourite places. He has also visited some of the places that feature in his historical fiction. To date, however, he has not had the opportunity of visiting anywhere outside the Earth that might feature in his futuristic writing.

Richard currently lives in Grasmere, Cumbria. When not writing, he works in the family hospitality business. He enjoys spending time with family, walking and wildlife - ideally combining all three of those pursuits at the same time. Much of the inspiration for Quarry has come while out and about in the central lakeland hills, which he loves.

Follow the author on:

- Instagram – @richardbabbott

- YouTube – @RichardAbbott

- Web site – richardabbottauthor.uk

- Facebook – www.facebook.com/RichardAbbottAuthor/

Look out for his other works, which are available from most online retailers and general booksellers, and include the following.

*Author's note*

## Historical Fantasy – full-length novel

*Half Sick of Shadows*

- soft-cover – ISBN 978-0993-1684-9-9

- ebook format – ISBN 978-0993-1684-8-2

    *Who is The Lady?*
    In ancient Britain, a Lady is living in a stone-walled house on an island in the middle of a river. So far as the people know, she has always been there. They sense her power, they hear her singing, but they never meet her.
    At first her life is idyllic. She wakes, she watches, she wanders in her garden, she weaves a complex web of what she sees, and she sleeps again. But as she grows, this pattern becomes narrow and frustrating. She longs to meet those who cherish her, but she cannot. The scenes beyond the walls of her home are different every time she wakes, and everyone she encounters is lost, swallowed up by the past.
    But when she finds the courage to break the cycle, there is no going back. Can she bear the cost of finding freedom? And what will her people do, when they finally come face to face with a lady of legend who is not at all what they have imagined?
    *A retelling – and metamorphosis – of Tennyson's Lady of Shalott.*

## Science Fiction – full-length novels

*Far from the Spaceports*

- soft-cover – ISBN 978-0993-1684-4-4

- ebook format – ISBN 978-0993-1684-5-1

    *Quick wits and loyalty confront high-tech crime in space*
    Welcome to the Scilly Isles, a handful of asteroids bunched together in space, well beyond the orbit of Mars. This remote and isolated habitat is home to a diverse group of human settlers, and a whole flock of parakeets. But earth-based financial regulator ECRB suspects that it's also home to serious large scale fraud, and the reputation of the islands comes under threat.
    Enter Mitnash Thakur and his virtual partner Slate, sent out from Earth to investigate. Their ECRB colleagues are several weeks away at their ship's best speed, and even message signals take an hour for the round trip. Slate and Mitnash are on their own, until they can work out who on Scilly to trust. How will they cope when the threat gets personal?

## Timing

- soft-cover – ISBN 978-0993-1684-6-8

- ebook format – ISBN 978-0993-1684-7-5

    *When quick wits and loyalty are put to the test*
    Mitnash and his AI companion Slate, coders and investigators of interplanetary fraud, are at work again in *Timing*, the sequel to *Far from the Spaceports*.
    This time their travels take them from Jupiter to Mars, chasing a small-scale scam which seems a waste of their time. Then the case escalates dramatically into threats and extortion. Robin's Rebels, a new player in the game, is determined to bring down the financial world, and Slate's fellow AIs are the targets. Will Slate be the next victim?
    The clues lead them back to the asteroid belt, and to their friends on the Scilly Isles. The next attack will be here, and Mitnash and Slate must put themselves in the line of fire. To solve the case, they need to team up with an old adversary - the only person this far from Earth who has the necessary skills to help them. But can they trust somebody who keeps their own agenda so well hidden?

## The Liminal Zone

- soft-cover – ISBN 978-1838-0120-0-7

- ebook format – ISBN 978-1838-0120-1-4

    *Selkies in Space?*
    Nina Buraca, investigator of possible signs of alien life, has heard tales of mysterious events on Pluto's moon Charon, where a science outpost studies extrasolar planets. Facing opposition from her colleagues, she nevertheless travels from Earth to uncover the truth. Once there, she finds herself working with a team of people who have many secrets. To make progress, she has to take sides in an old dispute that she knows nothing about.
    Can she determine who – or what – is really behind the name *"selkies"*, that the station's staff have given to this uncanny phenomenon? And how will the discovery change her life?
    *The Liminal Zone*, a novel in the *Far from the Spaceports* series, takes you a further twenty years into the future – and out to the edge of our solar system – for an encounter with the unknown.

*Author's note*

# Historical Fiction – full-length novels

## *In a Milk and Honeyed Land*

- soft-cover – ISBN 978-0993-1684-2-0

- ebook format – ISBN 978-0993-1684-3-7

    *Life, love and conflict in the hill country*
    Damariel is apprenticed as a young man by the village priest, whose reckless actions lead to his disgrace. Damariel manages to avoid becoming implicated in the matter and carries on his training, marrying his childhood friend Qetirah shortly before they begin their shared ministry in the town.
    Feeling ashamed of their continuing inability to have children, Qetirah becomes pregnant by the chief of the four towns, but the pregnancy is difficult. Damariel's anger and outrage spills over into the marriage. He holds the chief responsible for the situation but cannot see how to get either justice or revenge.

## *Scenes from a Life*

- soft-cover – ISBN 978-0954-5535-9-3

- kindle format – ISBN 978-0954-5535-7-9

- epub format – ISBN 978-0954-5535-8-6

    *What journey would you make to encounter the meaning of a dream?*
    Makty-Rasut is a scribe in New Kingdom Egypt, fashioning tombs for the elite. He lives a comfortable but restless life, moving every few years further upstream along the river Nile. He is content to exercise his talent without examining his origins.
    Then a series of vivid dreams, interpreted with the help of a senior priest, disrupts this pattern. To solve the riddle, he must go on a journey that will take him outside the Beloved Land and away from the life that he knows. His travels take him into the neighbouring province of Canaan, to a hill-country village called Kephrath, and to a way of life he has never considered.

*The Flame Before Us*

- soft-cover – ISBN 978-0993-1684-1-3

- ebook format – ISBN 978-0993-1684-0-6

    *Conflict and commitment in the shadow of a city's downfall*
    The raiding ships have come before, but this time it is different. This time the attackers are coming to stay, and defensive walls will not hold them back. Nowhere is safe. One by one, the great kings and their vassal cities collapse as the newcomers advance.
    The land is already a patchwork of many different peoples, bound together in a fragile web of traditional alliances and rivalries. How will political and personal promises change with the arrival of the new clans? Is war inevitable, or can a different answer be found?
    Walk with refugees, migrants, and defenders of the land alike, as they struggle to create a different way of life beside the ruins of the old. Can alliance, commitment and love survive the turmoil?

## Historical Fiction – short stories

- *The Man in the Cistern*, a short story of Kephrath, published in ebook format by Matteh Publications, ISBN 978-0954-5535-1-7 (kindle) or 978-0954-5535-4-8 (epub).

- *The Lady of the Lions*, a short story of Kephrath, published in ebook format by Matteh Publications, ISBN 978-0954-5535-3-1 (kindle) or 978-0954-5535-5-5 (epub).

## Non-fiction

- *Triumphal Accounts in Hebrew and Egyptian*, published in ebook format by Matteh Publications, ISBN 978-0954-5535-2-4 (kindle) or 978-0954-5535-6-2 (epub).

*Author's note*

# About Matteh Publications

MATTEH PUBLICATIONS is a small publisher based in Cumbria offering a small range of specialised books. For information concerning current or forthcoming titles please see http://mattehpublications.datascenesdev.com/.

www.ingramcontent.com/pod-product-compliance
Lightning Source LLC
LaVergne TN
LVHW041620060526
838200LV00040B/1362